I0526171

Stolen Lies

Stolen Lies

WREN WESTON

TOPSY-TURVY PUBLISHING

Topsy-Turvy Publishing
512 West MLK Jr. Blvd, Suite 264
Austin, Texas 78701

Copyright © 2016 by Topsy-Turvy Publishing
Cover Design by Deranged Doctor Design

ISBN 978-1-68381-023-0 (print)
ISBN 978-1-68381-024-7 (epub)

All rights reserved. No part of this publication may be reproduced, distributed, or transmitted in any form or by any means, including photocopying, recording, or other electronic or mechanical methods, without the prior written permission of the publisher, except in the case of brief quotations embodied in critical reviews and certain other noncommercial uses permitted by copyright law.

Visit Topsy-Turvy Publishing on the World Wide Web at www.topsyturvypublishing.com.

Visit Wren Weston at www.wrenweston.com.

1

The only flaw in Lila's plan was Tristan.

Again.

She cast a not-so careless eye toward the LeBeau militia gathered at the base of the auction house stairs. The dozen women and men tugged at the collars of their formal uniforms, the sweaty fabric chafing in the muggy afternoon. The LeBeau coat of arms, a scorpion with its stinger poised to strike, had been stitched in lavender on the breast of their summer-weight blackcoats, cut in ankle-length cotton rather than leather. The group chugged bottles of ice water, a balm against the late October heat wave, and fanned their coats to reveal tranq guns underneath. One of the militia whispered something. They all chuckled before separating once more to pace.

As the chief of her family's militia, Lila had been party to such jokes for years. It was likely a barb against the paparazzi, or the so-called press behind the stanchions. Microphones in hand and cameras at the ready, they stood at attention while their flashing bulbs captured the scene. Of course, the joke might have been aimed at the heirs who flowed up the silver-carpeted stairs toward the auction house, wilting under their finery.

Predictably, the highborn had ignored the weather. The heirs wore their autumn dresses and well-tailored long coats while the men panted in their vests and coats and breeches, their cravats tied and pinned at their necks. Everyone wore their family colors. The highborn sparkled with jewels and sweat as they ran the gauntlet of press and photographers, vainly dabbing at their foreheads between photos and interviews, desperate to enter the cool lobby and the ballroom beyond.

And they all suffered.

All except Lila. She'd visited the family tailors, insisting they alter a dress from the year before. Obligingly, they'd scissored off half the blood-red fabric and dyed a pair of gloves to match. After all, she had to hide the stitches and bandages that crisscrossed her palms. She'd earned them the weekend before when she'd been trapped in the middle of a riot. Of course, few people knew the real story. She'd told everyone she'd been in a motorcycle accident. So far, everyone believed her.

The other highborn stared at her dress, half jealous, half grumbling that her clothes too closely resembled last year's fashions. Her tailors had been clever, though, expertly tying together the trends. The bodice of her backless dress hardly covered her breasts, and the silken skirts barely brushed her skin. The slit had been cut as high as was proper, allowing for a delightful breeze between her legs. She'd balked at the matching gossamer coat, but it might have been woven by magical spiders, for it didn't stifle her in the slightest.

With her dark hair set in tumbling waves and her makeup perfectly applied, she looked a great deal less like a militia chief and more like the eldest heir to one of the richest and most powerful families in New Bristol, and perhaps all of Saxony.

Which she was. Sort of. Only fifteen women in each generation could call themselves heirs in each family, all standing in line to become the next chairwoman. The current matron's eldest daughter stood first among them. Despite being the prime heir by birthright, Lila had traded away her spot a decade ago in order to join the Randolph militia. She shouldn't have been allowed on the silver carpet at all. Instead of an heir, she should only rank as a highborn.

Her mother would never suffer such an outrage, though. The Randolph family had only fourteen official heirs, but everyone understood who held the fifteenth spot, no matter how often Lila resisted the implication. And under the pretense of sparing her younger sister Jewel from failure on the New Bristol High Council of Judges, her mother had declared Lila the family's emissary, forcing her to sit on a council made up of matrons and prime heirs.

The fact that Lila had never officially accepted her position as heir rankled the others.

The fact that everyone accepted it for her rankled Lila.

It also made everything about her annoyingly fuzzy—except her place in the auction house line. Only matrons and primes could skip them at highborn functions. As an heir, even an unofficial one, she had to wait, just like the others.

But waiting in line had been part of Lila's plan, for it allowed her to study the LeBeau militia. She counted six blackcoats on the roof while another half-dozen kept the front secure. Lila couldn't tell if the LeBeau chief had reinforced the alley, but Shirley watched from a neighboring building. The old woman had a keen eye, and an even keener mind for trouble. She'd let Tristan know the moment she found it.

Toxic would too. Lila had hacked the auction house security cameras. Toxic now watched every feed, including the ones Lila had looped and fed back to the LeBeau militia. Unfortunately, Lila couldn't check them herself. She'd hidden her palm computer in her clutch, and she couldn't remove the device while she tarried in line. Not around the nosy highborn heirs.

With the way the afternoon had unfolded, the heist might be over before she even got into position. Too many heirs had shown up later than usual to escape the heat, tying her up outside when she should already be inside.

Until then, Tristan and his people were on their own, and that was never a good idea.

"Chief Randolph?" came an overly cheery voice on the opposite side of the stanchions. The voice belonged to a pale, slender blonde in an off-the-rack dress, holding a worn palm.

Lila tried not to frown. Every heir knew Marion Carpenter, a leading journalist for the *New Bristol Times*, and every journalist knew that Lila Randolph didn't give interviews. Giving one meant that Lila had officially taken up her role as heir, and, more importantly, it meant any news outlet could run her photo without consequence. Lila enjoyed her anonymity far too much to destroy it. She also enjoyed the gaping loophole it created. The Randolph militia chief was completely off-limits to the press. No photos. No videos. Not even a sound bite.

"An unofficial word," Ms. Carpenter pleaded.

Lila gripped her clutch tighter and motioned her forward. It was good for the Randolphs to court the local press, officially or unofficially.

Ms. Carpenter hopped the rope and rushed over. "You look quite healthy, chief."

"I feel healthy."

"So there's no truth to the rumor that Peter Kruger shot you in the chest last Friday?"

"I'm wearing a backless dress, Ms. Carpenter. I think you'd notice the bullet hole."

The journalist's gaze dipped to the low bodice of Lila's gown. "There were reports you were taken to Randolph General."

"Is that so?"

"Yes, conflicting reports. I heard you were shot. I also heard you were in a motorcycle accident. Care to elaborate?"

"Perhaps it was both. Perhaps I'm a fast healer." Lila smirked, glad it had only been a tranq that had felled her, rather than a bullet. "Perhaps you rely too heavily on your sources."

Ms. Carpenter bit her lip. "How does it feel to acquire the Wilson estate so early? Unofficially, of course."

Lila recalled the exact words her mother had beaten into her head at breakfast. "While the Randolphs obviously regret the fall of any highborn family, on occasion, one must step aside so that another can join our ranks."

"You feel regret for the Wilson family? The same Wilsons who rioted throughout the family's compound the night Celeste Wilson and her son were taken into custody? The same family who killed a Bullstow militiaman during their tantrum?" Ms. Carpenter crinkled her nose. The highborn did not express violence; it just wasn't done. Even the poorer classes avoided it like a young child copying its elders. "The woman defrauded her own family and tried to do business with our enemies. Her son tried to make a deal with the Roman Emperor, promising to return his long-lost nephew for a pile of riches and safe haven. They rioted and killed for that, yet you feel regret?"

"I sincerely hope that the men of Bullstow will see justice for their fallen brother," Lila said carefully. "I also feel pity for anyone betrayed by Celeste and Patrick Wilson, regardless of their bloodline. I hope the next matron will not be so careless with the futures of her family and those who serve it."

"You sit on the New Bristol High Council. The rumor is you'll discuss candidates for the next matron soon. Which lowborn family will you support?"

"I couldn't say."

"Bullshit. You could. You just won't. Give me a name, chief. Will it be the Parks? Everyone says it will be the Parks. Just confirm it for me. Unofficially."

"It's not my job to confirm things. You'll have to wait until the council announces its decision. Good day, Ms. Carpenter." Lila stepped forward in line, finding herself before the auction house sign. LeBeau's had been scrawled in an artsy cursive script. The branding served as a backdrop for photo ops during the event.

Ms. Carpenter made the poor choice of stepping with her, blocking the view of the press behind the stanchions.

"Madam, we need the shot!" a member of the paparazzi yelled, already snapping photos of the pair, not realizing which heir he'd captured on film. "Get out of the way!"

Others clamored at the ropes, shouting at the journalist to move aside. Bright lights flashed around the pair, searing Lila's eyes. She lifted her hand to block them. Light-shadows danced in her vision.

Ms. Carpenter turned at their continued boos and jeers. "Unless you want a slave's term and a lifetime suspension of your license, I'd suggest you put down your cameras."

The paparazzi snuck a peek at Lila, faces falling as they marked her blood-red dress. Most deleted her photos immediately, scared they might post one by accident.

Ms. Carpenter swiveled back to Lila. "My sources tell me that you were instrumental in the capture of Celeste and Patrick Wilson. Is that true?"

"Your sources have interesting imaginations." Lila didn't know where the rumor had come from, but it spurred a sense of unease and apprehension among the highborn. Lila enjoyed keeping the matrons and primes on their toes.

"Do you plan on attending their executions?"

Lila steeled her face. Patrick might have hired Peter Kruger to kill her, but he was her best friend's little brother. "It's a bit early to talk of executions. The High Council has not even confirmed the sentence yet. If you'll excuse me, I have my mother's auction to attend."

Before Lila turned away, Ms. Carpenter blurted out a last question. "Are you still friends with Alexandra Craft-Wilson? Have you two spoken since her family's fall?"

The journalist scanned Lila's face, then smiled at the expression she found.

Lila cleared her throat. "My feelings for Ms. Wilson have never wavered."

"Have Ms. Wilson's? After all, it is her mother and brother who will be executed, some say due to your own maneuvering."

"You'd have to ask Ms. Wilson that, wouldn't you?"

"I've tried to get an interview with Ms. Wilson all week. Your matron has denied it time and time again. I—"

Lila's jaw locked. "That's what this is about, isn't it? You want an interview with Alex."

Ms. Carpenter took a step back.

The auction house door opened. A short, chubby woman appeared at the top of the stairs, wearing a long silvercoat and a formfitting green dress. Her gaze lingered over the line of highborns, landing on Lila.

"Ah, there you are, Chief Randolph," Chairwoman Masson called out, crooking her finger. Though only a dozen years Lila's senior, the chairwoman had dyed her hair silver, coloring it in stages over the years to attain the much-desired look of wisdom, maturity, and experience. Today it hung in thick curls around her calm, serene face.

A little too serene, actually. Lila sometimes wondered if she smoked just enough weed to render her unflappable. It had always been impossible to ruffle the elegant woman, not that Lila hadn't tried.

"Come," the matron said, ignoring the journalist. "We have council business to discuss."

Lila stifled her grin and jogged upstairs in her heels. The heirs on the silver carpet stared at her jealously as she passed, but no one said a word. Grace Masson was a matron, after all.

"I owe you," Lila whispered as the chairwoman clasped her arm.

"Yes, you do. I thought you might pull a tranq gun from gods know where and shoot her. Not that I would have minded. Dreadful woman, that one."

"Dreadful is too polite a word."

"Well, you may pay me back for my kindness this very afternoon. Take my son for the season. He's beautiful, sweet, and in need of a good match."

"He's very beautiful and very sweet, and also barely twenty."

"Twenty and twenty-eight aren't that far off. Besides, younger is better. You get stronger genes that way. You'll care about these things soon." The chairwoman eyed Lila's face and broke out into a wide grin. "A mother has to try. I promised. You'll tell him so?"

"I will tell him you gave it your very best shot."

"Excellent. That is payback enough." The chairwoman squeezed Lila's arm and led her into the blessed coolness of the lobby. The room stood as a monument to marble, gold trim, and Renaissance paintings. The line outside continued inside, stretching to the ballroom's entrance. Each heir waited impatiently to be announced.

"Such a horrid line in horrid weather. Why didn't you come earlier?"

"Work," Lila fibbed.

"You should take a vacation, darling. You look tired." The chairwoman led her to the front of the line as if she were prime once more and gave her a quick wink. "Once you're announced, we'll talk about tomorrow's council meeting. I'll find you in the ballroom directly."

Lila watched Chairwoman Masson walk away, years of ballet training in every step.

The rest of the heirs looked at Lila as though she'd cheated at cards.

Lila ignored them.

The teenage boy standing at the ballroom door turned to face Lila, his back straight, his chest open. "Elizabeth Victoria Lemaire-Randolph," he announced over the tittering in the ballroom and the clinking of champagne glasses. Though the boy's breeches, tailored jacket, and accent placed him in the upper echelons of highborn society, the tremble in his voice betrayed his true class, marking him as far too overwhelmed with the crowd around him.

A well-trained and beautiful lowborn, then, putting on airs.

Lila couldn't blame him for being overwhelmed. The crowd in the ballroom might have been composed of vultures, glamoured by Puck himself for his own amusement. Every heir within two hundred kilometers had assembled, all to bid on items the Randolphs had seized from the Wilson compound. LeBeau's staff hadn't even placed chairs inside the ballroom, knowing all too well the whims and the fancy of their kind. It wasn't often the heirs had a chance to gather en masse outside of the season.

The fall of the Wilson family had brought them all out for business with a side of gossip. The sea of whitecoats and silvercoats and bold family colors churned like a raging sea, with groups breaking away to join other groups that then broke apart again, a shifting foam of rich indigos, bold blues, hunter greens, and monarch oranges. The matrons and their daughters bid with upraised paddles or discussed business amongst themselves in the lull between items. Designer dresses marched back and forth over the polished oak floor, whisked back and forth on missions of scandalous importance. The occasional male from the great families dotted the crowd, whispering in hushed tones, smoothing over proposals, or laying the groundwork for new deals, hopeful to bring his matron another for consideration.

Of course, wherever highborn women ventured, the senators congregated as well. New Bristol and Saxony senators alike had crowded into the ballroom. The New Bristol senators wore their silver city medallions with pride, puffing out their chests in their tailored burgundy coats, black breeches, and black boots, the last polished to a fine gleam. Not to be outdone, the Saxony senators wore their hard-won black coats and gray vests, prowling around the ballroom as kings on a hunt. Both groups of men had likely arrived early, all to flirt for as long as possible with the heirs, all under the pretense of legislation and society, all trying to make a match before the season had even begun.

It was not a vain hope. A man did not attain a position in the capitol by accident. These were among the most beautiful, charming, intelligent, and well-spoken senators in the state.

And many of them had shifted to their gaze to Lila the moment she'd been announced.

Wrongly.

"That's *Chief* Elizabeth Victoria Lemaire-Randolph," Lila corrected, a note of annoyance entering her voice. Introducing her incorrectly was not only a snub, but it might make the senators inside overeager. A few jaws had already dropped at her dress and family colors. Hope strained in their breeches that perhaps tonight, Lila Randolph would retire from the militia and take her place as prime and president of Wolf Industries, elbowing her baby sister out of the way at last. Perhaps tonight the childless heir would select a senator for the season, intent on providing Chairwoman

Randolph with her first granddaughter and carrying on the Randolph legacy to another generation.

Whoever seeded such an heir would have his career handed to him on a silver platter, propelling him all the way to the Saxony senate or perhaps to the nation's capital.

All on the strength of his cock.

And should Lila have a boy, the senator responsible would retain full custody of the child, for the firstborn sons of heirs became the sons of Bullstow.

But Lila's plans didn't include any of that. She didn't want a place at Wolf Industries, she didn't want a senator for the season, and she sure didn't want a child.

Lila didn't just shoot the overeager senators a look of daggers—she shot them a look of scissors snipping off their precious, sperm-giving balls.

The men looked away. Quickly.

So did the boy at the door, who gulped when Lila's gaze turned back to him. He turned his head to Ms. Olivia LeBeau and helplessly looked for guidance. Like the boy, she'd been coiffed far above her station, a fine lavender dress covering a highborn who strained at the fringes of high society, forever wanting more.

Unfortunately for Lila, Olivia ran the auction house. This woman, one of her oldest friends from university.

Olivia grinned, showing her teeth.

Oldest friend did not mean current.

"Try not to confuse the boy needlessly, Lila," Olivia drawled, raising a brow. "It's not his fault that you insist on slumming it up as a militia chief. You were born the prime heir, for oracle's sake. Don't you have any pride?"

Lila narrowed her eyes and returned the woman's smile, glad that Olivia's auction house had been selected for the heist. The fallout from this break-in would pay her back for…

For what? Lila couldn't even remember why they'd become cross with one another. Knowing Olivia, it had been about a boy.

Olivia was territorial about men, which was an awful trait for a highborn. Of course, that wouldn't matter much after the night was over. Olivia would never bed another highborn again, not unless she found a rare love match. The family's precious little auction house might never recover after the heist, and her matron would make her suffer for it.

It was Olivia's own fault, really. If security had been tighter, Lila and Tristan never would found a way in. The LeBeaus, and Olivia in particular, had no business running an auction house. They should have stuck with groceries and meat and mines.

"I could say the same about you, Olivia, slipping into the Wabash fundraiser."

"I was a guest of Senator Cole." She sniffed. "Why are you even here? I thought you were too good for these things."

"I'm serving as my matron's escort."

Olivia's gaze slid into the ballroom. "Yes, I see how well you are escorting her. You do realize she hasn't yet arrived?"

"I'm checking the place out first, you ignorant twat." Lila didn't even bother to give Olivia a second glance before plunging into the room.

Opening her clutch, she retrieved her palm computer, glad she wasn't escorting her mother after all. The chairwoman hadn't even bothered to arrive on time for her own auction. After recovering the relatively few antiques and art pieces that Celeste Wilson hadn't already sold, her mother had taken what she wanted, then put up the rest for auction throughout the Allied Lands. She'd strategically placed each item where it would fetch the best price or draw the most attention. Some things she'd chosen to sell in New Bristol, mostly for the show of it, mostly for the excuse of having the event. Mostly to demand that Lila join the festivities, to prove to the other families and the press that she wasn't dead.

The Randolphs also had several dozen highborn to sell, Wilson highborn, who hadn't had the funds to rebuy their marks from the Randolphs. It had prompted quite a bit of talk in the press about the rumored Slave Bill. If the legislation actually existed and passed the senate, then highborn from fallen houses would no longer be sold into slavery if they didn't have enough money to purchase their mark. Failed business owners wouldn't automatically lose their marks, either.

Lila knew such legislation wouldn't pass, though. The highborn enjoyed the embarrassment and the shame and the show too much.

Leaning against the wall, she positioned herself near the ballroom's entrance, turning so she had a clear view of the pacing militia outside. She then slipped in an earpiece and tousled her hair over it, dipping her gaze to her palm. The thin, flexible device had much the same computing power as her desktop, though in a much smaller package. Tapping and swiping, she hurriedly pulled up the security feeds while heirs bid on a Rembrandt. A stooped auctioneer in a navy coat tossed out number after number onstage, his words blurring together.

He ended on a number that seemed much too high. Lila glanced up at the painting on display, a painting she'd seen often on the Wilson estate during highborn parties, a ship braving a storm on choppy seas. No doubt everyone else in the room had seen it as well. No doubt that was the very reason her mother had chosen to sell it in New Bristol. The Weberlys and Holguíns would want a token to remember their ally; the Wilson family's rivals would want a souvenir from her fall.

It seemed the rivals had won this particular round. Chairwoman Hardwicke lifted her paddle in triumph. The painting would likely be hung in her office by Monday, money traded for sentimentality and ego.

Lila turned her gaze back to the security feeds, stopping on one in particular that she'd looped and hidden from the militia. Two men stood in front of the LeBeau holding cells, both working on separate doors, both dressed in black t-shirts, matching trousers, and work boots. Knitted balaclavas covered everything but their eyes, though Lila hardly needed to see their faces to tell them apart.

The smaller, rangier man gripped his blowtorch and started severing the last bar that would free the fifteen-year-old boy inside.

The boy was not Oskar Kruger, the boy Tristan had actually gone to rescue, but Phillip Wilson. Phillip's scowl betrayed his conflicted feelings. On one hand, some petty thief from the poorer classes might save him from many years of slavery. On the other, his rescuer was some petty thief from the poorer classes.

Leave it to a Wilson to find fault with his rescuer.

"Stop it," Lila whispered, unmuting her mic. Only Tristan could hear her words, for he was the only one on his team who knew her identity. "There's barely enough time to free Oskar."

"He's being seen to," Tristan growled, his vowels long and rolling with a Bordeaux accent. "I'm not going to leave a child behind."

"What will you do with him after the auction? Take him back to the shop?"

"I don't know. Stop nagging me."

"Then stop being stupid. Get the one you came for and get out now. You're lucky you haven't been caught already, what with the—"

An alarm blinked on her palm.

"You're too late. The militia has caught on to the loop. Leave now."

"We don't have—"

"Get out now!" Lila opened her clutch and slipped in a second earpiece, tuned to the LeBeau militia's audio feed.

"Baxter to Wendy, over?"

Lila held her breath.

"Wendy? Who tranqed that one?" Toxic snickered in her other ear. The young woman pumped the militia's audio through their earpieces, audio Lila had captured before the auction.

"I think I did," Fry grunted, not turning away from his work. Tristan broke away from Phillip's cell and joined him. He pointed his blowtorch toward the last steel bar holding the slave inside.

"Baxter to Wendy?" the man asked again impatiently. After a slight pause, he tried again. "Baxter to Thomas?"

"I believe our fearless leader got Thomas."

"Baxter to Lewis?" the man pleaded, naming another downed blackcoat. Frustration replaced panic when no one answered. "Doesn't anyone have their damn radios on down there?"

"Ah, Hood tranqed Lewis. That guy really needed a bath."

"So everyone got a point?" Toxic asked.

"It's generally not good to get a point. It means someone found you when they shouldn't have. It means we're out of time."

"Natasha to Baxter, what seems to be the problem?" Another voice had broken in on the militia's channel.

"We're being robbed, that's the problem. Go check on the art."

Lila flicked to the relevant security footage, watching a capable-looking blackcoat in a hallway near the basement. Upon her whistle, a half-dozen blackcoats trotted to her position and fell in line. "Switch to the emergency frequency," she ordered Baxter. "Someone might be listening in."

"I'm on it!" Toxic squeaked, all humor gone from her voice.

"Abort now," Lila hissed at Tristan as the militia's audio fell silent. "You have one minute before they realize you're not here for the art. Maybe less if they get the basement cameras back up."

"Not yet. We just need more time."

"There is no more time! Get out, and get out now!"

Tristan turned off his blowtorch.

The small-framed teen inside the holding cell stepped forward, his cheap trousers and gray t-shirt too big and too new.

"Please," Oskar wailed, tears running down his cheek. Once again, freedom had slipped through his fingers. He shook the last steel bar madly as though he might be able to break it. "Don't leave me, please. I'll do anything!"

Tristan hesitated before the red-faced, crying boy.

"We'll fetch him later," Fry promised, shoving his boss toward the hole in the floor, a hole Dice had cut while the others had worked on the bars. "Hood, if you're still there, we need you. Tell the boss what the militia is doing."

Lila looked up to check.
A well-manicured hand snatched her palm.

2

"Whatever work you have on the compound can wait," Chairwoman Randolph said, turning off the device without looking at the screen. "You're surrounded by the most eligible senators in all of Saxony, Elizabeth. Do try to appear interested."

Lila snatched back her palm and slipped it into her clutch. "I was just about to visit the ladies' room."

"No, you weren't." Her mother straightened her silvercoat as though the matter had been decided. The garment marked her as the matron of the Randolph family and the CEO of Wolf Industries. As such, its fabric was even finer than Lila's tonight. Its hue matched her silver hair, which had been curled to perfection on the ends.

The chairwoman took Lila's arm and dragged her further into the room. "You expect me to think highly of Commander Sutton, yet you seem to believe she cannot fill in as chief for a few hours without supervision. The woman spent ten years in the infantry. She's not a toddler."

A crash sounded in Lila's earpiece, followed by a muffled curse. If Tristan had just been caught, then one prick from a DNA wand would ferret out his true identity, that of a long-escaped slave. It was only luck that he'd never been caught before. "Get out of the ballroom and keep an eye on the militia!" he shouted.

Lila took a quick look at the front of the auction house. "A lot can go on if a blackcoat isn't paying attention, madam. It's not like every blackcoat just paces around with their thumb up their—"

"Elizabeth!"

"Hood says the militia isn't onto us yet," Tristan told Fry. "Shirley, there's not enough fuel left in the blowtorches! We won't be able to collapse the tunnel."

"I didn't tell you to waste the fuel on some highborn snob, now did I? Get to the rendezvous point. I'll meet you there. We'll take off the regulators and make do."

Lila tuned out Shirley while she gave the others more instructions. "Don't start with me, Mother. I agreed to come to your little auction, didn't I?" She grabbed a glass of champagne from a passing servant and took the lead, finding another perch that offered a decent view of the militia outside. She stopped, took a sip, and pretended interest in the senators.

"Yes, you barely argued at all. I'm still trying to figure out why."

Lila ignored her. "The Rembrandt went for quite a bit."

"As I knew it would. Ah, look, there's Chairwoman Holguín." Her mother smiled and inclined her head slightly. The woman in question nodded pleasantly from across the room.

"Why smile when you hate her? Why not walk over and tell her she's a—"

"Elizabeth, don't bait me this evening."

"You started it. I put away my blackcoat for this. Don't make me put away my humor."

"What humor? Is it so hard to go out for one afternoon with your mother?"

"You didn't want quality time. You wanted to show the other families that I'm not dead yet and prod me to find a bedmate for the season."

"A what?" Tristan blurted over the sound of splashing.

"Focus," Fry shouted.

The chairwoman took a sip of champagne. "Yes, I suppose I should—"

The militia stopped pacing out front.

Lila cursed under her breath. "Mother, look. The militia is running to the back of the auction house. Running very, very quickly."

The chairwoman narrowed her eyes. "Really, Elizabeth? Commenting on the militia rather than your peers? Can't you put away your occupation for one afternoon?"

"I suspect a robbery. I should go inspect the art."

Lila took a step away from her mother.

The chairwoman grabbed her shoulder and snatched her back. "Think of the long game. All of highborn society is here this afternoon, and the LeBeau family insured my property for quite a sum. Their public failure is worth more than the loss of a few pieces of art. It will bankrupt the auction house, and I'll still get a good return."

"Couldn't happen to nicer people."

"Couldn't happen to us. We should open a replacement. You'd be far more competent to run its security. Isn't this the second robbery of LeBeau's in the last two years?"

"The third, actually," Lila answered as another crash sounded in her ear. "You're really thinking about it, aren't you?"

"When a void appears and you have the capital…"

"How much of that capital do you want to waste in security? How much do you want to throw away on art appraisers?"

"There's always Jewel."

"Jewel's far too busy for a second full-time job. And when she doesn't get a chance to engage in this new experience you'll inevitably offer someone else, she'll make our lives miserable."

"Fair point."

The crashing in Lila's earpiece grew louder. Tristan, Fry, and Shirley must have reached the tunnel, collapsed it, and cut off LeBeau's pursuit.

"There's Senator Langston. We should say hello."

Lila didn't budge. Tristan and his people might not have gotten away. She fumbled, trying to think of an excuse not to abandon her post.

"Elizabeth, come along. Senator Langston is an important—"

An engine choked in her earpiece.

Her part in the heist had officially ended. Five days and nights spent searching and planning, and Tristan had thrown it all away.

"Langston is a self-important blowhard, just like the rest of them," Lila muttered, staring at the young senator with long blond hair and a perfectly knotted cravat.

"Elizabeth!"

Lila drained the rest of her champagne and placed it on a waiter's tray. When her mother turned her back to do the same, she discreetly slipped out her earpieces and dropped them into her clutch.

She wordlessly took the fresh glass her mother handed her, then followed the chairwoman deeper into the room.

It took all her discipline to attend to Senator Langston's conversation, and even then, she failed to pay attention. Her mother nudged her elbow and made appropriate remarks, continuing the conversation when Lila did not. It wasn't that he annoyed her. He merely lacked a certain pair of brown eyes—brown eyes she'd grown far too attached to over the last week, brown eyes she kept thinking about even when she left their presence, brown eyes attached to a rangy body she currently wanted to throttle.

And not in the fun way.

Not that she really had the option. Tristan had not touched her since the hospital the week before, despite how closely they'd worked on their plan to free Oskar, despite how many nights she'd spent with him in his bed.

Both clothed.

Once again, her thoughts slipped from annoyance to hunger.

"So would you like to go with me, Chief Randolph?" Senator Langston asked, offering a slight, hopeful smile.

Lila blinked, her mind slowly shifting from a naked Tristan to the clothed Bullstow senator before her. "Excuse me?"

"Would you like to come with me to Senator Dubois's party next month? It'll be at the Masson's winery, a jewel, as you well know."

Oh great, a pun on her sister's name. That never got old.

Lila tried not to vomit.

She'd almost forgotten about the stupid party. Senator Dubois tried every year to tie her to one of his kin. It should have been enough that he had a claim to her younger sister, but senators could be just as ambitious as their matrons.

"No," Lila answered.

The chairwoman eyed her daughter in annoyance. "What my daughter means is that Senator Dubois would rather she remain unescorted to this particular event."

The senator's expression changed from confusion to acceptance immediately. "Of course. I should have guessed." He bowed and excused himself, no doubt searching for a more receptive heir for his flirtations.

"Really, Elizabeth? At least try to be civil."

"Since when does civility preclude bluntness?"

"Since always, you heathen," the chairwoman snapped as the auctioneer climbed down from the stage, conferring with Olivia. The slave auction would no doubt begin soon. "I have half a mind to drop you in St. Kitts for the next two weeks. Chef is right. You're starved, and it's making you act like a bratty teenager."

Lila frowned. The three highborn resorts on St. Kitts catered to a certain clientele, the sort who could appreciate their special touches: sheets made of the finest Egyptian cotton, tubes of lube on the bed pillows, and sheets of condoms in the bedside drawer. One needed an appetite, a flush bank account, and a fresh STD screening and vaccination for admission, the latter two provided on site.

Apparently the food wasn't bad either—not that anyone booked a room for that reason.

"I'm not starved," she lied, trying to shake Tristan from her mind once more.

A naked Tristan.

"See to your attitude, then, or you'll choose between St. Kitts or taking a lover for the season, for all our sakes." Her mother dragged her to the back of the ballroom, toward a man who wore the most beautifully tailored coat and breeches in the room: pure snow white, unspoiled by any family's colors, unmarked by any coat of arms. He had the shoulders to carry it well, with the cut unable to hide the body of the athlete inside. His salt-and-pepper hair matched all the experience he had gained during his time in the New Bristol, Saxony, and Unity senates.

Now he ruled them all as prime minister.

"Lila, girl." Lemaire pulled her into a bear hug. Lila had missed seeing her father over the last few weeks. He spent most of his time at Unity but governed from Bullstow during Father's Week each month, for the bulk of his children resided in or near New Bristol. "I hated watching the news last week. I couldn't help feeling like I'd really lost my daughter. The senators and highborn in Unity offered me their condolences for two days straight. I worked from my suite because I couldn't listen to it anymore."

"I'm okay."

He squeezed her one more time, then reluctantly let her go. "Never do that for real."

"Same to you," she said with a smile. "I heard your plane landed this morning. I knew you'd turn up early."

"I always do, don't I?" He turned and smiled at the chairwoman. The smile was not the smile of romantic love but the smile of equals, the smile of soul mates, the smile of many roads traveled in the company of a friend. He kissed the chairwoman's cheeks, lingering too long on each. "Bea, you look stunning as usual."

"Likewise. It's been weeks since you've seen the compound. You should come back with me after the auction. We could share a bottle of wine and watch the leaves fall."

"Your offer is tempting. It's so tempting that I'll have to accept."

Her mother chuckled, a real chuckle for once. Lila knew the difference.

The prime minister laughed back, pleased to hear it as well.

"Where's your security force?" Lila asked, thankful they had not entered the room during the failed heist. Their practiced eyes would have deemed her suspicious as soon as she'd pulled out her palm.

"I gave them an hour off for a late lunch. The LeBeaus seemed to have everything well in hand."

"I doubt that sincerely."

Her father let the comment slide. "Bea, I see that you've put up Oskar Kruger for auction."

The chairwoman inclined her head.

"Unity wants him."

"Everyone wants him. Does Unity want him enough to pay?"

"Yes."

"Enough to pay what the others won't?"

Lemaire eyed the chairwoman. "The government cannot compete with the whims of the matrons. You know I'll not be able to outbid anyone in this room."

"Then have this conversation with the winning matron. Perhaps she'll gift him to you."

"I could push something through Unity. Some bit of legislation favorable to your interests?"

"You do that for me already. It was one of the perks of pushing through Lila and Shiloh."

The prime minister sipped his wine. "Let me explain the big picture, Bea. Oskar Kruger has the potential to mend fences between the Allied Lands and the Holy Roman Empire. Perhaps he might even stop this war for a century or two. If I get him for Head Councilman Abbot, then the Allied Lands will have quite the bargaining chip with the emperor. As an ancillary benefit, America would rise above the rest of the commonwealth. I could trade that child for more independence for us all, and the boy could return to his father. Everyone wins."

"You rise. You win. It seems you aim to rule the Allied Lands one day."

"Abbot will step down soon. Why shouldn't I try for the council? I hear Paris is nice this time of year."

"You want to pave your way to the council by helping Peter Kruger? The man's a terrorist, Henri, and he tried to kill your daughter. Do you really want to help him and his spawn have a happily ever after?"

"Alleged terrorist," Lila offered before shrinking under the combined weight of her parents' stares. She looked away, her eyes following a pale member of the militia who squelched toward the ballroom's entrance. Olivia crinkled her nose at his drenched uniform and muddy boots. She barely listened, then waved him away with a firm shake of the head.

Unless Lila was very much mistaken, Olivia had disagreed with the man's plea to double the militia's presence.

How very sloppy.

"That's none of my concern." Her mother shrugged as Lila turned back to her parents' conversation. "There's nothing you can offer me at the moment, Henri. Besides, a senator's role is to smooth the paths of the matrons, not dictate them. Prime minister or not, your role is the same. Don't be crass."

"Don't be petulant just because I asked for a favor. I didn't know Wolf Industries needed the capital from Oskar's sale."

"I don't, but I'm not going to give the government something for nothing. Tell it to me straight. What's your best offer?"

Lemaire's mouth twitched. "One million."

"One? The boy could one day take the German throne one day and play emperor, and yet you offer one million?"

"I had to try money first." He shrugged.

"What's second?"

"The Ashburys have decided to close Unity Memorial and their associated clinics. The hospital's become too unwieldy to make a profit with the demands I set in their contract. I'll soon solicit proposals for another family to take over what they leave behind. Imagine Randolph General on a wider scale and in the nation's capital."

The chairwoman gauged Lemaire's face. "I'd need a lot of land to make it work, Henri."

"Give me Oskar, and I'll get you the land and the contract."

Lila stared openly at her parents. Her father could lose his position and his mark for making such an offer. On the other hand, taking over a hospital in Unity could launch the Randolphs onto the national stage, offering a foothold into the other three American states. The Randolphs wouldn't just be a powerhouse in Saxony, they might become one of the top families in the country. Her mother had always dreamed of sitting on Unity's High Council of Judges. She'd worked diligently over the last ten years to get there.

"You insult me as a woman, a judge, and a CEO with those words."

The prime minister caught her wrist before she could turn away. "I'm sorry, Bea. I'm desperate."

"Desperate enough to display a shocking disregard for the law? And in front of our daughter, no less? I don't need for you to cheat for me, Henri. I can win that contract and procure the land on my own merits. Or do you think I'm incapable?"

"You're more than capable."

The chairwoman looked down at her wrist.

Lemaire dropped his hold.

Lila looked away in embarrassment. She'd never seen her father engage in any sort of impropriety before, save the work he and Shaw brought her. Now this? Would her father offer a similar deal to the winning matron?

Had he tried already?

Most matrons would consider turning him into the senate disciplinary committee for such a transgression. A few might take the deal, though.

Others might blackmail him for it.

Lila scanned the crowd for such matrons as Oskar appeared at a side door flanked by two LeBeau militia. Everyone else watched the boy's progress toward the stage, but Lila watched the highborn and the foreign proxies, sent to bid on their master's behalf.

If Lila hadn't been worried over who else her father might have approached, she might not have noticed the man forty paces away, standing near Olivia LeBeau. She might not have noticed his crooked nose and small pot belly, which clashed with the beautiful, fit senators and highborn men in the room. She might not have noticed his breeches, his poorly tied cravat, and his ill-fitting jacket, all of which were too threadbare to belong to any highborn, and cut two years out of fashion. She might not have noticed his boots, which were well worn and unpolished.

Made for working. Made for running.

Lila's gaze swept up to the man's eyes. They were a little too intent on the raw-eyed Oskar and the LeBeau blackcoats who escorted him onstage.

Lila had already started running by the time he shoved his hand in his jacket pocket. She ran even harder when he withdrew an ivory-handled revolver, a model not used in the Allied Lands because it didn't accept tranqs.

She reached into her clutch and drew her Colt, dropping the purse as she wove around an oblivious heir.

She sprinted even faster as the man raised his trembling gun toward the stage.

3

Lila aimed, shooting three times in quick succession, three little puffs of air that barely made a noise over the still-chattering crowd.

Her first dart skewed wide, but the second hit the gunman's chin, startling him and frustrating his aim. Simultaneously, a sharp blast from his revolver echoed throughout the room.

Her third tranq hit his neck perfectly.

The man flicked it off and did not fall down.

The distraction allowed her to get closer, though. She didn't have time to wonder why the tranq hadn't worked or if anyone had been hit. Dropping her Colt, she sprinted closer, leaping into the air as he aimed again.

Another shot rang out as she barreled into the man's hips.

The pair collided. The gun shot rang far too loudly in her ears.

His weapon skittered across the floor.

Lila rolled onto the gunman's chest, unable to remember the complicated grappling moves from hand-to-hand training. Instead, she sprawled out on top of him and punched at his face, hoping her weight and fist would do the trick.

Predictably, it didn't. He shoved her off like an unruly child and crawled toward Senator Langston. In a brave moment, the politician had chosen to guard the man's gun, keeping it locked between his boots as if he were a hen roosting on a rotten egg. When he saw the would-be assassin heading toward him, he yipped and froze.

"Take it to the militia!" Lila shouted as she clasped her arms around the gunman's ankle. She yanked the man back, her stitches pulling, her palm screaming out with a dull ache. The gunman slid on the wooden floor, his hands whacking against it as he tried to stop the pull.

All at once, he sat up on his hands and knees, kicking back hard with his ensnared boot. It caught Lila in the stomach.

"Oof!" The champagne she'd drunk struggled at her throat, but Lila refused to let go.

In a panic, her fumbling mind landed on a move that would certainly have an effect.

Rolling on her ass, she kicked out, nailing the shooter in the balls.

"Ugh," the man cried out.

Lila winced. She'd hit his balls, all right, but her heel had also struck, stabbing him in the thigh. She nearly gagged as she pulled her foot back, her heel almost refusing to dislodge from his leg.

The gunman didn't seem all that concerned about the trickle of blood, running down his thigh. His boot grew heavy in her arms, and he finally flopped onto his stomach.

Finally, the tranqs had kicked in.

Lila let go of his foot and crawled toward his shoulder, ready to flip him over and check his breathing.

The gunman's elbow smashed into her jaw, stunning her.

Gods, she was horrible at hand-to-hand.

Lunging again, Lila grasped at the man's wrist and jerked, finally recalling at least one hold she'd learned in training. She quickly curled herself into an arm lock, twisting her legs on either side of his arm, pushing her ass into his neck and folding her ankles across his opposite shoulder.

The intruder flailed, pumping his torso off the ground, trying to break free. Seams ripped in her dress, but the lock held.

So did Lila.

She turned a frantic eye around the ballroom, waiting for someone to charge across the room and help her hold down the stranger. It wouldn't be Olivia LeBeau, for it appeared that Lila's first misfire had struck the woman. One little black dart had lodged itself between her perfectly sculpted eyebrows.

The heirs and senators weren't much help, either. Several hundred heads had jerked at the first shot, their eyes latching on to the struggling pair. Some watched with detached interest, assuming Lila would deal with the man, just as blackcoats and workborn always dealt with anything unpleasant in their lives. Others had frozen, refusing to flee out of shock or fear they'd be captured on film looking like an idiot. A quarter of the crowd had no such qualms. They'd run screaming to the exits, shoving one another out of the way in a bid to escape first.

The rest of their peers held up their palms, filming the panic for leverage.

Then there was Oskar Kruger. He trembled on stage, two holes buried in the wood beside his boots. He did nothing at all. He'd been left alone and unregarded when the auctioneer dove off the stage. Oskar hadn't even hidden behind the useless podium. He'd merely closed his eyes while the shots rang out, ready or willing or hoping to die.

Perhaps all three.

The two blackcoats guarding him wouldn't help, either. They'd changed priorities at the first shot and rushed to the prime minister's side, dragging him toward an exit. Her father fought against the pair, his arms sweeping against the blackcoats. "That's my daughter," he shouted, his voice booming amid the high-pitched screams. "Let me go!"

Only her mother had walked toward her. She looked down and calmly pointed at Lila's chest. "Your left breast is hanging out of your dress, Elizabeth."

"Thanks." Lila panted as the intruder continued to flail underneath her. "Could you at least be useful and sit on him?"

"It would be undignified. Fix your dress. There are cameras."

"Fuck my boob and fuck the cameras. No one can publish the damn photos anyway."

"Fix your—"

"Damn it, Mother, I'm a little busy!"

"Watch your language." Her mother's gaze slipped from her breast to her legs. "You are wearing something underneath that dress, aren't you?"

The intruder's muscles finally went limp. Lila swiveled on the wooden floor, twisting the man's arm in another lock, just to be safe.

"Elizabeth, your breast is still—"

"Shut up, Mother."

The gunman tried to bat Lila away as she flipped him on his back and patted down his coat. Finding nothing, she turned out his trouser pockets.

"Is that supposed to happen?" her mother asked, pointing at the man's face.

White foam trickled from his mouth. The small river turned into a flood, little bubbles spewing out onto the floor. A tremor passed over the man, and he began to twitch and shake.

"No, it's not." Lila slid away from the growing puddle, unsure whether it was safe. Adjusting her bodice at last, she turned toward the blackcoats who still struggled against her father. "Fetch a doctor."

One of the blackcoats reluctantly let go of the prime minister and reached for the radio perched on her shoulder.

The other couldn't hold Lemaire back. He sprinted toward his daughter, his boots clomping loudly in the quiet room.

By the time he arrived, the shooter no longer moved.

Everyone else in the room did, though. Now that the prime minister had gotten involved, the heirs considered the matter dealt with. The buzz started up again.

Lila turned back to the gunman and crouched over him. She smacked his cheek, jerking back when foam flew from his mouth and landed on her skin. Wiping it off quickly with her hem, she checked the man's pulse.

She cursed when she could not feel it.

His chest no longer rose, either.

Her stomach churned. She'd killed a man. A living, breathing soul. It didn't matter that she hadn't meant to do it. It didn't matter that he would have been executed for attempted murder in a few weeks. She'd still killed him.

She, Chief Elizabeth Victoria Lemaire-Randolph, had killed a man on a random Saturday afternoon in front of the crème de la crème of highborn society.

In front of her parents.

How could she look anyone in the eye again?

She smacked the man's cheek once more, though she knew it wouldn't do any good. Her tranq had malfunctioned. One of the sensors had failed, not taking into account the state of her target, his imbalance, his weight, his condition, the fact that he'd already been tranqed. It must have given him the full dose on top of another full dose. She'd heard about tranqs failing; she'd just never seen it. She'd never heard about it happening after two shots, either.

But it had happened to her and the gunman.

She'd killed him.

She'd killed a man.

Perhaps she hadn't cleaned her gun properly. Perhaps she hadn't loaded the tranqs correctly. If she'd taken better care, then the man would still be alive.

Oh, gods, he might have kids. He might have people who would miss him.

She cut a quick look back at Oskar Kruger, his slight, bony frame still shivering on the stage, so lost, so unsure of what he should do. He seemed almost disappointed to find himself alive and the danger over.

No one in the ballroom reached out to him.

No one patted his back to tell him that he'd be okay. Why would they? In their eyes, he wasn't a boy. He was another member of the poorer classes who should be so lucky to find himself amid the highborn. For wasn't a servant's contract in one of the great houses an ambition of their stock? Wasn't it the rare and lucky slave who got to see an heir at all?

No one moved, not in the entire ballroom, and Oskar stared around the room, unsure of what to do.

Lila finally understood what Tristan had been through, his entire childhood held up by one lone boy onstage, too confused and too embarrassed to speak or weep, so desperately alone in a room of hundreds. Now she understood why Tristan hadn't reached for her for years and why he'd stolen her palm over and over again.

It hadn't been because he thought it was funny, but because he wanted her to notice him, to touch him, even in anger or annoyance. He'd been exactly like the boy on stage once, though much younger, clinging to his mother as an auctioneer shouted out the bids.

Perhaps he was still like that little boy sometimes, even now, even when they shared a bed.

Perhaps it was also why Tristan had argued in favor of intercepting Oskar before he arrived at the auction house. He'd wanted to spare the boy the same trauma he'd been through years before.

He just hadn't said it.

Perhaps he didn't even know the reason himself.

Lila hadn't understood then, but she understood now.

Oskar looked back at her, probably because it seemed like the closest thing to comfort he'd receive in the room, not that he likely expected any. His father had run away to Germany, hadn't he? His sister Maria had gone missing as well, perhaps never to be seen again. They'd both run away and left him behind. Patrick had done the same, promising to take him away to a far-off land where he wouldn't be a slave. But even Patrick had left him in the end. Tristan and Fry had done the same.

No one would ever come for him. She saw the lesson tattooed in his eyes.

This was the price of Tristan's failure, of their failure. She'd not understood that Tristan's emotions had been far too heavily involved.

A group of senators hopped on stage at last, obscuring her vision. As was their way with children, they surrounded him, speaking to him softly, rubbing his back to comfort him. One gave up on that approach altogether and just took the boy into his arms, holding on to him fiercely.

Oskar collapsed into the senator, his tears rising and swelling, his shoulders shaking.

Lila turned back to the gunman and began chest compressions. She worked, annoyed at Tristan, annoyed at herself, annoyed by her stupid dress and coat as they got in the way. Her knees ached on the oak floor, and she wanted to stop.

But she didn't.

Her father bit his thumb as his entire security detail pounded into the room, a LeBeau militia captain trailing after them. Luckily, Lila didn't have to worry about closing off the auction house and searching for conspirators, for her father's security took over immediately.

Taking over also meant trying to get a defiant prime minister to safety. "I'll leave when my daughter leaves," her father told the group.

The man in charge glanced down at Lila, the wrinkles in his face signaling his intentions.

"Do it, and you'll never work again," Lila threatened as she pumped the gunman's chest. "I'll find all the things you don't want anyone to know, all the things you thought you'd buried years ago, and I'll show them to the world. You and anyone else who lays a finger on me."

The man had been around Lemaire long enough to know his daughter's reputation. "You six, stay and guard the prime minister."

Half the security detail surrounded Lila, her father, and her mother. Their faces turned toward the crowd as they laid their hands on their tranqs.

"See what I mean?" her mother whispered to Lemaire. "Lila needs a vacation. May I suggest St. Kitts?"

The chairwoman clasped her father's hand.

Lila ignored her. She had bigger problems. Her father's people would soon go through every frame of security footage from every camera in the auction house. If she'd missed one, they'd find it. They'd also likely notice her preoccupation with her palm and her hushed whispers to no one in particular.

She wouldn't be charged with freeing a slave.

She'd be charged with attempted murder.

Sweat broke out as she worked on the gunman, and her arms flagged long before a finely dressed woman knelt on his other side.

"I'm the LeBeaus' private physician." The doctor removed her blazer. She popped open the dead man's mouth to check his airway, something Lila had forgotten to do. Or perhaps she'd been too disgusted by the foam pouring from his mouth.

Lila saw the broken capsule as soon as the doctor did.

"Poison," the doctor said, her brown eyes flitting to Lila's before she took over chest compressions.

They said nothing to one another about the futility of it.

Sweat beaded down the side of Lila's face as they switched back and forth. It was important to save the man, even though she understood now she probably hadn't killed him after all.

It still felt like she had.

Lila and the doctor worked until the ambulance arrived. The EMTs' boots squeaked as they lugged a clattering stretcher across the ballroom, the wheels marking the wooden floor with black streaks. Their simple Randolph General polos and black trousers looked out of place among the highborn finery around them.

The EMTs only continued chest compressions because their boss had begun them. They connected sticky pads to the man's chest and shocked him with a tiny electrical box. Lila jerked at the noise, the sound seeming louder than the gunshot moments before.

They lifted him onto the stretcher and continued their work.

"Do you want to come with us?" one of the EMTs asked, a man who likely regretted not shaving that morning. He skimmed her face then stared at the floor, not meeting her eyes.

Lila shook her head, and the LeBeaus' doctor volunteered to go in her place.

A second ambulance arrived a few moments later for Olivia. She'd wake up with the worst hangover she'd ever have in her life, as well as the full force of her matron's wrath.

An hour before, Lila might have found Olivia's situation funny.

The EMTs also checked Lila's hands before they left, confirming that she didn't need more stitches. Lila watched them go and looked around for something useful to do. Since the gunman had been taken away and her father's security had already been handled, she had nothing to occupy her mind. Instead, she waved off her parents, collected her Colt and clutch, then retreated to the ladies' room on the top floor. It looked much like the lobby of the auction house, except it contained a few couches and dressing tables.

Underneath a painting of sunset, Lila took off her gloves and shoved her fingers under the faucet, splashing cool water on her arms where the gunman's spit had landed. A bruise had already formed across her jaw, and Lila winced every time she brushed the bone.

She didn't want to look at her stomach. The gunman's kick still throbbed.

Patting her arms dry, she slipped in her earpiece, listening to the militia while she carefully added more concealer to her jaw. Toxic must have cracked their new signal.

It appeared that her father's security personnel had ordered a thorough search of the auction house. It didn't take them long to find the body, some man found in a ground-floor closet, strangled, his clothes stolen. His wallet had been tossed onto his naked chest as though the killer thought himself above petty theft.

It made the death seem worse somehow, a man killed only for his clothes.

A DNA stick had established the lowborn's identity: some proxy for a foreign bidder.

Lila took out her palm and nearly typed Tristan a message, but she had no idea what to say. She felt as if she'd just relived Reaper's death all over again.

Except this time she had held the gun, rather than Tristan.

Her palm vibrated before she could put it back in her clutch. She opened it immediately, expecting little more than a message from the Randolph security office.

Good evening, Prolix. I trust you've had a few days' rest? Interesting stuff on the news lately. Fallen highborn are so very entertaining, don't you think?

Lila swallowed. Reaper had been the only one who knew about her fake Prolix account, and he was dead. She'd suspected that he had a partner, though, for Reaper's tech had been wiped the day he died, including all evidence of his misdeeds.

Hers too. He'd written an article about her activities in BullNet and hosted it on his private server. The only saving grace was that it had been unconnected to any other webpage.

Lila could only assume it had been a message to his partner, a way of passing information back and forth without the pair meeting. If that were true, then his partner had finally gotten bored. If he grew bored enough to release the article, then she'd be arrested and hanged for treason. She'd only dodge the noose if her father and Chief Shaw admitted the truth. They'd been the ones who'd given her permission to infiltrate BullNet and find Reaper in the first place.

Searching for Reaper had put Lila on his radar.

The public wouldn't care about any of that, though. They'd only see the scandal. They'd only hear that a highborn heir had been given unfettered access to BullNet and all the sensitive government data inside. They'd demand arrests. They'd likely demand executions.

Two lives traded for hers.

If she didn't join them, she'd lose her career, her reputation, her family, and her home, for her mother would exile Lila from the family when the public turned against them.

It was what any matron would do.

Lila tried to put it all out of her mind. She quickly configured her snoop programs to do a cursory search of the sender's ID, cross-referenced against a master list of all official logins.

She found no hits.

The ID was a fake.

Sitting down on a couch, Lila turned her back on the mirror, glad no one had barged into the bathroom yet. She'd been too busy with Oskar and Tristan all week to plug the last hole in her father's job. This was the price. Some asshole now taunted her from afar.

Rubbing her jaw, she stood up, knowing she couldn't stay locked away in the bathroom forever. She put on her gloves, jammed her earpiece into her clutch, and finger-combed her curls. She was a Randolph heir as well as the chief of her mother's militia. Chiefs and Randolphs and heirs didn't hide, and they certainly didn't wallow.

As she padded downstairs, her father peeked his head around the ballroom door. His security watched her every step, obviously unhappy that the prime minister still insisted on remaining in the auction house.

"I was worried," he said. "You were gone for quite a while."

"I had to fix my makeup."

"That man hurt you. I'm calling Dr. Booth to—"

"Father, I'm fine. I just needed a few moments to collect myself."

Her father grabbed her chin, carefully avoiding her bruise. "I'm proud of you, Lila. You showed everyone today why you're chief. You showed everyone what the Lemaires and Randolphs are made of."

"You also managed to make the LeBeau militia look like incompetent fools," her mother added. The chairwoman hadn't even bothered to modulate her tone, causing a few LeBeau militia nearby to frown. "Come inside. People are starting to talk."

"We can't have that." Lila sighed.

"Not when a rumor has spread that someone shot you again. It's getting tedious."

Lemaire took her arm and escorted her into the ballroom. Her mother stood on the other side, obviously intent on meeting the crowd as a united family. Half the crowd quieted when they entered. The other half trailed off in broken conversation. Even the LeBeau and Bullstow militias lowered their palms, enjoying the welcome break from recording witness statements.

Lila wasn't sure who started it. A member of the Bullstow militia, if she had to guess. One clap turned into two, and the militia and senators broke into applause.

The heirs joined in out of politeness.

Lila fought the urge to stare at the floor. Gracefully, she inclined her head.

The applause petered out.

The militia turned back to their unhelpful witnesses, and the heirs resumed their endless shuffling around the ballroom, still gossiping, perhaps gossiping more now that Lila had returned.

Lila was grateful not to be in charge. The highborn were annoying enough when their events hadn't been spoiled by the militia and the poorer classes.

"No telling who might have gotten shot if you hadn't taken down the gunman," her father grumbled. "The heirs should be more grateful."

"I saved Oskar, Father. He was the only target." A worry nagged at her, though. What if the gunman had planned on a second target? Everyone knew what the white coat and breeches meant in the Allied Lands. Most knew what it meant outside of the Allied Lands too, especially in the empire. The German and Italian kings would never dare attack the prime minister of a commonwealth nation, would they?

She held on to her father a little tighter. She couldn't lose him. Not today. Not ever.

"One lone assassin sent for a slave," her mother mused. "Odd that. He didn't seem that professional. Even Lila managed to pin him."

"Thanks, Mother." Lila stared at the spot where the stranger had died, now mopped and cleared of blood and foam. "I've never seen someone last so long after being hit by a tranq. He must have taken a suppresser before the auction. That's neither cheap nor easy to come by."

"Loyalists?" her father asked.

"Loyalists wouldn't want Oskar to return to Germany. King Lucas himself might have given the order. I can't think of anyone else who would go after him."

Her mother took a glass of wine, offered by the frantic auction house staff. A LeBeau heir had finally taken charge in Olivia's absence, intent on soothing the crowd with booze and food. Little sandwiches and pastries now circled the room.

Beatrice handed Lila a glass, inclining her head at Lila's hands. Her fingers had begun to shake.

Randolphs didn't tremble before other heirs.

Lila took a long sip of the wine. She needed to get out of the building. She needed to get back home and trace the snoop's message. She had to find Reaper's partner and figure out the game before another message appeared on her palm.

"This is exactly why I didn't advertise Oskar's sale and why I wanted to get rid of him so quickly," her mother said. "One slave is not worth the increased security costs, no matter the bragging rights. The others are fools if they bid at all."

Lemaire cocked a brow. "Just say the word, and my people will take Oskar."

"Have you told your security detail that?" Lila asked.

"They'll adjust."

"How can it be that no one's shot you yet?"

"Henri, I'll not give you the boy. I'd never have another successful auction again. You can't promise to sell things and not sell them."

Six LeBeau blackcoats brought Oskar back to the stage, for the LeBeau now running the show must have been eager to conclude the auction. The blackcoats stood on either side of him, covering the ragged bullet holes in the stage, their stern gazes panning the crowd.

The auctioneer walked to the podium, weaving a tad on his feet. He carried a glass of amber liquid with him, and the militia eyed it knowingly. Perhaps they'd taken a drink or two as well. The people of the Allied Lands weren't used to bullets, not unless you'd taken a tour in the infantry, and few among the highborn joined the military.

The auctioneer tapped on the microphone. After a brief speech about the LeBeaus' commitment to security, he opened a folder and began to read quickly, giving them a brief outline of Oskar's medical history, his parentage, and his skills. Oskar stared at the floor, reddening as the auctioneer mentioned he suffered from anxiety and stomach problems.

Tristan must have endured the same as a child, listening as some stranger read details of his personal life to a bored crowd.

Had he gone red, too?

Lila tried to catch the boy's eye again, but he refused to look up. He just kept his hands in his pockets, fidgeting as fifteen-year-old boys tended to do.

"Of course, as a German citizen, Oskar Kruger will never be allowed to purchase his mark," the auctioneer concluded.

Onstage, Oskar frowned.

"I'll start the bidding at ten thousand."

Chairwoman Hardwicke raised her paddle.

A man beside them countered it, another proxy for a foreign bidder, by the look of his coat. "The boy doesn't belong here," he hissed, his desperation overriding his propriety.

"He doesn't belong in Germany either," Lila said. "I suppose you'll help shuffle him along if your patron wins the bid."

"Of course not. It would be illegal for me to conduct business on behalf of a Roman citizen. The laws are strict—too strict, if you ask me."

"That's almost treason."

The laws weren't too strict, and they both knew it. Only citizens of the Allied Lands had the right to bid on slaves. If a non-American won the auction, Chief Shaw would have to verify everything before allowing Oskar out of the country. Papers would be signed, contracts would be validated by both governments, and many promises and assurances would be made on both sides.

None of that set Lila's mind at ease. Some of the less scrupulous matrons likely had a plan for smuggling Oskar out of the country, right under Bullstow's nose.

The lowborn ignored her parting shot. He turned on his heel, stalking closer to the stage.

Lila wondered whom he represented.

She could find out. It wouldn't be that hard.

"Fifty thousand to Chairwoman Hardwicke," the auctioneer said, offering a slightly inebriated chuckle. "I bet that flawless opal around her neck cost more."

After his comment, so many bids came in that he could hardly keep track. But as the amount pushed higher and higher, fewer paddles flashed throughout the room. Oskar's price had quickly soared above what most were willing to spend. The winner would still have to pay for the boy's education, medical fees, and security. Oskar Kruger would cost a great deal in upkeep.

That lesson had been burned into the heirs less than an hour before.

It didn't take long for the bids to dwindle away. Soon only Chairwoman Hardwicke and Chairwoman Holguín flashed their paddles.

"Six point five million to Chairwoman Hardwicke."

Chairwoman Holguín narrowed her eyes, peering at her rival. "Seven," she called out.

Half the room clucked their tongues. Calling out over the crowd was tacky. Highborn eyes bounced back and forth as though they watched a tennis match.

"Do I hear seven point five, Chairwoman Hardwicke?" the auctioneer asked.

The matron nodded, and the bidding started anew.

After Chairwoman Holguín raised her paddle for ten million, Chairwoman Hardwicke shook her head, letting her rival take the boy.

"I didn't know the Hardwickes were interested in Oskar," Lila said.

"They aren't," her mother replied. "Everyone knows that Chairwoman Holguín likes ones and fives and tens at these things. Chairwoman Hardwicke just wanted to drain her coffers."

As soon as the gavel banged against the podium, Chairwoman Holguín click-clacked toward the ballroom entrance, the handcrafted lace on her orange dress swaying with every step. The twin tigers on her coat of arms, stitched on the breast of her silvercoat, snarled at one another.

"It's the loyalists," her father said as the LeBeau militia led Oskar back to the holding cells. Phillip Wilson stepped up beside the podium next, his chin raised, his lips frozen in a pout. "I suspect killing Oskar was Plan A. Plan B is dealing with the Holguíns. They'll buy the boy and murder him to secure the empire, and it will only cost them ten million to do it. I should never have let you sell him, Bea."

"The prime minister does not let the matrons do anything. And I sincerely doubt that Chairwoman Holguín has found a loophole around the slave regulations. She's not smart enough for that."

"She doesn't need a loophole," Lila reminded them. "If I wanted the boy dead, I'd promise one of the families whatever it took, just so I knew where the boy would be after the auction ended. It would only take one shot from a high-powered rifle a kilometer away. A trained sniper—someone like Commander Sutton—could make that shot easily."

Her mother's face paled. Clearly, she hadn't thought of the most obvious solution.

Perhaps there was hope for her yet.

"Lila, you need a vacation."

"I'm only saying what someone has already planned, Mother. An assassin doesn't even have to take the shot tonight, especially if half the journalists in New Bristol follow the boy. They can just keep him in sight and wait for a clear shot. My advice, Father? Get Chief Shaw on it, and advise the Holguíns to keep the boy underground. It's hard to find someone on thermal through several tons of dirt."

Her father pulled out his palm and began typing a message. "I'll have Chief Shaw escort the boy to the Holguín compound and keep a few patrols in t   he area. The chairwoman can contest our interference with the council later."

"She will," her mother predicted. "I suspect two groups are out tonight, Henri. The loyalists want Oskar dead, but the traditionalists will want him alive. At ten million credits, the boy would make for a cheap and grateful puppet, one still young enough to be molded."

"It beats being a slave, doesn't it?" Lila asked.

"It's just a different kind of slavery. We should all be more concerned with the empire's aristocracy. If they fetch Oskar and take his father from King Lucas, then they could gain control of the empire, so long as they can sway public sentiment and gain the support of their clergy. Warmongers, the lot of them. King Lucas does a fair job of holding them all in check, but if he loses the reins…"

The chairwoman took a sip of wine and fixed her daughter with a stare. "War is generally bad for business, unless you're the one supplying the bullets and the rations and tossing someone else's children into the breach. It only takes one excuse to beat the drums."

"Well, let's hope they don't find an excuse."

"Let's hope they take up a new pastime and stop playing at politics."

"You dabble all the time, Mother."

"Dabbling isn't what they do. We push through favorable zoning laws and pollution regulations. That's a lot different than poking at foreign leaders and governments. It's why we let the senate handle such things. Buffers, if you will. Buffers who have too many children scattered among the highborn and lowborn alike to risk their offspring falling on the front lines of a war without reason. It gives us boundaries, Lila. That's the difference. Ask Commander Sutton if you still don't understand." She drained her glass and nodded at Lemaire. "Are you ready to leave, Henri?"

He tapped out one last message on his palm. "Yes. Lila, would you like to ride with us?"

Lila frowned. The pair seemed to have made up. "As much as I love trying to carry on a conversation while you both paw at one another, I have my own car and a prior appointment."

"Such a grouch. Maybe she does need a vacation, Bea."

The chairwoman looked smugly at Lila.

"Come to Falcon Home tomorrow morning for breakfast, Lila girl. Nine o'clock. I have an early meeting, but I'll wait to eat until you arrive."

Lila nodded, steeling her face so that she would not tip off her mother. Her father didn't want breakfast. He wanted her help with Oskar.

And that was too bad, for Lila had every intention of stealing the boy herself.

"I'd love to have breakfast with you, Father."

"Good. Perhaps I'll even try my hand at making pancakes."

Lila tried to smile. Though she appreciated the effort, she'd eaten burned pancakes too many times as a child. "*Hmmm*," she answered diplomatically.

"Fine, I'll ask Chef Mathieu make them instead."

"No sausage?"

"No sausage," he promised, his hand over his heart.

"Well, in that case, I'd be delighted to attend."

4

Lila exited the bathroom, her silken white robe light upon her skin. Two wolves had been stitched in red upon the breast, both snarling and biting in different directions. She dried her damp hair with a towel and sat upon her bed.

She had a blackmailer to catch, but all she wanted to do was sleep. Tristan had promised her a long rest after they caught Oskar. Her mother had promised the same after the auction.

Now she'd have another hard few days recovering the boy.

Her back hit the mattress, the gray and white paint on her walls calming her, the emptiness of the room soothing. She'd always kept her decorations simple and orderly. Bedding in black with little pops of crimson in the pillows. A black leather couch along one wall. A headboard, desk, coffee table, dresser, and bedside table, all carved in ebony. Jewel had crafted a small Randolph coat of arms out of silver, much like the one stitched upon her clothes, and Lila had hung it above her couch. That, and a collection of framed photos on her dresser, rounded out the room's decor.

Her palm buzzed upon her desk, reminding her of the blackmailer's message.

Reluctantly, she returned to her desk and checked her message. Commander Sutton had sent her an update from the security office. Luckily, she hadn't mentioned the gunman.

Lila switched on her desktop computer. She sent out spies to watch the Holguín compound and, for the next hour, fiddled with her snoop programs, altering them slightly to gather what she could from the blackmailer's message. After setting them to run their searches, she pulled open a secret compartment in the back of her closet. She withdrew a pair of black trousers, gray gloves, and a long-sleeved gray shirt, none of which displayed the family's coat of arms. After dressing quickly, she added a pair of worn boots. Though cheap, the boots felt like pillows and clouds after spending so many hours in heels. The unmarked, drab clothes would be a damn sight more anonymous than faffing about in Randolph red on Shippers Lane, and faffing about was exactly what she intended to do. She had a few choice words for Tristan. She also had no desire to be alone after what she'd done—what it felt like she'd done.

It would only make her dreams worse. She'd had a steady stream of disturbing ones the week before, dreams of an ancient oracle prodding her to visit the New Bristol temple, dreams of Reaper holding a knife to her throat, dreams of Tristan stabbing the hacker and firing a bullet into his neck, dreams of Dixon writhing on the floor. She had no interest in crawling into bed and risking another.

A giggle pierced the air as she opened her bedroom door. Her mother and father must have moved their wine drinking upstairs. Perhaps Lemaire would spend the next week in the chairwoman's bed, rendering them both too busy to bother Lila about silly things, leaving her free to rescue a potential monarch of their country's sworn enemy.

Lila slipped downstairs, passing under the full-length version of her sister's silver coat of arms and a few centuries of Randolph family portraits. When she thought about her life like that, she wondered who she'd become in the last couple of years. She certainly wasn't the woman her mother raised her to be. That didn't bother her much, for she'd never wanted to be that person, but the fact that she was drifting away from her father's notions of right and wrong did. Her father had always been her moral compass. If he looked at her tonight, really looked at her and all the things she'd done recently, what would he say?

He certainly wouldn't be proud.

If he was just, he'd most likely ask Shaw to arrest her.

Then again, he'd tried to bribe her mother a few hours before, all to save a boy from a lifetime of slavery. Perhaps he'd understand.

Lila slipped through the great house scullery, avoiding the footman in their coats and breeches. She jogged down a rose-strewn gravel path to the garage. It contained the cars of the chairwoman and her daughters, most shared between the three women. But no one dared touch the chairwoman's sleek Blanc convertible, just as no one dared touch Lila's Adessi roadster or her silver Firefly, a motorcycle full of curves and moxie. Unfortunately, she could not ride it due to the stitches on her palms. Instead she stopped before a nondescript Cruz sedan, one of the cheaper models the workborn could attain, so long as they belonged to a profession. There were thousands of such cars in New Bristol, which meant that it would afford her some degree of anonymity.

Pulling out her palm, she brought up her snoop programs and searched for her mother's ubiquitous bugs. Finding an audio bug and a GPS tracker, she tossed them onto her sister's Firefly in an ever-growing pile, then sped through the Randolph estate. A stone wall topped with iron surrounded the compound, just like the other eleven highborn compounds in New Bristol.

The Randolph estate shone just a bit brighter than the others, though. It spanned ten kilometers in each direction, far wider than any other compound. Wolf Tower soared above it all near the center of the compound, housing her mother's penthouse office as well as the offices of the other Randolph executives. No other skyscraper in the city came close to reaching its forty-five stories. Her mother wouldn't allow it.

Other skyscrapers crowded around Wolf Tower in the north, including the twin Garza buildings and several condos covered in glass. The south held the palatial homes of the heirs, including the chairwoman's great house, named Villanueva House after the architect who designed it. The Greens housed the legion of slaves who toiled as groundskeepers. They were all needed, for much of the compound contained nothing but lawns and flowers and trees. It made for a nice jog in the morning, but it took a great deal of care to maintain.

She reached the south gate quickly and flashed a distracted wave to Sergeant Tripp and his rookie.

The two blackcoats drew themselves up tighter when they glimpsed their chief. Sergeant Tripp bent at the rolled-down window and inclined his head. His pipe peeked from his coat pocket. "Evening, chief. Heard there was a fuss at the auction tonight."

"A bit."

"The security office is buzzing about it. Great save, chief." A ghost of a grin appeared on his face. "Were you really wearing heels at the time?"

"Yeah, I stole them from your closet." Lila sped off, knowing the security office would be covered in ribbons and heels when she arrived the next morning.

She drove the sedan along the darkening downtown streets, speeding past the lowborn and workborn crowds who had ventured out for dinner dates and anniversaries. Couples lined up with intertwined hands, young and old alike, waiting to enter restaurants they could barely afford. With little knowledge of the season's trends, they did not judge their partners for their attire, only noting it with simple descriptors: sexy, cute, sporty, and smart.

Lila knew they used more, she just couldn't think of them. She tried, though, all so she didn't have to think of the gunman's face while he lay on the ballroom floor, the way he'd looked when she—

Lila licked her lips and hit the gas, speeding toward the entrance for the interstate. Few cars drove upon it so late in the evening, and she slalomed through what little traffic remained.

Sexy, cute, sporty, and smart. What else had she read in those teen magazines all those years ago?

Ah, trendy. It described those from the poorer classes who snatched up counterfeit designer goods and try to pass them off as highborn ware.

Gods, she and Holly used to—

Lila swallowed hard. She didn't want to think about her, either. Mashing the gas, Lila sped along, not caring a whit about her speed.

It didn't take long for her to reach Shippers Lane. She parked in a parking garage near a Chinese restaurant called the Plum Luck Dragon, hoping her car would still be there when she returned. Plastic bags and cigarette packages skittered past her boots on the sidewalk. Today her stomach rolled at the smell of pork lo mein and stir-fried rice. Usually after a job, Tristan and Dixon celebrated with enough food to launch her into an MSG coma, but this job had not gone well. She hoped he hadn't bought food at all, for the last thing she wanted to do was eat.

Perhaps Tristan wouldn't want food either. Perhaps he was too busy explaining to Maria why her brother had not been brought back from the job as promised. Perhaps he was too busy bringing her tissue after tissue after tissue.

She and Tristan would fight about that. The fighting would annoy her even more than usual. They'd been getting along so well lately, ever since they'd narrowly escaped the Wilson compound. Reaper had bluffed that he'd poisoned Tristan's brother and that only he held the antidote. He'd also lunged at Lila with a knife. Tristan had shot Reaper, not realizing the gun held bullets, rather than tranqs. He'd killed a man and condemned Dixon to death with one shot.

Luckily, Dixon had only been given an anesthetic. A harsh one, but it hadn't killed him.

Reaper's death had amped Tristan up, though, had made him nervous and fidgety. It weighed on him but not as much as his split-second decision to save Lila's life at the expense of his brother's. Though he claimed he didn't regret it, he still hadn't come to terms with it.

He hadn't come to terms with Lila, either. Sleeping in bed together, curling up in one another's arms, was a welcome change from their perpetual arguing, but Lila still didn't know how to feel about it.

Highborns were much more casual about sex than the poorer classes, and he obviously didn't know how difficult their new normal was for her. To be so near someone and not have sex was torture.

It was even worse when you'd begun to develop feelings for them.

Lila slipped on her mesh hood and rounded the corner, the fabric stifling in the heat. A woman in a derby hat hopped up from a wooden chair when she saw Lila, the bulge of a tranq gun peeking out from both their pockets. Without a word, Samantha opened the front door of the mechanic shop, half medieval church, half dilapidated building. At least, it had been dilapidated before Tristan threw himself into restoring it with nervous abandon. Now the lights that spelled *Mechanic* had been fixed, the front door painted, the graffiti-covered plywood behind the iron-barred window taken away in favor of a glass pane. New thick drapes waved behind it.

The purple feather in Samantha's hat bowed as Lila entered, and the scent of grease and oil filled Lila's nose. The shop functioned as a mechanic's business during the day. As a consequence, a tangle of cars and trucks and motorcycles filled the back, parked so close that only a professional could pull them out again.

"The trucks all look nice, Shirley," Lila said, pitching her voice a bit lower than natural. She jutted her chin toward the row of blue Cruz trucks, recently painted.

"Thanks, Hood." The old woman sat on a stool under a sign that read *Clean up or Suffer.* Part of her ear and a few fingers had been severed, not that she seemed bothered by it. Shirley was more than capable of fixing a motorcycle engine and holding a knife with what fingers she had left. And according to Sam, she could hear a mouse fart across the room with her one good ear.

"Maria, come here," Shirley said, tugging at the neck of her coveralls.

The fifteen-year-old had been earnestly sweeping the garage when Lila came in, keeping her head down as she ducked between the trucks to catch every speck of dust and dirt. Likely before she'd come in as well, for the floor looked cleaner than Lila had ever seen it.

Maria immediately raced to Shirley. Her eyes never rose from the floor, and her loose gray dress twirled around her legs when she stopped. A healing gash peeked from her collar, for Doc had cut out her slave's chip, the ID and homing beacon that bound slaves to their masters.

The girl sniffled and gripped the broom like a shield, her shoulders tense, her eyes raw and red. As Peter Kruger's daughter, she should have been a princess of the Holy Roman Empire, but had instead lived with her twin brother as a slave under the spiteful hand of Chairwoman Wilson.

Shirley shook her head at the girl's speed. "Maria, I didn't mean you had to run. You can walk when you feel like it, remember?"

"Yes, madam. Sorry, madam."

"Maria, this is a friend of Tristan's. Her name's Hood. She's one of people who helped your daddy get to Germany."

Maria bowed low. "Thank you, madam."

"We're going to get your brother back," Lila vowed. "We won't fail again. I promise."

"Thank you, madam." Maria's shoulders rose as she gripped the broom.

Lila and Shirley sighed simultaneously. It was difficult talking to Maria. She only said a few phrases, never failing to attach a *madam* or *sir* to the end. Worse than that, her shoulders rose higher and higher the longer you spoke to her. It was a bit like conversing with a human hourglass. When her shoulders reached her ears, you had to let her go. If you didn't, the shaking would begin.

"Your hair is different," Lila said. "I like the red."

"Thank you, madam."

"It does look good, doesn't it, Hood?" Shirley said. "She wouldn't choose a new hair color, so Zoe recommended this. Maria let him do it. I nearly had a heart attack, thinking it wouldn't look natural, but it looks quite good. You made a good choice, didn't you, Maria?"

The girl stared at the ground. Her shoulders had reached her ears. They'd run out of time.

"Okay, go on, then," Shirley said. "Go on back to your sweeping if that's taken your fancy."

Maria scooted away and swept faster.

Lila studied her face, her body. Most slaves eavesdropped continuously, whether from curiosity or because they spied for another family.

Maria didn't seem interested, though. She didn't seem interested in anything.

"Hood, if they don't kill that bitch Wilson soon, I'm going to break into Bullstow and do it for them. I can't stop the girl from cleaning. We tried to explain that she doesn't have to do slave's work anymore, but she doesn't seem to understand what that means."

"Maybe she doesn't know what normal girls do."

"Maybe. I can't even get her to tell me what she wants for dinner, much less what she wants to wear or do for the day. She won't speak unless she's spoken to, and she doesn't say much beyond yes, no, thank you, and I'm sorry. It's breaking my heart."

"You're good with her."

Shirley shifted at the unexpected compliment.

"Perhaps it would be best to limit her options. Ease her into decision making. Have her choose among three things to eat, have her pick what to wear from three options, have her decide what to do each hour or so from a few choices."

"Like a toddler?"

Lila shrugged.

"Seems patronizing, but you have a point."

"Get her a tutor, too. I imagine she's woefully behind."

"Hard to find a tutor we can trust. Although, to be fair, no one seems to care that she's gone missing. They only care about Oskar." Shirley scratched at what was left of her ear. "Perhaps I could work with her a little and drag Dixon into it. Tongueless fool can't spook her if he can't speak. He's got a whole lot of book-learning in him."

She picked up a wrench and pointed a half-knuckle at the door in the back. "The boss man's upstairs. He's not in a good mood. Telling Maria he'd failed…it damn near killed him."

Lila dodged the tangle of cars and trucks to get to the shop's back door. She climbed the staircase, marveling at how nice the building had become in the last week. Tristan had repaired everything from baseboards to doorknobs to windows, painting every wall and trim. With Maria around, the place sparkled and shined.

Lila opened the door to Tristan and Dixon's apartment on the top floor and tossed her mesh hood upon the kitchen counter. It had been made from a thick slab of wood, which balanced on a pair of old wine barrels. The wood had been polished with a dark stain. Every other table had been made in the same way, leaving the room smelling of wine. Comfortable black couches swallowed the room.

Lila squinted at the dark purple paint on the walls, a project Tristan had finished only a few days before. Through an open door in the back, she saw Dixon's room, painted in stripes of varying lengths and colors: green, blue, purple, the occasional swatch of orange and yellow and gold. Tristan had called the job tacky, but he had painted them anyway. It was a gift for his brother, an I'm-sorry-I-chose-to-rescue-Lila-instead-of-you present.

As a result, things were definitely weird and forced between her and Dixon. His normal good mood and banter had been replaced by thoughtful, brooding silences whenever she entered the room. Worse was when he tried to joke like he used to.

Things were just so horribly forced.

Hot, too. Dixon had cranked up the heat again, and Tristan hadn't said a word against it. Neither would Lila. She took off her jacket and t-shirt, already prepared with a black tank underneath.

She then plopped between the pair, each sitting on either end of the couch. Tristan wore nothing but black cotton pajama pants, his dark hair mussed, his dark eyes heavy, his arms crossed tight around his chest like a pouting child. Dixon lounged in purple, rubbing his closely shaved head, his blue eyes exhausted.

The bright light caught the silver scars on their necks.

Dixon inclined his head, uncurling from his perch to study her face.

"Tired?" she asked.

Dixon nodded.

"Me too." She dropped her head onto the back of the couch.

He pointed at the bruise on her jaw.

"It's nothing a glass of wine won't fix."

Tristan took the hint and fetched a bottle of La Sangre de las Flores from a locker in the corner. Then he ventured into the kitchen. The freezer opened and closed with a sticky pop. "Did you see Maria?" he asked, handing her a bag of frozen peas as he sat back down.

"I see that she's still here. It's not safe for her. It's not safe for you and your people either if you keep her." Lila held the bag to her jaw, welcoming the burst of cold.

"She stays until I find her brother." He uncorked the bottle of wine with a hollow thump and filled a Jolly Roger mug. Another sat on the coffee table in front his place, filled with whiskey, by the smell of Tristan's breath. "She's been crying off and on all evening."

"I imagine so. She thought her brother would be free tonight."

Tristan handed her the mug of wine. "You should have let us break him out of your family's holding cells."

Lila frowned, the sweet taste of the blackberry wine soured by his mood. Tonight, Tristan was the old Tristan. She'd been waiting for their truce to expire, for him to begin arguing with her once more. She had hoped things wouldn't go back to how they'd been before, that they'd move to a new place instead, that they'd reach some new understanding.

Apparently, Tristan had other plans.

"No, I shouldn't have let you break in."

"Why? Because you couldn't bear a hit to your perfect record, even to save a child?"

"No, because my entire family would be investigated. I'm far too good at my job for someone like you to break into my compound. It would have raised suspicions, and you know it."

"Oracle's light, you're arrogant."

"I'm not arrogant. I'm correct."

"That's not the real reason," Tristan said, hopping up to pace. "I heard you speaking to your mother over the mic. You told her the robbery would force LeBeau's to close its doors. Had a good laugh about it, even planned to open a new auction house in its—"

"I had to say something so my mother didn't realize I was feeding you information, you nitwit. Don't blame me for your mistakes. I told you a hundred times that you only had enough time to break out Oskar, even with Fry's help. Somehow in your mind that translated into—"

"I couldn't leave him there. He's just a kid."

"A kid who has the opportunity to work off his mark. A kid who isn't in danger of being murdered." An image came to Lila's mind. The gunman's face as he'd raised the gun to kill Oskar, his eyes fading as he died.

An image of Reaper after he'd been shot.

An image of Dixon when they couldn't wake him.

"Yeah, I heard about what happened after we left. They keep showing it on the news. They say you saved Oskar's life."

Lila sat up, eyes wide. "Showing it? Showing what?"

"Showing nothing. They must have had a whole team pixilating you out in time for the evening news. It makes you even more obvious."

Dixon scribbled on his notepad. *You leapt like a flailing housecat but classier.* The joke belied his face, which hadn't twisted into his usual playful smile.

"So they have footage of it?"

Dixon nodded.

"Let me see."

"Great. You want to revel in your newfound fame." Tristan rolled his eyes and took another swig of his whiskey.

"No, I want to see what else was going on in the room, nitwit. I was a bit preoccupied."

"Stop calling me nitwit."

"Okay, jackass. Is that better?"

Tristan turned away and peered out the window.

Dixon passed Lila his palm, and she studied the shaky footage. It had likely come from a highborn's palm or from one of the servants. Unfortunately, she saw nothing except a pixelated ghost leaping atop the gunman.

Dixon was right. Her blobby form did look like a flailing house-cat, hurling itself toward the gunman, not that she'd admit it.

Gods, she hoped the Randolph militia hadn't gotten hold of the unedited footage.

Lila scrolled the video back to the beginning and watched it through again, focusing on the would-be assassin. She saw the same look in the gunman's eyes as before. Conviction. He truly believed that killing the boy was a necessary evil, that it was the best thing for everyone.

"He's a loyalist for the crown," Lila guessed, scrolling back through the footage to watch it again. "He's not conflicted about what he's doing. He believes."

Dixon gave thumbs-up, and Tristan nodded. "That was our guess as well."

Lila watched it a few more times, peering at the crowd. Only Chairwoman Holguín looked the least bit odd. Her mouth had widened in alarm after the assassin had lifted his gun, her eyes on fire, as though someone held a lighter to ten million credits on stage.

Her ten million.

Lila sent the footage to her palm and returned Dixon's device. Then she brought up the footage of their heist, scanning it frame by frame.

"What's that?" Tristan asked, peeking over her shoulder.

"Security footage from tonight. He didn't appear out of nowhere."

Tristan grabbed a cable and connected her palm to the screen in the front of the room. They sat in a row on the couch, watching the basement footage.

It was Tristan who saw it. The gunman peeked around the door, spied the heist-in-progress and the impotent cameras, then scowled and left.

The LeBeaus discovered the loop a moment later.

"Oracle's wrath! He tipped them off. He's why the plan went to shit," Lila said. "You saved Oskar's life, you know. The gunman had to find another way to carry out his plan."

"By creating a distraction so he could kill some innocent lowborn instead." Tristan kicked up his legs on the coffee table. "If I'd seen him, I could have—"

"That man's death is not your fault. It's the fault of the man who pulled the trigger."

"I'm getting Oskar out of there. I'm not leaving him with those people."

Lila glanced at Tristan's face and saw the darkness that passed over it. "What did the Holguíns do to you? To both of you."

Tristan's eyes traveled to Dixon. His brother stood up and walked to the window, brooding once more, the crisscross of scars marring his back like raised, writhing serpents. Dixon had never hidden them from her, but he'd never explained them, either.

Tristan had kept his brother's secrets.

"What I don't get is why the loyalists tried to kill Oskar now," Lila said, changing the subject. "He's been a slave in the Wilson compound for years without attention."

"Yes, but the German masses have been a bit too interested in their long-lost king lately. That makes all sorts of important people nervous. It provides hope to the traditionalists, too. After all, Oskar is young enough to be molded."

"My mother said the same thing."

"Also, King Lucas got caught with his mistress a few days ago. Photos of the kissing couple are all over the news in the empire."

"Romans are bizarre. My father has seeded children for eight different women over the years, and my mother has had children with three different men. That's not even counting all the lovers they—"

"Sometimes I don't understand how you can be so smart and yet not understand the very simplest of things."

"What's to understand? The empire labors under some misguided pretense of monogamy. Whatever happened is an issue between him and his wife, if she cares at all. Not his country."

"It's not like the wife knew," Tristan said. "It's cheating, and Romans consider it a personal failing. So do the workborn. If a man cheats in one part of his life, he probably cheats in others."

"How do they know the king and queen don't have an arrangement? If the queen is smart, she has lovers of her own. She lives in a palace full of young, virile bodyguards. You can't seriously expect me to believe she doesn't dabble with one or two."

"Why not seven, if we're throwing out numbers? Perhaps a different lover for every night of the week?"

"Seven? I admire her stamina." Lila grinned. At Tristan's narrowed eyes, she took a sip of her Sangre and cleared her throat. "So how badly do they consider cheating in the empire?"

"It's a public disgrace. Someone likely had the photos ready, waiting for the right time to embarrass the emperor." Tristan rubbed at his evening stubble. "Have you eaten?"

Lila shook her head.

"You should eat." He picked up his palm from the coffee table and typed in an ID, most likely for the Plum Luck Dragon next door.

"I'm not hungry."

"That's okay. You don't have to eat all of it. I'll get you some pork lo mein. You like lo mein. You order it all the time."

"Really, I don't want anything. I just want to sit."

Dixon shook his head too, and Tristan tossed his palm back on the coffee table with a dull thump. "Are you okay? That asshole didn't—"

"I'm fine."

His eyes snaked to her jaw, but he didn't say another word. "Fine, we'll start planning how we'll get into the Holguín estate. The news vans followed Oskar. He's in there."

"Doesn't mean he'll stay. The boy is a security nightmare, and Chief Holguín will certainly want him moved as quickly as possible. They just won't do it tonight. One leak and the press will follow them down the interstate. My father has stationed Bullstow militia around the compound. They'll keep an eye on him for us. I put a few spies on it too. They're monitoring the news vans and ferreting out his location on the compound."

"I'll get my spies on it as well." Tristan grabbed his palm and typed out a few messages.

Lila did not say a word against his rare note of caution. She was surprised he hadn't suggested infiltrating the compound that very night. Then again, he'd become more conservative over the last week even though he'd been rash in trying to save Phillip. Peering at Dixon, she couldn't help but think she knew the reason why.

Dixon avoided her eyes and trundled toward his room, yawning, ready for bed. It was a place he'd likely been for half the day.

Lila glanced at Tristan, not ready to leave. She hadn't come just to talk about their failure at LeBeau's. She'd come to talk with him about the gunman, about how she'd felt when she thought she'd killed him.

He'd be one of the few people who would understand.

But now that she was with him, she didn't know how to begin the conversation.

Instead, she kept silent. She didn't share the message she'd received, either. It wasn't like Tristan could do anything about it, and it was all a little too much, too suddenly. She needed to get back home and work on it, to trace it back to the source.

She stood up to go.

Predictably, Tristan tugged on her hand before she could step away. They had done the same dance for nearly a week.

Lila didn't say a word.

Neither did he.

She let Tristan guide her into his bedroom and close the door. A string of bottle caps swayed in the window as he cracked it open, the metal rattling like bells as it shook back and forth on a warm breeze. The crossbows and knives and mace on the walls glinted as he turned off the lights. Papers peeked from an open door on the filing cabinet in the corner.

She'd spend one more night curled around him, their fingers touching nothing but sheets, their lips unused.

She couldn't keep doing this to herself, being so close to him without skin and motion and whispers and more.

But she couldn't leave, either.

5

Lila yawned and crept up the stairs of the great house well before dawn, careful on the third and ninth steps to avoid squeaky boards. The show of it annoyed her. The fact that she had to pretend to sneak back into her own house at six o'clock in the morning—somewhat badly—just to give her mother's spies something to report back to the chairwoman, just so that they all thought they could still catch her if she was up to something.

Lila wasn't sure why she even bothered. For fuck's sake, she was the chief of Randolph security. She could do better than this. Her mother should expect more.

As she turned to slink down the hall toward her room, her younger brother Pax hopped up from the floor, a questioning look in his eyes.

Busted.

And not by whom she wanted.

"You were out all night again," he whispered, his loose brown waves falling over his eyes. He fidgeted with the drawstring of his pajama bottoms. His t-shirt stretched across his chest, already tight even though he'd just gone up a size. At sixteen, his body was already too large for his age. He'd grown clumsier and clumsier, too, as though a mouse lived inside him, working the levers.

A perpetually inebriated mouse.

But a happy one. Pax had always been joyful and sweet, even as a toddler. That joy had changed to sorrow several months before, the night his best friend had died, a best friend that Lila knew wasn't a best friend at all, not that Pax likely understood his own feelings.

Unfortunately, most of his mirth had perished along with his friend.

Lila shrugged under his scrutiny, feeling guilty that she'd spent time with Tristan while Pax mourned his loss alone. After Dixon had nearly died in front of her, she promised herself that she'd spend more time with Pax. She had followed through, but it didn't feel like enough.

"I had work. We just took over another family's compound, remember?"

"Work? Lie all you want, Lila Randolph, but I'm onto you." Pax circled her, brow raised. "Work hasn't kept you away the last few nights. I know how you look when you don't sleep."

"Oh really?"

"Yeah. When you're really busy, you get these heavy, dark circles under your eyes." He pointed at her face. "The ones you have now are just a little dark, which means you're still sleeping some. Besides, you're not nearly cranky enough."

"I'm taking naps at the office. I have my own apartment there," she reminded him, annoyed that she couldn't reside in the security office all the time. It was the rare chief of security who lived in her chairwoman's great house, though. Most would jump at her arrangement, but those chiefs didn't have to deal with a network of spies always peeking into her life. It didn't matter that they were rarely successful. It was the fact that her mother believed that Lila's business was her business, too. She also seemed to believe that if she kept Lila safe and close, then her daughter might one day decide to toss her career away and become the prime heir.

Her mother had the patience of a tortoise.

"Naps in your office? I don't believe you. I suspect you're up to something more than work, and I think it's about time."

Pax tried to smile, his own private tragedy scrawled all over his face. It made it worse that he was trying so hard to be happy for her. This young boy who'd lost his best friend and his first love all at once, making such an effort because he cared so much about her.

Gods, she was a horrible sister.

Lila put her arms around her brother, squeezing him as tightly as she could. "Come visit with me."

"No. I have to get ready." He pulled away and dug his thumb into his doorjamb.

She doubted Pax needed to be ready for anything. He just wasn't up to talking this morning. She could see his eyes turning a bit red, and knew he'd be gone in a few minutes.

Alone. Lying on his bed. Staring at the wall. Trying not to cry.

"You can always knock on my door for a chat, Pax. I'll never be too busy for you."

"I know, but you have places to be, just like I do." Pax smiled softly. "Life goes on and all that. Breakfast and work come around each morning, and they'll come around tomorrow, just like the next day and the next day after that."

"Pax—"

"That man died yesterday."

Lila nodded.

"You saved that boy. Perhaps Mother too, and the prime minster. You could have died."

"I didn't."

"You got hurt." He jutted his chin at the purple bruise on her jaw.

"It looks far worse than it is."

"That's what you said about your hands. You have to go around in gloves now. I'm glad you can't ride your Firefly for a while. You go too fast on it."

"I'm careful." Lila grabbed his chin. "Everyone is okay, Pax. Did you sleep?"

The boy shrugged.

Ah, it would be one of those days. A day when Pax just went through the motions. She'd get nothing out of him.

"Are you going to the hospital?"

Pax nodded. "I'm observing an appendectomy today, but first Ms. Beaumont is coming by for more drilling of pointless subjects."

Lila hoped he'd take a shower and change out of his pajamas before his tutor arrived. She'd rousted him out of bed for the first month after Trevor died, standing in his room and making herself an unavoidable nuisance until he took care of himself.

Was he backsliding now?

"I'm going to take a shower. Don't give me that look."

"What look?"

"That look. Like you're about to drop a bucket of ice water on my head."

"I don't have a look," she said, knowing she did. Pax was one of the few who could recognize it. "You pay attention to Ms. Beaumont. You have to study hard if you want to become a doctor."

Lila straightened his hair and squeezed his shoulder. She wanted to ask when he would return to boarding school, but she knew that he'd only shut down. The halls of his school reminded him too much of Trevor, and he couldn't bear the thought of going back without him.

She wouldn't push. Not yet.

"Geography and grammar and art? I don't need to know any of that to be a trauma surgeon."

"Oh really? I wouldn't want someone working on my body who sounded like an ignorant fool or who couldn't read a map of my innards."

"You wouldn't want anyone working on your body anyway." He grinned, a sliver of the old Pax showing through. "Except for the person working on it last night. Who was that again?"

"You don't know him."

"Are you sure? I know a lot of people."

"I know where I can find a pot of cold water."

His lips twitched. "On that note, I should get ready for Ms. Beaumont."

"A shower—"

"And clothes, I know. Geesh, you can be so annoying sometimes," he muttered as he slid back into his room.

Lila turned back to hers, glimpsing a flash of white and black at the end of the hallway. Alex had ironed her skirt and blouse perfectly, and she'd fashioned her hair into a bun without a hair out of place. She always looked put together, no matter what time you looked in on her. Lila had never learned her secret.

The slave nearly dropped her duster, and her mouth opened in surprise. Her eyes dipped, roving over Lila's lack of pajamas. She cocked her head to the side, curiosity flashing for one brief second.

Then it was gone.

A week ago, Alex would have grinned immediately. She would have grabbed Lila's hand and dragged her into her room, instantly peppering her with question after question after question. Where had she been? What had she done?

More importantly, who had she done?

Lila might have shared a few details, venting about her partner's disinterest, even if Lila kept his identity to herself. They'd laugh about things. They'd have hot chocolate. Lila would share her feelings about shooting the gunman, even though she hadn't killed him after all. They'd finally talk about Alex's mother and brother, and Alex would forgive her. She'd cry on Lila's shoulder about poor, wayward Patrick. They'd wonder how they'd never seen his true nature before.

But that would never happen now. They weren't best friends anymore. Perhaps they hadn't been for a very long time. Tristan had said once that they were on a different level now, that a slave and a highborn couldn't be friends, not when one owned the other.

Alex's eyes grew hard as Lila stepped forward. "Alex, I—"

"Ms. Wilson," she reminded Lila, the first words she'd spoken since the argument in Lila's room, the night of the Wilson riot. She gripped her duster and forced her lips into a smile, her eyes narrowing with every passing second. "I saw the news. You've moved on, haven't you? You're killing them yourself these days, in front of audiences, rather than letting Bullstow do your dirty work. I heard they clapped afterward."

"Ale— Ms. Wilson, I—"

Alex didn't stay. She turned on her heel and click-clacked down-stairs, leaving the railing undusted.

Leaving Lila with her thoughts.

That's how it was with Alex now. Anger and betrayal etched all over her face.

Lila deserved such treatment, though, didn't she? She hadn't just been a part of the investigation that had netted her friend's mother and brother. She'd been behind it, had spurred it on.

Lila stepped inside her bedroom and checked for bugs, then opened her snoop programs.

They'd netted no results.

Sighing, she plopped down in her desk chair and pulled off her gloves and boots. She spent nearly two hours altering the program and setting it to run again. Sliding back the panel to the secret compartment in the closet, she hid her clothes in a canvas sports bag. Then she shuffled to the bathroom, stretching her slashed fingers, wincing as she opened and closed her palms.

A long, hot shower washed the sweat from her skin. Tristan's open window had only done so much to combat the heat from his body and the lack of air conditioning—air conditioning that Tristan would not turn on because of Dixon.

Lila drained the tub and wrapped her hair in a towel, searching for something casual to wear to breakfast with her father, stitched with her family's coat of arms on the right breast. It would look too official if she wore her blackcoat to Bullstow this morning, and odd if she wore unmarked clothes. She only did that when meeting with spies or Tristan's organization.

She only wore them when she needed to be anonymous.

She only hid them so her mother wouldn't send in a slave to burn them.

After settling on a crimson blouse and a pair of black trousers, Lila slipped on a pair of knee-high boots while her computer read out the latest article from Alexandre Bouchard. Tristan used the pen name, as well as a second, to write for the *New Bristol Times*. It was his attempt to subvert the conversation, to warp public opinion on many issues important to the workborn by using two writers on opposite sides of the same issues, one just a bit more reasoned and persuasive than the other. He did a damn fine job of it, too. Not only could he live well off his salaries, but Mael Faucheux and Alexendre Bouchard were frequently quoted throughout Saxony. It was quite a feat for the son of a slave and a highborn father, a father who had never acknowledged him but had provided for his education.

Tristan had used it well.

After drying her hair, she put her daily coating of ointment on her hands, bandaged them, and slipped on her black gloves, all to keep dirt and germs from her wounds. Then she stared at the ugly purple bruise on her jaw. Concealer had only muted it.

There was a timid knock at the door before it burst open.

Lila peeked out from the bathroom as Isabel entered with a pile of fresh linens. Her red hair had been pulled into a bun, and the white blouse and black skirt she wore fit a bit loosely. The young woman enjoyed Chef's cooking far too much to miss meals. Alex's recent attitude had forced her to work harder, to pick up the slack.

"I'm sorry, madam." Isabel gasped and bowed, desperately backing out of the room. "I thought you'd gone already to Falcon Home."

"I'm running a bit late. Will you stay for a moment, please? I need a word."

Isabel fumbled with the linens uncertainly.

"If you need to work while we talk, do so. I know you're busy lately."

Busy and too shy to sit down and have a relaxed conversation with the chief of security and former prime. Lila was never sure which title made Isabel more nervous.

Isabel had come into the compound at eighteen, convicted of stealing from a Randolph department store. Bullstow had turned the girl over to the Randolph militia after sentencing, and Lila had nearly signed the paperwork to send her to the auction house.

Chef had vouched for her, had vowed to supervise the girl and take responsibility if the family would retain the girl's mark. She didn't give Lila any more information than that.

Predictably, Lila had dug a little deeper.

It turned out the girl had stolen for her little brother and sister, both on the cusp of attending school. Isabel had been raising the pair all alone, or alone in principle, as their father was a useless drunk. The man rarely crawled from their shared apartment, and lately, the money from their inheritance had begun to run out sooner and sooner at the end of every month.

Since the family didn't have money for school supplies and uniforms, Isabel had tried to steal them. She'd managed the supplies but hadn't quite gotten away with stealing the clothes. She'd been caught, and only a few days later, her sister and brother had gone into foster care. The neighbors had found them roaming the halls with soiled clothes and empty bellies, crying for their big sister. They still didn't understand why she'd been taken. Their father hadn't bothered to explain it, and he'd been too drunk to notice that the children had slipped out.

After meeting Isabel, it became obvious that she was far too dreamy and nervous to spy for another family. Lila had set up a frightening meeting with the chairwoman, and because Isabel was docile and sweet and pretty, she'd been assigned to the great house. The chairwoman had even pulled a few strings with New Bristol's Family Protection Services. Isabel's siblings were put in her care while she served her year-long sentence for theft.

It might not have happened at all if Chef hadn't agreed to sponsor the young family, peeking in and writing the necessary reports, vowing she'd ensure the children got to school, and ensuring that Isabel would work through her online parenting courses.

Isabel was so appreciative that she'd signed a servant's contract right after her slave's term ended. It was a damn good job for someone like her, finding herself in the great house of Randolphs despite her poor education, making plenty of money to care for her young family. Plus she was fond of Chef's food. In fact, that was pretty much all Isabel would talk about if pressed. Books and food.

Lila and Chef saw to it that she had plenty.

"I saw Ms. Wilson today," Lila said as Isabel removed the comforter from the bed, a comforter she hadn't slept under much recently.

"Yes, madam. Ms. O'Malley asked her to dust the stairs. She asked me to do it for her, but I was fetching the laundry." Isabel frowned, her face paling. "Should I have done the dusting?"

Isabel looked so tired. She'd likely been up early, getting her brother and sister ready for school. Lila remembered poking at Pax often when she began her militia training, for he refused to get out of bed for anyone else. Likely because she'd had never asked nicely. She'd once pulled him out of bed by an ankle and dunked him into a bathtub filled with cold water. After that, he'd always gotten out of bed the moment she knocked.

At least until he'd become a teenager. When he decided she was too small to pull him to the bath, he'd tested it. She'd ripped off his blankets and dumped a pitcher of ice water over his head, promising to call for more if he didn't get his ass out of bed.

He'd gotten up immediately and never tried it again.

"Isabel, don't take on Ms. Wilson's work because of me. I don't mind seeing her in the corridor. Where has she been working lately?"

"She mostly does whatever needs doing in the kitchens or…"

"Or anywhere that's not the top floor? She's only doing this so she doesn't run into me. You know that, don't you?"

"I wouldn't want to speculate, madam." Isabel tugged the last sheet off Lila's bed.

"Wouldn't, but could."

Isabel chewed on the inside of her check.

"I wronged her. She has a right to be angry, but she doesn't have a right to inconvenience you."

"Ms. Wilson has a lot on her plate at the moment." Isabel blushed, looking every bit like the twenty-year-old she was. "Her brother arrived yesterday. I saw him. He seems like a charming boy."

"Simon spent the last six months doing manual labor. I'm sure he's grown very charming indeed."

Isabel blushed harder.

"If you asked Chef to babysit, she'd do it in a heartbeat. You can't take care of your brother and sister all the time. You're young. You should go out."

"They don't like it when I'm gone."

"All the more reason for you to go. Chef practically raised me, and I turned out okay."

Isabel nodded, and Lila felt like an ass for interfering. Her mother had warned her about it for years, said it wasn't her place to comment on the lives of the help.

It was too late now.

"Isabel, you'd tell me if Ms. Wilson didn't want to be here, wouldn't you? I could move her to another compound for a fresh start. I have to know if that's what she needs. If it helps, you're not the only one I'm asking."

"You think she won't tell you herself?"

"I think she's never going to speak to me again. But if I find out she wants to go, and I put the question to her, I'm hoping she'll at least nod or shake her head."

Isabel bowed. "I'll try to figure it out, madam."

"Thank you. I value your opinion."

Lila stopped herself from meddling further in Isabel's personal life and jogged downstairs, already knowing she'd be late to breakfast. Instead of darting out the front door and making up the time, she entered the kitchen. The stout, middle-aged Chef bobbed her head to an odd French polka and spread out dough with her rolling pin. "Breakfast get cancelled?" she asked, using a flour-dusted finger to turn down her music.

"No," Lila answered, leaning on the door to the kitchen. "I'm just running late."

"I heard about the auction. How are you doing?"

"As well as I can after spending the evening with my mother."

Chef put down her rolling pin. "Word is some man died in front of you. It's too soon after all that mess with Peter Kruger. How are you really doing, child?"

"I'm fine."

"I wouldn't be."

Lila looked away. "Isabel mentioned seeing Simon."

"Did she blush terribly?" Chef snickered, letting the subject drop. "The girl needs to get out and find herself a man instead of a boy. I tell her all the time. Go out, meet someone. She's a starved little bunny."

"Babysit for her, then."

"I offer all the time, but I think I'll need to dangle the carrot first. A very big carrot with a very manly man attached to it." She dangled her rolling pin between her legs and cut her eyes to it. "Very manly."

"You're nothing if not subtle."

"Subtlety is boring." Chef laughed. "Everything went fine with Simon, by the way. I picked him up at the winery, and he and his sister had dinner together in her room. They even celebrated his visit with a nice, long walk around the compound."

"That's good." Lila nodded, a bit sad that she wouldn't get to see Simon.

But he'd likely hate her as well.

"That admin of yours…Sergeant Jenkins? He called last night. Told me Simon has been enrolled at Sturluson's. He'll start in a few days. They're still hammering out the details. Poor kid will have to repeat most of his senior year, but what can you do?"

Lila nodded. Sturluson's School for Young Men was a lowborn boarding school two hundred and fifty kilometers away. It was the best that Lila could hope for, though. The school trained boys from elite lowborn families, families like the Parks, who struggled to attain highborn status. Likely the young man working the door at LeBeau's had attended Sturluson's.

Her mother flatly refused to draw on her connections to get Simon back into his old highborn boarding school, the same school Pax had attended until Trevor's death.

She'd even been annoyed that Lila had dared to ask.

"I'm taking him to Randolph General this afternoon to get his physical and medical clearance," Chef said.

"Good, take Alex along if she wants to go."

As if summoned, the slave entered the room, eyes widening at the sight of Lila. She turned and walked right back out of the kitchen.

Two sightings in one day. That was a record.

"Alex," Lila called out.

"Ms. Wilson," her old friend corrected her, straightening her skirt. Only her eyes revealed the depth of her hatred. She managed to school the rest of her face into blankness.

"Ms. Wilson. I'm attending an emergency High Council meeting tonight. Your mother and brother will be on the agenda. I can sneak you in as my attendant if you wish. It only seems right to give you an opportunity to attend."

Lila hoped she'd say no. She couldn't imagine the torture of watching the group of matrons and heirs condemn members of her family to death, a death Alex clearly didn't believe they deserved, a death she could not accept, a death she could do absolutely nothing to prevent.

Alex stood straighter, resolved, and Lila's heart plummeted to the kitchen floor. "I'll go. The Wilson family does not wilt." With that, she marched from the room.

Lila sighed and tugged at the top of her gloves.

"That girl needs to grow up," Chef said. "Her mother bankrupted her entire family and has treated her like crap for years. Her brother turned out even worse in the end. It boggles my mind how she can hate you for all that now. She'll come to her senses eventually."

"Before or after our hair turns gray?"

"You're a convenient target for her anger right now, but she's not an heir any longer. Her attitude has no place in the great house. I've been meaning to talk to you about it."

"I just asked Isabel if she's mentioned wanting to move to another compound. I won't do it unless it's her choice."

Chef worked the dough on the counter. "You are a master of this house and of the compound, Lila. If you let her behavior slide for too long, the other workborn will notice. It won't end well. You have to make a decision before your mother makes one for you."

6

Lila winced as she came upon Bullstow in her Adessi roadster. The stone wall encircling the compound had been pockmarked by hundreds of pebble-shaped dents, dents not made by gunfire or acid but by a bomb. Across the street, the law offices of Slack & Roberts had been cordoned off, construction equipment and wrecking balls already chipping away at the skeletal remains. The few walls left standing had been knocked into a pile, the occasional back of an office chair or picture frame protruding from the mess of wire and concrete and sooty insulation.

Engine grease and gasoline covered most of the smell of the perfumery next door, but the discordant mix curled Lila's restless stomach. She rolled up her window, muting the incessant beeping of trucks reversing for another load. While she waited to be waved past, she tapped her steering wheel. At least traffic was light this morning, for the businesses around Slack & Roberts had closed down while the demolition teams worked.

The job would be completed soon, though, what with her father using his connections to rush the work. In a few more days, the office would be completely leveled, and a different set of people would come to the site to rebuild. All evidence of Tristan's bomb would be erased.

Few people would know the real story.

Even the conspiracy nut-jobs hadn't gotten close. The blogosphere had already divided themselves into two camps: those who believed Peter Kruger had earned his rescue by following a missive from King Lucas, and those who believed Bullstow had set it up to drag the country into war. Lila had used a fake account to stir the latter group up and make them look more idiotic.

None had managed a peek at Tristan's AAS flyer. If they had, they might have realized that the law offices had been misusing their poorer clients, fabricating evidence against them, and providing nothing more than a fumbling defense at court. After Bullstow arbiters pronounced their judgments, the client could be sent to the mines. They'd die slowly, black lungs suffocating any proclamations of innocence.

Tristan's heart had been in the right place when he detonated the bomb that destroyed the building, even though his methods had not.

Someone honked behind her, and a workman with a green sign waved her on, barely managing his jealous stare at the roadster.

Lila snaked around Bullstow's north gate, her engine rumbling while she waited in line to enter the compound. Oaks and maples peeked over the stone wall and the estate's familiar marble buildings, all cut with well-worn stairs, thick columns, grand arches, and thin-slit windows. Ivy crept where it was allowed, embracing the cold buildings within. The dome of the legislature rose above it like royalty lifting its scepter for another day at court.

Withdrawing her palm from her pocket, Lila checked for updates from her spies, but she'd only received the first wave of messages from the Randolph security office. She replied to as many as possible, yawning as a knuckle rapped on her window.

"ID?" a young blackcoat asked as she rolled it down, his chin too soft for the first stirrings of a beard. He scanned her ID, then blushed furiously when he saw her name.

"Chief Randolph." He dropped his palm computer, which skittered on the asphalt. After a quick bow, he snatched it up again and typed madly upon the screen. He barely looked old enough to have reached his senior year, much less complete his cadet training. "Are you here to see Chief Shaw or the prime minister?"

Lila rested her elbow on the roadster's window frame and said nothing, wondering where Sergeant Daniels had wandered off to this morning. He usually worked the gate in the mornings, and now he'd left his rookie to work the gate alone.

Slack & Roberts hadn't even been demolished yet.

Very sloppy.

"I'm supposed to keep a record." The rookie blushed again, his finger poised over the screen.

"And I'm supposed to get tetchy about it," she countered, finally feeling sorry for the poor kid. "I'm here to see my father. I'll be in Falcon Home this morning."

The boy typed in her license plate number, a relieved grin twisting his face. "I saw you on the news last night."

"And?"

The boy's mouth worked as though he didn't know what to say. "We live in interesting times. Made me want to join up, I guess."

"Join the army?"

"I'd be promoted directly to officer after boot camp. Right on time, too. War is coming."

"Who says that?"

"People here and there."

"People have been saying war is coming for a hundred years."

"Doesn't mean they won't be right this time."

"What does Chief Shaw say about that? Or your matron?"

"Does it matter? The army needs those of us with militia training."

"No, they don't. The army needs people with military training. There's a difference between those of us who keep the peace and those of us who don't."

A horn honked behind her, and the boy bowed. "See you on the way out, chief."

Lila pulled past the gate, sliding down the streets of Bullstow. Much like the Randolph estate, the compound had been sectioned off for different purposes. State government buildings clustered around the north gate, while the east held the city government. The boys' schools, university, and dorms clustered together in the south. The west part of the complex held everything else: cafes, restaurants, a hotel, even a grand ballroom for parties. In the center, Falcon Home stood tall and proud. On the outside, it appeared as a sprawling mansion, but it had been cut into suites inside. It housed Governor Lecomte, the men of Saxony's High Senate, and the prime minister whenever he stayed in New Bristol.

Her father almost always returned during Father's Week, that week each month when every senator in the Allied Lands turned away from government and spent time with his brood. Meetings still occurred, they just had to be important enough to warrant the interruption.

Few things were more important to senators than their families.

Lila pulled outside the senate's garage. As she disembarked from the car, she spied two familiar faces marching past, people she never thought she'd see again on the streets of Bullstow, much less in blackcoats. Sergeant Muller and Sergeant Davies shared a laugh, then passed into the security office behind Falcon Home, a plain, brown-bricked building with no frills and only eight stories.

Surely Chief Shaw's investigation had been completed? Surely their termination papers had already been signed? The men were dirty. Both she and Chief Shaw knew it.

Lila gave her keys to the mechanic outside the garage. He grinned immediately at the chance to play valet. He'd sheepishly asked the first time, and it had become a ritual over time, a ritual she didn't mind because the gifted man sometimes found problems with her roadster that her own mechanics hadn't. Sometimes, he'd even fixed them before she left the compound.

Besides, she hated parking next to the more practical sedans favored by the senators. She might have hated it more if her father didn't enjoy taking the roadster out for a joyride whenever she gave him the chance. He was like Senator Dubois, giddily riding Jewel's red Firefly whenever her sister gave him the opportunity.

Lila tugged her gloves and jogged up the stone steps of Falcon Home, shaking her head as a stiff footman extended a hand to take them. Turning, he led her toward the central staircase, a creaking oaken beauty stained in dark cherry, the newel posts carved into rosebuds. She'd given up brushing the servants off inside the mansion, for she'd gained quite the reputation as a child for mischief, and this particular gray-haired footman had been put through most of it.

At least until she'd stopped getting caught. The staff didn't know half of what she'd done or half of the places she'd been on the compound.

Especially as an adult.

Lila followed him to the top floor, past priceless oils and water-colors, past two-hundred-year-old vases filled with bouquets of hydrangeas and tulips, past rugs woven in countries Lila had never seen.

He finally stopped before a gilded rose knocker and rapped upon the door with three brief taps. "Chief Randolph has arrived, sir," the footman announced when her father opened the door. He gave another stiff bow and scurried away.

"Lila girl." Her father grinned, embracing her in a warm hug. He led her through his parlor, decorated with even more care than the rest of Falcon Home, a priceless painting of the great oracle battle queen Mildthrylth hanging in the room. The dark-haired, fur-clad woman had impaled a Roman general with a spear, a bloody, knowing smile on her lips. Her people slaughtered his men in the background.

Lila remembered staring at it for hours as a child. She and Alex had even taken turns as the oracle queen and as the fallen Roman general. Sometimes they fought as Mildthrylth. Other times they chose the moniker of a different oracle queen who had done the same, cutting down the Romans as they liberated their queendoms a millennia and a half ago. The oracles had attacked on the same hour of the same day, though no one claimed to have planned it, driven by the strength and whim of their gods. They'd left only one soldier alive in each city, bidding him to run home and tell their masters not to try again.

They hadn't, not until centuries later.

The Romans and the Allied Lands were still fighting the same damn war, although the Allied Lands had come together centuries ago with the Declaration of Peace. They were so enmeshed now that they'd become one, with pockets of languages and cultural quirks that merely triggered eye rolls rather than duels and confusion. It was a swirling mix of languages as well as shared history, enemies, gods, and oracles.

Not that Lila believed in that oracle crap, regardless of her recent dreams.

Her father led her into his dining room, and she raised a brow at Chief Shaw, sipping coffee at her father's table. The militia chief rubbed his moustache and folded his arms over his potbelly, his stern face seeming unfamiliar this morning without his sentry cap perched on his head. If Shaw had been summoned, it meant that she wasn't having breakfast, but an official meeting about a job.

She'd been right to suspect as much.

Sighing, she plopped in a padded chair across from Shaw, staring at an empty china plate with roses scrawled around the edges. She had no intention of rescuing Oskar just to give him to her father. Besides, as much as she usually enjoyed her father's jobs, the last one had worn her out. Not only was she still tired, but she still bore the marks from it, not to mention she still had to track down the person sending her cryptic messages from its aftermath.

Lila drummed her fingers on the table. There was another reason why she hoped they hadn't called her in for help with Oskar. Stealing a slave from a highborn family crossed a line, a line he'd slipped a foot over last night with her mother.

"Father, Chief Shaw," she said, inclining her head. The staff at Falcon Home had piled the table high with pancakes, eggs, bacon, blueberries, yogurt, maple syrup, and orange juice. A bottle of Sangre had been added in the middle.

All her favorite breakfast accoutrements.

It wasn't a good sign.

"Chief Randolph," Shaw echoed, nodding.

Her father looked back and forth between them. A guilty expression crossed his face as he sat beside her. "I thought Chief Shaw might have breakfast with us."

"A working breakfast, I take it? Usually you warn me first."

"I didn't know myself until last night. I should have sent you a message this morning, but I didn't want to wake you early."

Lila shook hands with Shaw and cut her chin toward the bacon. "You promised, Father."

"I promised no sausage."

"I can't be assed this morning. Ignore your doctors' orders, stuff your face, and have a heart attack for all I care." She turned her attention to Chief Shaw. "I saw something very interesting on my way in. Mr. Muller and Mr. Davies, both wearing blackcoats."

"The lawyers got involved, chief, and the Parks and Weberlys have better ones than we do. The men have been disciplined. We'll weed them out after they mess up again. I'm giving them plenty of rope to hang themselves."

"Before they hang someone else?"

"We're watching. Bullstow doesn't exile lightly."

Lila piled two small pancakes onto her plate, pancakes she had no desire to eat.

"By the way, excellent work last night," Shaw said, his gaze traveling to her jaw. "Oskar Kruger would have been killed if you hadn't taken out that gunman."

Lila poured a tiny amount of maple syrup on her pancakes, stopping as the sweet smell hit her nose. She placed the jar back on the table, far away from her place.

Her father clapped her on the back, glowing proudly, a smile lighting up his face. "That's my daughter. She was the only one in the whole ballroom who saw him."

"It wasn't like the room was full of blackcoats, Father."

"Yes, but the LeBeau militia let him in. Even my security didn't notice him when they took a turn around the ballroom."

"He might not have been inside at the time. Have you learned anything about him?"

"Nothing much," Chief Shaw answered, chewing on a piece of bacon. "His name was Hans Schulte. He was a merchant from Burgundy. Southeastern Burgundy."

"A German sympathizer?"

"One better, actually. He moved from Germany to Burgundy as a teen. The fool left behind a wife and two kids on this little crusade."

"So he was a loyalist living in Burgundy? A sleeper for the crown?"

Her father nodded. "That's our guess."

Lila sipped her wine. "I suspect he's not the only one on Saxon soil. Just the first."

"Bullstow is on it. We've stepped up security," Shaw assured her. "By the way, you were right about the suppressers and the poison. He didn't want a tranq to slow him down, nor did he want to get caught and interrogated. He entered LeBeau's ready to die."

"That's comforting."

Shaw steepled his fingers. "There was another incident last night."

"Was there?"

"Yes. Someone broke into one of the holding cells in LeBeau's and tried to free Oskar before he hit the stage. This person took out the entire security system and put it on a loop, covering their activities. They cut some cameras completely. We have little usable footage for the evening, including the ballroom."

Lila breathed a sigh of relief.

No one would spot her on tape, whispering to the void.

"You wouldn't know anything about that, would you?" Shaw asked.

"So Mr. Schulte tried to bust Oskar out first?" Lila asked, schooling her face. "That changes things."

"I doubt he was involved. I think someone else interrupted his first plan, which is why he killed the Burgundy proxy and took his clothes. He needed a way into the ballroom."

"Mr. Schulte didn't come to the auction with a backup plan? That's sloppy. It's not like a Roman, either."

"I think you know what I'm getting at, Chief Randolph."

"Breaking out Oskar is something your friend might do," her father prodded. "Thwarting the entire block's security is something you could manage."

"I was inside the ballroom at the time, remember? Besides, *our* friend steals cars and wine. Where's the profit in stealing a prince when he has no way to fence him? I can assure you, he's not nearly that well connected."

"So you haven't spoken to him since your last job together?"

"Why wouldn't I?" Since her father had told her not to do something, he could be assured that she would do the very opposite. "The man is a colleague, and I might need his services again. It's common sense to keep the door open."

"Lila."

She dropped her fork loudly on the china. "Don't channel Mother. It does you both a disservice. Peter Kruger bombed that office building, not our friend. What's your complaint with him now?"

"I don't trust him, and I don't like him."

"You've never met him, and you don't have to like him. I don't even have to like him." She picked up her glass. "I'm tired of being your first suspect when neither of you has another. It is tedious."

"My apologies," Shaw said, inclining his head. "I've become far too casual since we've begun working together."

Lila retrieved her fork. "There are two sides in Germany who have an interest in Oskar. One side wants him dead. One side wants him alive. Since this group in the basement didn't shoot him, they obviously want him alive. They must be traditionalists."

"Which means that we have German agents inside Saxony. I told you last night, prime minister. You'll have to call in the local militias for assistance. Bullstow can't handle the increases to port security alone. The airports alone would overtax us."

"And I told you that I refuse to call in the militias," Lemaire said. "It would make everyone afraid for no reason, not to mention the cost. Besides, the matrons would have a field day with it."

Lila donned her best matron voice. "All this fuss for one little slave? The prime minister is merely using it as an excuse. He's up to something." She pointed her fork at Shaw. "That's what they'll say after supplying their guess as to my father's real objective. It will be worse when the media gets hold of the story and talks it to death."

"I don't care what *they* say," Shaw said. "*They* can let us do our jobs."

"You should care what I say, chief, and I say no." Her father punched a few buttons on his palm and slid it across the table with a little grin. "Look at this, Lila."

She did, then wished she had not. Her father had gotten hold of the unedited video from the night before and saved a frame as his palm's desktop. She had already leapt toward Mr. Schulte. Her crimson dress and arms flailed at odd angles, and a comical expression covered her face.

Out of every possible frame, he'd chosen that one.

"You either suck at technology, or I'm even less photogenic than I thought."

Shaw snickered. "A little from column A, a little from column—"

"You look noble," her father said. "Heroic."

"I have it on good authority that I looked like a flailing housecat."

"No, a lioness."

Lila raised a brow.

"An alley cat, at least." When Lila did not relent, her father grunted and stared at the image again. "The boy's safe now, isn't he?"

Lila didn't know how to answer. Oskar hadn't been killed, but would he truly be safe at the Holguín compound?

Lemaire slipped his palm into his pocket. "Enough talk of Oskar. The boy is a job for me and Chief Shaw."

Lila nearly choked on her wine. Wasn't that why he'd called her to breakfast?

"As you might recall, I visited with the oracles last week," he said, stealing another piece of bacon from the tray.

"Yes, I remember." By law, the prime minister had to meet with oracles from each state, reviewing a list of their grievances and making vows to address each one. Luckily, the women rarely wanted anything more than a quick acceptance of their budget so that they could return home to their compounds and their work. Given her father's obsession with the women, she could only imagine how those visits had gone this year. "Father, what did you do?"

"Why do you assume that I did something?"

"Because you don't like the idea of the oracles handling their own business on their own sovereign compounds? Because they're outside of your purview, and you don't like that?"

"You make me sound like a meddlesome grandparent."

Lila shrugged and bit into her pancake.

"I could be a meddlesome grandparent." His gaze dropped to her belly.

"You have other children for that. Some of them are in the next room. Go bug one of them." She made a move to stand up, but her father gripped her arm, holding her in place.

"Must you do that every time I mention grandkids?"

"Yes. It's like training a rather dimwitted puppy. Consistency is—"

"Your sisters and brothers are already at the park, and they're far too young for this conversation anyway." He let go of her arm. "Back to the point. The oracles are hiding something. I want to know what."

"They're always hiding something," Lila said, sitting back down. "They're mysterious and misty and annoyingly full of crap."

Shaw snorted.

"They're disappearing," her father said.

"Everyone knows that."

"Yes, but no one's bothered to run the numbers. I had a few data crunchers check the public records. Female relatives of the oracles have had a shockingly high mortality rate in the last few decades. Sisters, nieces, daughters, cousins. It's twenty times the national average, and they have ten times the chance of being kidnapped."

"They are oracles, Father. They're targeted more often, and their illness brings its own complications. Their seizures can't always be controlled and some of them refuse to take it, claiming it stops their so-called visions. It makes them vulnerable." Lila sighed, annoyed at what her father would eventually ask. Though the ancient queens might have ridden victoriously into battle, their modern-day kin were little more than state-sponsored con women, or they would be if they didn't believe their own tripe. Each city retained its own oracle with a compound paid for by the people. Inside, her family and relatives resided like the highborn, the little girls inside waiting for the gods to bless them with the sight.

Or curse them. Gaining the visions meant a lifetime of seizures. The ones not chosen were absorbed into helping roles, running the temples, and assisting with administrative tasks. It took a great deal of time and energy to run a religion.

And money.

Lila privately thought the oracles should be disbanded, but the poorer classes believed that the oracles were the only way to commune with the gods. Even some highborn believed it.

Because of their special status as sovereign nations, the militias couldn't touch them, nor could the government pass laws against them, not unless every member of the High and Low Houses in Unity agreed on the proposal. In addition, the prime minister and the High and Low Councils of Judges must approve the matter.

Such a majority was nearly impossible to attain.

"If the oracles were really clairvoyant, they wouldn't lose so many children."

"Lila, don't—"

"You and I both know they can't see a damn thing. They might have had power once, but not anymore." She raised a brow when her father did not answer. "Don't tell me that you believe now."

"I'm privy to their visions, Lila, at least the ones they share. I'm not sure what I believe anymore, but I don't disbelieve. These women need our help even if they won't ask for it. I mentioned the statistics, and none of them seemed that concerned. They said they were handling things on their own, teaching their daughters to be more careful, putting them through self-defense courses, rolling out a few health initiatives, and funding extra research."

"Sounds like excellent first steps."

"It's bullshit, Lila."

She shoved her plate away. Bullstow men rarely cursed, and her father was no exception. "Okay, fine. What exactly do you want me to do?"

"A few days ago, a woman in Sioux Falls witnessed a girl being taken from the local oracle's compound and shoved into a black Cruz sedan. The woman followed the car, directing the local militia until they could pull it over. They barely got to the little girl in time."

"What did the kidnapper say?"

"Nothing."

Lila tilted her head. "Even under the truth serum?"

"No chance. The kidnapper disappeared on scene. How does that happen?"

Shaw poured himself another glass of wine. "Chief Vance said the mother's story was fishy as well."

Lila had met Chief Vance, the man who ran the government militia for all of La Verde, the northern American state. He was a lot like Shaw, except younger and a lot more attractive. "Don't ask this of me, Father. I have better things to do than chase fairies."

"Like what?"

"Like wash my hair." Or help rescue Oskar. Or find Reaper's partner. Or figure out how make amends with Alex. Or spend some time with Pax. Perhaps spend a little time with Tristan after they sent Oskar back to Germany.

"Your hair looks clean to me."

"The girl's name is Rebecca," Shaw said. "Her mother is the Sioux Falls oracle, so none of us can press too deeply. The girl also happens to be a future oracle. Chief Vance will keep investigating that specific case, but we want you to investigate these disappearances more generally. The Bullstow and the La Verde militias are at a loss. Your father wants answers before the next legislative session ends."

"That's six weeks away."

The side of her father's mouth twisted in a grin. "I thought you liked challenges."

"Don't mock me."

Shaw reached into a satchel on the table and pulled out two files. "Here are the most recent cases, prior to the one in Sioux Falls. One girl died four months ago during a seizure; another was killed in a car accident a few days later. My men are having no luck digging into the cases. We can't even verify the girls' deaths."

"So dig up the coffins."

"We did. Dr. Booth and the specialist who went along with us thought the ages and sizes of the corpses weren't quite right."

"DNA?"

"They both matched."

"So you're saying someone broke into the DNA database and changed the data?"

"Maybe. If someone did hack the DNA database, you'd be able to figure it out."

"Fine. Set up a meet with the Sioux Falls oracle. I want to speak with her personally."

Shaw eyed the prime minister, and her father looked away.

"There's more, isn't there?"

"She's not talking to us anymore," Shaw said.

"Why?"

"Because your father put her daughter into foster care."

Lila's eyes snapped open. "You did what?"

"It's for her own good," her father said. "Someone has—"

"What on earth were you thinking? You can't just take away an oracle's child! These women are the spiritual backbone of our entire society. The oracles might be charlatans, but they're a placebo for our society, and a necessary one at that. Don't you understand what sort of press this will bring down on your head if the oracles take it to the media?"

Shaw avoided her glare.

"Oracle's light, the press already knows?"

"It hasn't spread far," Lemaire said. "I don't care if it does, though. The oracles and their daughters are a resource. They must be protected."

"They aren't resources. They're children. This is why you can't get any further in the case, isn't it? This is why you want to hire me. You think they'll talk to me."

"It's not like they ever said all that much to me, but now they won't even speak to the militia. Two more girls have disappeared near New Bristol in the last week. You're our last hope."

"The oracles have been handling their own affairs for thousands of years. Of course they don't wish to talk to you. It's demeaning, and now you've taken one of their children on top of that?"

"You're really not going to look into it?"

Lila rubbed at her eyes. She'd always done whatever her father asked, whatever he needed, but she had too much on her plate at the moment.

His pleading stare worked at her, though. It wasn't like she had to figure it out in the next few days. Rebecca was safe in foster care, and the oracles and state militias were handling the girls' disappearances. She could rescue Oskar first.

Her father snatched the bottle of Sangre from the middle of the table. "Chief Shaw, could you please step outside for a moment while I speak with my daughter?"

"Certainly." The chief wiped his mouth with his napkin, bowed, and slipped on his sentry cap.

Lemaire poured more Sangre into her glass as the apartment door closed. "Help me with this, and I'll give you something you want."

"What could you possibly buy that my dividends can't purchase, Father?"

"Your contract. Permanently."

Lila sipped her wine. Her mother had signed her contract years ago, promising only an indefinite commission in the Randolph militia, a commission she could legally rescind at any time. The only reason why she hadn't was because Lila had been granted a boon in front of the entire Randolph family. Lila had taken advantage of that boon and, more importantly, the thousands of heirs who had heard her mother's answer.

Chairwoman Randolph had granted the contract to preserve her honor and her word. She could not destroy the contract unless she wanted to lose her family's esteem, unless she wanted the world to question the word of a Randolph. Her mother wouldn't break their contract, not without a damn good reason.

Lila might be the only person in history to ever get one over on Beatrice Randolph.

"How can you get Mother to agree to that?"

"By offering her something she wants more. The hospital contract is still up for grabs. Your mother might not want me to give her the deal, but she'll certainly ask for my help to earn it. No more holding the prime heir spot over your head. No more forcing you to attend High Council meetings because she thinks Jewel isn't savvy enough to manage them. She'll have to accept Jewel's shortcomings or pick a new prime. That's how important the oracles are, Lila."

"Oskar, too? Mother won't go for it, just like she didn't go for it yesterday. She'll earn that contract on her own merits or not at all."

"Your mother has always dreamed of earning a spot on Unity's High Council."

"She doesn't want a seat that badly. Not badly enough to drop the idea of me as prime. Not badly enough to cheat, either."

"Cheating and using her resources aren't the same thing. I'm a resource, Lila." He put a few more slices of bacon on his plate. "You don't know your mother half as well as you think. She might be middle-aged, but she's always retained the dreams of a child. I'll worry about the deal. You just worry about the oracles."

"Do you really need the information this much?"

"Yes. It's important, Lila."

She thumbed her sapphire ring under her glove. "Okay, I'll look into it."

7

It was nearly ten o'clock before Lila jogged down the steps of Falcon Home, her father and Chief Shaw trailing behind in hushed whispers, chests open and wide, hands folded behind their backs in the elegant pose of Bullstow.

Shaw excused himself once they reached the front door, begging his blackcoat from the footman, then headed off toward his security office.

"I should do the same," Lila muttered on the stone steps outside. Shaw disappeared around the side of the building. His boots clacked on the sidewalk.

"Not yet. It's Father Week." Lemaire grinned and nudged her with his elbow. "Come on, let's go to the park like we used to."

"I took the entire afternoon off yesterday to go to the auction, and Commander Sutton has already had to fill in for me at the commanders' meeting this morning. She's had to do that too much lately, mostly due to Bullstow and Unity business."

"That's what she's there for. You have to learn to delegate more, Lila. It's unhealthy to try to handle everything yourself."

"Unhealthy? I'm getting health tips from a man who just ate an entire plate of bacon?"

"It was only a few pieces. I'll work it off in the gym later. I always do."

"That's not your doctors' concern, and you know it."

"Let's go play with the little ones just for an hour," he said, changing the subject. "You haven't been to the park in ages. Shiloh will be there. Claire might have arrived as well."

Lila smiled at the mention of Shiloh. She used to visit him often when her father still resided in Bullstow. He had been shaped in the same mold as his father, even taking after Chairwoman Randolph in some rather fortunate ways. He'd taken their intelligence, their shrewdness, their serious nature. Barely older than Pax, he had every intention of becoming prime minister, just like his father. He'd already started his two-year internship with the New Bristol and Saxon High House, and after he finished, he'd cast his lot in the senate elections, allowing his brethren to place him in a city where his particular skillsets would be of most use. He'd spend the next decade working his way back to the New Bristol High House, and perhaps even Saxony one day, though Lemaire had managed it in only five years.

Lila had to take advantage of what little time they had left.

As for Claire and the youngest of her father's brood? Lila hardly cared, if she had to be honest. Half-siblings on your father's side drifted away from your awareness, just like old friends from university. You occasionally saw one another and caught up, but usually they had their lives and you had yours.

Unless someone tried to mess with them, of course. Then you might have been best friends for life.

Lila followed her father reluctantly, her dwindling time with Shiloh fresh on her mind. The pair turned on a cedar-lined path and strolled toward the southern area of the compound toward Bullstow's elementary school, where the youngest sons of the senate were housed and educated. Lila hadn't walked by it in several summers, and that was a shame, for summer was the best time to visit. The high school principal always charged the graduating senior class with creating some new contraption for the elementary students to play on every year. Part of the project involved speaking with the younger children and taking their needs and wants into account as the seniors planned and designed the equipment.

It was supposed to teach the seniors a fair number of life lessons: how to take your constituents' opinions into consideration, how to listen more than you speak, how to reach a consensus with so many hands stirring the pot, and how to ensure your work always secured the safety and happiness of the next generation. But mostly they learned that you couldn't please everyone and that children had the attention spans of gnats, just like the masses.

And like most things, it had become a contest over the years.

Shiloh had helped build his class's project, since he'd taken the relevant math, art, and shop classes. It'd been up for months, and Lila hadn't had a chance to stop by and see it. She'd only seen pictures, proudly slid over the table when he and her father came to dinner.

Lila had a feeling pictures hadn't done it justice.

They both heard the park before they saw it, surrounded by the hulking high school, junior high, and dorms. Screaming, squealing, and crying erupted in their ears.

Where there was screaming and crying, there must be Father's Week.

Lila paused at the line of shrubs around the park and checked her watch, a long list of excuses sliding through her mind.

"Oh no you don't. You promised," her father said, already searching the crowd for his children. His Saxon children, anyway. The ones from Unity and other states did not always come for Father's Week, due to the distance.

Given his happy face, Oskar Kruger and the oracles had retreated from his mind.

Lila wished she had the same off switch.

Sighing, she gave herself over to her father's mood, promising to stay for an hour.

An hour might have been too optimistic, though. Children screamed down slides or chased one another across the playground, kicking balls or bouncing them. Strollers lay abandoned in the grass, overturned and forgotten on the edges of the melee. Diaper bags lay scattered among them. Senators bounced among the chaos, encouraging it and swapping supplies with one another. They'd abandoned their coats and breeches for soft t-shirts and worn jeans, all so they could chase the children around the park, some with hands raised to the sky as though they'd been turned into monsters, growling and picking young ones up under their arms. Others tossed children over their shoulders, holding them like sacks of flour while the child giggled and smacked their father's back. The same men who gave stirring speeches on the floor of the High Senate, the same men who had been so charming at the last highborn party, every one of them turned into absolute goobers during Father's Week.

Those who weren't busy in the melee treated bumps and bruises or hurt fingers and toes along the edges of the fray, or changed the diapers of the tiniest children, the wiggling crawlers chewing their fingers and staring vaguely around them while the men worked. It was easy to tell the first-time fathers, so gentle they might have been handling fine china.

There was plenty of experience here, and they soon learned better.

Not all the senators were so enamored of the little ones, though. One senator had made a potato gun, and a crowd of girls and boys had lined up to fire it. Other senators had spread out among a sulky row of teenagers on the grass. The teens refused to get dirty with their younger sisters and brothers. Instead, they tapped on their palm computers, ignoring everyone around them, including their peers and fathers and uncles.

Lila had spent many an hour during Father's Week the same way. Except instead of being sulky, she'd been poking at Bullstow's defenses, ignoring her younger half-siblings while she played on a different sort of playground. She'd only been sullen when her father, knowing exactly what she was up to, made her put down her palm, stay in the park, and interact.

He didn't really care with whom.

With so many children, he had to turn his back at some point, though, and she'd be off seconds later, chasing a decent signal with more gusto than the senators chased after the toddlers, running deeper in Bullstow, breaking into buildings and offices she had no right to be in.

Poking, reading, and digging.

If Shaw knew half the rooms she'd been in during Father's Week, if he knew half the codes she'd stolen, he wouldn't be so blasé about inviting her into the compound.

Even her father didn't know that she could get into his and the governor's offices any time she damn well pleased, even without forcing the lock. She could even break into the holding cells and knew her way around the tunnels underneath the compound.

That was before she turned fourteen, before her mother gave her Our Lady of Light. Running the hospital and meeting with her advisors had taken up much of her time. When she wasn't busy with the hospital or attending school, she'd been accompanying her mother to Saxony High Council meetings and her Aunt Georgina to New Bristol High Council meetings. She had to learn as much as she could before taking Georgina's spot at sixteen.

It had angered her father that she was too busy to spend more than a day or two with him during Father's Week. He could hardly complain, though. When her mother was fourteen, she'd assumed responsibility for the entire Randolph family, for Lila's grandmother had passed suddenly during childbirth, leaving all responsibility on her mother's shoulders.

He'd gritted his teeth every time Lila sent a hurried message to her advisors, always working to shape the direction of the hospital. He wasn't angry that she was distracted. He'd been proud of her work, but he frequently despaired that she was missing her youth. It was likely the only reason why he allowed her to penetrate Bullstow so often. It was the only chance she got to be a stupid, reckless child.

Lila wandered away from her father toward a mass of brightly colored netting, strung out across a ring of trees and sunk posts nearly thirty meters in diameter at the edge of the park. It was as if an egg sac full of spiders had burst apart in the center, making a series of horizontal webs with thick, velvety strands, weaving holes in the middle. A mass of children already climbed upon them, using the holes to climb up to a higher level, sometimes slipping through a higher hole to fall on the netting below, crouching and bouncing as though it were some sort of trampoline. Some used the netting to climb up to the top branches of the trees, then jumped and rolled down the top layers of netting, toppling their friends.

Lila crept near and grabbed the netting, examining it, a bit jealous that she didn't have something similar in her militia's gym. Perhaps she'd send someone out to copy it.

"I don't mean to be biased, but I don't think any group will ever top Shiloh's creation," her father said. "Did you know he came up with the winning proposal? The kids were getting into trouble for climbing the trees, and now they can do it safely. They'd also studied spiders in their science classes and had become obsessed with the horrid things."

"Yes, I know he came up with the idea." She chuckled. "You haven't shut up about it all summer."

"The boys had quite a bit of fun learning how to weave the nets. They must have made a dozen prototypes. Shiloh even taught me how to do it." He crouched down and pointed to the two bottom layers. "Those are his. He weaved the strongest nets, so they put his on the bottom. Even the Massons have even been in for a look. They've gotten permission to use the idea for a new line of playground equipment."

"Any of that money going to Shiloh?"

"You think like a chairwoman too much," he chided. "The seniors decided their portion of the profits should go toward funding swings and slides for the poorer classes. The local senates even agreed to install the equipment during Volunteer Month, and the Massons are giving it to us at cost. It's too bad the poorer children can't have something like this in their playgrounds, but it requires a level of supervision that the poorer classes don't enjoy."

Lila turned and eyed the senators underneath the shade trees, watching the children play, Senator Dubois among them.

Lila nudged her father, and the pair strolled toward him. The senator inclined his head in greeting, barely taking his eyes off the raw-faced two-year-old on his lap, rubbing the little boy's back as he hiccupped at the end of his crying fit. Dubois had always had a penchant for distraught toddlers, able to set them to rights before they entered into a full-blown meltdown. Other senators constantly bugged him for tips or, in their frustration, simply handed off their children and watched him work.

He'd be an amazing father once he and Jewel finally conceived.

"What happened to this little one?" her father asked.

"He smooshed his finger in the swing set chain." Dubois wrapped his hand around the boy's fist and gave him a kiss on the cheek. "Gabriel will be okay. It's not broken, and he likes the swings too much to stay away. Don't you?"

Gabriel nodded and buried his face in Dubois's neck, turning shy.

"Whose is he?"

"I'm actually related to this one. Gabriel is my cousin's boy. Unfortunately, Bilsby is delayed in Beaulac. He'll be here tomorrow morning. I get to play the favorite uncle until then." A happy smile lit up Dubois's face.

"You'll have your own soon enough. Jewel is too enamored of you to stop trying so easily. She'll go to the doctors soon and do what she must."

Dubois nodded, a forced smile on his face.

Lila knew what he would not say. Even though he'd been fertility tested and cleared before his appointment as a senate intern, he feared that he was the reason for the couple's childless state. Randolph women were known to conceive quickly and easily when they wanted, as were the women of the Hardwicke clan, Jewel's family on her father's side.

It was likely why he hadn't taken other lovers. He feared he'd be found out.

"After my hands heal up, you should borrow Jewel's Firefly," Lila suggested. "We could go on a ride somewhere."

Dubois's face lit up again. "Gods, it's been months since we've done that."

Lila and her father chatted with Dubois for a few more moments, then drifted among the children. Lila managed to catch up with a few of her half-siblings, and she even saw Shiloh in the mix, wrangling a four-year-old over his shoulder before tossing him back into the netting.

He'd grown bigger since she saw him last, and begun filling out his clothes. He wasn't nearly as large as Pax, but taller than most. Unlike Pax, he'd started spending more and more time in the gym, widening his shoulders and thickening his legs with rep after rep. It was a pastime of Bullstow senate interns, and a religion to those ambitious enough to enter the heir carousel early.

Clearly, Shiloh hoped to make his first match when the season began next month.

Gods, she remembered changing his diaper. She'd always been too scared he would leak on whatever new gadget lurked in her pocket to manage the task with any degree of competency, but when had he gotten old enough for his first season?

Oracle's light! Little Shiloh might be a father soon.

When her palm's alarm vibrated discreetly in her pocket, Lila gave Shiloh and her father one last hug and dashed away, winding through the laughing and squealing and crying children. She drove through Sunday afternoon traffic to the Randolph estate, parking in the family's garage before marching down Villanueva Lane toward the security office. The twelve-story steel and glass tower rose high above the mansions in the southern part of the compound. It stretched like a nest of glass and steel, all arcs and curves, a gem cleaned and polished.

Lila loved the building, which was a good thing, since she spent most of her time there. It had been designed as the home of the Randolph militia, housing the barracks, cafeteria, training facilities, and department offices, as well as the private apartments of its senior officers.

Including her private apartment, if her mother had allowed her to sleep there.

She pulled open the metal front door, sculpted into the Randolph coat of arms, her boots clicking on the white tiles underneath a crisscross of steel arches. Since she hadn't worn her militia uniform, it felt too odd for her to take the staircase. Instead, she broke for the glass elevators, which would offer her a peek into every department on every floor, for the walls had also been made of glass.

Lila stopped as soon as the doors opened.

Several dozen blown-up pictures of her leaping across the LeBeau's ballroom had been taped along the walls of the car, even worse pictures than her father had saved on his palm. *Our Hero* had been scrawled across the top of each one, and around the edges of the posters, semicircles within semicircles had been drawn. A pert little dot sat at the center.

Thinly disguised breasts.

At least no one had put up pictures of that.

The same treatment had been given to the other three elevators. Surrendering to the inevitable, Lila stepped into the nearest car and slid her elevator key into the slot. She pushed the button for the twelfth floor, waving away strips of red silk and ribbon that dangled in her face from the ceiling. Luckily, very few people could access her office and apartment without the proper key. She'd not find any posters or dangly ribbons there.

As the car rose slowly through the building, everyone inside rushed the stair rails around the middle of the building, crowding in groups to watch her ride up in the glass-paneled elevator, all laughing as their handiwork floated past, some clapping, some hooting, some hollering. Many took pictures on their palm and patted one another on their backs for a job well done. She waved, playing the good sport until she finally passed into the private floors of the building. Then she sank against the wall and passed into welcome darkness.

She'd never noticed how slowly the elevator moved.

Once she hit the top, she entered her apartment, styled exactly the same as her room in the great house: gray and white walls, black furniture, little flares of Randolph crimson. She quickly changed into workout clothes before descending in the elevator again.

Luckily, few people noticed her descent.

She stalked out of the elevator into the basement training facility and grabbed a bottle of water from the front desk before walking toward the track. She often did her best thinking as she raced around the outer ring, hopping over foam-covered fire hydrants, racing up ramps, and scrambling over walls to jump to the next mock roof. She had her people change it up every week, to keep her fresh, to keep her people fresh too. Today, it was more challenging than usual, and she found herself falling and landing on the thick mats below more than once, pulling at her stitches as she hit the ground and slapped the padding.

Lila winced and pulled off one of her gloves, checking her hands for blood. Perhaps it wasn't so challenging. Perhaps she was just off since she couldn't grab at the terrain for balance. Or perhaps she just had a great deal on her mind. The botched assassination, Mr. Schulte's death, Reaper, Reaper's partner, Dixon, Oskar, the oracles, her father, Tristan, Alex, Pax, perhaps even Dubois.

She kicked a foam-covered streetlight and pulled herself off the mat, finally giving up. Instead, she ventured into the weight room, choosing to keep her feet on the floor.

Commander Sutton found her an hour later while she prepped for a last set of leg presses, entering the room with all the elegance of Chairwoman Masson. Lila said nothing as the commander pulled up a bench and sat down, her gray hair wrapped in a twist, her eyes dropping to Lila's jaw. "You sweated half your concealer off."

"How'd you know where I was?" Lila grunted as she straightened her legs and lifted the weight.

"Tim called me. Said you were falling so much you must be enjoying it. Are you going to tell me what's going on?" The shrewd, wrinkled commander stared at her knowingly.

Lila straightened her legs again. "There's nothing to tell. By the way, thanks for taking the commanders' meeting this morning."

"That's what I'm here for. One of these days you'll realize that I make a good enough chief for you to retire early."

"Anything come up that I should know about?"

"Nothing the other commanders and I couldn't handle. It's just another boring day on the Randolph compounds. If you don't stir up something soon, I'll have to go home to the Beast for dinner."

Lila couldn't help but chuckle at her old partner. She'd heard earful after earful about the Beast while they patrolled the compound over the years. "He's your husband, commander. Shouldn't you want to go home to him?"

"We work better when we don't see one another. When we're together, we're like two alley cats thrown into the same dumpster."

"Horny alley cats. How many kids do you have again?"

The woman locked the weight as soon as Lila straightened her legs.

"Hey, I'm not finished," Lila yelped, her hand going to the locking bar.

"Yes, you are," Sutton said, swatting Lila's hand away. "You're a woman. You're not going to get any more muscle on your bones unless you resort to steroids."

"I don't lift to gain muscle."

"Well, you already meet the militia's strength requirements and then some. Let's go have lunch. I'm hungry, and you're making me look bad with all this running and jumping and lifting weights."

"Maybe you should do so some—"

"If you finish that sentence, I will beat you. I brought you into this militia, and I can take you right out again. I don't give a damn who your mother is."

Lila snickered and followed Sutton from the room, wishing she could have a shower before facing her militia, but it wasn't like they hadn't seen her looking worse.

Plastered all across the elevators.

While Lila nibbled on a turkey sandwich and fries, Sutton filled her in on the commanders' meeting and other matters she'd taken care of, or would take care of if Lila needed. She had worked with Lila long enough to know when she needed to pick up the slack.

It was a good thing Sutton didn't know why Lila was so busy. Sutton was more or less a straight arrow, someone who only bent the rules so far. If she ever found out some of the things Lila had done recently…

"Hey, space case," Sutton said, rapping her knuckle on the table.

"*Hmmm?*" Lila mumbled, looking up into the face of the militia's chef and her team. The group chuckled, smug expressions pasted on their faces. Their little white caps tilted as each one laid tiny paper plates in front of her, each containing a cookie.

All shaped like breasts with chocolate chip nipples.

"All hail the conquering breast. I mean, hero." Chef Sasha giggled, unable to keep a straight face.

The entire cafeteria snickered, holding up their own breast cookies.

Sutton winked, picked up a cookie, and bit off the nipple. "Hey, look, there's fudge inside."

Chef Sasha bowed as Lila took a bite and gave an appreciative nod. Still chuckling, the group ambled away back to their stations.

"Traitor," Lila said when the staff was out of earshot.

"Ah, give them a break. It's rare they get a chance to razz you. They're proud and celebrating. Their chief made the LeBeau militia and the prime minister's security detail look like idiots." Sutton eyed Lila's face, and Lila knew the commander was about to do a bit of razzing of her own. "You usually have a much better sense of humor about this stuff. You need a vacation. You haven't had a proper one in ages. Perhaps you could some time off for the beginning of the season, find a senator, and enjoy yourself for a few weeks."

"Don't go there."

"Why not? I'm around you more often than my daughters. I'm too busy to bug them for grand—"

Lila stood up. She dumped the rest of her meal in the trash, then slid her tray in a slot in the back of the room for cleaning. She'd barely eaten and wasn't hungry, anyway. She practically welcomed an excuse to get rid of her food without comment.

Regardless, she collected half a dozen breast cookies from the table before leaving, all for the show of it.

Sutton followed along behind her in the corridor. "I guess your father bugged you about children at breakfast?"

"You guys teaming up now?"

"Perhaps he can take weekends from now on, so we don't overlap. It's better than you flying into a snit and running away whenever I bring it up."

Lila withdrew her elevator card from her pocket. "You could stop bringing it up."

"Life finds a way."

"Yeah, well, life can find a way up someone else's vagina." Lila would not get pregnant without a small miracle. She'd had a CUT on her twenty-first birthday. The operation had dropped her chances of having children to almost zero, and had been worth every credit.

Her womb wasn't open for business, and it would remain that way.

8

After a quick shower in her private apartments, Lila changed into her officer's uniform: black trousers, white blouse, crimson officer's coat, all stretching with every movement to allow her to chase, to leap, to kick, to punch. She tucked her trouser legs into her boots, fixed her concealer, put on a fresh pair of gloves, pinned her four silver stars to her neck, and rammed her Colt and officer's short sword into her holster, then added her leather blackcoat. Only Randolph sentries were allowed to skip the leather in the heat.

Riding down to the eleventh floor, she bustled past the receptionist and the empty waiting room, then turned into her office. Or, at least, her admin's office. Sergeant Jenkins sat at his desk, typing, his long fingers dashing across the keyboard, his tanned skin contrasting nicely with his crisply laundered militia coat. Sunlight gleamed off the spokes of his wheelchair and the Colt at his hip.

"Good evening, chief." He nodded, barely looking up. "You have good timing. I've almost finished the edits on yesterday's reports."

"I can't have you sitting around with nothing to do."

Jenkins smirked. "Captain McKinley wants to speak with you again. I could go down and get her right now."

"Touché."

"I'll make a deal with you. Have Ms. Harris buy more of my special coffee, and the next time the captain comes, I'll protect you to death. It'll be quieter for us all."

"We need her, and I can't afford to lose you to a lengthy investigation. Please, try not to kill my officers." It was lucky Jenkins only joked about protecting her to death. Though Lila might be one of the best shots in Saxony and a quick draw, Jenkins was faster. He could pull his Colt, aim, and fire accurately in less than a quarter of a second. Most people had a healthy fear of the man once they saw him on the shooting range.

"Do you have a class tonight?" she asked.

"Yes, another crop of idiots who can't be bothered to practice throughout the year. Speaking of which, I haven't seen you at the range for two weeks."

"I'll make time."

"You're going to get rusty. You already are. Only two out of three shots landed?"

"I was running."

"Why? You were well within range," he chided, turning back to his screen. "I taught you better than that."

Lila opened the door to her office, then sighed at the stack of papers on her ebony desk. The stack would have been larger if Commander Sutton hadn't taken care of what she could. Lila hadn't been lying to Pax; her workload had increased after they'd taken over the Wilson estate. Luckily, she'd passed most of the work on to a capable officer, one she had designs on promoting soon. If the woman did well, she'd run the Wilson estate as its commander.

Lila took out her palm, pulled up her snoop programs, and walked around her office, ensuring it hadn't been bugged overnight. She'd decorated the room exactly like her bedroom and private apartment: an ebony desk and shelves dominated one side, and a black leather couch and coffee table took up the other. A few pops of Randolph red completed the room.

Sitting down at her desk, she scanned the budgets of three militia commanders in charge of family compounds in other cities. She approved each with little fuss, for the figures hadn't changed much from the year before. She chuckled at the next budget and scribbled a note for Sergeant Jenkins to send it back to the optimistic commander. Commander Ashen Randolph had just been promoted six months ago, and she still needed help learning her position.

She'd have to get it from the other commanders this time. Lila made a quick call to the commander in Beaulac, a woman used to streamlining her own budget. She promised to make time for Ashen the very next day.

The reports of recent online attacks from Captain McKinley's tech department took longer to wade through, but her people were on the right track in solving them. If they didn't figure out the culprits in a few days, she'd have to get involved, but the attacks had already been thwarted. It was just a matter of ferreting out the perpetrators, and she'd leave them to it.

Lila shuffled through various other slips of paper, skimmed the reports from the commander-in-waiting at the Wilson estate, called and threatened a few highborn who'd dared yell at her militia over trifles, approved the promotion of a senior officer at the La Porte compound, and reviewed a few arrest reports that would be sent to Bullstow in the coming week: a disgruntled servant caught pocketing cash from her master in full view of cameras, a slave who punched a servant over a card game, and a spy from another family. He'd fallen over the wall after a tranq turret had knocked him out.

He'd pissed himself, too.

Could a spy that inept really be called a spy?

Lila grabbed her pen and signed off on the arrest reports. The investigations had been complete, diligent, and thorough, just as she'd come to expect.

The last thing in her inbox was the updated crime statistics for the compounds. She noted that domestic abuse calls among the poorer workborn had gone up for the sixth month in a row. Noting the pattern, she sent the report to her mother with a recommendation to increase the servants' minimum wage as well as the slaves' stipend.

At last, the entire stack of papers had finally migrated to her outbox. As much as she loved being chief of security, her father's jobs had always appealed to her more. She'd wanted to be in charge of the family's compounds to make them safe, and she had. The Randolphs were safer than they'd ever been.

But the reams and reams of paperwork, as well as the tedious flow of reports and messages on her palm, made life much more boring. She longed for the thrill of breaking into another compound, trying to figure out puzzles like the oracles, like Oskar, like Reaper's partner—so long as she caught him before he wreaked havoc on her life. If her father and Tristan ever stopped wanting her help, she wasn't sure what she would do with herself. Perhaps that was why she broke into her own compounds so often.

Security checks, she'd always called them.

"Security checks, my ass. Your chief of security is bored, my darling militia. Deal with it."

Bored and busy at the same time.

She checked the time. It was already half past three, and she'd done nothing to help Oskar, to find Reaper's partner, or to investigate the oracles.

She grabbed her palm and cycled through her messages. Her spies had not found any information about where the Holguíns had taken Oskar. She might have to get involved herself, and she didn't have the time for it. Of course, there was always Max Earlwell. An expense for sure, but she could trust him to get the job done.

Lila scrolled to the next message. *Tests came back negative. Nothing wrong that I could find, and there's nothing left to run at this point.* It was the last in a long line of messages from Dr. Booth and Dr. Adams at Bullstow. They'd run a barrage of medical tests on Patrick, for Lila could scarcely believe the man had been so altered from how she knew him as a child. Unfortunately, it had happened without an identifiable medical cause. She had no way to sway the council from his pending execution and no way to excuse his actions. Patrick didn't suffer from a brain tumor or an infection or a concussion or…

Or anything medical.

Dr. Adams had not found a psychological cause either, not some small excuse for his personality change. "Manipulative" was how the psychologist had characterized him. Manipulative, completely self-interested, and completely unaware of his own intellectual defects.

Like not realizing he shouldn't allow a random hacker to dictate his criminal activities.

In an effort to answer the question for herself, she'd hacked into Patrick's life, including his time at university. Since he'd never been that bright and had a great many brothers and male cousins, his matron had allowed him to study whatever he wanted, likely assuming he'd marry into an elite lowborn family.

He'd chosen to study philosophy. *Skepticism and Self-interest* had been the title of his senior thesis. In it, he'd deduced that nothing actually existed in the world except for the self. He'd examined common ethical problems through that lens, a lens dirtied by four years of grasping, misused, and misapplied logic, granting himself carte blanche for the worst sorts of selfish behavior.

His instructor had given him a C-minus for his effort, probably because she worried for her safety. One section had mentioned that criminal activity, including murder, was moral if the crime benefitted the self. It was merely in one's best interests not to get caught. His professor had sent his work to the university's psychologist, but Patrick had graduated before the woman had received the first page.

Dr. Adams had called it a window into his internal logic. "It explains how he thinks. It doesn't excuse it," he'd said. "It doesn't make him crazy, either. He doesn't function as if he actually believes that nothing exists in the world but his own mind."

Lila sent Dr. Booth a message, thanking him for his diligence.

She then turned on her desktop and searched for information on the oracles. As an agnostic highborn from a long line of agnostics, she'd never bothered to learn about them before, not even after her dreams the week before. All she knew was that the oracles' clairvoyant gene traveled along family lines. Nicknamed "oracles' disease" by the researcher who'd found it, it had turned out to be a specific type of epilepsy passed from female carrier to female offspring.

Lila believed the scientific facts. She didn't doubt the women had seizures, but she didn't believe in their so-called visions. There was the vision paradox for one thing. Though there were fewer oracles in the modern era, the number of visions for each one had gone up.

Substantially.

A few religious experts had studied the phenomenon, claiming that the gods talked to the oracles just as much as they always had, there were merely fewer oracles to receive the messages. Lila privately believed that the oracles had merely begun making up even more bullshit for attention, all to justify the expense of their compounds.

Lila typed in a few search terms about the vision paradox.

She jumped when her palm vibrated.

"I've made cookies," Chef crooned, her face coming on screen. "A dozen chocolate chip and another dozen peanut butter. I know how much you like them."

Lila narrowed her eyes. "What do you want?"

"You're so suspicious."

"What do you want?"

"Rosemary found a restaurant that's going out of business down south. I'd like you to check it out with me. You're so fond of saying that I should open a bakery. I could use some business advice."

Lila cocked her head to the side. There was no way that Chef had suddenly decided to open her own bakery, but Lila owed her far too much not to play along. Besides, Chef knew more about the oracles than anyone on the compound. It was a nice coincidence, though Lila normally didn't believe in them.

"I'll be right over." Lila disconnected and shut down her desktop computer, picking up the entire stack of reports before she left. Sergeant Jenkins was still typing away at his desk when she dropped them in his inbox. "Gods, that feels so good."

"Post-its again? You know I hate that. Your handwriting is tragic."

"I sent you voice messages about some of them," Lila said, shoving open the door with her butt. "You'll get to hear my melodious voice—"

"Rambling about stuff I barely understand."

"Nah, not today. Nothing's technical."

He brightened. "Well in that case, have a lovely day."

Lila twirled around, waved to the receptionist, and marched to the elevator. She sent a few more messages as she walked to Villanueva House, managing to completely clear the backlog before she stepped through the front door.

"Chef?" she called out in the kitchen

"Don't bellow, Lila," Chef muttered as she peered around an open cabinet. "It's not what highborns do."

"I'm the chief of security. We bellow. We have special permission."

Chef shook her head and closed the cabinet door, wrapping four loaves of fresh bread in plastic wrap.

Lila peeked through a stack of containers filled with cookies, sugared nuts, and fudge. "This is all for Rosemary?"

Chef averted her eyes. "She's gotten too thin since she moved out on her own."

Lila knew without a doubt that Chef was lying. She wouldn't have made bags of sugar for Rosemary. She would have stocked her fridge with meaty stew and lasagna. "So where are my noshes for the road? I'm to drive hungry? Starving?"

"You'll spoil your dinner."

"I'm a grown woman, not a five-year-old. I can't spoil my—"

"You're acting like a five-year-old."

Lila stilled her lips. Protesting at this point would make her sound like a five-year-old. Chef was far too crafty. "Who's making dinner?"

"Isabel. Everything's laid out already. She just needs to babysit the soup and assemble the chicken salad. She can't screw it up, so don't give me that look."

"I wasn't giving you a look."

Chef handed her a bag to carry, and picked up the rest. "You were giving a look."

Once in the garage, Lila grabbed the keys for an Adessi sedan, for her silver roadster was too small to accommodate the food. She quickly checked for bugs, then pulled out of the compound.

"Where am I going?"

"Go south," Chef answered vaguely, adjusting the radio, stopping as someone rapped in French. "Take the interstate."

Lila pulled onto the road, dodging cars as she stole sidelong glances at Chef in the passenger seat. Finally, she turned down the music. "What can you tell me about the oracles?"

"The oracles? You've never shown an interest in the oracles. Why do you want to talk about them now?"

"Just making conversation."

"Why now?"

Lila drummed her fingers on the wheel. "I'm having a religious experience. Right now. In this car."

"The gods are speaking to you?"

"Yes. It tickles."

Chef turned up the music. "We'll talk about them on the way back," she said, waving Lila's questions away. Rotting buildings and fields of bluebonnets flashed past the windows.

Lila shifted in her seat. "Okay, fine. Where am I going, then?"

"South, dear. Just a little farther."

"Bakery, my ass."

Just a little farther became a maze of shifting streets that Chef directed her through, almost too late for Lila to navigate properly. Gas stations and mega stores turned into large homes crowded around a lake, which soon turned into a collection of weathered wooden buildings, buildings that looked more like sheds than homes.

Lila soon understood where Chef had led her. When Lila's shoulders slumped in recognition, Chef stopped giving her directions at all.

"I hate you," Lila grumbled. While the Adessi bobbled and bounced down the pock-marked road, she couldn't help but feel as though Chef's insistence about the trip was awfully convenient.

"Maybe you hate me now, but soon you'll have your cookies, and you'll forget all about the rest."

"Not likely."

"Fudge too?"

Lila considered the offer. "How much fudge?"

The pair soon found themselves in the middle of nowhere, the horizon obscured by thick patches of cedar and ash. Wild, dry undergrowth lurked below the trees.

Lila parked on a disjointed, broken slab of cement marked with faded yellow paint, her Adessi sandwiched among several dozen other cars. The engine spat and hissed in the quiet as she took out the key.

She grabbed a bag of baked goods and followed Chef toward the trailhead past a sign that read *Home of the New Bristol Oracle*. A pair of wings attached to an eye had been painted above it, serving as the coat of arms for all American oracles.

They'd have to hike a kilometer before they even reached the temple.

"I have a High Council meeting this evening. I'll come back for you later," Lila said, hoping the reminder would work. She didn't know what was happening, but she didn't like it.

"It'll only be a moment, dear. I just need to drop a few things off."

"I'll wait back at the car, then."

Chef stopped and narrowed her eyes. "Elizabeth Victoria Lemaire-Randolph, you'll help me carry these offerings to the temple, or you'll get your lunch from the security office from now on. Do you hear me?"

Lila frowned. It wasn't often the good-natured Chef threatened her, especially when her threats were empty. "Insufferable woman," she grunted, not sure which woman she meant.

"I know what you and your mother think of the oracles, but don't you dare embarrass me in there. Just think of the cookies and fudge."

Lila clutched her bag and hiked over mismatched and uneven stones in the muggy heat. She'd always hated the hike, not because it was particularly hard, but because she thought it was horribly unfair to people like Sergeant Jenkins. Though she heard the oracles sometimes made house calls, Lila suspected they only did it for a generous donation.

Soon, the pair reached the dock.

They weren't the only ones waiting for the rowboat this afternoon. A young couple sat on the end of the dock, their shoeless feet skimming the water. They'd intertwined their fingers, murmuring softly to one another, stealing languid kisses before they glimpsed Lila and Chef.

Soon to be married, by the looks of them.

For a brief moment, Lila wished that she were back in Tristan's apartment, just so she could lie on his bed again, stealing kisses, stealing more. When would things begin for them? Why were things taking so long?

Why hadn't she just taken what she wanted?

Because he was workborn? Because she didn't know what he wanted? Because she was too used to reaching for someone who reached for her as well? Because he might want more from her than she could give?

It wasn't just about sex with Tristan, and it had frozen her.

Perhaps they needed to have a talk, a long talk, about why she kept going over to his place and spending the night with no climax to the evening, a talk about what he actually wanted.

Tonight. When she went over to his place after the council meeting, they'd have it out.

Wiping the sweat from her brow, Lila realized that the thought of not going to see him had never entered her mind. Things were moving too quickly and too slowly with Tristan all at the same time. She'd never let someone get under skin like this before.

She didn't like the feeling. She didn't like it one bit.

Her palm vibrated, and she swiped the screen. *How's your day going, Prolix?*

"Bad news?"

Lila swallowed and jammed her palm back into her pockets. "No, everything's fine," she answered as a man in brown pants and a black t-shirt rowed a little boat to the dock. A long scar ran from his eyebrow to his chin, barely missing his eye.

The group gingerly climbed inside, careful not to rock the boat and overturn it.

The scarred man rowed toward a building floating in the middle of the lake. It appeared like Lila's security office, all steel and glass and curves, except that it was shaped like a tear, peeking out of the water and coming to a point at the top. Four docks jutted out like compass points around it. Several empty rowboats bobbled in the rolling waves, the vessels tied off and abandoned.

Lila helped Chef from the boat when they finally reached the dock, tipping a bit of cash to the oarsman. Chef pulled out a loaf of bread from one of the bags. "For your service to the oracles."

The man bowed his head. "Thank you, Chef Ana," he said as they stepped toward the tear-shaped building.

"He knows your name? How often do you come here?"

"Enough."

The two lovers from the shore followed behind them, unconcerned with darting ahead and stealing their place in line. There was no such thing as a queue with the oracles. They saw you when they wished, and perhaps they wouldn't see you at all.

There was no sense in hurrying.

The building opened into a reception area and lobby filled with plush lilac couches, matching rugs, sturdy wooden tables, and the smell of incense. A few women in white robes and lilac lace trim wandered among the small crowd, shushing anyone who talked too loudly, passing out paper cups filled with water to the adults. Many pilgrims sat on the floor, legs crossed, vainly trying to clear their minds.

No such silence was required in the children's room. An occasional squeal broke through the quiet as a few excited children played with the toys inside. The children also got juice instead of water, and weren't asked to meditate.

Lucky them.

"Your mind must be clearer if you wish to see the oracle," one of the women whispered to a man in a green shirt. It likely wasn't the first time he'd been told. The man gritted his teeth and closed his eyes more tightly.

It was a neat trick, making people believe it was their own fault they hadn't been seen.

If only that worked in the real world.

One of the robed women smiled at Chef and pulled the pair into a separate room, styled like the lobby, only much smaller. "Chef Ana, it's so good to see you," she said, embracing Chef and kissing her on the cheek.

"I made some sweets and bread for everyone." Chef placed her bags on the little table near the couch. Lila did the same.

The woman's face lit up as she peeked into the bags. "You didn't have to do this, Chef Ana. Bringing Chief Randolph for the oracle was quite enough."

"Bringing me?"

Chef refused to look up while she unloaded the food onto the table. "The oracle called me this morning, Lila. She called me personally. You know when the gods speak—"

"You lose all common sense. I'll be going now. If the oracle wishes to see me, she can make an appointment like everyone else. I have a council meeting to get back for, and I haven't the time, the energy, or the desire to wait around."

Plus, she hadn't had time to review anything about the oracles.

"I'll start making pancakes twice a week," Chef promised quickly.

Lila paused, considering the proposal.

A palm beeped. The attendant pulled hers from her pocket and skimmed the message. "The oracle will see you now, Chief Randolph."

"Go with it," Chef said, tugging Lila's sleeve. "It might be fun."

"That's what Thomas Baskins said when I was thirteen. He was wrong too. I want pancakes or waffles twice a week from now on. You gave your word."

Chef inclined her head.

Lila followed the attendant back into the lobby. They passed through the waiting crowd and entered a room that held nothing but a staircase, leading into darkness.

Lila clomped noisily down the stairs, letting her boot strike each stair as loudly as possible. She found herself approaching a small, dimly lit room, each wall made of glass. Fish swam outside it, bobbing and darting in the cloudy water. A sudden bout of claustrophobia struck her as she reached the last few steps.

A woman, not much older than Lila, sat on a white leather couch watching her descend. She wore a floor-length lilac robe, and her jet-black hair fell in loose waves around her face. She had few wrinkles, perhaps because she schooled her face so often that lines had not had time to develop.

"I don't enjoy being summoned." Lila plopped down on a plush chair across from the couch. The leather crinkled as she folded an ankle over her knee.

"*Summoned* isn't the word that I would use. If I had contacted you directly, then you wouldn't have come. Not without digging and poking us apart first, though I daresay you've already started. It's how you highborn operate, and you're the worst of the lot."

"What makes you think I've taken an interest?"

"I'm an oracle, Chief Randolph. I know your father has asked you to look into us, specifically into the disappearances of our young."

"Is that so?" Only a few trusted servants had access to her father's apartments and offices in Bullstow and Unity, but workborn tended to be quite loyal to the oracles. It stood to reason that some of them might act as the women's spies.

"Let's not waste time with tiresome circling," she said, waving Lila off before she could get started. "I know, chief."

"How do you know what you think you know? By poking and prying?"

"I didn't have to pry, chief. I deduced it by watching the prime minister during our meeting last week and asking a few pointed questions. His thoughts jumped straight to you."

"So my father has a passing thought about me, and you decide—"

"Deduced, and deduced correctly."

"Is that how you oracles operate? By making deductions?" Lila shifted in her seat, outwardly calm on the outside, but the room had begun to creep in on her. It was too quiet and too dead, especially with the fish swirling around them, their eyes shifting and unblinking.

"You believe us to be charlatans."

"Did you also deduce that?"

"Your feelings are obvious. Though in this case, Chef Ana told me how you felt ages ago. She talks about you. She despairs of how she might bring you to the gods."

Lila bit the side of her cheek, uncomfortable at the thought of Chef chatting about her with outsiders. She'd never thought of her as a spy before, not with their history.

"Stop fretting. Chef Ana is utterly loyal to the Randolph family. She only requested my help in bringing you and your siblings to the gods, a mighty task after you'd been schooled so heavily against us."

"How did you reply?"

"I told her not to bother."

Lila lifted a brow. She hadn't been expecting that answer.

"I don't have time to undo years of suspicion, chief. Fate will decide if you should come toward us or not." The oracle stretched her arms across the back of the couch. "Your father is correct. Our numbers are dwindling. As a result, the oracles have more faithful than we have time for. I hardly need another, no matter how rich or well connected you might be."

Lila leaned forward. "You know what I think?"

"Enlighten me."

"I think you and your sisters dabble in psychology and theater, just like fortune tellers. I think that you read people very, very well and tell people exactly what they want to hear, pretending it comes from the so-called gods. I think you're the most well-paid and well-protected actresses on the planet. What I don't know is if you actually believe your own hype."

"Yes, we dabble. And no, not all of us believe."

Lila chewed on her lip. "Then you don't deny that you're a fake?"

"No, but I am an honest fake. As are you. And when I walk back up those stairs, I'll deny saying that with every breath in my lungs, but I can read you well enough to know I won't have to. You respect my candor even if you don't respect my words."

Lila cocked her head. "People come to you frightened and worried, sometimes sick and in pain or dying. They come to you with questions, and you lie to them. Do you really think I could respect you for that?"

"It's rare that anyone wants to talk to me, chief. Most of the time, they just need someone to listen. I do that for them, without judgment, no matter what has happened, no matter what choices they've made in the past, no matter what they're deciding now or might have to choose in the future. I'm safe, I'm impartial, and I'm omniscient, at least in their eyes. They have no reason to lie to me. People need that."

Lila drummed her fingers on her knee.

"I steer people toward decisions they've already made, chief, toward people they're already in love with, toward their own fumbling ambition. I trust them to use their own good sense. I help clear away the fog, so they can see their options for what they truly are, and I let them choose among those options without all the fluff getting in the way. I don't judge their choices, nor do I try to sway them unless their actions will harm another person or themselves. Oracles do have a code of ethics. Who are we to say what's best for anyone?"

"You tell them their choices have been blessed by the gods."

"If our choices are predestined, then everything we do is blessed by the gods. People can do great things when they believe the gods are behind them."

"And terrible."

"People do terrible things anyway. But you'd be surprised how much hardship a person can tolerate when life falls apart around them, once pain and misfortune befalls them, so long as they believe a higher power is involved."

"You're all nothing but liars. Have you no shame at all?"

"You would know a great deal about lying, wouldn't you? Perhaps you should turn your discomfort inward and evaluate the choices you've been making lately."

Lila's gaze locked on the oracle, but she found no condemnation in the woman's hazel eyes. Was she reading her? How else would she know all the things she'd been up to?

She couldn't, not unless she was tossing out bait.

The fish lurked behind the windows.

"People lie all the time," the oracle said. "I just put my lies to better use."

"Do you even believe in the gods?"

"I don't know. It's not all lies and psychology and guesswork. When the seizures take hold, I have visions, and they certainly don't come from me. What I see comes to pass, at least in some form. All I can do is guide what I've seen to the best conclusion."

"So you believe that your visions are true?"

"I know they are. Even so, I wonder about the machine in the basement. Perhaps more so than others who aren't afflicted with the visions. Should we worship the ones who send me these glimpses of the future? Are there even beings behind them at all? You'd be surprised how many oracles are agnostics and atheists."

Lila raised a brow. "Is this the part where you tell me to back off and—"

"I'd rather not waste my breath. I daresay you wouldn't back off even if I bothered. No, I asked you here for a different reason."

"Ah, and what's that?"

"I had a vision this morning."

"Did you now? What happened in this so-called vision?"

"That's none of your concern. Not yet, anyway." The oracle pinned Lila with a severe gaze. "A person makes thousands of decisions every day, but only a handful might decide how a vision comes to pass. I don't mean what shoes you'll wear on Monday or if you'll turn right or left at an intersection. I mean decisions on a more primal level: who you'll choose to align yourself with, how far you'll go to defend a friend, what you believe, and how far you'll go to defend those beliefs. It's obvious that you haven't made some of these decisions yet, for this particular vision was far murkier than I've seen in a long while. I believe it was murkier because of you, chief. Much that surrounds you is a blur. I don't like it. I don't feel comfortable with it."

The oracle studied Lila with the same shrewdness her mother offered those in a business deal. "This conversation will push you to make decisions. It will put you on a path whether you want it to or not. My next vision will be clearer, and you'll have some honest information about my kind, rather than the crap spread over the net."

"If I'm not mistaken, your order is responsible for most of that crap."

"No doubt. We either wrote it or deserve most of it," she admitted. "Come back and see me sometime, chief. I don't mind sparing an hour to help you clear your thoughts."

"What thoughts?"

"Thoughts about watching a man you tranqed die. I've seen the news."

"That wasn't my fault."

"No, it wasn't. Doesn't mean you're not picking it apart in your mind, though. I wager that's not the only thing you're picking apart. How about handing over your best friend's mother and brother to Bullstow for execution? That would brew a fair amount of drama and discontent. Perhaps it is for the best."

"What is that supposed to mean?"

"Not all friendships are destined for a lifetime. I don't believe that you and Ms. Wilson were meant for it."

"How do you know?"

"Because there are some things you can't forgive, nor forget."

Lila's gaze strayed to the fish. "You think she won't forgive me?"

"Who said I was talking about her?"

Lila turned back to the oracle. "What do you mean?"

"I suspect your future with a certain man will last much longer. Dark hair, dark eyes, and a long brown coat? I saw him in my vision too. Your paths cross over and over again, melding into a blur, but there are too many unmade decisions between the pair of you to get a clear glimpse. You're both intertwined, just as you, chief, are intertwined with the oracles. Unfortunately, I don't know how yet. But mark my words, you will be important to us, whether for good or for ill. If I'd known sooner, I might have encouraged Chef Ana a great deal more."

Lila swallowed hard, thinking of her dreams the week before. "What do you mean that I'm intertwined with the oracles?"

"The vagueness is annoying, isn't it? Try living in it." The oracle ushered Lila to the stairs. "All I know about the dark-haired man is that he has killed once and will kill again. It wasn't his fault last time, but next time he'll mean it. He'll keep doing it, over and over again. His path isn't a blur. He's making choices while you spin your wheels, and I fear he's making the wrong ones. He's going to drown in the mire if he's not careful, and he'll take you with him."

"What's that supposed to mean?"

"It's a warning. I fear you'll become like him."

Lila didn't like the oracle's pitying tone.

"I won't tell you more until the visions tell me you are safe and trustworthy. I might question who sends them, but I believe in their validity. You have your family, and I have mine."

9

It was nearly six before Lila pulled into her family's garage, a curious Chef trailing behind her as they returned to the great house. Chef hadn't said much on the way home, likely understanding from Lila's quiet manner that the oracle had given her much to think about. Or perhaps Chef was only happy that Lila hadn't argued for the closing of the oracles' compounds on the way home, believing the women to be a drain on the state's coffers.

It had been Lila's opinion when she was young and too full of her own budding understanding of the world. Chef's continued high praise of the oracles had been what changed her mind. Now Lila understood how important they were spiritually to the majority of the country. Symbolism, if not truth, was important.

Perhaps even more important.

Now the oracle had glimpsed her future, had forced her to think about her place in the grand scheme of things, not just as an heir dodging the path she'd been born to run down, but as a woman rushing toward another, a path set by the gods.

But it was all bullshit, wasn't it? A con to amuse the masses? None of it was real, it was mere entertainment, like horoscopes and crystal balls and Tarot cards. The oracle was a brilliant actress, and she'd been playing her role for a very long time.

She'd been right about one thing, though. There were some things you couldn't forgive or forget. Lila had thoroughly ruined things with Alex. Maybe it would have happened anyway, a slow friendship death over years, rather than an incomplete fracture that lingered only because of circumstance. Tristan had told her that a highborn and a slave could never be friends. They were simply on different levels. Even Alex had alluded to it recently.

Lila had been appalled at the idea, but perhaps she didn't feel the imbalance because she was settled in the higher station. Perhaps you only felt it when you crashed to the bottom or when you were born there.

Alex had certainly fallen. Perhaps the kindest thing Lila could do for her friend was transfer her to a compound closer to Simon and Sturluson's. Maybe if she really loved Alex, she had to let her move on.

But then why did it feel like throwing Alex away?

When Lila and Chef entered the great house, Chef bustled quickly to the kitchens to check on her soup and salad, while Lila jogged upstairs and plopped down in front of her desktop.

Once again, her search for Reaper's partner had yielded no results.

Lila cradled her head. She didn't have time for this now. She didn't have time to concentrate on a potential blackmailer.

Isabel knocked on the door, and Lila's head shot up. The servant carried a little clinking tray, which she placed on Lila's desk. "Chef feared it would be one of those days, madam. Not that you can't eat downstairs with—"

"No, this is wonderful, Isabel. You and Chef always take such good care of me." Lila spied quite a large block of fudge next to her soup and salad.

Isabel bowed and scurried from the room.

Between a few mouthfuls here and there, Lila cycled through messages from her spies. None of them had any news about Oskar. Tristan's didn't either.

Considering that he had turned more than a few workborn inside the Holguín compound, it surprised her that he hadn't found anything. She'd anticipated a race, that they'd rib one another over who had found Oskar first.

Both of them coming up dry could only mean one thing. Chairwoman Holguín had done the deal the night before, smuggling

Oskar from the compound with no one being the wiser, including the Bullstow representative assigned to his case.

Lila turned toward her desktop. She visited the Pirate's Cove, a black-market online auction house, and searched their history for mentions of Oskar. It was a stupid, last-ditch effort, but she had no other ideas.

Unsurprisingly, she came up empty. Whoever wanted Oskar must have contacted the Holguíns directly. If she could break into HolNet, she could peek at their servers and copy every message sent and received by every device for the last two weeks, then execute a global search on the data. If that didn't work, she could read every damn message herself.

Unfortunately, the approach was completely illegal and unethical.

A few years ago, she would have balked at such measures, balked at destroying the privacy of several hundred people. She then recalled Oskar, clutching his blue teddy bear while being led away from Patrick's car. She recalled him standing on the stage, eyes closed, not caring whether Hans Schulte shot him through the heart. Perhaps wanting it to happen.

Ethics be damned.

Lila stared at the pixels on her screen, thinking of everything she'd need to steal their data. She wouldn't need physical access to their servers; she'd just need access to the network. They'd never see her if she did it right.

The last time she'd done something like that, the Wilson militia had seen Tristan's truck. They'd nearly been caught.

Lila choked on her fudge, the chocolate going down the wrong way in her surprise, settling in her windpipe like hands squeezing her neck. She wrapped her napkin around her mouth and coughed, trying to free it, her eyes tearing up as she struggled to breathe.

She had been caught, after all. One of the Wilson militia had put her ruse together, had started the rumor of Lila being involved in their family's downfall because she had enough sense to believe that Lila Randolph had ripped information from their network.

But even if Bullstow believed her story and chose to investigate it, even if Shaw didn't stop the investigation outright, the computer techs wouldn't find anything. She hadn't taken information. She'd just borrowed their connection for a little investigation of her own, covering her tracks well.

Besides, the Wilson militia no longer had access to their own servers. Most of them didn't even live in New Bristol any longer. They'd been snatched up quickly by lowborn families and private security firms throughout Saxony.

Lila finally coughed up the fudge and wiped her mouth, gulping half a glass of water to still the burning in her throat.

Her eyes strayed back to her computer. The messages from Reaper's partner stared back at her. Apathetic. Innocuous.

Perhaps she should call Max to find Oskar. He was better than her at finding things, and she had other matters demanding her attention.

Lila rubbed her eyes and sent Max a message, ignoring the tray of food she'd barely eaten. Hopping out of her chair, she shut down her computer and brushed her hair into a sleek ponytail. She then added more concealer and changed into her formal militia uniform. It was the same as her everyday uniform, only shinier and better tailored. She then pulled on a pair of polished black militia boots and matching white cotton gloves, then added her leather blackcoat and shoved her Colt and her short sword back into their holsters.

Straightening the four silver officer's stars on her collar, she stared at herself in the mirror. She was ready to go toe to toe with ten chairwomen and primes from the other families.

She was ready to condemn her best friend's mother and brother to death.

Lila turned away and trundled down the corridor, passing her sister's door. It should have been Jewel going to the meeting. Unfortunately, her sister had flopped so badly on the High Council that her mother had given up on the idea of Jewel representing the Randolphs. The chairwoman had nearly torn up Lila's contract in a moment of resolve, forcing her to take over the prime spot. In the end, Lila had agreed to assume the prime's role at High Council meetings while Jewel spent more time in training.

It had twisted Lila's stomach to accept. It felt like she'd begun to roll down a hill, gathering moss and snow and weeds that would turn her into something else. But it had been five years, and her mother hadn't asked more of her.

But she hadn't asked less, either.

Lila put her ear to Jewel's door, wondering where she'd gone. Perhaps she'd had a late dinner with Senator Dubois and Gabriel.

Turning away, Lila jogged downstairs and trotted into the kitchen. Chef took off her apron and handed it to Isabel, whose face had gone pale.

It went even paler when a sulking Alex entered seconds later, clad in her best outfit, an old black dress of Lila's and black tights. Lila had liked the dress because it made her feel anonymous. She'd given it to Alex for the same reason, especially now that her friend wasn't allowed to wear color anymore. Her life would be an endless collection of black, gray, brown, and white.

Lila spied a golden serpent brooch pinned to Alex's breast as though her friend still belonged to the Wilsons. It had been the first time she'd been so supportive in a decade.

It must have stung Alex's pride to wear Lila's clothes, but it would have stung her even more to show up in her housemaid's uniform, no matter how fine the clothes might have been. She'd walked among heirs for years, after all, as a prime and an equal, attending the same parties, attending the same schools. All before she'd left her family to go into business for herself, all before her business had fallen apart, all before Lila's mother had seen an opportunity to strike at a weak family.

All before Lila had finished them off.

"Chief, why don't I drive Ms. Wilson?" Chef offered, her presence making more sense now. "You were kind enough to indulge me earlier this afternoon. It's only fair."

Lila inclined her head and trudged from the kitchen, leaving a scowling Alex behind. Lila didn't want to fight, nor did she want to sit in a too-cold or too-quiet car. She didn't even bother to check for bugs or deactivate the GPS from her roadster this time. Everyone knew where she'd be going.

She parked in her reserved spot in the judges' parking lot, only a few meters away from the capitol. The domed structure was composed of marble, arrogance, and ambition. The senators and judges who held session in the east wing longed to be in the west, the one devoted to Saxony. Those in the west longed to be called away to Unity.

It seemed that everyone else wanted to move up in the world.

Lila's boots padded against the marble floor as she entered the building, a muffled sound underneath the chattering of several New Bristol senators. They'd gathered in a hallway, all four taking long looks at her. Perhaps they hoped to speak to her about some piece of legislation waiting for the High Council's signature, or perhaps they wanted to ask her about the season.

Either way, Lila couldn't be bothered. She turned to the nearest stairwell and climbed to the next floor, trotting down the empty corridor to dodge them.

She hung a right and jogged downstairs again, ending up by the door to the High Council chamber. Most of New Bristol likely believed the judges met in a far grander room, with stained glass and expensive art and gilded trim, but the High Council hadn't bothered with such frippery. The small room contained thick drapes and expensive rugs, not bought for beauty but for thickness, all to drown out their voices from curious ears.

The damn rugs didn't even match.

Lila skirted the long table inside, the only furniture the room contained. Twelve different chairs of varying lavishness sat around it, all matched to each house's color. Celeste Wilson's golden chair had been shoved to the back of the room, discarded and waiting to be thrown out.

Lila sat down in her crimson chair, eyeing the women around her. Their ages spanned from twenty-five to seventy. All but three were matrons, clad in their silvercoats. The others wore white-coats, the primes attached the New Bristol council because their matrons had been elevated to the Saxony High Council, just like Lila's mother.

Lila enjoyed wearing her blackcoat in the council room. It kept the other women on edge, knowing that she had the authority to arrest them. It also kept them confused about the exact rank of the Randolph heirs, since tradition dictated that Lila should not even be on the council if she was no longer prime.

Confusion and nervousness were good things sometimes.

In any case, it kept her amused enough to get through the meetings.

She grabbed the folder before her and peeked at the typed agenda, noting the first few items dealt with legislation passed by the Low and High Senates in the last week. The Randolphs had no issues with them, for they were all trifles. A building renamed, a memorial planned. Everything substantial had already been debated and passed earlier in the legislative session: the budget, next year's educational standards, new health concerns, environ-mental regulations, and transportation initiatives. The last two months of the session tended to be nothing but pomp.

Lila's gaze dropped to the last three items.

4. Review Celeste Wilson's conviction by both chambers of the senate.
5. Review Patrick Wilson's conviction by both chambers of the senate.
6. Nominate a new family to ascend to the New Bristol highborn.

Alex entered the room as Lila finished reading, her heels clicking across the chambers. She'd borrowed Lila's shoes and hadn't even asked. She stopped behind Lila, surveying the rest of the room with the proud scowl she'd worn all week long.

"Chief Randolph," Chairwoman Weberly said, her eyes straying to Alex. "I see you've brought a guest to visit with the council before we begin. We should drink to old times before we get down to business. Perhaps President Holguín has a spare bottle of Sangre?"

Lila didn't rise to the bait. Hardly older than Lila, Johanna Weberly had only recently succeeded her newly retired mother. She was still drunk with power, still prodding where she shouldn't. "You know why she's here, madam. Ms. Wilson will stay for the duration. Her mother and brother are to be condemned today. The least we can do is let her witness it."

"No, the least we can do is kick her out of the chambers," Johanna muttered, her gaze meeting the face of each whitecoat and silver-coat in the room, contemplating her next move.

None of the women joined her cause, not even Élise Holguín, prime of the Holguín family, president of Holguín Enterprises, chair of the New Bristol Council, and Johanna's usual ally.

The table's reluctance wasn't much of surprise. The other judges rarely engaged Lila directly at the best of times, for Lila rarely spoke up in council. Whenever Lila did voice a position, they knew she meant it and that it was important to her, the Randolphs, or their allies. They were usually too cautious of her position to protest merely for the sake of protesting.

In any case, these weren't the best of times. For all anyone knew, Lila had just masterminded the Wilson sting out of nothing more than impatience. Everyone in the room probably had information they didn't want Lila to seek out.

Johanna sniffled and adjusted her silvercoat. "This is most irregular."

"No, it's not. Heirs of a fallen house have a habit of barging into senate and council deliberations. The only thing not typical this time is that we only have one."

Élise sat up primly, taking over her role as head of the council, and banged her gavel on its sounding block. "Let's begin, shall we? Perhaps we should start with agenda items four and five so that Ms. Wilson will not be overburdened?"

The judges picked through the files of Celeste and Patrick Wilson, reviewing Bullstow's position as well the position of the defendant's lawyers. They couldn't decide guilt or innocence, but they could judge whether or not all the evidence had been considered, if the punishment fit the crime, if the judgment should be returned to the senate chambers for further review. But Bullstow had been diligent in their paperwork and more than fair to both of the accused. Since they'd only been charged with treason for doing business with citizens of the empire, there was no penalty the state could levy except death.

A screen descended from the ceiling. The women watched an abridged version of the Wilsons' interrogations. Lila recoiled when Patrick turned to the double-sided glass, suspecting that she had been the one behind Shaw's questions.

Alex suspected it too, murmuring several choice words. Someone must have shown her the tape. Even now, she chose to blame Lila for their mistakes.

Or perhaps just Patrick's.

Perhaps he'd always be a little boy to her, a boy who'd been led by their mother and wronged by Lila. A scapegoat, rather than a co-conspirator. A fool, rather than a murderer.

Just like Lila had trouble seeing Shiloh as a father and senator.

"The House of the Golden Serpent has fallen," Élise proclaimed after the screen darkened and rose back into the ceiling. "Celeste and Patrick Wilson have both confessed to treason. Celeste, under the truth serum, and Patrick, of his own free will and in the presence of his advocate and Chief Shaw. A special council of the High Senate and Low Senate each ruled to convict. After viewing the interrogation, I see no reason why we should overturn their decision. Would anyone like to speak before we vote?"

"You're damn right I wish to speak," Alex snapped before anyone else had a chance to say a word. She grabbed a file before Lila and waved it in the air. "My brother wouldn't do any of this. You know him. You've been to parties with him. You've worked with him. A few of you or your daughters have even slept with him. How could you even think he'd be mixed up in—"

"Bedrooms do not make boardrooms," Chairwoman Grace Masson gently reminded her.

"My mother made him do this, and you know it. You can't execute him for being easily led. He doesn't have the sense for any of this. Put him in the auction house if you must, but don't condemn an innocent man to death." It wasn't pleading that entered Alex's voice. It was rage. Pure rage directed at every woman in the room who still had power she did not, the power to rule, the power to kill her brother with a simple vote. If she were still prime, several of the women might have hid under the table.

Élise swallowed hard and lifted her gavel. "Chief Randolph, rein in your pet, or we'll be forced to have the militia escort her out."

"She's neither a pet nor a child. She's a grown woman who used to stand among us not so long ago. Show her some damn respect."

"You go too far," Johanna growled. "I think Ms. Wilson has said enough for one evening."

Lila swiveled her chair and faced her old friend. "Ms. Wilson, if you have anything, anything at all to corroborate your claims, to prove that your brother was led, to prove that he didn't have the sense to make these decisions for himself, then speak now."

"You know him," Alex said, fumbling.

"I thought I knew him. He admitted to all charges."

"Not under the serum."

"Would that satisfy you?"

"Yes."

Lila considered her agreement, considered how she might talk Shaw into giving Patrick the serum and sneaking Alex inside the holding cells to witness it.

But Shaw would never go for it. Bullstow had already gotten a confession.

Chairwoman Masson gave Alex a pitying look. "Your brother must agree to the serum, Ms. Wilson. He did not. No sane person would, given the side effects. Chief Shaw cannot force it on a person just because the accused's sister cannot—"

Alex slammed the file on the table.

Everyone winced at the loud slap.

"Ms. Wilson," Lila began, "unless you have some piece of evidence to present to us, then I'm afraid there is nothing we can do to stop this. He made his decisions. Now he has to face the consequences, as do you. I ask again, do you have any evidence to present to this council?"

"Chief," Johanna hissed. "The time for evidence has passed. This is most irregular."

"No, what would be most irregular is if a militia chief tossed a chairwoman out the window."

The women gasped, and Johanna's eyes dropped to the recorder in the middle of the table. "You would dare threaten me?"

"Johanna, shut up," Lila replied tiredly, spinning once more in her chair. "Ms. Wilson, help us help you. We have Patrick's confession. How do you counter that?"

"It's just the boastings of a young boy. A boy who was angry because his sister was wronged. A boy who was confused by his mother."

"He's a twenty-three-year-old man. That's hardly a boy."

"Don't throw Johnny back in my face."

"I didn't mean... I just mean that we can't excuse his actions on age alone. Is there anything you have that could excuse his behavior? Anything at all?"

All eyes turned to Alex. Her eyes clouded—not that she'd allow tears to fall in front of the matrons and primes. "Don't do this, Lila," she said finally, a note of pleading finally entering her voice. "What did my brother ever do to you?"

Lila opened her mouth to answer, but she wasn't sure what to say. It seemed important to say the right thing, because if she didn't, she knew the right time would never come again.

But the perfect words didn't come. "I'm sorry. It's out of my hands."

"No, it's not!" Alex shouted, kicking the bottom of Lila's chair. "Tell them. Tell them it wasn't his fault!" She kicked again, shoving Lila's chair into the table. Her third blow landed on Lila's shin.

Lila sucked in her breath but did not call out.

Nor did anyone else as more kicks landed, as Alex ignored the chair in favor of her former best friend. Perhaps the women were frightened of what Alex would do if they intervened. If she'd assaulted her best friend, what would she do to people she hated?

"Ms. Wilson, I'd say that is enough," Chairwoman Masson said at last. "I think I speak for the rest of the council when I say our patience has come to an end. This isn't the time or the place to settle private arguments or to work through your grief. I'm sorry for the loss of your brother and your mother, but neither Lila nor her chair is at fault for Mr. Wilson's actions. Perhaps you should see the oracle."

"Fuck you," Alex yelled, finally breaking off her assault. "Fuck you and fuck the oracle. Fuck the whole damn lot of you."

Élise's eyes widened, but she said nothing. Alex had gone so far over the line that the council now looked to Lila to discipline her.

But Lila couldn't, just as she couldn't at the great house. She should call for the Bullstow militia and charge Alex with assault against her master. If she didn't, rumors of her leniency would go round and round the city before the sun rose. What was worse, a second rumor would accompany it, claiming that she'd allowed Alex to abuse the High Council of Judges unchecked.

When Lila didn't rise to summon the militia, Élise snatched up her gavel. "All who find no fault with the conviction of Celeste Wilson, raise your hand."

Ten hands went up around the table.

"All opposed?"

Lila did not vote.

"Abstained?"

Lila finally raised her hand. She couldn't vote to condemn Alex's mother, but she couldn't vote for her to go free, either. What else she could do for her friend but this one trifle?

"The council upholds the senate's decision, ten in favor, one abstention. All who find no fault with the conviction of Patrick Wilson, raise your hand."

Again, everyone raised their hands but Lila.

"Abstained?" Élise asked.

Lila inclined her head.

"The council upholds the senate's decision, ten in favor, one abstention."

Alex shoved Lila's chair away from the table. It rocked her violently to and fro, her vision shaking with every wobble. "You've killed them both. Is this what you wanted?"

"Ms. Wilson, Chief Randolph didn't even vote," Chairwoman Masson pointed out.

Alex didn't seem to care. She turned on her heel and dashed from the room.

The door hadn't even closed before Lila stood. She chased after her friend, her boots heavy on the marble as they reached the middle of the corridor. "Alex, stop!"

The slave turned, her face locked in stone.

"Alex."

"No," she shouted, shoving Lila back. "For the millionth time, you don't get to call me that ever again. You fucking bitch, you made me help you!"

She shoved Lila again and dropped her voice to a hiss, anger and regret and shame in every word. "Patrick would be at home right now if I hadn't taken you to the compound. Instead he's rotting away in a holding cell, waiting to be hanged like a criminal, and three of my cousins are dead. You made me do that! You!"

She shoved Lila again, as tears fell heavy on her cheek. "How could you do that to me? How could you make me help you? You've made me worse than her. You did that, Lila. How could do that to me?"

Lila didn't fight back. She let Alex shove her farther and farther down the hall, back toward the council chambers.

Lila took it, even when Alex slapped her, the sound echoing in the corridor.

"Say something!" Alex shouted at last, punching Lila in the jaw, right where Hans Schulte had elbowed her.

Lila took a step back at last, holding her face.

Alex winced and held her fist, reddened from the blow.

Neither of them moved.

From the corner of her eye, Lila saw the unblinking eyes from the High Council chamber, disgust etched in all ten faces. Several senators gaped at the end of the hall, unsure if they should intervene. A few militia hovered twenty meters away, staring at one another, ears cocked for orders ungiven, tranqs wavering, well aware that the chief had not drawn hers in self-defense.

Lila hadn't even seen the blackcoats approach.

Her jaw hurt badly.

Her cheekbone still throbbed.

After walking several steps to the High Council chamber, she slammed the door on the matrons and primes before returning. "Alex Craft-Wilson," she said quietly, "I charge you with assault against your master. You have the right to—"

"You've got to be kidding me! But you're not, are you? You're serious. Gods, Lila, how do you look at yourself in the mirror? How do you sleep at night?"

When Lila didn't respond, Alex started forward. "I said how do you—"

Lila grabbed her old friend's shoulder and guided her toward the wall. The militia ran forward to assist, cuffing Alex's hands behind her back and patting her down for weapons.

"Take her directly to Chief Shaw's office, nowhere else," Lila ordered, already sending him a message on her palm. Perhaps it wasn't fair to disrupt his evening, but he'd disrupted plenty of hers. He owed her.

"As you wish, Chief Randolph," one of the militiamen said, bowing before they escorted Alex from the building.

Lila sent another message to Chef, telling her to return home. Then, rubbing her jaw, she slipped back into the council chambers.

"Oracle's light, did you see her face?" Élise snickered. "It's like she was possessed. It's clear now the whole family suffers from poor breeding and aggression. They never should have been admitted into the highborn. They've been an embarrassment to us all."

Lila didn't even tell her to shut up. She merely looked at Élise, pouring all her anger into the glare.

Élise closed her mouth.

"Perhaps we should move on the last item on the agenda," Chairwoman Masson suggested.

"That sounds like an excellent idea," Élise said, trying to smile. "Since the House of the Golden Serpent has fallen, we now have cause to add another family into our ranks. There is one lowborn family in New Bristol who has shown decorum in the face of adversity, who has proven their worth, wealth, and quality. If it pleases the council, I nominate Suji Park to join the highborn."

"I second that motion," Johanna agreed.

"All in favor?"

Everyone raised their hands, even Lila this time.

"Any other New Bristol families to consider?"

No one said a word. The elevation of Suji Park had already been decided in restaurants, in country clubs, on the lake, among little groups of heirs sipping wine at the end of the day. No further discussion would be needed; the rest was merely a formality.

"All right, Ms. Park will be invited to give a proposal to the High Council of Judges two days hence at our regular meeting. Now, for the other items on the agenda…"

The women quickly passed the legislation sent from the senates, and the meeting broke apart. Lila hopped up as soon as Élise slapped her gavel upon the sounding block.

As Lila slipped into the parking lot, she pulled out her palm to check her messages. After scrolling through quite a few from Tristan, she tapped on the ID of one of her best spies.

Oskar Kruger had gone missing.

10

After checking her roadster for bugs and turning off the GPS, Lila left Bullstow and drove to Max Earlwell's home, which looked like the interior of a dollhouse displayed under a massive, overturned tumbler, surrounded by kilometers of trees and woods and cameras. A finely tailored servant let her inside, then disappeared in the bowels of his master's house. Lila padded over the cream-colored carpet, ignoring the sky-blue chairs, the marble statuary, and the paintings in the parlor. She leaned upon one of the thin metal beams that framed the curved glass panes of the home, each the size of garage doors.

Trees and darkness surrounded the house like arms and blankets hiding a coy woman's flesh from her lover's eyes. Fifteen meters away from the parlor wall, a dark Lake Bristol lapped at the shore. It would have been five, but the drought had stolen ten meters, likely the only thing in the world Max couldn't steal back.

Turning away at last, she sat upon a couch, musing again upon the bulletproof glass surrounding her. The entire outside layer of Max's home had been plated in it, leaving the majority of his life exposed to anyone with a set of binoculars. He was a little bird in a cage that watched you long before you glimpsed it.

For a spy, Max had certainly built the strangest house of all.

Born John Poole, Max had grown up on the Randolph estate, studying with Lila under the tutelage of Trudy Poole, John's mother. Busted for several dozen counts of corporate espionage, fraud, and blackmail, she had been surrendered to the auction house with a lifetime sentence. Not a single highborn had bid upon her, not even to put her into the mines out of revenge. Ms. Poole was a loaded gun, and no one wanted a daily game of Russian roulette.

Given the severity of her sentence, Ms. Poole would have hanged if someone had not taken her. Unfortunately, the Massons could not handle the negative PR, given the embarrassing secrets that had been exposed about Chairwoman Masson's youngest daughter, the only one of her brood that had not inherited their mother's sense of elegance and propriety. At the last moment, Chairwoman Randolph had stepped forward to take charge of Ms. Poole as a favor to a longtime ally. What no one had understood was that Lila's mother had actually wanted Ms. Poole all along, she just knew she wouldn't have to pay.

Ms. Poole wouldn't do a damn thing against the Randolphs, for if Chairwoman Randolph became the slightest bit unhappy, she could turn her back over to Bullstow. If no one bid on the spy once, they damn sure wouldn't bid after she'd been tossed away.

She'd be hanged this time, and her son would become an orphan.

The only thing Ms. Poole had ever cared about had been John, a fact Chairwoman Randolph had paid well to ascertain. Ms. Poole had been the sort of mother who kissed her son on the cheek whenever they parted, who put little notes in his luggage whenever he slept at a friend's home, who watched him too closely at the park. She also had the nerve to share his baby pictures, including the naked ones, with anyone who would sit still for more than ten minutes.

Lila had sat still for ten minutes. She'd blushed, unsure what to say, but she hadn't looked away.

John had blushed harder. It had been the first time they'd met after all, and he'd tried to kiss her only moments before.

He'd gotten a swollen eye for his trouble, though Lila had been aiming for his nose.

She'd sucked at hand-to-hand even as a six-year-old.

She couldn't leave, either. The condo on the edge of the Randolph estate was supposed to be out of bounds for Lila, but that made her desperate to visit it. Her mother had known that about her daughter, even back then. Though the chairwoman had intended for Ms Poole to teach Lila corporate defense, Ms. Poole had taught Lila whatever she wanted to learn. What young Lila had really wanted to know, other than how to keep her family safe from people like Ms. Poole, was how to sneak into wherever she wasn't supposed to be.

Lila had always been too curious and nosy for her own good.

Ms. Poole had been more than happy to comply. She thought it funny. She also thought learning how to attack a system was a far better use of Lila's time, and far more instructive than learning how to counter.

John had learned alongside Lila, though Ms. Poole had clearly taught her son more tricks than she'd offered Lila. The pair eventually took up Ms. Poole's assignments as homework. As a consultant to the Randolph militia, she'd occasionally been charged with puzzling out how certain blackmailers and intruders had compromised WolfNet. She'd been well kept for her trouble, and John had been treated like a little prince. That had endeared Chairwoman Randolph to Ms. Poole somewhat, or at least tempered her urge to steal from the Randolphs and flee to Burgundy.

That, and the fact that John refused to leave his friend.

Rather than follow in his mother's footsteps when he grew up, John had chosen the safer route. He merely watched, both people and systems. He'd quickly earned his fortunes as the best spy in Saxony, growing rich off the highborn and others who could afford to pay for the best.

Lila, too, as she hadn't the time to watch everyone she needed to watch.

Max slowly descended the glass staircase in the middle of the house, his steps barely making a noise as he entered the room, his path visible through several panes of glass. He had dressed in a pair of nondescript trousers and a plain white t-shirt, both commissioned from a tailor. His shirt's fabric was a silk blend and incredibly soft, not that anyone would notice it, just like his black boots. They'd been crafted by a cobbler in Greece. Max's wardrobe looked as common as his face, though far more lurked beyond the surface. If anyone met him on the street, they'd forget him and his clothes less than five seconds later.

That was exactly how Max liked it.

His hazel eyes fixed on Lila as soon as he entered the room, the corners crinkling as he smiled and gave her a bear hug. "Lila, you little minx, I'm so glad you could join me for a glass of wine. I can't remember the last time you came over for a chat."

Lila's hand twisted in her pocket, and she thumbed her jammer. The little pendant-like device would prevent any audio from being recorded, either from bugs that Max's enemies had planted or the ones he'd planted himself. "Wine? What sort of wine?"

"The best." Max led her through a glass corridor. He always claimed the soundproofing was better inside the kitchen, covered with some new glass from Asia. Glass and stainless steel appliances filled the kitchen, everything clear and sparkling. "Let's have some Sangre, my darling, before we muse about poor Oskar Kruger and the scoundrel who gave you that nasty bruise on your jaw. How long has it been since you had a glass?"

Lila smirked.

"Ah, you bought a crate from Natalie recently? One of these days your mother will catch you at it."

"I had breakfast with my father. Bullstow doesn't care about my mother's ban. Have I mentioned how much I love visiting my father?"

Max picked up a bottle of wine on the counter. "I hope you plan on visiting your father a whole lot more this week, because I fear your source has dried up." He dug through a drawer for a corkscrew. The serving spoons and spatulas rattled against one another.

Lila shrugged and sat on the barstool across from him. "I know, but it won't be hard to acquire a new source. Natalie was merely the cheapest option. I don't have much sympathy for the woman. She's difficult."

"Women always are." Max popped the cork with a hollow *thunk*. "Especially when they've been disowned. It happened right after her arrest warrant came down from Bullstow on Tuesday, and no one has seen her since. By the way, my sources tell me that you were right in the middle of that kerfuffle."

"Kerfuffle? No one uses that word anymore, Max."

"Kerfuffle, kerfuffle, kerfuffle." He raised his eyes to the ceiling, unable to peer through the metal floor. "Mr. Vimes, please use the word 'kerfuffle' in a sentence for our darling Lila."

A muffled voice came from somewhere upstairs. "I'll get into a kerfuffle with my boss if I do not use this word in a sentence. I'll get into a worse kerfuffle if I remind him that rich people do not shout."

"Thank you, Mr. Vimes." Max winked at Lila. "Chef Ana always said the same thing. I think the only reason why the rich do not raise their voices is because the poorer among us do not wish it. They train us as easily as spoiled puppies with diamond collars."

"I didn't say I didn't know what kerfuffle meant, smartass, I just said no one uses the word." She shoved her empty glass closer to the wine.

Max held the bottle back. "You didn't answer my question about Natalie's arrest. Did you have something to do with it?"

"I have no intention of answering. It's more fun to watch your little wheels work."

"Brat. All of New Bristol is buzzing about what part you might have played in Natalie's arrest, as well as the Wilsons' downfall, and you won't tell me? Me, Lila? I'm your oldest friend."

"Alex is my oldest friend. You're merely the most annoying."

"Even after she assaulted you before the High Council?"

"How do you know about that already?"

Max grinned. "I know everything, my darling Lila, except where Natalie is. What do you know?"

"What makes you think I know anything about her arrest or her disappearance?"

Max stared at her for several long seconds, studying her face.

Lila didn't flinch, and searched his face at the same time. They'd engaged in such contests frequently over the years, each claiming they knew when the other told a lie.

This time it was Max who pulled away first, finally pouring the wine, leaving Lila to wonder what he had gathered. "You usually know what I do not, and vice versa. That's why I think you know. Of course, maybe you don't. The rumor is that Chairwoman Holguín's blood squad disappeared Natalie for dishonoring the family."

Lila raised a brow. Every matron had a blood squad, reserved for violent and serious crimes against the family, usually perpetrated by the family itself. The group punished assassins and thieves, closing the gap between a family's safety and what the law could prove. So long as the blood squad only operated on a family's property and left no physical evidence behind, Bullstow left them alone. They even found a little innocent blood acceptable, so long as it kept their matrons, mothers, lovers, and children safe.

"Since when does that family care about dishonor?" Lila asked. "Even if the chairwoman did send her brutes, Natalie would have slipped away before they closed in. Follow the Sangre if you wish to find her. She still has a whole warehouse full of it."

Max stopped mid-pour. "Where did you hear that?"

"It's basic human psychology. A woman like Natalie will have an insurance policy set up somewhere. Mark my words, she has plenty of wine set aside to tide her over. She just won't sell it here. There are other families in the commonwealth who boycott the Holguíns."

"It's almost as if you have firsthand experience with such insurance policies."

"Now who's fishing?"

"I'm always fishing." He smirked, circling the counter to sit next to her. "I just don't sell the information when it's about you."

"Well, put aside your fishing pole. Both of them," she said, grabbing her glass and casting a languid eye at his trousers. "Mark my words, Natalie will have put some of her money in reserve to pay for lawyers and sent the rest to Burgundy."

"She doesn't have an account in Burgundy."

"What happened to it?"

"Perhaps you should ask your dear father. He's stepping outside the bounds of his role as prime minister more and more these days. Perhaps his heart is in the right place, but it's going to get him into trouble if he moves against the matrons, trying to govern as a king rather than as a satellite of the highborn. You should warn him if it's not already too late."

"You're claiming that my father froze Natalie's account? The entire banking industry in that country hasn't frozen the accounts of any Allied criminal in two hundred years, not unless the courts have found them guilty. Why would they do it for my father? And why now? They only exist so that the shadiest among the Allied Lands and the Holy Roman Empire can do business together without risking the hangman's noose. It would put the entire country out of business in an instant if word leaked that they'd become anything less than neutral. They'd be bankrupt."

"Perhaps they were under the mistaken impression that the account belonged to your mother. Or perhaps they weren't so mistaken after all."

"You want me to pay for information that I can get by asking my father?" Lila pinched Max's cheek. "Are you that hard up for a shiny, new Adessi of your own?"

"No. Where would I drive it? It's far too flashy," Max said, brushing her hand away. "Do you honestly believe your father tells you everything? You're smarter than that, Lila. For his entire adult life, he's been best friends with one of the sneakiest matrons in the commonwealth. I know you see him as a plodding idiot, Lila, but he didn't become the prime minister on his cock alone. Don't be so gullible."

"Don't talk about my father's…thing. And I don't think he's an idiot."

"Fine. You think he's a golden retriever, but even happy dogs can growl and bite."

Lila sipped her wine and ignored the slights against her father. They weren't the first Max had ever made. "So Natalie's accounts have been frozen. Big deal. She'll have more money soon. Natalie, of all people, wouldn't want to see the auction house. She's pissed off too many people for that. She'll have a way out of this jam. Just follow the wine, and you'll find her."

"I've been trying, but Natalie's usual hideouts are empty and I don't think she's in the wine business anymore. More than a few Randolphs have been asking my minions to procure Sangre. It's beneath my people, Lila. They just stroll into a liquor store, buy a few bottles, and sell it at an obscene markup. I think the highborn merely like throwing their money away."

"It's safer. They can't exactly ask their servants to buy it for them. It might get around." Lila didn't have that problem anymore. Tristan had cleared out a Holguín warehouse filled with wine the previous month. He'd offer her crates of Sangre if she asked.

"Just like the rest of the highborn. You'd never ask anyone to buy it for you. Word might get out. How would it look for the future prime of Wolf Industries—"

"I'm not prime."

"You will be. On that, I'm certain." Max poured himself another glass. "My mother taught us human psychology on the playground, Lila. Your mother is like the child who never learned to share. She won't let the militia keep you for much longer."

"She's not sharing me. I'm not a toy."

"You could be. Why haven't we slept together?"

"Because we grew up like siblings?"

"I can get past anything if the lights are off. Maybe even if we leave them on."

"Fine, because you'd probably film it without me knowing and sell the tape?"

"Hey, that's a good idea." He grinned. "I bet it'd go for quite a bit, too. I'd ask you to wear a costume. A pretty little dress with—"

"Focus, you perv."

"Fine. Natalie has no money and isn't moving any product. What does that mean?"

"It means that she has another source of funds we haven't found yet, or she found a better way of making…" Lila put down her wine. A blush rose on her cheeks. "Gods, you think she took Oskar, don't you?"

"It was a bit obvious, Lila. You're slipping."

Lila didn't even bother contradicting him. "It's a bit obvious for her as well. It won't take long for people to put two and two together."

"By then, she'll be gone. It's a risk, but not too risky for a pissed-off niece with nothing to lose. I bet you'd try to screw over your matron in her spot, so long as it didn't involve selling a child."

"The big difference is that I have the skills to pull it off."

"Natalie might not have our skills, but she isn't as inept as you believe. In any case, the Holguíns have their suspicions about who took Oskar. They just won't release a word of it to Bullstow. They don't want the press, and I'm betting Chairwoman Holguín still wants to complete her deal, which they can't do if her buyer thinks she's lost Oskar. She's stalling until she finds him."

"What do you know about a deal?"

Max shrugged, his hazel eyes coyly tracing the floor. "Lila, Lila, Lila… Do you really expect me to answer that?"

"You're telling me far too much already. They didn't hire you to find Natalie, so you're blabbing everything to me as an act of petty revenge."

Max cleared his throat. "It's not petty."

Lila said nothing, and poured another glass of wine.

"It's not," he muttered, and sipped his wine. "It's costing them far more than it's costing me, and I'm not just talking about money."

"Now who's pissed?"

"I'm not pissed. I'm just free to say what I will."

"How many families know that Natalie and Oskar are both missing?"

"None that I can tell. You and your mother's spies always scoop theirs, but I'll make sure my clients know soon. Four of the families pay me quite well, after all. The other six can't afford me or refuse to spend the money. Cheap fools."

"What about Ms. Park?"

"She's not cheap, nor is she a fool."

Lila drummed her fingers on the counter. "Natalie's going to use Patrick's plan, or some version of it, only she'll remain in Burgundy. No one can extradite her there, and Chairwoman Holguín will be out much more than ten million credits. It's smart and bitchy, just like Natalie."

"Maybe she'll move to Burgundy, maybe she'll move somewhere else, but one thing is for sure. She won't stay in New Bristol for very long." Max stilled Lila's fingers on the countertop. "You're tired and nervous, Lila. What's got you so wound up? Was it that man last night at the auction?"

"No, just work."

"Good, because he did it to himself. Take a vacation. I don't like seeing you like this. I don't like seeing bruises all over your face and your hands torn up, either."

"I have too much work to take a vacation. Part of that work is locating Natalie. Could you do it?"

Max shook his head and played with the stem of his glass. "Ask me to do something else, Lila. Anything else."

She narrowed her eyes. Max rarely refused to take a job from her.

"You don't want to find Natalie. You want to find Oskar. I'm not an idiot, Lila. Unfortunately for you, the boy destabilizes the playing field too much. A looming war? Families in a tizzy? It only helps my bottom line if the boy remains missing. Surely you understand."

"I know you like chaos, sometimes you even create it, but I don't care about your hobbies tonight. That boy could die if he's not found soon."

"You want to rescue him, is that it? What will you do when you find him? Give him back to the Holguíns? No, you want him for something else, and I don't like where that will lead. Not for my bottom line and certainly not for your future. Stay out of politics.

The world gets messier the farther away you get from New Bristol. Riskier, too."

Lila hopped off the stool, annoyed at how much Max sounded like her whenever she spoke to Tristan. "Don't tell me what to do, Max."

"Fine, but I'm not going to help you find Oskar. Ask me to do anything but that." When she turned to leave, he grabbed her arm. "Let me help. I want to help."

Lila eyed her friend. He'd never betrayed her trust in all the time she'd known him, but she still didn't trust him. Not completely.

Perhaps she didn't have the luxury of focusing on herself. Missing kids needed her attention, attention she could not give them if she spent her hours searching for a ghost.

Something in her eyes made him frown. He pulled her close and put his arms around her, resting his chin against her forehead. His stubble grazed her skin, and his embrace tightened around her so hard that she couldn't help but melt into him.

Kissing her hair, he rubbed a calming hand over her back. "I'm not your brother. Not even close. Let's get that straight right now."

Lila snorted and broke away.

He leaned against the counter and crossed his arms over his chest, a satisfied smile on his face. "Let me help, Lila. You look like you need it, even if you refuse to admit it. You have my full discretion. You know that."

Lila recalled the messages from Reaper's partner, something Max could handle just as quickly as she could, perhaps faster. She could strip the text, but Max could easily find them in the logs. *Would* find them, eventually.

But he'd never betrayed her.

"Your discretion is what I would need. I want to trace a few messages back to their source, but I haven't the time to do so."

"Is it about Oskar?"

She waved his concerns away. "It's nothing to do with Natalie and Oskar. Just me, but other things take priority. It's not a favor. It's a job. I'll pay at my usual rate."

"As you wish."

"I'll send you the details tonight. Find the sender, Max, as quickly as possible."

He nodded, curiosity evident in every line in his face. To his credit, he didn't ask any questions, but Lila couldn't help but feel that getting Max involved was a mistake.

What other choice did she have, though?

She thumbed off her jammer as she left the glass house. Opening the door to her roadster, she whipped out her palm computer and checked for bugs. Max's minions often went behind their boss's back and planted one.

Finding nothing amiss, she sped down Max's driveway, thinking about taking a detour to Tristan's shop. She always stashed servant's clothes in the trunk in case she needed sudden anonymity. Unfortunately, the oracle's warning still unnerved her, melting the small ache in her chest that had tightened throughout the day, an ache she'd begun to feel more and more acutely over the last week whenever she left Tristan's side.

She hated the feeling. It didn't befit a highborn to moon after a lover. Lovers should be enjoyed and cast aside when whim or family politics necessitated it. Having one you couldn't cast aside meant marriage, and she'd never let that bind her.

They weren't even lovers yet. Somehow that made her feelings worse, to feel so altered when they'd barely touched.

As she cruised through an orange light, her thoughts lost to Tristan, a motorcycle ran the red behind her. The cheap, beaten-up Barracuda looked as though it'd been ditched and rolled on the streets of New Bristol.

Often.

She could have sworn she'd seen same bike recently, perhaps coming home from the oracle or on the way to her council meeting.

Had Max put a tail on her?

Frowning, she turned on LaSalle, annoyed to find the bike still following. After a few more turns, it was obvious the rider didn't belong to Max. The spy lord would never take on someone so clumsy.

Lila stopped near a convenience store, parking her roadster at the mouth of an alley. As she dug through piles of candy inside, she watched the front window out of the corner of her eye. The bike zoomed by and parked a few stores up in plain view. The rider didn't remove his helmet, though. He locked his gaze on the register and the door, waiting for her to emerge.

Lila memorized the license plate. While the woman at the register rang up another patron, Lila put back the candy and snuck through the store's side exit, emerging back in the alley.

The stench of piss and vomit nearly choked her. She held her breath until she returned to her car. Then she popped the parking brake, shifted into neutral, and let the heavy car roll to the end of the alley before slipping the key into the ignition. After starting her car, she hung a left at the corner. She had little desire and even less time to chase someone down. She had too many other things to do.

Fifteen minutes later, she slipped into her bedroom and removed her Colt and sword, placing them on her desk before sitting in front of her computer. She traced the rider's plate in the militia database, letting it search while slipped off her gloves and boots.

It didn't take long to get a hit.

Finn Nottingham, 2404 East Third Street.

A familiar stare and familiar scar appeared onscreen. They belonged to the same workborn who'd rowed her to the oracle's temple that afternoon.

Mr. Nottingham should have known better than to follow a blackcoat, and the oracle shouldn't have ordered it in the first place. Perhaps this was how she made her predictions.

After all, lies worked best when surrounded by truths.

That didn't make much sense, though. The oracle had known about Tristan, at least enough to offer a vague description. But Lila had always careful when she visited him, far more careful than she needed to be. She'd always made sure her GPS was disabled and that she had no bugs attached to her car. She always took many twists and turns to get to his part of town, dodging every security camera as she walked to his shop, and employing her jammer when she could not. If Max had never been able to follow her, if her mother had never been able to track her, then the bumbling Mr. Nottingham could never have managed it.

She would have to find out more.

Later.

He might have bumbled his pursuit for a reason.

Unfortunately, Mr. Nottingham would have to wait. Lila had other matters to attend to.

11

Lila woke to a staccato knock at the door. She groaned and curled deeper under her crimson blankets and sheets, covering her head with her pillow as Isabel entered. Fresh linens filled her arms, and the newly risen sun peeked through the drapes.

"Sorry, madam," Isabel squeaked as she took in the bed and the person still sleeping in it. She darted from the room and nearly slammed the door.

Lila peeked out from under the pillow, far too late to catch a peek of red hair.

Alex wouldn't have retreated. She would have come in, shaking Lila awake and telling her to get out of bed like a grown woman, asking her why she'd slept in.

She would have wanted gossip.

She would have demanded it.

Unfortunately, Alex would never speak to her again, not after last night. If someone forced the slave to do so, she'd become a bitter, angry version of Maria, only saying yes, no, sorry, and thank you. She'd keep her hands busy, eyes burning, throat choking on the words.

Lila patted the bed, searching for her palm. Eight o'clock had come far too early. She should have left for the security office half an hour before, but she'd been researching until half past three.

Barely awake, Lila crawled from between the sheets, checking her messages as she stumbled into the bathroom. Instead of looking at her new messages, she opened the ones she'd already memorized. The ones from Tristan. The first asked her what she wanted for dinner, the second asked when she'd be coming over, the third asked if she'd come over at all.

The last, sent at one in the morning, said that he'd missed her. It was a lot coming from him.

It was too much, coming from someone who wouldn't even have sex with her. He was playing some sort of game, and the game was growing old.

Lila hadn't responded to the messages, especially the last one. At first because she feared she might drive to Shippers Lane as soon as he asked, and then later because the last message had confounded her and twisted her stomach all at the same time. Part of her had grinned when she read it, and wanted to return the sentiment. The other part, the highborn part, had been annoyed with the entire thing. She needed to take another lover, or she'd get too attached. Perhaps she already was. After all, the first thing she'd done when she woke up was grab her palm to see if he'd sent her anything else.

That wasn't her, and it wasn't highborn behavior.

Not only that, but the oracle's words had unnerved her.

Sighing, she cycled through the rest of her messages. Nothing of value had come in from her spies, but Reaper's partner had not been silent. *Prolix, I waited all day for you to reply. Perhaps you aren't taking me seriously because I haven't asked for anything? I could, you know. I could ask, and you'd have to dance.*

Lila dropped her palm onto her bed and threw on a militia tank, workout pants, and stretchy gloves, wincing at the blotches of purple on her shin and arms. Then she trudged downstairs.

She left her palm behind.

Isabel bowed at the entryway. "Chief Randolph, I apologize for—"

"It happens, Isabel. It's nothing to worry about."

"Thank you, madam." She smoothed her hair behind her ear, blush fading. "The chairwoman has requested your presence at breakfast."

"Damn it to…" Lila rubbed her sleep-filled eyes, too tired to finish her rant. "Why? When? And who's suffering with me?"

"The prime minister is in residence this morning. I believe Pax will be joining you as well. Your matron wishes the family to breakfast together in one hour."

"Where's Jewel?"

"President Randolph had prior plans with Senator Dubois."

"Prior plans, my—" Lila bit off yet another curse, hoping rumors of Alex's confinement had not yet reached her mother's ears. "Fine. If I can't think of decent excuse to get out of it, I'll be back for breakfast. Has Chef bailed Alex out of Bullstow yet?"

Isabel shook her head. "She said she had to make breakfast first. She said it would serve Ms. Wilson right if she stayed in a holding cell all month."

"She can't stay in there. She's our responsibility. Ask Chef to call Mr. Norris and send him to Bullstow, will you? He usually handles these matters."

Isabel nodded, watching as Lila stalked from the great house.

Since she wouldn't have much time for a workout, Lila jogged to the security office as a warmup in the muggy heat, hating her mother's careless demand that she accommodate her whim and change her morning schedule. Chairwomen. All that power tended to go to their heads. Maybe her mother didn't notice when she did such things. Perhaps she did and didn't care.

Lila entered the security office, giving curt nods to her militia as she jogged downstairs to the basement, hoping she wouldn't fall on her ass so much. That hope dwindled as she fell on her first jump across a platform and many times after. Her arms stung as she slapped the mats to spread out her weight, the stitches pulling on her gloved fingers.

After fifteen minutes, she gave up and ran the flat track instead.

She'd been about as successful in her workout as she had in her research the night before. Since Natalie needed a bank account and, in theory, a net ID to trade Oskar, Lila had focused on finding them first. She'd prodded into Natalie's financial data but discovered that every bank account had been frozen, including her

Burgundy account at the Liberté. Not only were Natalie's accounts frozen, but she hadn't used her net ID since the day she disappeared.

It was odd that Natalie hadn't used the net, but she was in hiding.

Lila turned her attention to Natalie's fake ID after that, the one that had started her troubles, the one Bullstow knew about because it had been included in her list of official charges, released earlier in the week. Natalie hadn't used it either, probably fearing that Bullstow had been keeping tabs on it.

Which they most certainly were.

Once she'd gotten the obvious out of the way, Lila had fine-tuned some of her snoop programs to ferret out other IDs for Natalie, finally locating a badly faked ID that had once belonged to her. It was likely Natalie's first attempt at faking a net login. It wasn't hard to track the illegal activity attributed to it, but Lila hadn't found anything recent. The account hadn't been used in months, most likely abandoned when Natalie made a better fake that hadn't turned out much better after all.

With no other ideas, Lila had reviewed Natalie's bank account data from the previous case with her father. She opened the transaction history from the Liberté and pored over the data, as well as the data from three other bank accounts in Saxony. Natalie was staying somewhere, and Lila would use the data she had to find her hideout. She didn't waste time focusing on properties Natalie had been renting, though she dutifully jotted down the addresses. Natalie wouldn't stay anywhere with her name on the lease, even a fake one. Instead, Lila followed the people Natalie associated with, the people she gave money to, and the people who gave money to her.

Unsurprisingly, Natalie associated with a lot of unsavory people. Too many for Lila to get through in one night. She'd finally abandoned the task, promising herself that she'd pick it back up after a few hours of sleep.

Before she called it a night, she'd run Finn Nottingham's name through the militia database. Her stalker had been suspected in two kidnappings in the last five years, but Lila was far outside his preferred age group. Mr. Nottingham liked little girls. Chief Quinn, Shaw's counterpart in Bordeaux, had suspected him of kidnapping a five-year-old and a nine-year-old.

The five-year-old's aunt was an oracle.

Why would the New Bristol oracle let someone like Mr. Nottingham near her and her family? Didn't they do background checks on the rowers? Perhaps the woman believed her own hype, thinking she'd get a vision if Mr. Nottingham decided to act against her, her family, or her visitors. Or perhaps she wanted him nearby so that she'd get a bead on where the missing girls might be, assuming the kids might still be alive.

That was a dangerous game to play.

None of that explained why Mr. Nottingham had followed Lila. She wasn't just some random woman who had visited the oracle; she was a childless militia chief with the most secure compound in all of Saxony. She'd even been wearing her militia uniform, so there would have been no confusion as to her identity. Was he an idiot or did he have a purpose?

Or was he not working for the oracle at all? Perhaps he was connected to Reaper's partner instead.

Lila didn't have the time or the manpower to launch a surveillance operation against Mr. Nottingham and find the answers. Her spies were busy digging up what they could about Natalie and Oskar, and she'd have to send a few more to check out the properties that Natalie had rented under own name and her fake IDs, just to cross them off her list.

And Max? Not only was he busy digging into Reaper's partner, but he'd be offended if she asked him to check out the bumbling Mr. Nottingham, just as he'd been offended that members of the Randolph family had used his minions to buy wine.

Regardless, Mr. Nottingham needed to be checked out.

Lila jogged to the great house, the air even warmer and muggier. Before she hopped into the shower, she sent Tristan a message. He replied as she dried herself off. *Of course I'll help. When have I ever said no?* He'd added a smiley face at the end.

That smiley face made her feel like an ass.

Yet again, she realized that Tristan had always been there for her. He might have been a jerk or a grouch at times, but whenever she needed help, he'd always come through. Even now, when she'd ignored every message he'd sent the night before.

Why had she let a con woman she barely knew alter the way she thought about Tristan? The oracle had never even met him.

Lila had let the woman mess with her mind.

She vowed never to see the oracle again.

Lila scrolled to the next message on her palm. It was an update from Chef, saying that Mr. Norris had brought Alex back to the compound. They'd confined her to her room for the time being, not willing to give her the chance to assault Lila again.

Luckily, Reaper's partner had not sent another message. Stalling seemed to be the best strategy for now, at least until she knew more.

Lila sent a quick message to Sutton, asking her to take the commanders' meeting, as she'd be out all morning. Then she dried her hair, put a thick layer of concealer over her jaw, slipped on a formal militia uniform, and hurried downstairs.

Giggles erupted from the morning room. A deep answering rumble followed.

Good. They'd started without her.

"Lila girl," her father said when she peeked into the morning room. "We were waiting."

"Not so much that we didn't start eating, though," Pax said. "We know how you are."

"Oh, how am I?" Lila hugged her father and Pax, happy that her brother seemed distracted from his troubles this morning. Her father had worked a bit of magic on him, and he had almost finished an entire plate of French toast and bacon.

"Unable to find an excuse to miss breakfast."

Pax grinned proudly as the prime minister winked in agreement.

Lila sat across from her brother. "Sometimes I think you like my father more than you like your own."

"Mine's too serious. You have all the luck. Mine usually just rambles on and on about legislation."

"Senator Blanc is an important man with important thoughts," the chairwoman said.

"Boring thoughts."

"He merely respects you enough to converse about adult matters," Lemaire said. "He was better with you when you were a toddler. He knew what to talk about then."

Pax shrugged and chewed on his French toast while Isabel put Lila's plate down before her. True to her word, Chef had made a few pancakes and doused them in maple syrup.

The chairwoman clucked her tongue as soon as she saw it. "Was it too much to ask that you eat the same as the rest of the family?"

"I'm here, aren't I?"

"Yes, we should be so honored."

"Perhaps I'd join you for breakfast more often if you actually woke up early enough to have it. Usually you're still snoring when I leave for the security office."

"I do not snore."

"You snore."

The chairwoman sighed. "I have a condition, Lila."

"Didn't you just claim that you didn't snore?"

"Ladies." The prime minister cleared his throat.

"She started it." Lila shrugged, nibbling her bacon, glad her mother had been too busy with her father last night to learn about Alex. Regardless, it would be one of those breakfasts. Since she couldn't get out of it, she'd eat quickly and leave.

Not that she was all that hungry.

"Is that sausage on your plate, Father?"

The prime minister poked at a link and chewed heartily. "Of course it is. I can't miss Chef's best dish. I'll do a bit of extra running later."

"Exercise isn't the issue. Neither is your weight."

"Your mother tells me you haven't been sleeping here lately. Care to elaborate?"

"No. Nice dodge, though."

"Lila?"

"It's called work, Father. It's also called privacy and being a grown woman."

Her mother lifted her fork. "Prime heirs tell their matrons when—"

"Prime heirs don't bother after they've been cut. Besides, I'm not prime any longer. We could talk about your private life instead, if you want." Lila smiled innocently as her mother picked up her wine glass. "Hey, Pax, do you think we're getting a new heir in nine months?"

"Probably," Pax whispered a little too loudly, his eyes bouncing from mother to daughter, full of his old mirth. "They were both really loud for a really long time."

"Yes, I heard spanking."

Her mother's face reddened, and not from embarrassment. "Elizabeth Victoria Lemaire-Randolph, you—"

"You started it."

"I love it when you come to breakfast, Lila." Pax smirked, patting his belly as he leaned back in his chair to watch the show.

Her father finally surrendered and took the same approach.

It took ten minutes and many more volleys and spikes on both their sides before Lila could slip back upstairs and change. Luckily, the chairwoman had said nothing about Alex.

The clothes in Lila's closet swung like a pendulum as she pushed them aside to open her secret compartment. She donned bland, unmarked clothes and stuffed her servant's garb into her satchel, as well as everything she might need to break into Mr. Nottingham's home. She also grabbed her Colt and tucked her knife into her boot.

Her father caught her at the door, asking for an update, but she only shrugged and said that she hadn't found anything yet. It wasn't the time or the place to talk at length or in specifics.

What could she tell him, anyway? That she hadn't done any research at all? That she'd let the New Bristol oracle screw with her mind? That the woman had said awful things about the man she wanted to take as a lover, a man he also wanted her to stay away from?

Screw both of them.

Lila hadn't made it ten steps from the great house before someone else sought an audience. Her cousin Johnny Beaulieu put down a stack of flower-filled pots and hurried over.

"I'd almost believe you were waiting for me," Lila said when he approached, his muscles sleek, his skin tan and sweaty from the sun. As the man in charge of every landscaper and every blade of grass on the Randolph compounds, he spent a great deal of time in it.

"I was. Can I walk you to the garage?"

Lila nodded. They followed the gravel path, their feet crunching the rocks underfoot. The sticklike rose bushes he'd planted the week before waved in the warm breeze beside them, still budless and brown. "I have to ask you something, chief, but it's not really appropriate."

"When has that ever stopped either of us before?"

"You may regret encouraging me before we're done."

Lila knew his question already. "I don't know anything of Ms. Wilson's current feelings toward you. I'll probably never know anything about her again."

He nodded, seemingly unsurprised at the news.

"She broke things off with you, didn't she?"

He offered another frustrated nod. "Last week. She said that she wants nothing to do with the Randolphs anymore. She said the Randolphs had fucked her for long enough. Now whenever I see her on the compound, she hurries off in a different direction."

"You and me both." Lila opened the garage door. It screeched as it rose to the top. "You didn't do anything wrong, Johnny. I did."

"You had some part in her mother and brother being charged, didn't you?"

Lila didn't answer.

"So the rumors are true? You're thinking of sending her away, aren't you?"

"After the executions. It's cruel to keep her here, and it's hurting her. She deserves a fresh start somewhere new."

"Really? How's she supposed to get that now?" He pressed his palm into her hand. "It's all over the compound. Gossip channels, too."

Lila skimmed the headlines on his newsfeed. Alex appeared in several. So did Lila. "It didn't take the matrons long, didn't it?" Her mother had known about Alex at breakfast, and she hadn't even broached the topic.

That was not a good sign.

"Did she really do what they claim? Did she hit you?"

Lila nodded.

"The article made it seem like a brutal attack, like she'd gone crazy." His eyes trailed along her face, as though he didn't believe she'd been struck at all.

Lila had no desire to show him the bruises. "The High Council pushes drama, but it was assault. Alex forced my hand, whether she intended to or not."

"So you had to arrest her? I'm pretty sure the Randolph heir and chief of security can do whatever the fuck she wants."

"That's what you wanted to talk about, wasn't it?"

He stepped into her space, his mouth far too close to her nose. "Drop the charges. Drop them or so help me—"

"So help you, you'll do what?"

A patrol of six passed by the garage. The blackcoats cast a wary eye at Johnny. One even gripped the tranq gun at his side.

Lila waved them on. She didn't need anyone to witness Johnny's lapse in propriety.

The audience slinked away, as did Johnny's temper. "Drop the charges. If she's ever been your friend, drop them and let me go pick her up."

"So you can rush in and play the hero?"

"Fuck you."

"She's already back at the compound. There's nothing to be done."

"Drop the charges."

"No. Let me remind you of something. Alex chose to assault me in front of the High Council. Not just in front of one judge, or two judges, but all of them. She gave me few options. Do you know what sort of headlines would have been in the news if I hadn't? The Allied Lands takes a dim view of assault, but it takes an even dimmer view of a chief or a High Council judge who lets it go unpunished right under her nose."

"You arrested your own friend to preserve your reputation?"

"Not my reputation. Do you know what sort of problems would begin creeping up on the compound if I hadn't? Problems with the slaves, with the servants, even with criminals picked up by the militia? I did what I could. I spared her from arrest in front of the matrons. I let her salvage that much pride, but she chose this. Don't forget it."

"How very generous of you."

"I don't get to pick and choose who to arrest, you ass. If she had done it at the great house when we were alone, then I would have gotten that choice, just like the last time her temper got the better of her. I didn't have a choice there."

"Keep telling yourself that. Now that we've gotten the Wilson fortune, Alex is useless. The chairwoman will sell her to the LeBeaus at auction, and they'll put her in the mines."

"I'm not going to let that happen. Alex is my best friend, regardless of how she feels about me right now, regardless of what you believe. So long as I'm an heir, she'll stay on a Randolph compound where I can ensure that she's safe and that no one's making a mockery of her."

"Yes, because you've done so well lately." His nostrils flared. Before Lila could say anything else, he bowed slightly and dashed down the gravel path.

Lila watched him go. She couldn't chase after him. Even if she had the time, she didn't have the right words.

Instead, she pulled off a set of keys from the pegs near the garage door and wandered among the vehicles inside. She needed stealth and anonymity. She needed the Cruz sedan. After removing the bugs and disabling the GPS, she slipped on her sunglasses and drove from the garage.

When she stopped at the south gate, her eyes traveled toward Aunt Georgina's bridal block. A familiar Barracuda had stopped near a fire hydrant. Its scarred rider swiped at his palm as though he wasn't paying attention.

Lila rolled down her window and waited for Sergeant Hill to approach. "Sergeant, have you seen—"

"The silver Barracuda?"

"Yes."

Hill wiped the sweat from under his sentry cap. "We've been watching him for two hours. We just need to confirm his target so we can build a stalking case. Is he here for you?

"Yes."

"You leading him somewhere?"

"Nope."

"Do you want to?" He grinned. "It would help our case if he followed you a bit."

"Too busy today, sergeant. I'd be much obliged if your men intercepted him instead. Stash him in a holding cell for loitering until you hear from me." Though her militia could only hold Mr. Nottingham for a few hours before writing him a ticket and kicking him loose, it would be plenty of time to conduct an illegal search of his apartment, especially if she had help.

Hill took off his hat and scratched his ear. Seconds later, three motorcycles came at Mr. Nottingham from several different directions, pinning the Barracuda in before Mr. Nottingham could start the engine and get away. Two blackcoats emerged from the florists and tugged him off his bike, cuffing him without incident.

Hill pulled down the hem of his officer's jacket, standing up straight and tall as the blackcoats walked Mr. Nottingham toward the security office. "That's how we do things at the south gate."

"Damn straight. Great job as always, Sergeant Hill. Take your people to Juniper at close of shift. My treat. I'll tell the hostess to expect you."

Hill licked his lips. "Juniper? Are you kidding me?"

"I never kid about steak." Lila pulled away and sent a quick message to the manager of Juniper's Steakhouse, warning her to plan ahead for a dozen hungry and boisterous militia.

Ten minutes later, Lila parallel-parked in front of a lowborn convenience store and walked north for one block. Tristan opened his truck door with a squeak as she turned the corner, smiling warmly as he jogged to meet them. Dixon stayed inside, his gaze not meeting hers. Instead, he watched the people walking on the street, their thin, sweaty t-shirts waving in the warm breeze, their boots crumpling scraps of paper and cigarette butts underfoot.

"Fry's on the roof, Sam's in the back, and Dice is watching the front in case this guy decides to bolt," Tristan said, jutting his chin down the block.

Lila had no desire to wind a scarf around half her face in the heat, merely to hide from Tristan's people. "Pull them off. Our target is in a holding cell. My people picked him up for loitering just as I pulled out of the compound."

"A quick search, then?"

"Very. I have bigger fish, Tristan."

"So he's a little fish?"

"The smallest. A minnow. He's just some guy who followed me after the council meeting last night. I want to know why." When Dixon slipped from the truck, the group headed toward Mr. Nottingham's apartment building.

"What do you know?"

"Not much. I only had time to run his plates. I was busy with other things last night."

"Other things?"

"I'm digging into Natalie Holguín's disappearance. I suspect it might be connected to Oskar."

"So you were researching?"

"Yes. I didn't find out much, though. I found a few of her rental properties, but I doubt she'll use them due to the paper trail. I just need to cross them off my list."

"We could do it today. I could go with you."

"I have work, Tristan. Besides, I have a few people on it already."

"You could have done your research at the shop."

"I can't come over every night. People are already asking questions."

"So? Let them ask."

"When you get ambushed by your parents at breakfast about your sex life, then come talk to me about letting people ask questions."

The group entered the apartment building as soon as someone emerged from the locked door. The building was average and well maintained, with enough well-off workborns inside for light bulbs to survive night after night.

"According to official records, Finn Nottingham is single and lives alone," she whispered as they climbed upstairs. "The database isn't always current, though. We have to be careful."

Tristan and Dixon loitered in the stairwell while Lila strode to Mr. Nottingham's door. She knocked absently and slipped a lock-picking tool from the hem of her shirt with her other hand.

Lila wasn't prepared for the door to open. A blond man answered, a giant whose head and wide shoulders grazed the doorframe. He wore a thin t-shirt and a pair of jeans, almost like Max in attire, but certainly not body.

He looked at her expectantly and wiped his hands on a dishtowel. "Can I help you?"

Inside, a little girl screamed.

12

Lila dodged the man and rushed inside, searching for the child. She launched herself through a brightly lit kitchen, pots and pans still on the burners, and a dining room half set for breakfast. She found the girl in the den, her screams turning into laughter as an older girl chased her. Cartoons played on the screen in the front of the room.

"Freeze," the man called out behind Lila.

The two girls stopped instantly, leaking a few giggles unable to be bitten back. The smaller child might have been around five years old, stout and dark-haired and dressed in blackcoat costume. A plastic Colt flopped in a cloth holster around her middle. The older blonde wore a simple dress, with an oversized white robe atop it, the ends swirling around her legs. Neither looked like the girls Mr. Nottingham had been accused of kidnapping.

Lila held her breath, unsure what to do, and dropped her drawn Colt to her thigh.

The man walked to the middle of the den and crouched before the girls. "What did I say about running in the apartment? Especially this morning?"

The two girls looked at one another then scrambled to the couch, heavy-footed, with tiny toes slapping against the hardwood floor. They looked at him innocently, their feet disappearing underneath their laps.

The man sighed wearily and rubbed his eyes. "Your friends can come inside, madam."

"My friends?"

"The ones outside," he said, his words thick with a La Verde accent. "I'm going to stand up now, if it's okay with you. My knees aren't what they used to be. I'd appreciate it if you put that gun away. The girls are too young for it, and I have a heart condition."

He stood up slowly and extended his hand. "I'm Jake."

Lila put her Colt back in her holster. The apartment door closed with a little snick, and Tristan and Dixon watched from the kitchen, arms crossed over their chests.

Lila shook Jake's hand.

"I'm sorry about all the noise. We're moving into a house next month."

"I'm not a neighbor."

"I know. I've just gotten so used to apologizing that I guess it's become a habit. The whole building will throw a party as soon as we're gone. I never knew little girls could be so loud."

"Can I go to the party?" the younger girl asked.

"It's going to be a boring grownup party, Valerie," Jake replied, squatting down in front of them, blocking their cartoons. "You both have to be quiet here, remember?"

The girls nodded.

"If you aren't quiet, I'm going to turn off the cartoons for half an hour."

"Noooo," Valerie said.

"Then no more stampeding around the house with those tiny, tiny feet." Jake tickled her soles.

Valerie's protests turned into giggles.

"Vivian?"

The older girl nodded.

"Good. It's just for another week. I know it's hard, but we have to try, okay?"

Solemn nods answered him.

Jake led Lila back into the kitchen. She'd rarely been in a work-born dwelling, and the warmness and wornness of the spaces always surprised her. The counter had been scratched and dented as if it had been the casualty of many family dinners. Children's drawings had been framed and tacked to the walls, rather than art. Instead of a footman, someone had hung a little coat rack, all pegs full. The girls' brightly colored schoolbooks had been piled underneath.

Jake stood in front of the stove himself, rather than a workborn.

It all seemed so very odd and messy.

"I'm making extra for you and your friends."

Tristan cocked his head. "You're cooking us breakfast?"

"I figured it would confuse you, and I knew your confusion would amuse me." Jake stirred a mash of eggs and vegetables in a skillet. The spatula scraped against the pot.

"Can I have ice cream?" came a tiny voice behind them.

Jake didn't even turn around. "What did I say yesterday?"

"That I won't get tall if I eat ice cream. I don't want to be tall. I want ice cream."

Vivian strolled in behind Valerie and gave a long eye roll. "You can't eat ice cream for breakfast. You have to eat normal things, like eggs and waffles and stuff." Both girls had the same accent as Jake, the same rolling Rs and short vowels.

"My mother let me—"

"No, she didn't—"

"Did too—"

Jake winced at their raised voices. "Cartoons. Living room. Now. Unless you want me to turn them off? I need to talk with our new friends. Remember?"

Vivian's eyes flashed, and she looked the group up and down, her senses on alert. Lila knew she'd been prepped for their arrival.

Lila didn't like it one bit.

Valerie demanded a hug from Jake before she'd go, then left to watch cartoons once more, ice cream tantrum averted.

As soon as the girls moved out of the room, Jake held his hands behind his back as though preparing to be arrested. "You're still suspicious. I'll let you cuff me if you'd feel safer. Just don't let the girls see—"

Lila pulled out a DNA pen from her pocket and jabbed him in the neck. He cursed and whipped around. The needle jerked. A little trickle of blood ran down his neck.

"If you hadn't moved, you wouldn't have bled."

Jake rubbed his wound, frowning. "It's probably better you surprised me. I loathe needles. What's it for?"

Lila pulled up his file on her palm, watching as the pen broke down his DNA information bit by bit and transmitted it wirelessly. In less than one minute, it had already reported her subject as male. "Sit down. This will take a few moments."

"You could have just asked me for my full name. I would have told you." He kept hold of his neck and turned back to his skillets and pots. "If you don't mind, I'd like to finish cooking breakfast. I'd protest you trying to break into my home, but I know that would get me nowhere. Your family's influence goes far, Chief Randolph."

"You know my face?"

"I knew who you were before you even knocked."

Lila's gaze cut to Tristan, but he seemed equally confused by Jake's words. "You're going to bring those girls in here so I can test them, too."

"Do you have to?" Jake moved to the refrigerator. He took out some apple slices and dropped them into a pot, then sprinkled in a bit of cinnamon before closing the lid. "The girls have been through a lot recently. They're my sister's kids. She—"

"You expect me to believe those girls are related?"

"Not everyone looks it."

"No, they don't. How do you know Finn Nottingham?"

Jake raised a brow, concern in his eyes. "You know Finn?"

"How do you know him?" Lila watched as more information popped up on her palm. Probable hair and skin color, race, and body type. His name and picture would pop up as soon as the device matched his blood against the DNA records.

"Finn is my husband."

"I didn't see that in the database. Do you have the license?"

Jake pointed over his shoulder to the dining room wall. A marriage license had been framed and hung beside several pictures of them in tuxes on their wedding day, with large grins and even larger cravats. "Finn insisted we hang it. I think it throws off the entire room. I suppose your all-important database hasn't been updated since last January."

"I suppose it hasn't been. It's bad with marriages. It's great with arrest reports, though. You do know about the suspicions surrounding him?"

"The kidnapping thing? I'm aware of the reports, but it's all completely unfounded, just like I told Chief Quinn at the time. Finn would never hurt anyone, much less a child. You should see how great he is with my nieces."

"I'm not convinced they are your nieces." Lila left the DNA pen to do its work and opened up her snoop programs. Pulling his full name from the marriage license, she dug for Jake's biographical data. He had one sister, deceased. When Lila dug into the woman's records, she found that Jake's sister had not given birth.

Flipping back to the DNA results, she let out a grunt, surprised that Jake hadn't lied about his name. "Care to come up with a better story, Jake?"

He took the eggs off the stove. "You're fast with that thing."

"Stop fussing about with breakfast and sit."

Tristan turned off the burners and ushered Jake to the table. He and Dixon loomed behind him.

"Breakfast will get cold. Oatmeal has a short half-life."

Lila inserted a fresh needle into her DNA pen, then started toward the den. The two little girls stared at the screen like owls, watching a pair of animated figures chase one another across the desert.

"Don't," Jake said softly after she set a foot into the den. "Please."

Lila stopped and turned around, her hands on her hips.

"Please, they really have been through a lot. I'll tell you whatever you want to know—just let them be, will you? All anyone wants is for them to be safe."

Lila put down the pen and sat next to him at the table. "Safe from what?"

"From their destiny."

"Wow. Could you be any more melodramatic?"

"I could, actually," he said, playing with the silverware in front of him.

"Okay. I'll bite. What destiny?"

"Their destinies as determined by man. Is that better?"

"Not really. You said you knew who I was before I knocked. How?"

"The oracle called me thirty minutes ago."

Tristan and Dixon exchanged a confused glance.

"She said Chief Randolph would be along this morning with a couple of friends. She said you'd be suspicious of us at first, but I was to tell you what I could, since you had enough information to dig it all up anyway. I don't trust you, though, and I don't feel comfortable telling you a thing."

"But you'll talk?"

"Only because the oracle wills it. You're a highborn. You don't give a damn about the rest of us unless it affects your family's bottom line. You only serve yourself, your family, and your kind. If the news I saw this morning is true, then you just had your best friend arrested last night. So what does that mean for me and mine?"

Tristan studied her, questioning her with every blink.

"I have your husband in a holding cell right now," she said. "I can make his stay far more unpleasant with one call. Tell me what that means for you and yours."

"That really doesn't inspire me to talk."

"It should. As the oracle said, I'll just figure it all out anyway. You don't want me pissed off when I do."

Jake pursed his lips. "Fine. The little one is called Valerie. The older girl is Vivian. Finn and I changed their names, of course. It's why I'm tutoring them at home instead of enrolling them in school. They're struggling to remember their new names and identities. They're struggling with lying about who they are. It's all very hard for them. They don't understand yet."

"I don't either."

"According to the official records, Vivian was pronounced dead in a La Verde hospital several months ago. A car accident, from the original report. Valerie died from seizures."

"You took them."

"No, they were given to us. They have the sickness." Jake fiddled with the silverware in front of him once more.

"Seizures? The girls are future oracles?"

"Their mothers didn't want that future forced upon them. They wanted the girls to have a proper childhood, to have a choice when they came of age."

"If they have the seizures, they need to see a—"

"They have a doctor. One who is sympathetic to the New Bristol oracle. He's treating them, though you'll never see a record of it. Luckily, he's been able to control the girls' seizures with medication. They couldn't have been smuggled out otherwise."

"Smuggled?" Lila pinched the bridge of her nose. "So the oracles are responsible for the kidnappings and deaths of their own children?"

"That's alleged kidnappings and alleged deaths."

"Why did the women choose you and your husband to take care of the girls?"

"Finn and I wanted children. We both have fertility issues."

"You can't adopt?"

"Of course we can adopt. Chief Quinn had to drop those stupid charges on lack of evidence, but the adoption agency said we'd still be okay for a placement. We decided to move for a change of scenery and to get away from Quinn, though. About a month after we moved, we read through the adoption papers again, just to make sure we were on the same page about what we could deal with and what we couldn't. We were both fine with taking in a few older strays," he said, the corners of his mouth quirking. "The

New Bristol oracle called us the next day. She said that she had a vision of us, asked us to come see her."

He put down the silverware. "You see, they were already laying the groundwork to smuggle Valerie and Vivian out of La Verde. In her vision, the oracle saw us taking care of them. The girls were from La Verde. I had the right accent to make the ruse work. My sister died recently, giving us a plausible backstory."

"So they just handed the girls to you even though they barely knew you?"

"Finn wasn't unknown to the oracles or the ruse. He had helped them in Bordeaux, which is why he's a kidnapping suspect in the first place. He was the girl's driver, just some stranger driving an unmarked car, a show for the neighbors. I guess the neighbors got too good of a look this time, rather than a glimpse. He nearly got caught before he got the girl to the safe house. She's happy now, though, from what the oracle tells me."

"I'll bet."

"Quinn tried to tie Finn to another disappearance a few months later. That's why we decided to leave. Chief Quinn would have arrested him for something eventually."

"You don't expect me to believe this, do you?" Lila asked. "If what you're saying is true, then one of these girls somewhere would have been found out by now. All it would take is one prick from a DNA stick to reveal who they really are."

Jake shook his head. "The oracles took care of the DNA database, or I should say, one of their faithful has been doing it. If you took a sample of the girls' blood right now, they'd come up as Valerie and Vivian Vince, just as I claimed. I'll need to remind the oracle to fix my sister's data, though. That could be a problem in the future."

"Give me their mothers' names."

Jake handed over his palm reluctantly, and Lila retreated into the girls' bedroom for privacy, leaving Tristan and Dixon to watch the suspect. Or to help him finish breakfast, from the looks of things. They both believed him already, not a suspicious bone in their bodies.

Sloppy.

Lila moved past the pale pink beds, cringing at the green pastel walls, stenciled with overly happy bears and tigers. She had to admit, the men had dedicated a great deal of time and energy to build the girls a paradise. A full-length mirror stood in the corner surrounded by movie star lights. Costumes and boas spilled out of a trunk beside it. She counted at least a dozen stuffed animals piled on each girl's bed. A dollhouse stood in the corner, made far too well to be from a factory. Lila peeked in, amazed at the dolls and tiny furniture inside.

Had one of their adopted fathers built it himself?

Lila sat down on one of the beds and scrolled through Jake's palm, finding an entry marked *taxi*. A harried woman answered the palm on the first ring. She was an older copy of the little blackcoat in the living room.

"Where's Jake?" she asked in alarm.

"I thought you were an oracle. You should have seen this coming."

"My sister's the oracle, not me, thank the gods. Why are you calling?"

"You know why."

The woman licked her lips. "What are you going to do?"

"I don't know yet. I wanted to make sure that your daughter isn't really missing, that she was only given away."

"She's not missing. Please, I'm begging you. My husband and I have given up a great deal to make sure she has a future."

"A future you chose for her?"

"A future she'll choose for herself when she's old enough. I saw what my sister went through, what she still goes through. I'll not put my daughter through it unless she wants it. The predictions will still come even if she decides to take a different path. The meds might stop the seizures, but they don't stop the visions. They just make them gentler. She's already called upon the New Bristol oracle a dozen times. She understands her duty."

Lila raised a brow. That explained the vision paradox. If the missing girls relayed their visions to the oracles and the oracles claimed them, it stood to reason their counts would increase.

Lila flicked her thumb, ready to disconnect when the woman faltered. "Please, you've seen her? Does she look well? Is she—"

"They won't let you see her?"

"We all thought it would be for the best if we don't, at least not until she's a little older, not until she learns her name better, not until she's—"

"Old enough to lie well?"

"Don't you dare judge me. You have no idea what it's like. I'd have taken her away myself, but my face is too well known to those who follow the oracles."

"And her father?"

"His mother is a matron. He couldn't take her either. This was the only way."

Lila hung up on the woman a few moments later, too tired to talk further.

Vivian's mother was worse, for she hardly stopped crying. Same story, different women. She took her child to her cousin, shortly after Vivian had fallen ill with her first seizure. The oracle had given Vivian's mother a choice, and the woman had made it.

Lila didn't go back to the kitchen right away. She dug through clothes and toys and schoolbooks, not sure what she was looking for until she opened Vivian's dresser. Underneath a pile of cartoon-themed pajamas, she found a little notebook with a lock.

Vivian kept a diary.

Lila picked the lock and read through the girl's scribbles. Vivian had been anxious before she met the men, worried they might not be nice. She'd been happy when she finally met them, relieved that Jake could cook better than her mother, relieved that Valerie wasn't such an annoying little sister after all. She'd written whole pages about how much she missed her mother and how she didn't understand why she had to leave.

Her mother had kept her older brother. Why not keep her?

Had she been sent away because she had the same sickness as the oracles?

Did it make her bad? Didn't her mother want her anymore?

In the last few pages, she'd begun to muse on what she should call the men. Should she call Finn her uncle? She wasn't sure if it was a slight against her real uncles or if either of them even wanted it.

Lila closed the lock with a sharp little *click* and slipped it back into the girl's drawer.

Sneaking back into the den, she stood behind the two girls and watched their cartoon for a few minutes. "Do you like it here with your uncle?"

Valerie nodded shyly, then looked to her new big sister for help. Since she didn't know what she could say, she didn't say anything.

"It's okay," Vivian said. "I mean, Valerie doesn't like eating vegetables, and Finn and my uncle don't let her leave the table until she finishes them. They don't let her have ice cream all the time or candy every five seconds, but she still likes them. We both do. They're nice. They read to us. They let us make messes. Mother never let us do that. They said we can run and scream and shout until we make ourselves sick once we move into the new house, we just have to be quiet until then. That's the only bad part."

"Uncle Jake and Finn are nice." Valerie nodded.

"You call Finn by his first name?" When Vivian shrugged, Lila saw an opening. "I'd probably just start calling them both uncle. You know, if he was as nice as you claim."

"But Finn's not our uncle."

Lila shrugged. "Uncle and dad and sister just mean family. Sometimes you have to make your family where you can."

Vivian pulled at her lip, lost in thought. She wasn't old enough to realize that Lila had been fishing through her diary, or perhaps she was just too innocent to believe that someone could read it if there was a lock.

"Be nice to your uncles," Lila said, leaving them to their cartoons. She entered the dining room in time for Tristan to shovel a last bite of eggs into his mouth. Dixon spooned his bowl of oatmeal, squinting at the cartoons in the other room.

"Are we good?" Tristan asked around his food.

"His story checks out. The kids are happy enough here."

Jake turned his gaze on the two girls in the den. "They told you that?"

"They didn't have to. I read Vivian's diary."

Jake's mouth gaped. "That's an invasion of privacy. You shouldn't—"

"Take it down a notch, Jake. I had to make sure they were okay. I hope you'd do the same thing in my position."

"Are you going to arrest us? Are you going to take the girls away?"

"Why should I? You've become caretaker to two girls at the request of their parents. This isn't a matter for the militia or anyone else, as far as I'm concerned." She returned his palm and stalked toward the door. "I'll have my people release your husband. Tell him to stop following me, or I'll charge him."

"Wait," Jake called out, just as she reached the door. "The oracle wishes to see you as soon as possible."

"Well, the oracle can see me in a vision giving her the finger."

"You don't believe in the oracles?"

"No."

"She had a vision of you coming here. How else would I have known you were coming?"

"She didn't have a vision, Jake. She knew because your husband called her from a Randolph holding cell. He burned his one call on the oracle."

"How'd she know the others would come?"

"Because it would have been stupid of me to come alone."

"You're wrong." He frowned.

"When I was teenager, my best friend made me go see the oracle."

"You saw her mother?"

Lila nodded. "She claimed she had a vision about me, too. I was walking down the staircase in our family's great house. My hair was still dark, I had a toddler in my arms, and I wore a sad expression. I also wore the whitecoat. The woman is a fraud, Jake, just like her mother. They're all frauds."

"Don't be so sure," he called out while Tristan and Dixon followed her from the apartment.

13

"Thanks for helping out," Lila said as they reconvened in front of the lowborn convenience store a block from Jake's apartment. A trickle of people entered and left the store, small bags swinging, feet skipping.

Dixon held his hands out for the truck keys.

Tristan wordlessly tossed them to his brother.

"It was no problem really, but I want to know what's going on with you and the oracles."

A door slammed. An engine started. Tires squealed.

Tristan's truck pulled out into the street without him.

He chased Dixon for half a block before giving up. People on the sidewalk stared and giggled. One bored workborn held his beer aloft as a toast. "May you have better luck catching a cab." He snickered, cracking the tab with a hiss.

Lila grabbed Tristan's arm and tugged him down the street. "We'll take mine."

"Did you see that? He just took off without me!"

"Dixon interacted more with his oatmeal than with us. You should talk to him. An actual conversation, not just painting his room a rainbow of tacky colors and hoping the weirdness goes away."

"It's not that tacky."

"Yes, it is," Lila insisted, unlocking her sedan.

"How can any of it go away? It's never going away."

"Well, it's certainly won't get better if you let it fester." Lila could think of another conversation Tristan should have. The one where he confessed why he kept bringing her into his bed if he had no intention of touching her.

"Let's talk of something else." Tristan slipped inside the car and strapped on his seatbelt with a sharp little click. "The oracle, perhaps? How come you didn't tell me you were mixed up with her?"

Lila pulled out her palm and began to check for bugs. "Because it doesn't concern you? Because I don't need to run every job I have past you? Because—"

"Don't be snippy."

"I'm not being snippy."

"Your father asked you to investigate them, didn't he?"

Lila plopped in the driver's seat and started the sedan's engine. "Yes, Tristan. He did. I often take jobs for my father. You know that."

"You're exhausted, and you just took a job that almost killed you less than a week ago. You can't even ride your Firefly right now. Doesn't he care?"

"Should I forget about finding Oskar because I can't ride my damn motorcycle?" Lila replied, pulling out of the parking spot. "If I hadn't spent the last week planning how to break Oskar out of LeBeau's, then I would have had plenty of sleep."

"That's different. The oracles can wait. Oskar could die if we don't save him." He grazed her cheek as she drove. "Did you get any sleep at all last night, Lila?"

Her toes curled in her boots when he said her name, his mouth lingering on the vowels like one might tongue a sweet. He had just begun using it the week before, and even still, said it rarely. The man obviously had no idea of the effect it had on her.

She batted away his hand, unsure what might happen if she let him carry on. "I had a few hours. Besides, very little of what I researched last night had to do with the oracles, so don't blame my father just because I'm a little tired."

"You're not a little tired, and you're not fine. You already have dark circles under your eyes, and it's only going to get worse until we find Oskar. If your father saw you now, even he would notice, and—"

"He saw me this morning."

"Didn't he care?"

Lila nearly wanted to laugh at how uptight he'd become over a few hours of lost sleep. Such a fuss when he didn't care that he'd turned her away from his bed for a week.

The workborn really were different.

"I'm a grown adult, Tristan," she said, stopping at a red light. "Grown adults often have to work when they're tired."

"Good parents would give you time to recover. Good bosses, too. There's too much going on lately. He's going to lose you as a resource if he's not careful."

"What do you propose? If he put someone else on this case, they would have arrested Jake and returned the girls to their parents. Part of why he puts me on these cases is because he trusts my judgment."

"Your judgment or your moral flexibility?"

"Both."

"I propose a vacation when this is all over. We'll go somewhere nice, get away from everything for a few weeks."

"A few weeks?"

"You drive a hard bargain. A month, then."

"This isn't a negotiation."

"Isn't everything a negotiation with your kind?"

Lila studied Tristan, her gaze drawn to his long eyelashes. She couldn't imagine a vacation with Tristan being fun. Not now, anyway. He'd become a Winter Solstice gift she wasn't allowed to open, for the winter holiday never came.

She nearly longed for the days she couldn't stand him.

"Whatever you're thinking, stop." He frowned, turning up the air conditioning. "What's going on with the oracles?"

Lila quickly told him all that she knew. "There's really nothing to investigate, and I have no desire to trek all the way out to the temple."

"But she summoned you for help. She just wasn't sure if she could trust you."

"So?"

"The oracles don't summon outsiders for help. Doesn't that mean anything to you?"

"It means she wants me to back off from my father's investigation."

Tristan shook his head as the light turned green. "I don't believe that. We should go and see what she has to say."

"What about Oskar?"

Lila saw the struggle cross his face. "It's only a fifteen-minute drive. We're halfway there already."

Lila eyed the clock, remembering Oskar's face onstage.

"I don't like this."

"I don't either." He fiddled with the air conditioning again. "You never told me about that before."

"Never told you what?"

"What the oracle's mother said when you were a kid, about you holding a child and wearing the whitecoat."

"I'd mostly forgotten, Tristan. The oracles likely tell every prime the same thing. Yes, you'll be prime. Yes, you'll have heirs. They're con artists and charlatans. They tell people what they think they want to hear."

"What did she tell Alex?"

"I don't know. She didn't say. Do you actually believe in the oracles?"

"I never thought about it much. Slaves don't get much of a chance to visit them, much less the children of slaves. I would have had to get permission from my mother and my matron, then bribe someone to drive me to the temple and bring me back. Even then the oracle might not have seen me. How many slaves do you think want to waste a day off waiting for something that might never happen?"

"So slaves don't believe?"

"Oh, most do, they just don't often visit the temple. Can't say that I blame them."

"What about Dixon?"

"Funny you should mention that. I saw him with a book a few days ago. Apparently, he asked Samantha to fetch it for him.

It was a book about the oracles and the gods. A few more have turned up since."

"Is that odd?"

"He's never shown an interest before. I think what happened last weekend shook him up."

"What about your parents? Does your mother believe?" Lila turned down another street. They passed shop after shop, lowborns and servants carrying packages and sweating in the heat.

"Yes. Who knows what my father thinks, though."

"What do you mean? How can you not know if your father believes in the oracles?"

Tristan just shrugged. "When he came around, he only had eyes for my mother."

"So he ignored you?"

"Not exactly, but it wasn't like he could take me out. He'd married into the Holguíns. If he had acknowledged me publicly, his marriage would have been ruined and his matron never would have accepted him back. You know how your kind are, always believing the fallen have come back as spies, especially from a family like the Holguíns."

"It depends on how long they've been gone and the circumstances they married under."

"He left the Vargas family under less-than-ideal circumstances. He's little more than a pet to Chairwoman Holguín's youngest sister, thrown in to seal the deal on wine grapes. She's in love with him, though. He could have said no, but that Sangre you enjoy has to come from somewhere."

"Is he in love with her?"

Tristan shook his head. "My mother always kept his identity a secret in the BIRD, but when she was arrested and he arranged for our placement in Beaulac... Well, you can bet everyone on the Holguín compound knew exactly who my father was. The fact that I look like him never helped. Whenever he slipped away to visit, which wasn't often, he'd spend twenty minutes or so catching up with me, shove some new toy in my lap, then spend the rest of his night with my mother. By the time I was ten, I started disappearing before the visits."

"Your mother let you?"

"How could she stop me after I was already gone? I knew when he was coming by. She never knew how, but it was obvious. The smiles, the long shower, the perfume, the extra care with her hair and a bit of makeup. Sometimes I think she was relieved to find me gone. It meant they could be together longer, since he didn't have to waste his time with me."

"When was the last time you saw him?"

"I was fourteen. I saw him walking toward me on the compound. I was usually good about avoiding him, but I was thinking of other things. I didn't notice him until it was too late, but it was the same for him. I decided to walk right on by. Usually whenever I tried that, he'd stop me, at least for a few minutes, and chat. This time he didn't. No one else was even around."

"He gave up?"

Tristan rubbed his chin and didn't answer. He merely looked out his window as the lowborn shops turned into manufacturing plants.

"What did you do next?"

"Stole my first bottle of whiskey to celebrate."

"To celebrate or to mourn?"

Tristan didn't answer. "I didn't mean to tell you all that."

"Why not?"

"It's whiny."

"Life often is."

"What about you? Tell me something."

Lila pulled up to another light. She racked her brain for something to tell him, but her experiences with her own father weren't so horrible. What could she say about her mother without sounding like a spoiled heir? Boohoo, my mother constantly demanded that I run a multibillion-credit empire, but I just wanted to fiddle-fart around as a blackcoat for the rest of my life? Poor me, I was so oppressed?

"You're not going to share anything, are you?"

"I have nothing to match it."

"You don't have to match it, Lila. This isn't a competition. Just tell me something, anything. What's the most annoying thing you had to deal with growing up?"

"You already know." Lila shrugged as she merged onto the interstate, dodging the scattered traffic. "I didn't want to be prime. I wanted to be the militia chief for the entire Randolph family, so I fought for it."

"That's what I don't get about you. Why? Why join the militia at all?"

"Because I have no interest in my family's business dealings. I just want everyone to be safe and protected."

"You took over the hospital."

"That was for different reasons entirely. For starters, it was my mother's idea of a test."

"What about the other reasons?"

Lila didn't want to answer. She didn't want to remember Holly. "Let it go."

"I didn't want to tell you about my father. I thought we were friends."

Friends?

Lila cut her eyes to Tristan, more and more annoyed with herself. Perhaps there wasn't anything between them after all, not anymore, not after what had happened in the tunnels with Reaper. He'd cleared it all up with that one little word.

Friends.

Why on earth did he insist on sharing a bed with her, then? Sending her messages about how he missed her? Making jokes about going on vacation together?

The workborn were very, very different indeed.

But she'd lost Alex, and now Dixon wouldn't speak with her either. Maybe she needed another friend.

"Chef Ana has cooked for our family since before I was born," Lila began as the bluebonnets, cedar trees, broken-down gas stations, and workborn diners slipped past the car. "Her oldest daughter was named Holly. We were the same age, and as close as my mother would allow before propriety took over. If I had kept my damn mouth shut, we might have been closer."

"What does that mean?"

"I asked my mother once if Holly could be my sister instead of Jewel."

"How old were you?"

"Five or six. My mother didn't take it well. I had to sneak around more to play with Holly after that, but Chef didn't try very hard to keep us apart."

"Where's Holly now?"

"Dead. She got sick when we were eleven, and she never got better. Watching Holly spend her last few years dying was hard enough, but I saw what it did to Chef. It tore her apart a little more each day. And every day she grew a little more desperate. My mother saw it too. She sent Holly to the best doctors, even got her into an experimental trial in Our Lady of the Light."

"That was Randolph General before you took over?"

"Yes. But in the end, Holly still died."

"Most matrons wouldn't have bothered for a servant's child," Tristan said.

"I never said my mother was evil, Tristan. We just don't get along. We have different concerns about the family and different priorities, and she wants me to be someone I'm not."

"So you took over the hospital to save little girls like Holly?"

Lila shook her head. "No. When I watched my friend die, I learned that you can't save everyone. People just die sometimes, no matter what you do. And every morning, the sun still rises even when it shouldn't, and it laughs at whatever you've done to stop it."

"That might be the most depressing thing I've ever heard you say."

"Well, I became quite the angst-ridden teenager after she died."

"Anyone would be after losing their best friend. Why did you take over the hospital if it wasn't to save other kids?"

"I saw what my mother's persistence had done for Chef. It wasn't much of a consolation, but it gave her peace of mind in the end. Me too. And I think it helped Holly too, as horrible as that sounds. She couldn't keep reaching for treatments that weren't there because she knew that doctors didn't have the answers. Holly was able to go home for a while and be a stupid, goofy kid at the end, at least when she wasn't sleeping. It seemed like that's all she did, tubes in her nose, those stupid machines wheezing in the background." Lila frowned, remembering how she'd snuck into her friend's room some nights, just to snuggle next to her, terrified Holly might die alone.

She hadn't, as it turned out. Lila had been with her when she stopped breathing. She jumped up by her side, completely powerless and frantic to help her friend. Pax had run in after Lila began screaming. Only a toddler, he'd cried because he did not understand and cried more because he didn't know what to do or how to help. He claimed he didn't remember it, but Lila had to wonder.

Why on earth had the boy become so obsessed with being a doctor if not for that? She'd done that to him, and she didn't know if it was a good thing.

Chef had run into the room a moment later and shooed them out. She had only left the room for a second, just for a cup of coffee.

Perhaps Holly had known somehow, even though she'd been asleep for days. Perhaps she hadn't wanted her mother to see her last gasping breaths.

And she'd gasped, terrifyingly so.

"I remember Chef telling me that if you've tried everything, even if you fail, you're not left torturing yourself with what-ifs. It stuck with me. I wanted a way for everyone to feel like that. Tragedy sucks enough without spending the rest of your days bitter and angry because you might have saved someone you cared about, if only you'd had more money, if only you'd had a better doctor, if only, if only, if only…"

"So your mother gave you Our Lady of Light."

"It was my fourteenth birthday present. She even told me it was a test. To show her, the family, and myself what I could do if I became chairwoman someday. We'd never even been involved with hospitals before. The insufferable woman gave me the one thing that I couldn't say no to, all because she thought it might tempt me to take up the whitecoat. She's not evil, Tristan. She's just manipulative in the coldest, most infuriating ways possible."

"You passed her test, then, and got what you wanted from the process. From what I hear, the hospital is profitable. Zoe was treated for free when he broke his ankle."

"It's not the hospital that's profitable. We make our profits from the businesses around the hospital, from the drugs Grace Medical tests there, for overcharging the highborn. My mother was pleased when I asked for all the land two blocks around Our Lady of Light. She thought I was already getting a taste."

"The Randolphs owned those blocks?"

"Not back then. Not all of it. But my mother is very fond of acquiring land."

"Quite a stroke of inspiration for a teenager."

"It wasn't my idea. A few of my advisors came up the plan, Randolphs both of them, obviously. I thought they were crazy at first, but the numbers looked solid, and I wanted it to work so badly. I didn't care so much if it failed, either. I thought perhaps my mother would leave me alone if I failed spectacularly. She lent me the money to buy the blocks and set up what I needed. We bought a couple of lowborn apartment complexes and changed them to micro-leases for long-term patients and their families, leases that didn't gouge them senseless. We bought two more apartment complexes just for medical staff, to give them a place to live near the hospital at a fair price. Then I built other things, restaurants in different price ranges, a gym, a grocery store, a movie theater, a toy store, florists—everything patients and their exhausted families could want and everything my staff could want. It worked."

"Then Holly's death paved the way for a lot of good in the world, especially if other families adopt the model in other cities."

"Maybe." Lila shrugged, remembering how Holly's hair used to smell before she fell ill, like roses, and how it had smelled after, like damp. "I'd trade it all away for her."

"You miss her."

"Alex always understood the frustrations of being a highborn, but Holly always understood me."

"And now, Alex is in a holding cell in Bullstow."

"I had a footman bail her out this morning," Lila said, shifting in the driver's seat. "You're angry at me for that, aren't you?"

"Not if she hit you. If she did that, she deserves what she got." He pulled one of her gloved hands from the steering wheel and intertwined their fingers.

"I'm trying to drive," she muttered, pulling away.

"Trying is a good word for it. You don't have to speed to every red light in the city, you know. It'll still be red when you get there."

The pair didn't speak for the rest of the trip. Lila was glad for it, for her thoughts were consumed with two laughing children running through the grounds of the Randolph compound.

She soon pulled into the parking lot near the oracle's sign, sliding into a spot between a sports car and a beat-up pickup truck. They hiked past the sign, emerging at the dock. Lila noticed the same couple from the day before, holding hands, toes skimming the lake.

Luckily, the rower had just tied off his boat, and the group hopped inside.

When they entered the main room of the temple, it was already crowded with people muttering meditations or sipping water on the couches. A few parents even held babies tight to their chests.

One of the lilac-robed women approached the pair and bowed to Lila. "The oracle said to keep an eye out for you this morning. She'll only be a few moments."

A man nearby frowned at the exchange. At least she didn't have a Randolph coat of arms stitched onto her shirt this time.

Tristan sat on one of the couches and patted a seat beside him. Lila sat, worried he'd be inspired by the couple on the dock. Highborns never held hands in public or displayed affection outside of the bedroom. Only workborns staked a claim to one another so publicly.

But she and Tristan were just friends, weren't they?

Tristan sank back into the couch and closed his eyes. "I'm going in with you. I helped."

"No."

"I'll blow something up if—"

"Don't even joke about that."

"Too soon?" he asked, opening one eye.

Moments later a woman with a round belly emerged from the back of the room, waddling toward the front of the temple.

Another pregnancy blessed by the oracle. Lila wondered how many times a day the woman rubbed fat, baby-filled bellies.

She and Tristan dodged the pregnant woman and descended into the quiet fishbowl.

The oracle sat upon her couch and raised an eyebrow at Tristan's presence. "You brought a friend."

"He's like static. Whenever I try to peel him away, he shocks me."

"You trust him."

"He helps me sometimes," Lila said, refusing to sit.

Tristan had no such reservations. He plopped down on the couch beside the oracle and crossed one ankle over his knee. "She trusts me, or she never would have told me half the things she has. She just has problems admitting it."

Perhaps that was true. Perhaps no matter what the oracle had told her the day before, she did trust Tristan. Or at least, Lila trusted him far more than she trusted the oracle. The woman's mother had made a prediction that had already proved to be untrue. Since she'd been cut, the chance of Lila becoming pregnant was practically negligible. She would never become a whitecoat or a silvercoat either, especially with her father conspiring to make her contract more permanent, so long as she finished the job with the oracles.

If she finished the job.

"*Hmmm…* The girl is thinking so loudly I can see it cross her face. What do you suppose she's thinking about?"

"Something dangerous, I presume," Tristan answered. "It usually is."

"I trust him enough," Lila muttered, just to shut the pair up. "He knows what I know, anyway, so it's pointless to send him out."

Tristan grinned, the corners of his eyes crinkling. "I knew it."

Lila barely stilled her jaw. She'd always found it difficult not to smile whenever Tristan smiled at her. He had one of those grins that men sometimes had, the ones you couldn't help but return.

She turned her gaze on the oracle. "By the way, on behalf of every militia member in the country, we are thrilled to chase our tails for the pleasure of the oracles."

The oracle gestured for Lila to sit.

Lila crossed her arms over chest, still refusing.

"What do you know so that I can fill in the gaps?" the oracle said soothingly.

Lila was not soothed. "I know that future oracles are being kidnapped and placed in new homes to dodge their duty."

"Well, I'm not sure what I can add, then."

"The why, perhaps? Why are you doing this to your daughters?"

"Why does a prime give up her duty to become a blackcoat? Because you don't want to become prime?"

"Obviously."

"Then why can't our daughters do the same?"

"This isn't a case of firstborn dibs. If even half of what you said yesterday was true, then you're chosen by the gods."

"You were chosen by birth as well."

"I don't mean birth. I mean because of your disease."

The oracle winced at the term. "So not only would you have our daughters marked by seizures that drugs can barely control and visions of pain and death they should never be privy to, you'd take away their future as well?"

"It's not mine to take away. It's the gods'."

"So now you've become a believer?" the oracle said, cocking her head to the side.

"I'm playing devil's advocate."

"How nice that you have that luxury. I don't, and neither do our daughters. I want to change this life that we've been born into, and I'm not the only one among us who does. As you pointed out so elegantly yesterday, a great deal of what an oracle does has nothing to do with our gifts. My own sister hasn't the gift, but she's excellent at the rest of it. Far better than me, in fact."

Lila held her tongue, unsure how to proceed.

"Nothing is lost. The missing girls still pass on their visions. We talk and try to figure out what they mean, and at the end of the day, that girl can go back to being a child until she's old enough to decide for herself. Perhaps she'll become a doctor, a lawyer, a teacher, a soldier, or maybe even the oracle she was meant to be. Would you not give other girls the same opportunity you had to choose?"

"That's not even the point."

"I think it's the only point. Some girls wish to be an oracle with all their hearts. We keep those girls close. Others have seizures in public and get captured on film, or someone outside of our purview gains knowledge of their medical records. The press marks them as future oracles and shows them to the world before our lawyers can stop it. We have a chance to save the rest, and it's a rather small percentage."

"Girls like Valerie and Vivian?"

The oracle nodded. "I knew those men would take them and love them like their own children. The hardest part was changing the girls' government records."

"Well, you missed a spot." The words were out of Lila's mouth before she realized she'd said them. She should have been pissed that they'd altered government files. She shouldn't be offering tips.

The oracle barely contained her grin.

"How long do you think you can keep doing this before someone finds out?"

"I don't know, and I really don't care. We'll do it for as long as we can. We're tired of our girls running away at eighteen, never to be seen again because they don't want this life. We want them safe, and we want them to have a proper childhood. They can learn how to be oracles when they're older if they chose this path."

"You used Mr. Nottingham as bait. You dangled him in front of me so that I'd follow him and find the girls."

"I didn't use him as bait. He got scared when he saw your blackcoat. I told him not to worry, but he thought you'd come for the girls. He's not some criminal. He's a believer and a scared, overprotective father."

"What's my role in all this?"

"I had a vision, clearer than the first. I know now that I can trust you, and that I can rely on you. I was right to say you were intertwined with the oracles. I just didn't understand how intertwined. The oracles need someone we can trust now."

"Why?"

"Among other reasons, the militia intervened in one of our kidnappings in La Verde. The girl's birth parents are still under suspicion. Our lawyers will handle that end of it, but getting Rebecca back is proving more difficult. Your father put her into a foster home. I want you to retrieve her."

"You want me to waltz into that girl's foster home and kidnap her?"

"No. Her face has been splashed all over the news in La Verde. She'll never have a chance at what Valerie and Vivian have, but the least we can do is get her back with her parents. All I'm asking is that you convince your father to return the girl."

"That's not all, though, is it?"

"Ideally, he'd also drop his fixation with the oracles."

"You want me to go against the prime minister's direct orders?"

"He's your father."

"When he's hired me to do a job, he's the prime minister."

"I'm asking you to do what you've already decided. We wouldn't even be having this conversation if you hadn't." The oracle opened a folder on the table. "That's not all I'm asking of you."

"Wonderful. Should I start taking notes, or will you just hand me a list when you're done talking?"

The oracle ignored Lila's tone and passed the folder to Tristan. "The larger problem is that someone else has been stealing our girls. Two have gone missing in the last week, both around New Bristol, and we've had nothing to do with it. Obviously we can't go to Bullstow with this information. My purplecoats are looking everywhere, but so far, they've turned up nothing, and the gods are silent. This is everything we have on the girls' cases."

Lila averted her gaze. She'd almost feel sorry for the kidnappers if the purplecoats got hold of them. The oracles' security forces carried tranqs and guns loaded with bullets, and they had the immunity to do as they wished with those they caught.

Tristan flipped through the militia reports. "I'll look for them if she won't."

Lila snatched the folder from his hand.

"We can pay," the oracle said.

"I'm sure you can." Lila climbed upstairs, nearly leaving Tristan behind for the second time that day.

14

Lila reclined on Tristan's couch and worked her way through the list of Natalie's associates, her laptop warming her thighs. From time to time, she peeked at Tristan, who sat on the other end of the couch. He had been gone for the first four hours after she arrived, flitting in and out of the building, checking on the shop and Maria, then holding a couple of meetings downstairs. Now he seemed to have settled in, scrolling through a long list of messages from his spy network and inputting them into a spreadsheet on his laptop.

Even Tristan had tedious paperwork.

He'd been at it for over two hours already. Lila could have written a program in less than fifteen minutes that would have done the job for him, but she'd liked watching him go through the process. The way he cocked his head, considering the more interesting messages, the way he sighed occasionally at a particularly useless spy, the way he bit off a chuckle at something funny and turned his head, hoping he hadn't disturbed her.

Out of the corner of her eye, she saw him stifle yet another laugh and check her face again. She tensed as his eyes snaked across her body to focus on other things, and she longed to turn her head and watch him as he watched her.

How could he study her so completely and not even kiss her? How could he watch her with such intensity and not bed her? How could he call them friends?

More to the point, why hadn't she taken him? Perhaps she just needed to get him out of her system. Despite what Tristan claimed, they'd never had a friendship, and their peace was already ruined.

She had work, though, and work was far more important than satisfying her libido.

Tristan blushed suddenly, then turned back to his palm.

Had he been thinking about her? About sex?

Perhaps he hadn't been thinking about her at all. Perhaps he had been thinking about another woman. One smarter, funnier, with more daring eyes. Or perhaps he'd just recalled the punch line to a naughty joke.

Or maybe he'd been thinking about steak.

You never knew with men.

Lila leaned back deeper into the couch, so hard her shoulders blew past comfort into pain. She'd officially lost all willpower with Tristan. His smile had talked her into staying at the shop, rather than the security office. She should have been there, working her way through the list and her militia paperwork. At least there hadn't been much of the latter to finish. She'd blown through it all in an hour and a half.

That didn't change the fact that she should have worked some-where else, though.

It didn't change the fact that she hadn't seen Tristan the day before, and she'd barely gotten to see him after visiting the oracle.

Gods, she missed him when he wasn't around, no matter what the oracle said he might do. Despite the fact that she should take another lover.

Tristan closed his laptop and turned his head toward her, clearing his throat. "It's getting close to dinner. I'll get us something to eat."

"You might be done, but I'm not. Stop rubbing it in."

"You're never done." He set his laptop on the coffee table, stood, and stretched his arms into the air like a cat. His shirt rode up, exposing his flat belly and the ridge at his hips. She had an urge to grab him, to pull him toward her, to lick it.

Lick it and other things.

Lila looked back down at the screen. She should have gone back to the compound. She'd been distracted for most of the afternoon, and Oskar would pay for it. As would the missing girls, now that they'd been added to her plate.

He tugged on his shirt and yawned. "I'm going to order us something to eat. Whether you eat or not is your choice."

"I'm not hungry, especially for Chinese food."

"Actually, I thought I'd order something more mundane. How about pizza?"

"Pizza? I haven't eaten pizza…"

"Probably since the last time I ordered it for you. What's the point of having a fancy chef if she never makes anything good?" He dug into his pocket for his palm. "Did you like what I ordered last—"

The door opened, and Dixon strolled into the room.

Tristan's palm dangled at his thigh. Guilt flashed in his eyes. "Want some pizza? We were just going to eat."

Dixon shook his head and shuffled to his room. He emerged a few moments later, carrying a small bag, his purple scarf wrapped around his neck.

"Where are you going?"

Dixon dug out his notepad and a small pencil from his pocket. *Checking out the lead.*

"What lead?" Lila asked.

"You're not at one hundred percent. You need to rest."

We went out today.

"That apartment was supposed to be empty, and Lila and I were with you."

Fry and Dice are going too. We're only watching. No fighting. Dixon didn't look up as he wrote, neither requesting permission nor waiting to see if it was given. *See you tomorrow.*

"Just wait, okay? Let me get my things. I'll come—"

Dixon cut him off with a look, a look that plainly said he wasn't invited.

That wasn't the only look Dixon threw out. He glanced at Lila for only a split second, but that glance said volumes. Annoyance and frustration twisted his face.

They'd been friends before the incident in the tunnels. They'd laughed and joked. He'd once pushed her closer and closer toward his brother.

Now he didn't even want to be in the same room with her.

Dixon hitched the small bag on his shoulder and shuffled from the room.

Tristan followed him to the door. "Be careful," he called out, frowning as his brother's boots thudded on the stairs.

"What lead?" Lila asked again, instead of asking the question she wanted to ask. Of course, she already knew the answer. They hadn't talked yet, for the wound between them still festered.

What would Tristan do if they did talk and Dixon spoke against her? Who would he choose this time?

She could barely handle a day apart from him.

She stared at her thumbs, realizing the truth. When had her feelings turned so serious? For gods' sake, they hadn't even started anything, unless awkwardness and far-off stares counted.

"I have a lead on Natalie, but it's not much of one," Tristan said, stuffing his palm in his pocket, pizza forgotten. "One of my people overheard a matron talking to a spy. Chairwoman LeBeau, so you can guess how seriously I'm taking it."

"Seriously enough. You put two people on it."

"Not really. Fry and Dice are still smarting over losing Oskar at the auction house. They needed something productive to do, even if it's a fool's errand. I'm no different. We've chased ghosts ever since. I should never have gone for the other kid. I don't know what I was thinking."

"Your heart was in the right place."

"Sometimes it needs be somewhere else."

Lila looked down at her screen. "I've found a few places we can check out."

"Where?"

"It's not a short list, Tristan, and I'm not even done yet. I'll finish going through Natalie's account data tonight, and we can start tomorrow. I'll work on the rest from home." Lila tugged the star drive around her neck and stuck it in the port, saving her work. "I haven't even begun to look into the oracle's files."

"Someone's already looking for those girls. Oskar doesn't have anyone looking for him, not anyone who doesn't want him for their own uses. He's our priority." When Lila pulled the pendant from her laptop, Tristan took both from her and set them on the coffee table. Then he stood and offered his hand. "No. You're going to have something to eat and a nap before you go."

"You never ordered."

"You never told me what you wanted," he said, pulling her from the couch.

Tristan didn't drop her hand. He intertwined his fingers through hers and stared as though he longed to say something more.

Lila didn't push him away, even though she found it hard to breathe.

One minute their gazes were set upon one another; the next minute their lips were. He pulled her into his arms, hungrily sucking her lips, a wisp of a thumb trailing down her spine. The light warmth rolled down her back like the ghost of foreplay from lovers past.

She wove her arms around his neck, curling her fingers into his hair.

He sighed from it, jerked his head back, and closed his eyes as though dropping into early morning dreams. "Lila."

She breathed in her name, the vowels rolling off his tongue. A tongue that darted into her mouth tentatively, a tongue that felt like velvet as it snaked across hers, lighting her taste buds on fire. He'd had a shot of whiskey not too long ago, either for courage or out of habit.

When the smoothness retreated, she returned the favor, sliding her tongue along his lips as she sucked each one in turn. They were soft and silky in her mouth, his stubble prodding against her every exploration.

The contrast delighted her, as did the hardness of his jaw.

Tristan pulled her in tighter, his erect cock poking her in the thigh as he worked at her mouth.

"It's about time," Lila whispered once they finally broke away, foreheads still touching, both panting, their hungry lips barely apart.

"You never told me what you wanted. Is this what you want?"

"Not all of it," Lila said as she sucked at his bottom lip and pushed him toward his closed bedroom door. They'd go further than a nap today. She couldn't take it anymore. Damn the consequences; she wanted him inside her, needed him inside her. Either to get him out of her system or to get him into it, fully and completely.

"Dixon won't be back until tomorrow morning. We have plenty of time," he said when his back hit the door. He nibbled at her neck, fumbling behind himself to find the doorknob.

Lila pulled away. "Wait. That's why you haven't touched me?"

Tristan's head *thunked* against the door. "I can't when he's here. Not after what I did." Tristan's cock strained in his trousers, but his eyes had begun to lose their resolve.

His cock would as well if she didn't stop his brain with a kiss, perhaps more.

"Oh yes, you can," Lila growled, grasping his erection through the thin fabric of his trousers. She smirked as he jumped and breathed in sharply at her touch, his palms smacking against the bedroom door, his eyes closing in a surprised moan. "Open the damn door," she demanded, pressing her lips to his before he could second guess himself.

The door opened behind them, and Lila pushed him inside, flicking on the lights.

She closed and locked the door behind her in one fluid motion, kicking off her boots and peeling off her socks. Her tank, trousers, and gloves fell atop them seconds later, her palms still wrapped in a thin layer of gauze. Tristan's boots hit the ground with two quick *thumps*, and he fumbled with his belt, staring. When Lila tossed her bra onto her clothes and grabbed the waistband of her panties, he'd barely gotten off his socks.

"You're covered in bruises. Are you okay to—"

"They look worse than they are. You're overdressed. Are you shy?"

Tristan shook his head, licking his lips as she kicked off the last of her clothes.

Perhaps it was a good sign that he stared so hungrily, even with her bruises. His eyes snaked down her face, her breasts, her hips, her thighs. Usually the highborn didn't linger on one another's bodies; they were usually too busy tonguing them.

Playing was always more fun than staring at the wrapping.

Bored, she padded toward Tristan and unbuckled his belt, then lifted his thin shirt over his head and tossed it on the floor. She let her hands drop around his neck, tracing the broken, tanned skin around his scar before brushing across his shoulders. She moved down his chest and the ridges of his abdomen, each as hard as the erection she'd handled only moments before. "I'm going to lick you here," she said, letting her finger drift down toward his iliac ridge, which had tempted her earlier.

His hands stiffened at the buttons of his trousers. "Now?"

"Now. Later." She shrugged, unfastening his pants, yanking them and his boxer briefs down with one tug. They fell to the floor in a puddle, revealing his erect cock at last.

It was the only part of him she hadn't seen. She grasped the hard velvet, stroking him while she spoke. "I'm going to lick this too," she said before letting go and shoving him down on the bed.

She crawled atop him, sliding her chest and belly over his, liking the feel of his skin upon hers. It was smooth as silk in places, but he had the hands of a workman as they traveled down her back. Perhaps she would have the same sort of hands when they finally healed.

Gods, it'd been too long since she'd taken a lover inside her. Perhaps too long to take her time.

Tristan moaned at the contact, then wrapped his legs around her and whipped her onto her back in one quick motion, as if he'd thrown her onto a practice mat. He sat back on his heels and tugged at her ankles, yanking her toward him with a *whoosh* across his worn, soft sheets. He parted her thighs. His eyes traced her body again, and she grew wet from that alone.

A languid finger snaked from the back of her knee and up her thigh, deepening her arousal. Kisses landed next, full of warm breath and soft lips. He narrowly missed her clit and veered toward her thigh, her hips, her belly, and then her breasts.

He latched on to one, nibbling on her nipple, with just enough pressure. Her back arched off the bed, and he grabbed her wrists in a strong, insistent grip, bending them back over her head. His cock pressed against her thigh as his lips met hers again, kissing her, teasing her.

Lila grew wetter. Few senators would be so rough with a highborn heir.

Few senators would dare try to hold her down.

When she struggled against him, he released her. Her arms met behind his back, and she pressed him closer, too aroused to suffer through foreplay.

"Not yet," he said, rocking forward to nibble on her neck. It seemed every bit of her could be contained before his lips, his roving hands, his arms holding her so tightly as he breathed in her hair.

His teeth clenched around her earlobe. He tugged slightly, before returning to her neck.

Lila shuddered and gave him full access.

Tristan took advantage of it. He'd likely leave marks, as though she were a schoolgirl again—not that she could pry her mouth open to warn him against it; not that she could do much more than moan.

Especially when his fingers drifted between her legs. He stoked her clit, and little swirls of heat and ache trailed in his wake, one unremoved from the other. "Gods, you're so wet."

"Of course I am," she grumbled before her jaw opened in shock. "Oracle's light, you have done this before, haven't you?"

"Yes, Lila. I have had sex before. Lots of times. It's just that the other women I've bedded weren't quite this enthusiastic."

"Their loss," she said. "You've had the STD vaccine?"

"How very romantic."

"Have you?"

"Yes, Lila. I've had it."

"Good." She placed his hand over her clit as she lay back down. "Keep going."

"Stopping never crossed my mind," he said, his fingers continuing their exploration.

Lila's breath caught as he stumbled into touching her the right way. He planted whisper-kisses across her neck, her breasts, her belly, and her thighs before his tongue joined his practiced fingers. Her legs rocked and her back arched as his warmth slid over her, as his fingers entered her in her a rush.

She gasped, looked down, saw his eyes fixed on her, gauging her.

"There," she moaned, her thighs parting wider as his fingers slid inside her once more, his tongue lapping as though she were a cherry stem to be tied. As the waves of arousal crashed against her, as the heat of an orgasm burned within her, she fumbled at his headboard and gripped the bars, crying out "Tristan" over and over while she squirmed and bucked against him.

Tristan would not be thrown off, even after she stopped moaning and thrashing. She nearly told him to stop, but when his tongue lapped at her clit again, her voice went astray.

The warmth and aching came back quickly. She thrashed and bucked again, calling his name even louder. Her orgasm deepened as she rolled and crashed once more.

Tristan did not let up. She'd barely opened her eyes when she found him, staring at her face, dropping his lips to kiss her once more, brushing his body on skin too aroused and too sensitive to take it lightly. She could taste herself in his kiss and let her fingers fall to his cock. She gripped it, working it in her palm as he took her lips roughly.

He groaned against her mouth with each stroke, biting down on her lip.

"If you want a turn, you'll have to get off me."

"No." He shoved her hands above her head once more. "I like where I am, and I'm not done. I like when you writhe under me. I like when you shout my name."

Lila writhed underneath him twice more, coming from his mouth and fingers alone.

When he dipped his head for another pass, she closed her thighs before he could reach her, pinning his hand. "If you don't want my hands on it, then put it to better use. I want you inside me."

"I wasn't done."

"Yes, you are."

Grinning, he sat back on his heels and grabbed the back of her knees, pulling her toward him in one fluid motion, more strength in his arms than she would have guessed. He thrust inside her, finally quieting the need that had welled inside her all evening.

A need that grew as he rocked into her.

She wrapped her legs around his waist and rocked back.

Both stared at one another's eyes as they worked.

A thin sheen of sweat broke out on Tristan's forehead and over his chest.

In that moment, Lila knew she was ruined. Whenever she thought of Tristan, she'd return to this moment when he moaned and bucked against her, fierce and sweaty, all his attention fixed on her.

All at once, he thrust hard inside her as though sheathing a boot knife. He then sprawled atop her, settling his body against her arms as they kissed, still pumping inside her. "Say my name," he whispered into her ear. "Say my name and come for me."

"Tristan." She grabbed his ass and gave it a squeeze, directing him deeper and harder inside her. "Say my name and come for me," she whispered into his ear, biting the lobe as he had done to her.

Tristan paused. "Fuck, you have a mouth on you, don't you?"

"I didn't say anything you didn't say."

"It's not what you said, it's how you said it. All husky and sexy. It's hard not come inside you right now."

Lila moaned as he began stroking again. Faster this time, pushing her closer and closer toward the edge.

She came at last, shouting his name as she pawed at the headboard.

Tristan followed suit, whispering hers as he filled her.

15

Lila felt the arm around her waist before she saw it. She opened one eye and then the other in the cold, dark room. The little clock on Tristan's nightstand read three o'clock. They'd fallen asleep around ten, both exhausted from the last couple of weeks as well as several hours spent in one another's arms.

The ensuing five hours had been the best sleep that Lila had gotten in years.

Her eyes fell upon the string of bottle caps in the window. Tristan's arm tightened around her, tugging her closer.

She felt his naked body, warm across her back.

And his erection.

Stretching like a satisfied cat, she turned in his grasp, shaking the bed. He yawned and rolled over body. He said nothing, merely latched on to her lips, tracing them with his tongue.

Her breath hitched as his cock pressed against her, and she grew wet instantly.

She spread her legs, inviting him in.

Tristan didn't wait for any other signs. She gasped as he entered her, amazed she wasn't too sore for his languid thrusts. Lila reached around his waist as the bed rocked back and forth gently. His lips worked at her mouth, her ear, her neck.

They both came in a sleepy heap on Tristan's bed, all soft moans and hoarse voices.

"That's a nice way to wake up." Tristan yawned, pulling her back into his body. "It's even a better way to fall asleep."

"I can't."

"Shhh…" He yawned again. "Go back to sleep, Lila. Just for a little longer."

Lila knocked his arm away. "I can't, Tristan. I still need to finish my list. Oskar's still out there somewhere. So are the missing girls."

"You're no good to anyone if you're exhausted."

"I'll sleep after I find them."

"With me?"

Lila laughed and slid out of bed, leaving the warm sheets and Tristan's body behind. "One thing at a time," she said, eyeing the pile of clothes near the door.

"That's vague." Tristan turned on a lamp, wincing. He fiddled with the controls, and the bright light in the room faded to a welcome dimness.

"I can't find Oskar and the girls and figure out this too. Cut me a break." She knelt on the floor, finally finding her underclothes and digging through the pile for her trousers.

"You have to live sometime, Lila."

"Tell that to Oskar, and the kidnapped—"

"I know. I just meant—"

"I know what you meant." She turned, annoyed to find Tristan's hungry eyes following her every move. "Stop looking at me like I'm breakfast."

"Then stop looking so delicious."

Lila found her palm and scrolled through her messages. "Great. I'm to breakfast with my father. He gave me six weeks to look into the oracles, and he already wants an update."

"That will be hours away, and you didn't even have dinner. Let me make you something to eat," he said, slipping out of bed. "Maria taught me how to make pancakes. Sort of."

"Sort of?" Lila turned her eyes away, not wanting to stare after she'd just chastised him for doing the same thing.

"I asked her how to make them. Instead of teaching me, she cooked a bunch downstairs, tossed them in bags in my freezer, and told me how to heat them up. I think she's scared of me."

"It's Maria. Maria is afraid of mice."

"I would be too with those beady eyes and whiskers. Come on. Eat with me before you go."

"I'll eat later. I need to go home now."

"You're not eating much lately. I don't like it." Tristan helped her up and wrapped his arms around her. He smelled so good, felt so warm against her, both of them still mostly nude, both of them ready for another round.

Gods, what if she walked out now and it never happened again?

"Do you want to leave? Is that it?"

"No, I don't want to go home. I just have a great deal to do."

"You could work from the shop."

"I work better from home. There are too many distractions here."

"One of these days, I'm going to hop that wall and find you."

"Don't even joke about that," she said, pulling away.

But Tristan didn't let her go. He held her even more tightly. "Then come back tonight. I want to keep being with you. I miss you when you aren't around. I know I need to stop telling you that. I know it bothers you, but I can't help it."

But it didn't bother her. That was the problem.

"Go back to bed, Tristan. I'll send you a message after I finish the list, and we'll start working our way through it."

He opened his mouth to say something more, then thought better of it. "At least promise me that you'll eat something?"

"Sure."

After one last kiss, Lila slipped downstairs in the darkness, her fingers tracing the newly painted walls as she made her way to the back door. She cringed at the thought of seeing anyone else in the shop, especially any of the night guards that Tristan had placed outside the building.

Turning the door handle, she held her breath and peeked outside. Samantha paced away from her, deeper into the alley. Tristan's people always paced. It was sloppy, but it made it so much easier for her to get in and out undetected that she never said a thing.

Lila darted around to the mouth of the alley while Samantha's back was turned, her Colt jutting from her hip and creating the familiar bulge that would keep everyone she met away. But the street was empty in the hours before dawn, too early for the workborn and too late for criminals and drunkards.

She crept into the parking garage, thankful her sedan had not been vandalized or stolen, and hopped inside. The ride home would give her enough time to wipe the silly grin off her face and think.

Tristan certainly wanted to be more than friends.

She did too. She wasn't content with what had happened. She wanted more. Lots more.

She'd been worried about that. Getting too attached was a dangerous line to toe among highborn, a line Tristan had no experience navigating, a line Tristan wouldn't respect.

Frowning, she pulled into the compound, ignoring Sergeant Nolan's raised eyebrow, and parked in the garage. She slipped back upstairs, checking for bugs in her room. Then she turned on her desktop computer and pulled up the rest of Natalie's accounts, prepared to complete her research before she met with her father.

She managed to find a great deal in a few hours now that she'd been laid good and proper, now that she didn't have Tristan beside her, distracted by his grin, his smell, his little sighs, his lips, his cock.

Racing through every new contact she found, she tossed out anyone who turned out to be a highborn. Natalie wouldn't bother partnering with a highborn crony. None would aid her, for the ensuing scandal of stealing and selling Oskar might cost the entire family its highborn status.

And the one who lost it for them?

Their body would never be found.

Lila rubbed her chin. What if a Randolph had helped Natalie?

Gods, she didn't want to think about what would happen once the chairwoman found out. The punishment wouldn't go through Lila and the security office, that was for damn sure, and Lila wouldn't say a word against it.

No, a highborn wouldn't risk her matron's wrath—not anyone in the good graces of their family, anyway. The culprit might be a disgraced highborn, though, or perhaps another in the city who wouldn't mind getting back at the Holguíns.

Someone like Tristan, if he'd gone into crime rather than crusading.

As she composed her list, she rated both types as equally likely to harbor Natalie, adding every property they owned, including those they'd bought or rented using fake accounts.

Once she finished her work, she had nearly a hundred properties from two dozen people.

Lila rubbed her eyes and ran through the list once more, shuffling it until she had a list of the ten likeliest properties. Picking up her palm, she typed out a message to Tristan. They'd check them out together after she had breakfast with her father.

It was too late for a workout, so she hopped into the shower, tossed some unmarked clothes into a satchel, and dressed in the same clothes she'd worn to have breakfast with her father two days before. She wondered if he'd even notice.

Probably not.

Lila arrived at Falcon Home ten minutes early, just in time to witness Marie Masson, the youngest sister of Chairwoman Masson, slip out of her father's apartment, a last giggle still in her throat as he kissed him goodbye. She'd worn a thin burgundy dress and black boots, a color to honor her lover, rather than her family.

"Chief Randolph." Ms. Masson laughed, giving Lila a hug and a kiss on the cheek. "How are you this morning?"

"Well, and you?"

"Well, but I fear you are fibbing. You look tired, child. You must get more sleep." Ms. Masson stroked Lila's cheek. "Henri, look at her? Such pale skin! See that she gets more rest. It does no good for the Randolph prime to burn herself out before she's turned thirty."

Lila gritted her teeth but did not correct her. Ms. Masson was a silly woman, but very sweet. You couldn't help but love her, and her concern was genuine.

Because of that, Lila had always been secretly pleased at the match between Ms. Masson and her father. He needed someone light and joyful in his life, someone both silly and sweet. While her mother was her father's best friend and soul mate, Ms. Masson was more of a playmate. Always had been. Always would.

"Yes, Marie," her father said, patting her hand. "I'll be sure to do that."

Ms. Masson smiled and gave Lila and her father one last hug before trotting down the hall toward the stairs.

"Making the rounds, I see," Lila said as she followed her father into his apartment.

"I have to catch up with my family, my lovers, and my children when I can. I suppose it'll be easier when I retire. I can bounce back and forth between Unity and New Bristol and give everyone equal time." He closed the door and escorted her into the dining room while a servant finished setting the table.

"Is that what we're doing?" Lila asked when the servant bowed his way from the apartment. "Catching up?"

"As far as everyone knows. Everyone thinks that you're my favorite child, and I do nothing to dissuade them from that theory."

It wasn't until that moment that Lila realized her father hadn't asked a single personal question since he'd been in town. He'd nosed into who she was sleeping with, likely at her mother's urging, but that had been another bit of highborn business. It had been a very long time since he'd merely sat with her, as Tristan's father had tried to do, and spoken about her day.

They hadn't caught up in ages.

They'd had briefings.

When had it all changed?

Lila sat down at the table, pushing aside the question. She could worry about it next time he came into town. She had far more urgent problems.

"I ordered waffles," he said, pulling off the tops of the silver trays. "You can't eat pancakes every day. You're not five anymore."

He winked as he sat across from her.

Lila poured maple syrup over her breakfast and updated him on her progress with the oracles, eyeing his plate to ensure he hadn't added any sausage or bacon. She didn't mention that she'd met the oracle twice in as many days. Instead, she kept her information light and sparse, saying only that she'd looked into records of the kidnapped and murdered girls but hadn't drawn any conclusions yet. She'd only compiled lists and biographical data.

Lila sipped at her Sangre. "I disagree with your actions toward Rebecca. The oracles have had enough tragedy without you adding to it."

"I'm not convinced that the parents weren't involved," he retorted, and bit into his waffle. "I'll not give her back just to let it happen again. These girls need to be protected."

"By strangers?"

"My gut says I shouldn't give her back."

"Is your gut prepared for the shitstorm that will erupt if you don't? The oracles will not suffer the government stealing one of their own."

"Are the oracles threatening to act?"

"Not that I've heard, but they've lost enough daughters without having a target. You're giving them a big one. What do you think they'll do once word leaks to the press, assuming they don't leak it themselves? Do you honestly think they won't use it to their advantage? Do you want to give your rivals the ammunition?"

"I won reelection with three-quarters of the vote last season. I've never backed off from anything because of an election."

"Yes, that's one thing the senate and the matrons respect about you, but the matrons will withdraw their support the moment your decisions impact their bottom line. Pissing off the faithful so that they demonstrate rather than shop will certainly do that."

"I don't care about the matrons' attention on this one. My gut—"

"You can't arbitrarily take a child from her parents based on your gut," she snapped. "Your gut is not proof. Your gut isn't infallible."

"If something happens to that child—"

"Then it will be her parents' fault. My gut is telling me that you're wrong about this. My gut says that you're slipping away from the confines of your position."

He leaned back in his chair and snatched his wine, frowning. "You're probably the only person in the entire country who will tell me I'm being an idiot to my face without having some agenda lurking in the background. I value your opinion. Always have, from the day you earned the rank of captain. Perhaps even before that."

"But?"

"I don't know who's right about this one."

"Fine, you have a desperate urge to save a girl? Surrender this battle and charge into another that saves more. Like the hospital."

"That's a segue worthy of your mother." He swirled his wine. A thin purple sheen clung to the glass.

"I'm not lobbying. You know me better than that. All I'm saying is put your energies elsewhere while I look into things. Focus on the hospital. Pick a lowborn family for all I care, but find something else to do instead of obsessing about the oracles. It's going to end your career."

"Lots of things could end my career."

"Yes, like promising a deal to the Randolphs in exchange for Oskar Kruger? What were you thinking, Father? You don't think the matrons wouldn't figure that one out in two seconds? You don't have the political capital for these deals you're trying to pull. No one does. I suggest you not waste what you do have by chasing children."

"I just want a legacy, Lila. Is that so wrong?"

"You're fifty. There's time to worry about legacies later."

"Is there? I can't even eat bacon without a whole host of people muttering curses at me. If I don't make councilman in the next few years, then I'll be cast out of my position to make way for a younger prime minister. What do I have to show for it?"

"Fifteen well-placed children and the promise of grandchildren?"

"I mean professionally."

"Gods, this is a midlife crisis, isn't it?" Lila sighed. "Father, sometimes the best leaders can be defined by what they didn't do, rather than what they did do. The war has not resumed. You could have urged Head Councilman Abbot to declare war after Peter Kruger tried to murder me."

"I never wanted to be a quiet leader."

"So you'd rather be a stupid one?"

He snorted and returned to his breakfast. "You'll make a good matron one day."

"No, I'll continue to make a good chief. You can't save everyone, and it's not your responsibility to. You save who you can."

"Where'd you learn that?"

"From Holly? From Commander Sutton? The Randolphs aren't above domestic violence, you know. If I tried to take children away from their homes permanently instead of putting their parents through anger and relationship classes, we wouldn't have had the success we've had in treating the problem. Sometimes you have to trust people if you want them to surprise you."

"This isn't domestic violence, Lila. Too many children have gone missing lately. Not only the oracles, but Oskar and his sister Maria. Someone even snatched Phillip Wilson a few hours after the auction on Saturday night. He never made it to the Hardwicke factory outside of town. There are too many children missing on my watch. I can't suffer another one."

"You can't hold on to them so tightly that you break them, either. Trust me to look into the oracles and let Rebecca go back home to her parents."

Lemaire rubbed his chin and returned to his wine, not giving her an answer.

16

Lila parked her Cruz sedan in the same garage she'd used the night before. Rummaging in the back seat, she retrieved her satchel and trotted to Tristan's shop. She didn't slip on her hood until she'd darted into the alley behind the shop, waiting until the guard turned his back to slip through the door. The hallway smelled of sausage and biscuits and wine.

Creeping through the dim corridor, she slid into the garage, dodging the tangle of trucks and cars and motorcycles. Tristan and Fry called out to one another as they backed two trucks through the open dock doors.

"Hey, Hood," Shirley said, looking up from her perch. She settled a small motor on a table and waved her closer. "I heard you're taking the boys out hunting."

Lila nodded.

"Good. They've been driving me batshit insane the last few days. My team can finally get some work done without them hovering. I have four customers coming in at five o'clock, and we've barely started their repairs."

"Does it matter? This is just a cover, isn't it?"

"It's still a business. Keep them out all day, will you? I'd consider it a personal favor."

Lila laughed, drawing Tristan's attention. He peeked through the dock door and grinned, strolling across the shop. "How'd you slip in?"

"By being sneaky." She followed him to one of the trucks parked outside. She climbed into the passenger seat while he started the engine and pulled to the end of the street. Dixon and Frank stopped behind him. Fry and Dice backed a third truck from the shop's dock door, bringing up the rear.

"Are we splitting up the list?"

Tristan's eyes slid to the rearview mirror as they pulled into traffic. "No, I called them for backup. They'll stay close in case we run into Natalie and Oskar. I have another few teams on standby."

"You're worried about Dixon," she guessed, removing her hood as the other trucks made their own way to the first address.

"He's not at one hundred percent. Last night exhausted him. I shouldn't have let him come along."

"He's a grown man."

"He's my family, and he's unwell."

"And you don't want to let him out of your sight? Dixon can take care of himself. He's used to leading teams, not being watched like he's some invalid child."

Tristan's gaze flitted to his vibrating palm. "If he could manage to stay awake for more than five minutes, I might feel better about the situation. Apparently, he's already sawing logs in the front seat. Send them a message not to wake him, will you? I'm driving."

Lila tapped out the message. "A nap will do him some good. It'll take us twenty minutes to get to the first address."

A nap would have done her some good as well. She'd just begun to stretch her toes when Tristan intertwined his fingers with hers. He didn't seem to care that he had only one hand to steer.

Lila said nothing against it. Instead, she fought the urge to curl up against his shoulder.

Her palm vibrated. *Prolix, you're testing my patience. Surely you could have spared a moment before breakfast to send me a message. I'm sure you father wouldn't have minded.*

Lila swallowed.

Reaper's partner had followed her to Bullstow.

"What's wrong?" Tristan asked. "You just got pale."

"It's nothing. I'm just tired."

Moments later, Tristan pulled into an abandoned tire shop and stopped the truck, brakes squealing faintly in the morning heat. The building was one of many stand-alone businesses on the dying block, a row of loosely cracked and crumbling structures, lost amid fields of weeds. The businesses' names had once been painted on the buildings, but the lettering had faded on most. Perhaps the names had been lost to the neighborhood, just like the residents.

A pit bull barked nearby, already aware and unhappy with their presence. They closed the truck doors gently, and Tristan winced as the noise echoed off the empty buildings.

The pit bull barked louder.

"I should get a dog for the shop," he said. "I doubt you'd be able to get in so easily."

"Dogs love me."

"Barking or whining at the door, they'd still hear you coming. Dogs are good like that."

They padded down the sidewalk, the weeds thwacking against their knees. They did not wait for the others to join them. The two trucks circled the neighborhood several streets away, waiting to be called only if needed.

The pair walked along a chain link fence and slipped behind a junkyard. It smelled of engine grease and rotting food. Lila had to breathe through her mouth to avoid gagging.

The pit bull rushed, jaws clenching on the fence between them, his nose dotted with crimson flecks. Drool flew and landed with a splat on the sidewalk.

Lila backed away, her boots unscathed.

"He might have torn his nose up on the fence, but that doesn't look promising. What do you suppose—"

Lila sprayed a mist in the dog's direction, ensuring both she and Tristan were upwind. The dog whined and stumbled, falling in a cloud of dust.

"What the—"

"I told you." Lila grinned mischievously, sliding the metal container back into her pocket. "Dogs love me."

"Lila, just so we're clear, love doesn't mean that someone has a rabid desire to be tranqed."

She rolled her eyes and flipped on her jammer. "Come on, I estimate we have twenty minutes before it wakes up."

"Wait. Estimate? Explain estimate."

"Research is still in the testing phase. It's an aerated tranq solution. Works particularly well on little yappy dogs."

"A pit bull is not a little yappy dog, Lila!"

"Yeah, I know. There will be a much bigger mess when it wakes up." She hopped over the fence.

Tristan did not follow.

"Is it going to stay down?"

"I don't know. It's a mystery. That's what makes it science."

Tristan gave her a long stare before finally jumping over the fence and following along behind her. The pair crept toward a dilapidated structure in the center of the property, more wood pile than building. The smell grew worse and worse as they approached, the stench of piss and excrement cutting through the rot. The pair skirted piles of ripped batteries, coffee filters, and bottles of soda and drain opener.

"I don't think Natalie would have chosen this place. It stinks too much. I put it on the list because of its owner, but Natalie has her limits."

"Who owns it?"

"A disgraced Hardwicke. He was caught stealing funds from his wife and bugging her office. He passed information to his former matron and other families before getting caught."

"Chairwoman Hardwicke wouldn't take him back after that?"

"Of course not, both for sharing intel with other families and for getting caught. Turns out he had dividends stashed away that the government couldn't get to. He bought back his mark after he served his sentence."

"Where'd he stash the money while he served his slave's term? Burgundy?"

"Wasn't smart enough to do it and not get caught," she said, shaking her head. "He gave his money to Natalie Holguín to hide. They go way back, if you know what I mean. She still took thirty percent, but that's downright charitable for her. In any case, Mr. Hardwicke holds a few properties in East New Bristol—won them in card games, mostly. This property is an anomaly, though. It went out of business almost two years ago, and he hasn't tried to lease it."

The pair made a brief circle around the structure, peeking through broken shards in the painted-over windows. Nothing moved inside.

"I haven't seen any guards," Lila whispered, fishing her lock-picking tools from her pocket.

The door clicked open less than a minute later, and the pair stepped into a one-room structure. The dirty linoleum floor muffled their footsteps as they approached a long table in the back. Glassware and hoses spilled out of a box. Someone had stacked two large box fans in a corner.

"He doesn't even have a decent security system."

"Of course he wouldn't." Tristan sniffed the air. "It's smart to hide this place in the middle of a junkyard. Bravo, Mr. Hardwicke. It's just like a highborn to find a use for something this worthless."

"What use?"

"Do you smell that? This was a meth lab. Recently."

"Meth? How do you know what a meth lab smells like?"

"Not everyone I deal with is as sweet and carefree as you." He pushed her deeper into the room and curled his arms around her waist, grinning at the contact. "I've wanted to kiss you since I saw you at the shop this morning."

Lila squirmed out of his grasp. "No, my stomach can't handle that here. Besides, I don't have time. I haven't even begun to look for the oracles."

"Later, then. Are you going to call this into Shaw?"

"No. I'm bound to find more after we search the other properties. I can't call everything in today. Shaw will know exactly where it's coming from, and he'll know what I'm doing."

One spray to an unsteady pit bull later, and the pair returned to the truck, ready to scout the next location.

Lila pulled a laptop from her satchel, working through her inbox while they drove between locations. Before the clock struck noon, they'd ferreted out a hydroponic pot operation, a chop shop, and a dominatrix's secret dungeon. Although no one watched over the grow house, cameras had dominated the entire operation. Lila had merely turned her jammer up to maximum and peeked inside a few windows, satisfying her curiosity. They hadn't needed to go inside the chop shop either, for Tristan knew one of the men who worked inside. A quick call had ended that search. No one matching Natalie's description had been inside. As for the domi-natrix, she'd been surprisingly sweet, given her chosen occupation. Mistress Lola Whiplash had liked the look of Tristan, offering them a forty percent discount on her normal couples pricing.

Tristan had gone red immediately, and bowed from the chain-filled dungeon as though he'd become a slave once more. Mistress Lola had handed Lila a whip free of charge, claiming to be charmed. "You'll have to break that boy in slowly before you return." She elbowed Lila, her thigh-high leather boots creaking as the women watched him flee.

"I'll get right on that," Lila said, smacking the whip handle against her leg. "Thanks for the gift."

Despite his original reluctance, Tristan seemed quite comfortable with the whip after he got his hands on it. He'd already smacked her twice on the ass before they reached the truck.

"You're really good, you know. Someone's been doing something they shouldn't at every location we've checked so far, except for Mistress Lola. I don't really know what she was up to."

"Bribery. Information. Spying. I'm sure she made me as soon as I came through the door. Why do you think she offered the discount?"

Tristan stopped suddenly. "Is that bad? Do we need to—"

Lila shook her head. "My jammer was active, so she didn't get me on camera. Even if she had, who the heck would care? Her sort doesn't trade in that sort of blackmail. It would be bad for business. She pries information directly from the target's mouth. She wouldn't learn anything about me unless I was drugged, horny, and begging for release."

"I don't know whether to be terrified or incredibly turned on."

"How about frustrated? After all, Natalie wasn't there." Lila opened the truck door and vented the afternoon heat. Tristan tossed the whip into the back seat. "I can't believe you're keeping that. It should be dipped in disinfectant. Repeatedly."

"I like it."

"Fine, but stop smacking me in the ass with it. It's tedious."

"Make me."

"I have tranqs."

Tristan's grin faded. She'd shot him once before. "That's not even funny."

"It's a little funny." Lila leaned against the truck bed while Tristan pulled out his palm and made a quick call to Frank.

"Dixon's still asleep," he said when he finally disconnected. "He slept all morning."

"That's good, though. He needs to sleep."

"And we need to eat lunch. The others want a break for chow. It looks like we're going to have our first date."

"Date?"

"Yep." He slammed the truck door and wrapped a thin scarf around his slave's scar. "A quick one, just you and me. There's a great place up the street. If it can't tempt you, there's no hope for you at all. You'll just turn into sticks and bones, and I'll have to toss you into the lake and find a fluffier woman."

"You'll just rescue me again."

"No, I won't. Next time you fall in the water, you're on your own. I'll buy you one of those inflatable life vests to keep in your pocket."

"One of these days, I'm going to teach you how to swim."

"Never. The only thing that could get me into the water again is if you didn't have any clothes on. If you're going to drown, Lila, drown naked."

As Tristan led her down the street, Lila's thoughts filled with images she didn't want, of Tristan pushing her under a dock, shoving her against one of the thick wooden beams while he thrust into her, the sound of his muffled moans as he came, as he called out her name.

She grew wet between the legs, hungry for anything but food.

Soon the pair reached an unmarked, dilapidated structure, not unlike the buildings they'd trudged through all morning, except that this one had been cared for and cared about. Though the wooden building had weathered and warped over the years and needed a fresh coat of paint, Lila couldn't shake the feeling that it had been made to look that way.

Tristan led her through the swinging front doors. The walls had been painted in pastel blues and greens, hung with black-and-white photographs of Mexico City, the capital of the Mexican Commonwealth. Banners honoring their ancient gods hung beside saddles pegged to the wall. Stained glass filled the window, tiled into portraits of flowers and ivy.

Lila slid into a booth, making sure she faced the wall in case of spies. Tristan sat across from her and pushed a menu forward. "They have the best queso and fajitas in Saxony."

"And the worst architect."

"It's not as if the lowborns who run this place had a great deal of capital, Lila. Fry and Dice helped build this place."

"They should have helped more."

Tristan poked her on the nose. "Hush. It matches the picture of a little restaurant in Mexico City, a tribute to the owner's great grandmother. She opened the first El Dorado a hundred years ago."

"Sentimentality has no place in business."

"You're so highborn sometimes. Dice's little sister is probably in the back ordering the poor cooks around. She's married to the owner."

"His sister is gay?"

"No, the owner is male. She moved up in the world and became lowborn by marriage."

Lila raised a brow. "Interesting," she said as a young waitress stopped by their table.

She let Tristan order for them both, as she didn't know enough about the place to pick wisely, and she wasn't even sure that she was hungry. But when the waitress brought out a bowl full of queso, her stomach changed her mind. Even though it was the spiciest queso she'd ever eaten, she kept shoveling chip after chip into the golden sauce.

"Told you." Tristan slid his palm across the table.

"What's this?" Lila said, munching as he spun the device and tapped the screen. A video of a red-nosed Peter Kruger filled it. The camera quickly pulled back. The small man stood next to a mound of dirt with King Lucas, a golden shovel in his unsteady hands.

"A photo op?" Lila squinted at the captions that flew along the bottom. Her father had been forced to attend such occasions for years, usually to break ground on some major project for Unity or for a highborn family that he had tied himself to by seed. "Why am I watching this? It's just the empire, breaking ground on some government building."

"Keep watching," Tristan said, and sipped his water.

King Lucas finished his short speech and handed the microphone to his elder half-brother. Peter gripped it as though it were a weapon. He made a far different image than the budding revolutionary he'd been a week before. Gone was the mysterious, passionate twist to his face. Gone were his workmen's boots. His clothes had been tailored to fit his form. They might have fit better if he stopped fiddling with his collar and tie.

His eyes were bloodshot, too. Lila didn't need to understand German to hear the slurring.

"He's drunk," she said after the short video played out.

"Yes, but that's not the point. Watch his hand." Tristan tapped the screen, replaying the video.

As Peter spoke to the crowd, he tugged at his ear. Not just once, but on three separate occasions. "That was the sign, wasn't it? He's asking you to take care of his kids."

"Partly. To be more specific, he's signaling that Germany is unsafe for them, at least for the moment. I've seen him do it in the last two videos as well. We have to find Oskar, Lila. I promised Peter that I'd look after him. As much as I hate the guy for trying to kill you, he did save my people from Bullstow's attention."

"That makes you even, not indebted. I want to find Oskar as much as you do, but not for his father."

"I know. It could make us all safer, though. If Peter did get into power, perhaps he'd end this stupid war once and for all. It's always my people who pay when war thickens."

Lila wanted to disagree with him, but she could not. The workborn filled out the military, though a quarter came from the oracle children, the extended families of the oracles. Many left their compound to join, staying with the army until retirement. Most lowborn stayed away from conflict altogether, choosing to grow their family's business.

Almost no soldiers came from the highborn, not unless they'd been promoted directly to officer, and usually only if they'd been disgraced, exiled, and had nowhere else to go. Only the highborn senators participated in war, offering a hurried debate in High House whenever the Roman Empire poked a little too forcefully at the Allied Lands.

"Oskar and Maria aren't safe here, and they aren't safe in Germany," Lila said. "Where's safe?"

"Nowhere. That's why I'm going to make them disappear."

"How? People are never going to stop looking for them."

"I have a few ideas."

Lila narrowed her eyes.

"I do. Trust me."

"You'll run your plan by me before you decide to act. I don't want to get stuck cleaning up your mess again."

The waitress saved them from an argument, returning with sizzling plates of fajitas.

Tristan hadn't been lying about the food. If Lila had thought the queso had been amazing, it had nothing on the fajitas. "What'd they marinate this stuff in? Unicorns and rainbows?" she asked, wrapping up strips of steak in fresh tortillas.

Her mouth watered as she chewed, the slight tinge of lime biting her tongue. "I should send Chef over to ferret out the recipe. She's like a walking food analyzer."

Tristan gave her a long look. "If I'd thought your family might steal the recipes, I never would have brought you."

"We don't steal. We partner. Voluntarily. Our deals are very generous."

For a first date, it wasn't half bad. Tristan spent most of the meal rubbing his leg against hers under the table. She didn't pull away, though it made concentrating on her food more difficult. That and her constant worry that a spy might be watching.

After Tristan hopped up to visit the men's room, she finally sent a message to Reaper's partner. *Are you going to keep blowing up my palm, or will you actually tell me what you want?*

She received her answer a few seconds later.

One hundred thousand credits. You have two days.

She wrote back immediately. *Just money? Is that all you want?*

For now, my sweet. I'll send you my account number soon. Fail to pay, and you'll receive a very different sort of message.

Lila pinched the bridge of her nose. Paying would begin a dance she didn't want. She'd never paid a blackmailer in her life, and she refused to start now.

After the meal, the pair returned to the truck. Lila finished her work for the security office while Tristan drove them to the fifth location, then she returned her laptop to her satchel. Unfortunately, location five turned out to be a waste of time. It was nothing more than another chop shop. Lila scowled on the way back to the truck and said nothing as Tristan drove to the next address. Her unmarked servant's shirt scratched against her neck in the heat.

Twenty minutes later, Tristan parked a block from the corner of Antigua Way and Achilles Drive. The whole area had been filled with factories, though half had been shuttered when the last round of environmental regulations had passed a decade ago. She and Tristan were so far from downtown New Bristol that the skyline had pinched into a small cluster. Twelve towers poked out from the mass of metal and glass behind them.

Her mother would soon raze Wilson Tower, as dictated by tradition. The skyline would change again after the Parks built their tower inside their fledgling compound, marking them as newly highborn.

But Achilles Drive was far away from all that. The sidewalks had been matted by weeds and dirt and cigarette butts, and the voices on the street sounded tinny and quiet and eerie.

"It's that one." Lila jutted her chin to an abandoned factory. "There's another on my list nearby, but this one is more likely." The properties on all sides had been abandoned, leaving it inside a strange pocket of protection. Boot prints marked the dried mud around the perimeter.

"Guards," Lila whispered.

Tristan frowned. They'd been dodging the occasional guard all day.

Still they pressed on. Though Lila didn't spot any cameras, she turned on her jammer. They followed the prints, noting that none of them looked all that fresh. When they saw no evidence of a patrol, they peered into one of the dusty windows. Lila didn't see anything at first. Just a dirty floor and a few tables far in the back.

Then she saw the toe of a worn boot and a pool of crimson nearby.

Lila pulled away from the window and grabbed her tranq gun and hood, while Tristan tapped upon his palm and sent for the others.

Fry, Dice, Frank, and a yawning Dixon soon appeared behind them, just as Lila slid her mesh hood over her face.

"Hood and I will go around the back," Tristan said. "Fry, Dice, and Frank, take the front. Dixon, you're up top."

As Fry and Dice slipped around to the front of the building, a pale Dixon struggled up the fire escape, his boots quiet as he scrambled onto the roof.

Lila typed a code into the security box by the back door.

Tristan gagged slightly as it opened. The smell of rotting meat was light on the air but strong enough to claw at their throats.

Lila had smelled it before on patrol. "Pull the others back to the trucks," Lila said, dragging him away from the door before he vomited. "Call Frank. Have him retrieve my satchel."

Tristan nodded quickly, gulping quickly several times. After a long moment, he pulled out his palm and relayed her instructions.

Frank didn't do much better. He turned a rather odd shade of green as he stood near the door, and seemed more than happy to return to the truck.

Lila removed her hood, then pulled covers over her boots and donned latex gloves. "Are you better now, Tristan? Can you go inside?"

"I'm fine."

"If you throw up, you'll leave your DNA behind. Take a moment if you need it."

"I'm fine."

She helped Tristan fit covers over his boots and gave him a pair of latex gloves. "Don't touch anything if you don't have to," she whispered, handing him a camera.

Tristan took it uncertainly and followed her inside, the smell growing worse in the closed warmth of the heat wave.

The scene chilled her, not due to the violence but for the lack of it. It was as though Natalie and her people had fallen where they stood, not even wasting the time to face their attackers. A half-eaten donut lay near one of the guards, his mouth still full. Near another, a tranq gun had fallen from its owner's holster, unused. Laptop cords wound around a few tables in the room, the computers missing. A tray of croissants and pastries had been placed upon the tables, half the food uneaten.

More disturbingly, a blue teddy bear lay discarded at the side of the room near a large dog crate. If Oskar had been inside, he'd barely had room to stretch.

Knowing Natalie, she'd bought him a dog collar and a leash to complete the look.

"Oskar was here." Lila picked up the bear with gloved hands. She breathed out in relief when she turned the toy over and found no blood. "They took him."

"Are you sure?" Tristan said, his voice muffled as he pulled his scarf over his mouth.

"I know this teddy bear."

Tristan crouched in front of the crate. "No blood. If they wanted the boy dead, it would have been much easier to shoot him here. They didn't do that. He's still alive."

"Maybe." Lila tossed the toy into the crate and slammed the lid. Oskar had slipped further away. "I was supposed to find him today. I was supposed to bring him back safe, so I could start looking for the others."

"We'll find him. We'll find all of them," Tristan assured her, tugging her back from the crate. His gaze swept the room. "I count ten bodies."

Lila turned, counting as well, trying to keep her mind on the case. Natalie and her people had perished in the dim factory, bullet holes adorning their chests and foreheads, all lying in blood, little of it disturbed in last-minute death throes. One in the head, two in the heart.

"You think they were drugged first?"

Lila shook her head. Too many had died with their eyes open, their pupils seeming to follow her around the room.

It was Reaper all over again.

It was Hans Schulte.

"Take pictures of the scene. Make damn sure we aren't in them. Not even a finger or a hem."

While Tristan sent his people a short message to return to the shop, Lila took a blood sample from each body. If the food had been drugged, it might explain how ten experienced thugs had been slaughtered before they even managed to draw their weapons.

She put the samples into her satchel and searched each body. Unfortunately, it appeared that the killers had already done the job, though poorly. Lila managed to find a palm hidden in a bag of clothes in the back of the room, stitched into a hidden pocket.

That wasn't the only thing she found. In the corner of an office, she discovered a ladder propped against the wall, one so tall that it nearly scraped against the ceiling. After dragging it out, she scrambled to the highest rung, peeking over the steel beams that ran the length of the factory's ceiling.

"I'll be damned," she whispered, sliding out to snatch a palm. She found another on a second beam near the entrance. Taking out her laptop from her satchel, she backed up each palm's contents, then replaced them where she'd found them.

She did the same with a star drive around Natalie's wrist, lost amid a charm bracelet. "I knew her," Lila said while she worked. "She wasn't like Patrick. She never hid. She never pretended to be anything but what she was."

"A sociopath?"

"A monster. If someone pissed her off too badly at school, she'd kill their pets, even a teacher's once or twice. No one could ever prove she'd done it, though. Did you know her?"

"Not well, and for that I'm grateful. She didn't visit the Beaulac compound very often." He dropped the camera to his thigh. "When do you think they died?"

"No idea. We have daily wellness checks for the at-risk and elderly back at the compound. I'm used to fresher bodies. With this heat?" Lila considered the pastries on the table. "I'm guessing this morning from the food. It's still soft. If I'd just gone home last night and finished the list, we might have—"

"Stumbled into an execution? No, thank you. I'm happy with how things turned out. She deserved what she got. She ruined more than a few lives."

"I'd rather she be in a holding cell."

"Why? So she can be hanged after a drawn-out trial? She deserved death for more than just Oskar, you know. Someone should have shot her a long time ago."

Lila frowned, not sure whether she agreed with him, the oracle's words fresh on her mind. "You sound like you wish you could have done it yourself."

Tristan shrugged.

As much as she wanted to pry, it wasn't the time or the place. "Oskar was easier to track when we could follow Natalie. Now I don't have the faintest clue how to find him."

"You have a few palms and Natalie's star drive. That's a good start." He showed her the photos stored in the camera, and she pointed out a few shots he'd missed. "They used bullets, Lila. You know what that means."

"No, I don't. I need to look at all the data first. Then we can draw conclusions."

"You can draw a few already," Tristan said as he snapped the last photo. "Few in the Allied Lands use bullets. That means that unless the purplecoats have gone into buying princes, then Natalie tried to sell Oskar to German mercenaries. The mercs surprised her, offed her and her people, then took the boy and everything tying them to the scene."

"Anyone can use bullets."

"How many people do you think stormed in here, Lila? I could see two or three risking the hangman's noose for the promise of quick money, but not a dozen."

"At least a dozen." The pair tidied the scene and stepped through the back door. Lila tossed their gloves, booties, and the camera back into her satchel. "Just don't jump to conclusions before I look through the data, okay?"

"Fine," Tristan said as they stalked back to the truck, rubbing out their footprints. "How do you think they found her?"

"I have no idea, but I doubt they found her like I did. They probably followed her. Natalie wouldn't have held a drop in the same place she was staying. She would have taken precautions."

"They found her somehow."

"Yes, they did." Lila slipped into the truck and slammed her door. "I'm just not sure how yet."

17

Tristan parked a block away from the garage that held Lila's Adessi and promised to call Natalie's murder into Bullstow's anonymous tip line when he returned home. He snatched her hand before she could disembark. "Don't go. Come back to the shop with me."

"I can't. Time's ticking for Oskar," she said, unsure if she'd be able to say no if he asked again, but knowing full well she had to. If she and Tristan had not been together the night before, she might have found Natalie before the massacre. Oskar might have been saved.

She had to focus, and that meant staying away from Tristan.

"Time's ticking for all of them. Let us help you."

When she didn't answer, Tristan rubbed the back of her hand with his thumb. "Is it that you don't trust us, or you just think we're too stupid to be useful?"

"You're not stupid, just unskilled when it comes to militia business. When's the last time you went through crime scene data?" Lila handed him an extra star drive from her satchel. "If you want to help, then give this to Toxic. It's a copy of all the palm data. I don't know who the devices belonged to, so I'll be looking at Natalie's star drive first. Message me if she finds anything. I put the crime scene photos on it as well."

"Come back with me."

"I don't have time for sex, Tristan."

"I didn't ask for it." He dropped her hand. "Besides, I think my libido burned out from the smell and the sight of that place, Lila. I just want to make sure you eat dinner and sleep tonight."

"I might not have time for that, either."

"You have to live sometime."

"Those kids need to live too. Besides, I have a High Council meeting tonight."

"Fine. Give me something useful to do. I'm tired of chasing leads that go nowhere."

Lila opened her satchel, took out the oracle's files, and slid them over. "I don't have time for these right now. Look them over. See what you see."

She slipped out of the truck before he could say more.

Hopping into her sedan, she sped back to the compound, and parked in front of the security office. On the fifth floor, she filled out a request for lab work, marking the blood samples as a rush order, and handed them personally to Captain Regina Randolph. "Run the tests yourself and send me the results. Destroy all paperwork after."

Captain Regina raised a brow, but she wasn't so suspicious that she'd go against Lila's orders. She wasn't so suspicious that she'd send the data to the chairwoman, either. Lila had put loyal officers in charge of her departments. If loyalty wasn't enough, she'd made examples of two spies in her first week as chief, had ruined them so completely that her people were more afraid of turning on Lila than not spying for their matron.

Being thrown out of the militia had just been the beginning for the two women. Everyone had skeletons in their closets, and Lila was very good at finding them.

She was even better at seeing them prosecuted.

No highborn wanted to spend time as a slave.

Lila jogged down the steps and got back into her Adessi, wondering if Bullstow had arrived at Natalie's hideout. She planned to break into their records and go over their reports later. Shaw and his men sometimes caught things that she missed.

Besides, she had no idea how to trace bullets.

Isabel knocked as soon as Lila stepped from the shower, bearing a silver platter with none of Alex's grace or sarcasm.

She only bowed and waited for a reply.

Lila didn't have to peek underneath the platter to know what it hid, and it wasn't anything like the meal she'd eaten at El Dorado. "A missive from our illustrious matron for a family dinner, I suppose?"

Isabel bowed again. "Chef said you'll be dining on wild salmon."

"Well if we're having wild salmon, then how could I say no?" Lila snatched up the cream-colored envelope. She had absolutely no reason to say no to her mother's summons.

Why hadn't she stayed with Tristan at his shop?

"Chef is making petit fours. I saw those little chocolate ones you like so much."

Lila's mouth watered. Her appetite seemed to have recovered somewhat after her lunch with Tristan. "Have I mentioned how much I love Chef lately? The woman has a sixth sense for when I'll need chocolate or pancakes."

Isabel smiled shyly, took Lila's grin as an affirmative, then carried the silver platter away.

Still in her robe, Lila sent Max her last communications with Reaper's partner. She then flipped on her desktop computer and proceeded to hack into Natalie's data. After sending the decryption codes to Toxic, she poked through Natalie's star drive and skimmed through several spreadsheets of Sangre sales, black market absinthe, and another product she couldn't identify for half an hour.

People, she discovered after penetrating the star drive further. Natalie Holguín ran a brothel, perhaps more than one. Since there were no outgoing expenses for labor, it was obvious that her workers had never signed up for it. Natalie had been stealing them from auction houses across the region, slaves arrested for petty theft, shoplifting, vandalism, trespassing, minor in possession—

Minor in possession?

Teens?

Gods, Natalie was selling children.

Lila shook her head and kept digging. The kids were mostly workborn teens who had no one to prod Bullstow after they'd gone missing, no one to keep their cases fresh in the minds of the blackcoats. They existed as nothing more than torn and dirty fliers on a bulletin board, as ones and zeros in a computer file that hadn't been accessed in years, as nagging paperwork that no one could quite clean off their desks, but wasn't that bothersome so long as you put other paperwork on top of it.

You could almost forget about it entirely.

Now it seemed that Phillip Wilson had been among them, judging from the last line entered on Saturday night. It made sense. His parents had been casualties of the Wilson riot, and anyone close to him had been taken into custody for their actions. Given how the family had been split apart, most of them had too many problems in their own lives to worry about a child who never made it from the auction house to his new master. Perhaps they thought he'd slipped away on his own. Perhaps they cheered his mischief.

It wasn't mischief that got him out of his slave's term, though, a term that would have only lasted a few years after his eighteenth birthday. Now he'd go to work immediately, his body given over to anyone with a few credits, to workborns who wished to take out their frustrations with the highborn on a child.

Phillip would never have been so disdainful of Tristan's help if he'd known.

Lila wanted to call it in immediately, wanted to rush to his rescue and save him, to save them all. But that was the problem, wasn't it? If Natalie ran one brothel, she probably ran more. Calling in one location to Shaw would merely drive the others deeper underground. She had to dig deeper into Natalie's files, and she couldn't do that until after dinner and the council meeting.

Perhaps not until after she'd found Oskar.

What would Tristan have done if he'd found out before Natalie's death? Would he have killed her? He didn't seem that averse to the idea at the warehouse.

The oracle had claimed that Tristan would take to killing.

Was this how it started? A week ago, she wouldn't have believed it. Reaper's death still haunted him, and that had been an accident. The Wilson child still weighed on his mind as well, dead in the middle of a riot.

Then again, Tristan had wanted to kill Natalie at the factory for her crimes. He'd always believed that he and his people were locked in some class war against the highborn. That stealing from them wasn't wrong. That hurting them might not be wrong, either. The idea of casualties had not dissuaded him from planting a bomb at Slack & Roberts.

But hadn't he changed after the Wilson riot?

What if he hadn't? What if his misgivings were only temporary? What if he truly thought a highborn deserved death? Would he take the next step now that he had killed once? Would he seek it out? Would he begin to enjoy it?

Lila shook her head. She couldn't see it happening. Screw the oracle's vision—she wasn't about to take to killing, either. She would never kill anyone, not unless she must kill for self-defense, not unless her Colt malfunctioned and she must resort to her boot knife. After all, she would have killed Peter Kruger if she'd had a weapon. She hadn't wanted to die.

Lila rubbed her lips, watching the seconds tick by on her computer.

With great resolve, she pulled herself up in her seat. She couldn't beg off the High Council meeting. It just wasn't done. All judges attended a new family's proposal, regardless of health. An early slight against Ms. Park might turn the woman into a rival, rather than an ally.

She must spare the hour for the council meeting and for dinner as well. Not going downstairs would only lead to more interruptions later, and she needed to eat, anyway.

Before she left, she wrote a few lines of code to search for more information about Natalie's brothels, cross-checking the information she'd already found against every address and person on her unculled list of accomplices, the list she had not removed any highborn from.

At least her computer would do something useful during the council meeting.

Lila pulled on a formal uniform and dressed carefully for dinner, dabbing more concealer on her still purple jaw. Then she slowly descended the stairs and entered the dining room. Her family already sat at their places at the table. An artisan had carved a racing pack of wolves into the side. Their howling brethren had also been carved into the legs.

A matching chair had been pushed out beside her brother Shiloh, who wore the golden coat and breeches of a Bullstow graduate and senate intern. It wasn't often that her brother visited the family, finding his matron far less entertaining than his thousand fathers at Bullstow. It usually took the prime minister's visit during Family Week to drag him to the compound.

He winked at her as the rest of the family enjoyed their soup.

Senator Dubois had come too, and sat beside his lover. He sent Jewel long glances, her sister a far more beautiful copy of her older sister, with blonde hair and the same large eyes. Whenever Dubois looked away, Jewel did the same to him.

Lila nearly gagged.

In the corner, Alex stood before the hand-painted crimson wallpaper. It was as if her back had been glued to a board, she stood so straight and tall and unnaturally.

Lila took her place beside Shiloh. Her mother had chosen Alex to serve the family dinner for a reason. The move would only escalate matters. She'd push the slave to slip before the family and the prime minister, and have the perfect excuse to cast her aside.

Who would buy Alex at auction now? If she couldn't behave around the prime minister and had assaulted her best friend, then who would be safe? Besides, everyone knew that she had outlived her usefulness. She'd become a torn-up lottery ticket, a busted toy, useful for nothing except her family's humiliation. But even that would quickly expire, for after her matron's execution, there would be no one around to care about Alex. Indeed, everyone in the family had ended up as slaves or criminals or workborn in the end. They probably all blamed Alex, and would enjoy the thought of her humiliation.

If she'd continued as Lila's friend, then Alex might have been saved. But she'd separated herself from Lila's good graces, and the chairwoman would press the issue.

At dinner.

This, and many other reasons, was why Lila detested taking meals with her mother. It was never about the damn food.

Lila spooned her soup and tried not to look at Alex, for it might only set her temper off. Instead, she nodded to Senator Dubois, who had marked her presence with a smile. "You're joining us this evening, senator. It's a rare treat indeed."

"I was just telling Jewel how we were making plans to ride soon."

"Perhaps Jewel would like to join us," Lila offered, feeling gracious under the brewing storm cloud. "We could rent another bike."

"I have a bike now." Jewel shrugged.

"Ah, but you've only ridden on a Firefly. We could rent something more rugged, more pedestrian. Perhaps an Amazon or a Barracuda."

"Are they really all that different?"

"You could always check them out. If that doesn't suit you, we could always attach a sidecar to your Firefly." Lila intended it as a joke. She winked at Dubois, whose eyes bugged out at the thought of attaching a sidecar to such a fine motorbike.

That was when Lila realized her mistake. Jewel, ever the artist seeking new experiences, leaned back into her chair. "A sidecar?"

"Perhaps you could don a pair of goggles and a fetching scarf to complete the look. I'm sure it would add to the experience."

Jewel's face crumbled into annoyance. "Don't mock me."

"I wouldn't dream of it." Lila's gaze slipped automatically to Alex.

In years past, they would have shared a secret grin over Jewel's remarks. Perhaps even a little eye roll if her mother became particularly demanding and matronly over some frivolous event. But this time, Alex wouldn't meet her eyes. She stared at the opposite wall like a good little slave, waiting to clear away the dishes and bring out the next course.

The chairwoman would not be so appeased. "I think that's a lovely idea, Jewel. You need a break from the office. Perhaps you could turn it into a long weekend. I enjoy the idea of my daughters spending more time together." She cut her eyes to Lila, a checkmate playing on loop. She knew how much it would annoy Lila to spend so much time with Jewel.

It wasn't that Lila hated Jewel; she just didn't get her. Jewel's mind was composed of paint and canvas, of wax and wood, of blowtorches and metal. Lila, on the other hand, had never been creative. She bent code to her will, used it to peek into things she shouldn't, to work mischief. She used bravado and lockpicks to poke and prod where she didn't belong.

Lila only made an effort because Jewel had taken over as prime.

Her sister nodded. "That sounds lovely. Perhaps I will try a sidecar, though for a short afternoon trip rather than a long one. I might not enjoy it. Louis, you should go on a longer ride with Lila, if you can get away. You need to shake off the stress of the session."

Jewel had learned. She'd satisfied her sister, her mother, and her lover in one suggestion. Perhaps she wouldn't be such a useless matron after all. "That's a fine idea," Lila said.

"I do have them occasionally."

"You seem to have them more and more often lately, President Randolph."

Realizing what Lila meant, Jewel blushed. It was rare that Lila complimented anyone, and Jewel had always been particularly eager for her older sister's approval.

The chairwoman frowned and spooned her soup, somewhat defeated by her daughters. "So, Lila, the High Council meeting is tonight. You'll admit Ms. Park into the highborn?"

"Yes, madam."

"Good. She's the best candidate in all of New Bristol, and she owes us many favors already. The Randolphs have been instrumental in her family's rise. She'll make a find addition to the highborn and become an ally, rather than a rival."

"I concur. She has enough capital to become a major player in New Bristol within the next generation if her daughter is her equal."

"Agreed. The Parks are nothing like those disgraceful Wilsons. It was a bad decision for the High Council to admit them into the highborn. Your great-grandmother Ophelia was shrewd enough to vote against their inclusion, did you know that?"

"Yes, madam."

"It's a pity that no one else listened."

Alex kept her gaze on the wall.

The other diners shifted in discomfort.

"You've told me the story, madam." Lila scrambled to change the flow of the dinner conversation. "I'm extremely curious to see what colors Ms. Park will propose for her family. Her coat of arms, too. What do think, Pax?"

"A lime dragon? Perhaps a tigress atop a field of calming blue?"

"I think either choice would serve her family well," Senator Dubois replied.

Pax beamed and took a large spoonful of soup. Dubois had the same effect on the boy as her father, encouraging him to eat and smile when he otherwise wouldn't.

"How's Father's Week?" Lila asked the senator, forging ahead. "You spent some time with your cousin's children the other day. Was it nice having a practice run for the real thing?"

Dubois laughed and squeezed Jewel's hand. Her sister paled and sipped her soup, not saying a word in answer. Perhaps it was guilt. Perhaps her sister had begun wondering if she was the reason the pair couldn't conceive.

"It was very nice. We had a great deal of fun at the park. You should have come too, Pax. Your father misses you. Perhaps tomorrow?"

"Perhaps. I have a lot of studying to do."

"The boy is always studying," Chairwoman Randolph said off-handedly. She looked over her spoon to her eldest daughter. "Lila, don't do anything that slights Ms. Park tonight. The last thing we need is another—"

"You mean I shouldn't advise Ms. Park to select a mole for her family's coat of arms? Or a squirrel?"

"A sheep?" added Pax with a soft chuckle.

Lila poked her little brother in the belly. Her giggle was somewhat stunted when she realized how flat his stomach had gotten. Perhaps she'd buy some chocolate from Violet's to tempt him. The boy always had a sweet tooth. "A vulture?"

"A minnow?" Shiloh offered, not wanting to be left out but fighting all the decorum he'd learned at Bullstow.

"A tapeworm!"

"A flea!"

"A roach!"

"A stinkbug!" Lila said, raising her arms as though she'd won a race.

Her father pursed his lips, trying very hard not chuckle and encourage their impropriety.

Even Alex's face lit up with a fraction of a smirk.

Jewel frowned. "Why not a beautiful like a peacock or a—"

"Children." The chairwoman clapped for silence. "Ms. Park doesn't need your suggestions. She's likely had her coat of arms designed for years. Everyone has known the Wilsons would fall eventually. It has only happened sooner than expected, what with the executions looming."

"Madam," Lila said, a tone of warning entering her voice.

"What, Lila? We all knew they'd fall, given the family's poor breeding and poor business sense. They've never been anything but workborns and criminals putting on airs. Now they are back where they belong."

"Madam."

"Everyone's said it for years. Barely educated, barely refined, completely inelegant. You should have heard the stories about Celeste when I attended Bokington."

Lila put down her spoon, her gaze flashing quickly to Alex. Her old friend stared at the wall, her jaw tight. They'd heard plenty of stories when they attended the highborn university. None of them had been pleasant and most of them had been made up. Lila seriously doubted that Alex's mother had ever mixed her drinks with chicken blood or participated in orgies with workborn, much less film them.

Her mother noticed the rage in Alex's eyes, and grinned victoriously. "You know, I heard about this one time when Celeste—"

"Mother, you're being needlessly cruel."

"I'm just making conversation. Tell me, has Bullstow set a date for her and her son's execution? I think I should like to attend. Chairwoman Holguín might even tempt me into drinking a glass of Sangre. It's been two decades since I've—"

"Mother."

"What? I'd just like to pay my respects," she said, and took a sip of her Gregorie. "Can't a matron drink to another matron as she goes not so gently into that good night?"

Lila stood up and nodded to the others at the table. "Dinner was lovely, but I have a—"

"Sit down," her mother said sharply, her own tone of warning creeping into her voice. "We haven't even had the salmon yet. Besides, Chef has made some of her famous petit fours for dessert. Why let a little thing like the Wilson matron keep you from them?"

"It's not the Wilson matron who's keeping me from them. Who's the inelegant one now?"

"Sit down."

"Then stop baiting the help, Mother. It's low."

The rest of the room stared at their soup awkwardly. She couldn't believe her father hadn't jumped in yet, either to call out her mother or to support Lila while she forged ahead.

The chairwoman's nostrils flared. Lila hadn't seen her matron so angry in years. "Don't you dare 'Mother' me, Elizabeth. Not when Celeste and her bratty spawn tried to kill you. You, my

eldest daughter! Maybe you've forgiven them, but I haven't. If
they'd hired someone competent for the murder, you'd be dead
right now and none of us would have had the pleasure of your
company for dinner, such as it is."

"That has nothing to do with—"

"With Ms. Wilson?" her mother said, placing her spoon onto
the table. "Doesn't it? I'm not baiting her, Lila, I'm giving her one
last chance to prove that she can hold her temper. Some best friend
you chose. If you'd tossed her away like I'd advised and found one
of better quality, you could have a real friend at your side to work
through whatever it is you're feeling, whatever issues have crept up
from being nearly murdered a block away from your own compound,
from being tranqed and left for dead on the sidewalk like common
gutter trash. Instead you barely eat and you run off to do gods know
what in the middle of the night without telling any of us where
you are. Or all day when you should be safe in the security office."

"Mother—"

"If you had a real friend, she wouldn't have turned her back on
you after her mother and brother nearly killed you. If they'd had
their way, she'd be mourning your death instead of wishing for it.
Perhaps the little brat forgets that, but I certainly do not."

Lila dropped her gaze, not daring look at Alex's face.

"You dare ask me to spare her feelings? What about mine? What
about Pax's?"

Her brother looked down at his plate, his eyes reddening. It was
a red Lila had seen too often in the last week. She'd just chalked
it up to Trevor, to a relapse of grief. Perhaps she'd been wrong.
Perhaps it had been about almost losing his sister so soon after
losing his best friend.

"What of your own feelings? Her family almost killed you, and
you've done nothing but obsess about her. It makes me ill. Whatever happened between the pair of you is trivial compared to
attempted murder."

Dubois licked his lips and patted Jewel's back.

Her sister grew pale at his touch.

None of their discomfort seemed to bother her mother. She merely pushed harder and harder. "I've seen how the brat looks at you, when she bothers to look at you at all. Refusing to do her duty and serve you, forcing Isabel to do the job of two and take time away from her family." The chairwoman faced Alex, who immediately shifted her gaze to the floor. "Then she dares to assault you in front of the High Council? The fact that she laid her hands on you at all is revolting, much less her attitude after you arrested her. I would disgrace myself if I admitted the sort of punishments that have run through my mind since I found out."

"Mother—"

"The brat should be too ashamed to meet your eyes, Elizabeth, too horrified that you almost died by her family's own hand. A few hundred years ago, she would have offered you the sword of her family's militia chief, asking you to plunge it into her heart to free her from her family's shame. That is why she has poor breeding. You and I understand the depths and bounds of friendship and family. Workborns do not. She does not."

"No one does that any longer," Lila murmured.

"We understand the sentiment. We do it symbolically. Ms. Wilson does not, and she has the audacity to continue her little snit, not only in private, not only in front of you, but in front of the family and the High Council. She should be hanged with the rest, and good riddance. I could have dangled her before the highborn at parties, but I let her stay here with her dignity because you asked for it. You've done too much for the girl. You've been a far better friend to her than she's been to you because you are blind to her true nature. It's time you figured that out."

"She's my best friend. She's the most loyal, the most—"

"Holly was your best friend. Why do you think I let the girl stay on the compound? Why do you think I tried to save her when she grew ill? She had workborn breeding, but a highborn heart, and you dishonor her memory by sticking up for this trash now. Ms.

Wilson is not fit to serve the family. You say she's loyal? Loyal to whom? To you? To Jewel?"

Jewel swallowed and clenched her spoon.

"Ms. Wilson isn't loyal to anyone but herself."

"Even if she never speaks to me again, I trust her," Lila replied. "Until she tells me that she wishes to move to another compound or to another family, she stays."

Alex's eyes met hers for a few moments, then settled back to the floor.

"That decision is not yours to make, Elizabeth."

"Stop calling me Elizabeth, Mother. I'm not five, and I've done nothing wrong. But if you try and move Alex out of here, I just might. We're going to have a problem."

Her mother sipped her wine. "You mean this isn't already a problem?"

"She's my friend."

"You deserve better. You always have."

Lila stood up again and slowly pushed her chair under the table. "You've said what you wanted to say, madam. I do not wish to keep the High Council waiting."

She turned toward the door and heard the clack of high heels dashing forward.

"Ms. Wilson, stand at your place," her mother snapped as Lila retreated from the room.

18

Lila's stomach growled as she drove her roadster through downtown New Bristol, its street lamps bright, its lowborn crowd well dressed in tailored suits and tailored dresses, its storefronts clean and inviting. After her mother's lecture, she'd gone back to her room in an attempt to quell her rumbling belly, inhaling a few of Chef's cookies and a chunk of fudge.

Obviously, it hadn't been enough.

Her stomach protested again.

"Shut up," she grumbled, tapping on the roadster's steering wheel as she stopped at a light, eyeing a burger joint on the corner with a silly, fries-shaped neon sign and feasting patrons. She could have stopped at the militia cafeteria before she left, but she hated the idea of the chairwoman smirking at reports that she'd eaten somewhere else after storming out.

She'd been right to leave. Her mother shouldn't have attacked Alex, for her old friend had nothing to do with her family's crimes, nor was it fair when the slave couldn't defend herself without risking her master's wrath. Besides, her mother had no idea what Lila had done to deserve Alex's treatment. Regardless of whether Alex had been happy to help, it had been wrong to ask her friend to betray her family.

She hadn't been thinking. She'd merely wanted to solve the case.

When the light changed, Lila breezed through the intersection and sped to Bullstow. She parked her roadster in her usual spot and padded through the back door of the High Council wing. No senators lingered, hoping to flirt their way into a season.

What a shame. She'd spent practically the entire day with Tristan, and still he demanded more of her time. It didn't matter that she wanted to return to the shop instead of going to Bullstow, to slip back into his bed, to call out his name while his tongue and cock worked at her for hours, while they curled up together and fell asleep, hot and sticky and spent.

Lila shook her head. The entire situation was too much. She needed to take another lover or else her feelings for Tristan might spiral out of control.

She had to pull her head out of her pants. Soon.

Lila opened the door to the High Council chambers. The three women inside looked up, tilted their heads curiously, then checked their palms.

"What happened?" Johanna asked, showing her device to Lila. Large digital numbers blinked back. Six thirty-five. "You're never early. You're rarely even on time. Did the empire's hell freeze over?"

Chairwoman Masson giggled, then cleared her throat. "Sorry, chief, she does have a point. Not that you're late all the—"

Lila rolled her eyes and turned around, leaving the building once again. Twenty-five minutes might not be enough time to beg dinner from her father at Falcon Home, but it was enough time to stop at a café for a bagel and hot chocolate.

She'd probably be late, but apparently everyone expected it.

Screw the council.

Lila stumbled into Rosebuds, a café across the street filled with simple oak tables and benches under a hundred twinkling lights in the ceiling. They were set to simulate starlight, only bright enough to capture the text on a book or a palm or a laptop. She ordered a bagel and cream cheese and sipped at a mug of hot chocolate while groups of students studied. Their burgundy jackets had been embroidered with golden roses, their breeches slightly wrinkled from their day at school. Most had not a hair out of place, even so late in the afternoon, even as they puzzled over texts and papers.

These students were serious. These students aimed for the Saxony Senate, for Unity, for the prime minister's chair.

These students aimed to partner with women like her.

It didn't take long for the bravest boy to wander toward her, a boy who couldn't have been older than seventeen with his baby cheeks and smooth chin. She'd wanted a senator to take her mind off Tristan, not a boy who couldn't shave yet.

She shook her head and pointed back at his chair.

The boy's friends erupted into laughter, slapping him on the back when he returned, the reward for daring to approach Chief Randolph.

Her palm vibrated in her pocket as she finished her bagel. *Come see me after the High Council meeting*, Max had written.

Lila frowned. *No time. What did you find?*

Her palm vibrated again. He'd called instead of writing another message. "Lila, why didn't you tell me you were in trouble?" he said without his usual greeting. "What were you doing and where were you doing it when this asshole caught you?"

"It's none your concern. Just tell me what you found."

"This asshole is threatening my friend. It damn well is my concern."

"I'll deal with it."

"Will you? It doesn't seem like you are from my end. You didn't even call to check on my progress this morning."

"I didn't want to distract you," she lied, knowing she'd been too busy to devote time or energy to her blackmailer. "I have a council meeting in ten minutes. I don't have time to play twenty questions. Just tell me what you found."

"Blow it off and come over. We'll spend all night finding this asshole."

"I don't have time. Please, Max."

There was a long pause. Lila sipped her hot chocolate and checked her palm, wondering if he'd hung up on her, but the line remained open.

"The message came from a boy named Xavier Masson."

"A Masson boy?" Lila asked, barely able to hold her surprise. "Why don't I know that name?"

"Because he died five years ago, just a few weeks before his sixteenth birthday. There was a car accident near his family's compound in New Lisbon. Someone stole his ID and used it to contact you. I looked for other activity online. The thief has sent a few messages here and there in the last few years, all as cryptic as yours. Most receivers lived in New Bristol."

"That's impossible. My snoops flagged it as a fake account."

"Yes, and Xavier is the one who comes up when you dig through the layers. Why do you think it took me so long to find him?"

"Send me the information, would you?"

"No. Come over after your meeting. We'll figure this out together. I dug into the thief's bank account number. It's tied to a bank in Burgundy. The system isn't that sophisticated. We'll hack it. We'll—"

"I haven't the time, Max. I have other things on my plate."

"Make time. This is more important."

"I have to go."

"If you don't make time, Lila, what's going to become of you? I'm worried. You should be worried as well."

"I'll look into it more deeply after my meeting."

"If you don't find him tonight, then pay."

"I can't. I'm the damn chief of security. How can I—"

"Damn your pride, woman. This isn't a game. He's threatening to expose you. You don't have time to play the wounded heir. Where did you poke your nose?"

"Thanks, Max. I'll take it from here," she said before disconnecting.

Lila drained the rest of her chocolate and left the café.

A Masson boy might mean a Masson blackmailer.

When she returned to the High Council chamber and plopped into her crimson chair, Johanna held up her palm. Five minutes past seven flashed back at Lila.

"Let's begin," Élise said. "We have a few items to discuss before we call Ms. Park."

The group waded through the several items of expected legislation and court cases, weighing convictions and judging laws as
good or bad for business. The Low Council of Judges would do
the same, one wing over. Whenever the two groups didn't agree,
the highborn would look to the populace to make their decision.
If polling indicated a high surge of lowborn and workborn support and it wasn't too bad for business, the High Council often
allowed themselves to be swayed. That was rare, though. Usually,
they merely took the most prominent among the Low Council
out for tea, offering gentle reminders about who allowed their
businesses to run in the city unfettered.

Usually that solved the problem.

From time to time, though, a lowborn disobeyed the highborn
and charged ahead on a piece of legislation. From time to time,
that lowborn's business went under.

The matron who conquered the lowborn would win her in
the auction house by default, for the other matrons wouldn't bid.
It was one of those unwritten rules of being a highborn. A rare
instance of solidarity among rivals.

But nothing tonight was that contentious. The High Council
finished their last vote within an hour and sent a servant to fetch
Ms. Park from a nearby waiting room.

Lila checked her messages in the interlude, gratified to find
Max's information waiting, as promised. She'd also received a voice
message from Captain Regina Randolph, most likely Natalie's test
results. Unfortunately, Lila had no clever excuse to sneak from
the room.

The three messages the captain left afterward piqued her curiosity, though.

With effort, she put away her palm as Ms. Park entered, taking
her place at the podium, ready to walk them through her proposal.
Her silver hair had been tied into an elegant bun, and she wore a
simple dress cut in silver. It was daring, very daring to wear silver
on such an occasion, but the future chairwoman did not shrink

under any displeased looks that came her way. Instead, she matched them, chastising anyone who gave her a critical stare.

Finally, her gaze stopped on Lila's blackcoat. It was the first time Ms. Park lost her composure, though only for a split-second. As far as she was concerned, Lila had taken down an entire family, a family her mother had already put in checkmate years before. That was what happened to families who angered the Randolphs.

The blackcoat might be the most dangerous one of all.

Lila wondered if Ms. Park knew she could crush her dreams in an instant. Her eldest son had made a mockery of Bullstow, and the woman likely knew everything he'd been up to. She had to suspect that Lila could have found out as well, that she could stop the entire meeting and have her son brought before the council to answer for every piece of circumstantial nonsense he'd done in his not-so illustrious career. If that didn't work, she could always mention Bo Park, that distant cousin who had just been arrested in the same sting as Natalie Holguín. She too had been caught in Reaper's web.

After that, the council would balk at admitting her into the highborn.

But Lila didn't believe that Ms. Park should lose her shot due to an idiot son and a distant relation, though it did make for an awfully nice trump card until the Park family's confirmation became official.

Ms. Park cleared her throat and looked away, shuffling the papers on the podium.

"The next item on the agenda," Élise began, "is Ms. Suji Park's request to join New Bristol's highborn. Ms. Park, we have copies of your proposal. Begin when you are ready."

Lila flipped through the booklet, which described Ms. Park's tenure on the Low Council of Judges, as well as the facts and figures of her family, outlining every company and holding, at least the ones she wanted the rest of the highborn to know about. Her R&D departments seemed much too small, but they all knew the bulk of it would be hidden to stave off corporate espionage. Lila skimmed the sections detailing how the Parks might partner with each family, expanding upon their business interests and increasing everyone's revenue.

As Ms. Park droned on about her proposed expansions, Lila put down the booklet and studied the woman, ignoring the whole load of fluff and twaddle coming from the potential matron's mouth. Ms. Park would sit on the council in a few months. They'd throw her a party, and she'd be thrown into the viper pit.

Gods help the woman.

Lila's mother had called them potential allies, which meant that Lila would be sent to meet with her and her eldest daughter, to explain in blunt detail how to navigate the new world they'd been thrust into, to give them the cards of a few tailors, not tailors that impressed the lowborn, but tailors who were only acceptable to the highborn and their spoiled children.

Ms. Park had been ballsy to dress as she had, and she'd been ballsy to look the High Council in the eye and not flinch, except perhaps a bit with Lila. Ms. Park's daughter was a copy of her mother. She'd make a strong prime and a strong matron. Neither understood the show of it, though. Neither understood how to play their parts.

That was half the game.

One thing was for sure: if Ms. Park grew annoyed at the appalling waste of time Lila often encountered during High Council meetings, then Lila might have found a friend.

Well, not exactly a friend. Matrons and primes were never friends. Lila and Alex couldn't have been, not if Alex had become the Wilson's prime.

But they could be friendly.

"If you'll look on page forty-two," Ms. Park said, moving on to the most trivial bits of her proposal, "I have included the request for my family's colors."

Lila sat up, mildly curious what color the new family would wear. But when she turned the page, she couldn't help but laugh.

Gold. Ms. Park would ask for the Wilson family color before their matron had even been executed. She either had moxie, or she was completely blind to the significance of her play.

The rest of the council gasped, their gazes lifting to the potential matron. Though Ms. Park had schooled her expression, Lila could see that she'd expected the reaction. She knew exactly what she had done, and she stared back unflinchingly, showing the highborn that she'd take whatever she could get as soon as she could get it. She'd tossed out whatever girlish dreams she had in favor of what proved the most politically expedient, the most daring. The show of it didn't elude her at all.

Perhaps Ms. Park and her daughter wouldn't need as much coaching as Lila had thought.

Perhaps they wouldn't be as friendly as Lila had hoped, either.

The women in the room studied Lila. When a matron took down a house, the color belonged to the victor's family, free to grant or deny to the next matron who might desire it. Ms. Park must have known about this unofficial rule. She looked toward Lila, a little twist at the corner of her mouth. This was her first deal as a new matron, Lila realized. An olive branch to the Randolph family, and a very public one. She was declaring early, attempting to align herself.

Johanna and Élise seethed.

Ms. Park had chosen well. Only three New Bristol families had seats on the Saxony High Council, and the Randolphs were first among them. They had the other New Bristol families in their pocket.

At least most of the time.

"I think it would be a shame to let such a prosperous color wait for another family," Lila said, knowing her mother would approve. "I only ask that you endeavor to bring it more honor and integrity than its last owner."

"Certainly, Chief Randolph." Ms. Park bowed her head. "My proposed coat of arms is on the next page."

Lila turned the page, curiosity revived. From what she'd seen on television, lowborn and workborn girls constantly doodled coats of arms in the margins of their economics notes, at the bottom of their math homework, and signed every art project with the symbol. Ms. Park had likely been drawing this coat of arms for her entire life.

It was beautiful for something modified in a rush. A golden bear on a golden background, mouth open to rend and bite, paw lifted to punch and slice its opponent. Such a coat of arms would serve her and her family well.

Underneath, Lila read their proposed motto. *Loyalty preserved enriches.*

"A fair showing, Ms. Park," Élise said primly as the lowborn concluded her proposal. "You may now leave our chambers so that we may begin deliberations. Expect to hear back from us before the season ends."

Ms. Park bowed and left the council chambers.

As soon as she was gone, Élise swiveled in her chair. "Now that we've heard from Ms. Park, I believe we should discuss alternative—"

"Fine. Discuss them without me." Lila stood up and shoved her chair under the table. She then leaned on its back, eyeing Élise and Johanna grumpily. "This woman has attended nearly every highborn party in the last two decades because she's had enough money and favor to snake the invitations. She and her family conduct herself far better than the last family this council voted in, and she rakes in more money than some of the highborn families in this room. No other family in the city comes close to her qualifications. Let the record show that the House of the Crimson Wolves votes to include Ms. Suji Park among the highborn. I have better things to do than let you waste my time with candidates this council will ultimately reject."

"We might not reject—"

"We will. Her proposal outstrips any others you could find in Saxony, which is why we invited her here in the first place. And regardless of how she stacks up against any other candidate you could drag into this council room, she's the only potential matron in New Bristol who would have walked into this room and pulled the stunts she did. If nothing else, she should be admitted for brashness and style alone."

"This isn't a fashion show," Élise grumbled.

"And be glad for that," Johanna agreed, crinkling her nose at Lila's blackcoat.

"Call the vote, Élise," Chairwoman Masson said. "Chief Randolph has a point. This is tedious, and I'm sure we all have work to finish at home."

"Fine. All in favor of seeking more families for inclusion?"

Chairwoman Masson sighed heavily.

Only Élise and Johanna raised their hands.

Seeing little support, Élise didn't even bother to finish the vote or make it official. "All in favor of the Park family joining the highborn?"

The other nine families raised their hands.

Seeing they would be outnumbered, Élise and Johanna raised their hands as well. It wouldn't do for the public record to reflect the slight. Ms. Park and her family would always remember any family who dared vote against their entry.

Rarely did families vote against a nomination.

Not unless you were Ophelia Randolph.

"Fine," Élise said, banging her gavel. "Let the record show that the Park family will be admitted into our ranks during the first High Council meeting of next year's legislative session."

Just like that, Ms. Suji Park and her entire family became highborn.

19

After sweeping her bedroom for bugs, Lila changed into her comfiest pair of cotton pajamas pants and a worn t-shirt with the words *Randolph Militia* scrawled across her chest. She tended to do her best work in her pajamas, and the High Council meeting had drained her, as had replying to Tristan's message.

Or not replying.

He'd missed her. Again. And he wanted her to know it.

She'd fumbled for several moments after receiving it, unsure how to answer. When they'd first started up, she hoped things would become less confusing. Unfortunately, the opposite had occurred. Everything was more and more confusing the more they saw of one another. Tristan wanted a great deal from her, and all the messages about how he missed her were pressing down on her chest, suffocating her.

Her thumb hovered over *Delete*. Instead of tapping it, she moved the message to Tristan's folder. She'd not yet been able to get rid of any of them. To make matters worse, she almost wanted to back up the folder on her desktop computer, because if anyone else picked up her palm and didn't enter her code properly, her palm would erase itself.

She didn't care about most of her data, but she cared about Tristan's. His messages seemed important somehow. Perhaps that was what suffocated her—not necessarily Tristan's declarations, but that his words held power over her. They spurred her to do things she didn't want to do, like keeping a host of messages due to sentimentality.

She sent Tristan a message that she'd see him soon, then tossed her palm onto her desk. It slid, nearly falling off the other side. Seconds later, she found herself grabbing it again and backing up the damn folder, slamming the small device on her bed afterward.

Her cheeks warmed as she glared at her desktop computer, but at least she wasn't an obsessive idiot any longer.

Sipping on a mug of hot chocolate, she checked the search for Natalie's brothels. Since it hadn't finished, she pushed it to the background and pulled up the results of the blood tests. The numbers meant very little to Lila, but Captain Randolph had attached a brief voice message explaining them. Natalie had not had been under the influence of alcohol or drugs when she died. Neither had her guards. But the lab director had found something infinitely more interesting. She'd discovered a substance that might be a tracer in Natalie's blood, as well as the blood of several of her guards.

Tracers?

"Shit, shit, shit, shit, shit," Lila said, leaping from her seat as though she'd been burned, her hand covering her gaping mouth while she fumbled for her palm.

Tracers were a Roman technology the Allied Lands hadn't figured out yet, though not for lack of trying. Once they'd been injected or ingested, the target could be located for the next thirty-six hours, so long as they were within a few kilometers. Though GPS bugs might be more lasting and comprehensive, even lowborns had developed ways to detect and deactivate them.

No such counters existed for tracers. If you had a team large enough to murder almost a dozen thugs, then you had enough people to canvass all of New Bristol in a day and a half, searching for a tracer's signal.

"You stupid woman," Lila whispered as she typed Captain Randolph's ID into her palm. "You should have known better than to drink with mercs from the empire."

Tristan had been right. German mercs were involved. Not even the highborn families had ever been able to get their hands on tracers. The Germans had stolen Oskar, and they hadn't even been subtle about it. Perhaps they'd assumed that Bullstow wouldn't find the tracers. It wasn't as if the Allied Lands had a blood test to detect them.

"Walk the sample to the Burgess Building," Lila told Captain Randolph as soon as she picked up. "Personally."

Captain Randolph laughed. "No need. I'm in the lobby as we speak. I told Director Randolph to stay at work until you called her. She already knows something is up."

"Good. Share nothing except the sample, not even a hint of where it came from."

"Of course. I nearly beat down the door of Villanueva House until a footman told me you were at a High Council meeting," the captain said in a rush, the giddiness palpable in her voice. "I wouldn't even have suspected if my snoop programs hadn't caught a whiff of something strange when I scanned the lab. This is serious, chief. And seriously time sensitive. The sample will degrade substantially after thirty-six hours. How old is it?"

"Best guess? Around twelve hours old. Tell no one else about the sample. No one."

"You didn't procure it legally, did you?"

"I have to call Director Randolph."

Lila disconnected and called Viola Randolph, the director of her bioengineering R&D department, quickly explaining what the sample would contain. She'd barely gotten the words out before she heard frantic button-pushing and the dings of an elevator in the background.

The director made quick promises to rouse her entire team, assuring Lila that they'd spend the next twenty-fours working on the sample. Then she made the usual vow to not ID-test the blood, and quickly disconnected.

If Lila knew the group at all, they'd run to the lab and get started immediately without complaint even if stopped mid-orgasm. She'd just handed them the best Winter Solstice gift of their lives, nearly two months early. They'd talk about it for years, and they'd be famous throughout the Allied Lands if they managed to replicate the tracer.

No one would know where it came from, so long as no one ran a DNA test. The way she'd given the instructions would leave little doubt in anyone's mind. The sample was the product of corporate espionage. Running DNA tests would effectively incriminate the entire lab team, making them accessories. Neither lab director had gotten their jobs by being stupid, and both knew better than to move against the heirs.

No scientist had any desire to end up a slave. Slaves didn't win science prizes, and they certainly didn't end up in the history books. They'd do whatever it took to duplicate the tracer quietly. Once her people figured out how it worked, they'd figure out how to counter the stuff so it wouldn't affect the Randolph family.

Then they'd keep the antidote, sell the tracer, and make a fortune.

Lila sipped her chocolate and broke into Bullstow's database, peeking into Natalie's murder investigation. She and Tristan had been right. Natalie and her people had died around eight o'clock that morning. The ballistics team confirmed that the bullets lodged in the bodies were German-made and fired from German guns.

Not German hands, though. Bullstow believed that the Holguíns had killed Natalie for the shame she'd brought upon the family, knowing that more of her crimes would be revealed if her case went to court. They, like many highborn families, simply decided to spare their family the embarrassment of a trial and regain their family's honor and protect themselves from Natalie's wrath after exile.

They just hadn't done it legally. The family's blood squad should have taken Natalie while she tarried on the Holguín estate. She should have gone missing, never to be seen or heard from again. Instead, they'd surrounded Natalie off-compound, killing nearly a dozen workborn criminals in the process. Even worse, they'd left the bodies for Bullstow to clean up.

That rankled Bullstow. They could not ignore it, not that they believed they were meant to. The Holguíns had left Natalie there for a reason. Indeed, Bullstow thought they had the key to the elaborate death scene. Acquiring German guns might have been difficult but not impossible, certainly not when one had the resources of the entire Holguín family at their disposal. The Bullstow teddy bear at the scene had been an easy prop, for Oskar had taken it with him from the auction house. Both pointed to German mercs. With Natalie and the Germans as patsies and a believable cover story, Chairwoman Holguín would be free to make a deal for Oskar with anyone she liked, selling him without the stern eyes of Bullstow focused on her compound.

Indeed, Bullstow would be too busy chasing kidnappers who did not exist.

The plan was so thoroughly highborn and brilliant that Lila had to applaud Bullstow for coming up with it. It was certainly much more plausible than German mercenaries stealing into New Bristol, something Chief Shaw thought rather unlikely, given the number who would have to be hidden in the city to pull off the murders. Besides, he probably believed that Natalie was too clever to lead mercs back to her hideout.

Shaw didn't know about the tracers, though. He also didn't have the most discreet militia. Now that Bullstow knew Oskar was missing, the press and the matrons would know as soon as the first spies got hold of the information.

So would the empire.

Lila dug into the files submitted by Shaw's tech department next. The group hadn't been able to break into Natalie's star drive. They'd only managed to break the encryption on the palms, but they only found a few naughty photos and silly games.

Lila closed her connection to Bullstow and brought up the contents of Natalie's star drive once more. After an hour of digging, all she found that pertained to Oskar was a few incriminating messages. It appeared that Natalie had been contacted by a friend of a friend. For a small fee, that friend offered to connect Natalie with someone who would pay good money for the boy, so long as she didn't mind who might be buying him.

Natalie had replied that she didn't care who bought him or where he ended up, so long as she got paid on delivery. She just needed to know the amount and who was buying.

The messages made it easy to guess the buyers would be German. It also made it easier for Lila to deal with the image of Natalie and her thugs dead on the concrete.

Shaking her head, she delved into the palm data, looking for any clues about who might have brokered the deal. There were no blinking arrows, no flashing neon lights. All she found were naughty pictures and silly games, just like Bullstow. She even ran the pictures through a few programs that might extract codes or secret messages from the pixels, but found nothing.

In the end, she even looked at the games. Two appeared on all three palms. In the first, the player navigated a swiftly swimming fish through more and more precarious surroundings by turning the palm. Since *Fast Fish* had broken many sales records throughout the Allied Lands in the previous month, she wasn't that surprised. The second game confused her, though, for she'd never seen it and it seemed to be broken. Nearly a dozen cartoon aliens clumped in the center of the screen, which flickered every few seconds. The score didn't budge from three thousand no matter how many buttons she pushed, no matter how many times she turned her palm.

"Stupid game."

She poured out her chocolate in the bathroom sink, too full of sugar to drink the rest. Instead, she poured herself a glass of water and checked the results for Natalie's brothels. She found twelve probable locations, though by her estimates, there should only have been seven or eight.

Yawning, Lila considered pulling up Max's data and looking for Xavier, but she still had two days to dig into it. Instead, she began the search for Natalie's friend. The message Natalie had received had come from somewhere. Someone would be on the other end of the chain. She just had to dig deeply enough.

Lila was so engrossed in her task that she almost didn't hear the knock on her bedroom window. Startling, she shot up and grabbed her tranq gun in one fluid movement, aiming at the drapes.

Tristan waved behind the glass.

Lila looked down at her attire. He'd never seen her dressed down so completely, and she was dressed down. Way down. All the way to the basement down. Even her hair was a mess. At some point she had wound it into a messy bun with a pen.

Putting down her Colt, she opened the window and quickly herded him into her room, worried someone would see him before he hopped inside. He'd dressed in black trousers with a dark hoodie over a dark gray t-shirt, probably so he wouldn't be seen. But if anyone did see him, he'd look so suspicious they'd have to chase after him. "How did you get in here, you idiot?" she whispered, closing the window behind him.

"I walked. You seem to forget sometimes that I'm quite capable—"

"Of doing really stupid things? The first thing militias do is a DNA stick."

"They'd have to catch me first. You're never afraid of your identity being exposed when you come into my shop. Why should it stop me from waltzing into your compound?"

"Your people can't arrest me and throw me into slavery," she said, glad her sister had run off for the night with Senator Dubois. Pax and her mother slept like logs and the walls weren't thin, so it wasn't likely they'd hear Tristan's voice.

Not likely, but not impossible. Pax sometimes came into her room for a chat when he couldn't sleep. After her mother's words at dinner, Lila couldn't help but think he might.

"Any one of my people could ruin your career, and yet you still come."

Lila frowned and closed the drapes, carefully settling the cloth around the window.

"I shouldn't have said that." Tristan pushed a lock of hair from her face. "None of them would ever say a word if they found out. They'd respect you more for helping, for—"

"You were right the first time. How'd you get here? No one gets into my compound without me knowing about it."

"Even after all this time, you doubt my abilities?"

"Keep your voice down."

Tristan stepped away from the window and twirled around her room, his eyes locking on every piece of furniture, every pillow, every picture. He peeked inside her closet, studying every uniform and dress and pair of shoes. He even poked his head into her bathroom.

"It's not what I thought it would be."

"What did you think it would be?"

"I thought there would be more to it somehow. Bigger? Filled with expensive things? Like priceless art and a golden bathtub. You don't belong here, Lila. It's too drab. You're too alive for a place like this."

"The fewer things you have in a room, the easier and faster it is to scan for bugs."

"You do that nonsense in your own bedroom?"

"Every time I come home."

"I thought you said no one could get into your compound."

"I don't do it for outsiders."

Tristan tilted his head.

"I was six months old the first time someone tried to hurt me. A member of the family slipped poison into my bottle. I should have died, reducing the prime's queue. Checking for bugs is almost quaint in comparison."

His jaw dropped. "I can't believe you have to be that vigilant with your own family. You're supposed to trust them. Dixon never had to do that stuff."

"Dixon is male and probably wasn't that important in the grand scheme of things."

"He was important enough." He fingered the silver coat of arms above her couch. "Do you test this as well?"

"It's the first place anyone tries to plant a bug. It's symbolic, I suppose. I wouldn't even keep it on the wall, but my sister made it, and I couldn't put up anything else she made me."

"That bad?"

"No, her work is exquisite, but none of it is right for me."

He wandered back over to her dresser and picked up a picture among the two dozen frames. In it, a very young Lila and a fair-haired girl bowed their heads over a bowl of dough, cheeks brushed with flour. "Is this Holly?"

Lila took the photo and settled it carefully back on her dresser. "Why are you here, Tristan? Why are you on my compound?"

Tristan's arms snaked around her waist, and he dropped his chin on top of her head. "Because I missed you. You don't miss me when I'm not around, do you?"

Lila shrugged and lifted her lips, knowing why he'd really come. She wanted it too.

He pulled away. "I didn't come here for that, Lila."

"You found something?"

"No, but we're still looking."

"An update from me, then?" Lila returned to her desk, kicking her bare feet onto it while she clacked away at the keyboard.

Tristan stared, stifling a little grin.

"What?"

He sat at the edge of her desk. "It's just that I've imagined you at home so many times doing this, doing your research thing. And here you are." He wrapped his hand around her toes, warming them. "I've never really noticed your feet before."

"You saw them last night."

"I was busy looking at other things. They're sort of adorable."

"Focus, Tristan."

"You're blushing."

Lila looked away, but her gaze snapped back when he began massaging the balls of her feet. She slid down in her chair as he worked, trying not to moan.

"I didn't come here for an update, but go ahead. Update me if you can."

When she didn't immediately start speaking, he deepened the massage. "Focus, Lila."

Lila wiggled her ankles, but he held on, grinning wider. Oh, how she hated that grin, the grin that let him get away with so much, so often. "Why did you come? You used to be all about the job. You used to send me message after message about nothing but work. Kids are missing, and you don't seem to care."

His hands stopped. "I care. I care a great deal, but I almost lost you because of the job. I almost lost Dixon because of the job. I almost lost the two people I care about most because—" He looked away. "If I hadn't been so focused on the job, you wouldn't have nearly gotten pinched on Leclerc Street. Peter Kruger wouldn't have almost killed you. Reaper wouldn't have had a knife to your neck, either. I'm done living for the job, Lila. There's more to life than work. I want both. I'll have both."

"I applaud the sentiment, but there are children missing."

"We'll find them." He looked her in the eye and started rubbing her feet again. "I know I'm annoying you, but I can't help myself."

"Why?"

"Because tomorrow almost didn't come for you. Twice. Tomorrow almost didn't come for Dixon, either. I find myself unable to pretend patience."

Lila squirmed in her chair, unsure what to say.

"If you don't mind, I'd like to know what you've found now that you've mentioned it, but I'm going to keep playing with your feet. I like them."

"Great, you have a foot fetish. If you start licking my toes, I swear to the gods I'll beat you with my militia boots."

"Maybe I'll lick them too. Maybe I'll lick you in other places. You liked it last night."

Lila looked away, knowing she'd blushed again.

Gods, when had she begun to do that?

Lila tried to wiggle her toes away again unsuccessfully, then told him about the tracers, about everything that Shaw had found in his investigations, and about everything she'd found on Natalie's star drive and palms. Everything except the brothels. Tristan wouldn't have the patience to wait, and Lila needed more time to ensure she found them all.

Tristan didn't seem surprised about the rest. "So the Germans did take Oskar."

"Yes, but which faction? The traditionalist tried to buy him in the auction, and the loyalists tried to murder him. Perhaps King Lucas wants his corpse as proof."

"Perhaps the traditionalists are taking him to Germany."

"At least he'd be alive. Either way, you should prepare Maria. I don't think I'm going to find Oskar in time. Perhaps if I'd ordered my list differently."

"Lila, that wasn't your fault. They'd been dead all morning, and you know it."

"I fooled around too long with the oracle. I fooled around with you. If I hadn't—"

"The oracle needs our help too."

"Trying to save both groups means I'm failing both of them."

Tristan knelt beside her. "You can only do so much, Lila. You do too much."

"It doesn't look like I'm doing enough, or else I would have found them by now. You should go home. I have to find Natalie's friend. I have to look into the missing girls."

Tristan yanked her closer, and her butt slid forward in the wooden chair. He slipped his arms around her and put his lips against hers.

Lila couldn't help but kiss back, pushing all thought to the back of her mind. Only Tristan's mouth existed, his arms around her, stroking the small of her back. She jerked as his tongue entered her mouth. Every flick promised more than a kiss.

But she didn't have time for that.

"We'll find them," he said, resting his forehead upon hers. "Come to bed. You're long past exhaustion, and I've missed you." He stared at her eyes, looking for…something. Perhaps he wanted to see if she'd smile, pull away, or if she'd wince. She blanked her face, trying not to show anything.

Seemingly not completely annoyed at what he found in her eyes, he tilted his head and kissed her again. Pulling her to the front of her seat, he caught hold of her ass and stood with a little grunt. Lila wrapped her legs around his waist, but felt nothing press between her legs. He merely held on to her. Perhaps he hadn't come for sex after all.

He stopped before her bed and put her down gently. "You're going to sleep for the next four hours. I'm not taking no for an answer."

Lila knew she wasn't relaxed enough to sleep. "I'll take a nap later. I'm not tired yet. I should—"

"Four hours."

"I'm not tired."

He grabbed the waist of her workout pants. "Fine, I'll make you tired."

Lila glanced back at her desktop computer, her resolve wavering. Perhaps she did need some sleep before continuing her search. Her mind had grown fuzzier and fuzzier as the hours stretched on. Besides, her only lead was Natalie's friend, but that lead wasn't a great one.

And the missing girls? Bullstow and the purplecoats were trying to find them.

She reached for the hem of her militia shirt, but Tristan stilled her hand. "No, leave it on. You have no idea how hard it's making me right now."

Lila started to pull down her pajama pants, but she barely got a chance. A wave of heat snaked up her belly as Tristan slipped his hand under her shirt and grazed her nipples. They hardened into nubs as his tongue entered her mouth.

His mouth bobbled while he kicked off his boots.

Lila pulled away and unzipped his hoodie, the sharp hiss lost amid their labored breathing. His gray t-shirt came next, the fabric cheap and new, discarded onto the growing pile on the floor. She spread her hands over his smooth skin, her thumbs grazing his body just as he had grazed her nipple, exploring every bulge of his arm, every ridge of his abdomen.

She fumbled at the button of his trousers, the zipper another hiss in the quiet. They undressed one another piecemeal, the lights on, staring at one another with every item that came off their bodies, kissing the newly revealed flesh, their hands passing over the exposed skin in waves of heat.

It was a type of foreplay, a dance without music, and it lasted much longer than the hurried job the night before.

At last, Tristan stood in his boxer briefs before her. He tugged off her panties, falling down to his knees as he pulled them down, tracing a finger from her navel all the way down to her thigh. Before she could step out, he stared up at her eyes, slipping a curling tongue between her legs, seeking, searching.

Lila jumped as the warm wetness of his tongue brushed her clit. "Fuck."

"That's the general idea." He chuckled, moving back to lavish attention on it once more.

Lila pushed him away gently. "You're rushing ahead."

He hopped up, keen to finish the game they'd begun playing. Lila reached for his boxer briefs, tracing the erection within, already waiting to be used.

He breathed hard as she grasped his waistband, falling to her knees as he had done before her. Once his boxers hit the floor, she licked his cock underneath from base to tip, then let her fingers play in the wetness she'd left behind. Then she put her lips around the tip and sucked him in.

Tristan moaned, his fingers flexing as he gripped her shoulders. "No," he panted, freeing his cock and helping her from the floor.

"I told you. I didn't come for that. I'm trying to put you to sleep, not get off."

He yanked the blankets off her bed with one quick pull, then gently laid her onto the mattress. Tilting her head, she watched him kneel at the foot of the bed.

He grabbed her foot, kissed the bottom and the top of it, then moved up her ankle, her calf, the side of her knee. He kissed and licked his way up her thigh, and she breathed in, watching him make his way to her clit.

She grabbed her headboard and squeezed so hard she thought she might break the wood.

At the last moment, Tristan turned his mouth away. "Now who's rushing?"

"I—"

Any response she might have made was taken away as he kissed her hipbone and her navel. His tongue shot out and he slowly, carefully licked up her breasts, pushing her t-shirt up to her neck. Latching on, he sucked each one into his mouth, nibbling until her nipple swelled and hardened in his mouth.

She grew wet between her legs, and she began to ache.

Tristan's cock poked her in the hip, in the belly, and tickled between her thighs so often that she wrapped one leg around his hips in an effort to wiggle him in, but Tristan did not thrust inside her. He merely kissed her lips, her neck, and her breasts. His body warmed her. His chest rose and fell. The clock marched on as though mischievous sprites had taken charge.

His finger curled around her clit.

She gasped, sinking into the bed. His tongue reached farther into her mouth, arching and curling. One skillful finger slipped inside her, doing the same, moving so slowly that she gripped her headboard out of frustration, rather than to steady herself.

A booming chuckle worked itself down her navel, interrupted with a nip. He moved down her hips and the inside of her thigh, his stubble brushing her smooth skin, her blood pumping throughout her body, moaning as the voice inside her head screamed along. All at once, a welcome, warm mouth fastened on her clit, claiming it as his own.

His tongue brushed her.

Lila nearly came from the expectation alone.

Tristan pulled his head back, letting her pant herself calm, then leaned forward again. She writhed on the bed as he worked at her, the pressure building higher and higher. The bed rocked back and forth from her shivers, and she stopped worrying about what she might do or might say. She stopped worrying about his feelings or hers. No thoughts of pulling away entered her mind. All she wanted was everything that was him inside of her.

A wave rushed through her as she came.

Tristan let it pass this time, his mouth still working.

He didn't pull away once she was done. His fingers returned, slipping in and out. Over and over and over he licked and thrust, his stubble brushing her thighs.

Her clit swelled wide, and her moans carried farther than the bed.

She couldn't take not having him inside her.

"Enough." She panted, pulling him up to her chest. He grinned and crawled atop her as she removed her shirt.

His grin was far too cocky.

Lila rolled him onto his back. She slid up his body as though he were a pole, tonguing each ridge, letting her hair tickle his skin from his knees to his chest, loving the way he sucked in his breath, enjoying the feel of him on her body.

She took his mouth as he had taken hers.

He thrust his hips.

She dodged.

"Sucks, doesn't it." Lila snickered, retreating down his body.

"Absolutely nothing about this sucks. This is all things—"

Suddenly, Lila put her lips around his cock and sucked hard.

"Fuck," he growled, quietening his voice before she had a chance to admonish him. He gripped her headboard as she had gripped it while she ran her tongue up and down his cock, gripping the rest with her hands, tight and warm. She squeezed and licked and stroked and sucked as though it were all of him, as if she could place her tongue on his entire body from that one handle of flesh like a joystick in a game.

"Stop."

Lila pulled her hands and mouth away. "What do—"

He didn't even stop to explain. He tossed her under him on the bed and slid inside her, thrusting quick and hard.

Three times.

She only needed two.

They moaned together, a harmonious little tune, played quietly so as not to disturb anyone but the players.

"Fuck," Tristan said as he flopped onto the bed beside her. "That was supposed to last longer. A lot longer." He hid his face under his arm and grabbed himself absently, trying to inspire his cock to come back to life. "Fuck."

"We could try again."

Tristan peered out from under his arm, and Lila laughed. She'd never seen him look so dejected. "You're good with your mouth. Too good."

"You're good with yours as well. Your fingers, too."

Lila traced her finger from his chin and across his throat, grinning as his body jerked to meet it. She snaked down his chest, down his navel, and trailed toward his cock. A shiver ran along his skin. Her fingers drifted along his shaft languidly as though she were nearly bored.

"Hello," he said, turning his head at his erection. "That usually lasts longer too. I think he likes you."

"I like him too."

"Do you?"

"Yes." She climbed atop him, spreading her legs and guiding his cock into her. "It's my turn."

"My turn didn't last as long as I would have—"

"Tough." She chuckled as he gripped the headboard.

She thrust her hips, tilting and bobbing as if in a dance. Warm, strong hands gripped her waist, and he joined in, both hearing the same tune, louder this time, and fiercer. She covered his hands with hers, enjoying the feel of him, enjoying the strong grip, the pumping.

The determination on his face, as though he wanted to last for hours this time.

She bit back a chuckle as she came, arching her back as he pumped.

Her moans were not joined. Instead he rolled her on the bed. His tongue entered her mouth, and he thrust inside her, his hands tracing her thighs as she curled her legs around his waist, squeezing as he pumped over and over again, both of them pressing their bodies together in a crush of hips and a mixing of tongues and limbs.

He got what he wanted in the end. He lasted while she came again in quiet moans.

Lifting her head, she sucked on his ear. "Come for me, Tristan," she whispered.

It was calling him by name that did it. He moaned softly in her ear while he spent himself inside her.

20

Lila yawned and groggily sat up, her motion greatly retarded by the pair of arms fixed around her waist. She wormed out of Tristan's grip and slithered onto the floor, digging through a few stray pillows and extra sheets for her vibrating palm. It was likely Commander Sutton, calling with some bit of militia business that needed Lila's touch, an heir who had been placed in a holding cell in lieu of an arrest, the lenience of another heir demanded and required.

Screw that. They'd picked the wrong night for it. She didn't care if it was Jewel in a holding cell. She'd see them hanged for disturbing her, for disturbing this…whatever it was going on between her and Tristan.

Lila turned back around, eyeing her bedmate. Given the sleepy frown on his face, Tristan felt the same way. He ran a finger down her shoulders in silent protest and let her fumble with the knotted sheets on the floor, sore and annoyed.

When she turned on a light, both winced.

And snuck peeks at one another.

Tristan threw back the covers so she'd get a better view.

Snorting, Lila picked up the tangle of sheets and shook it, finally rewarded with a soft patter as her palm hit the floor. She snatched it up and sat on the bed to answer it while Tristan yawned and stroked his cock in that absent way men rubbed themselves in the morning. She'd never been able to understand it. Women didn't grab their crotches straight out of the gate. Why did men reach for theirs so often?

"Hello," she muttered sleepily into her palm, turning off video.

"Your father has requested your services, Chief Randolph. Our plane leaves shortly."

"Plane? What plane?"

"Are you drunk, chief?" he said, sounding both inconvenienced and amused at the same time.

"No, I'm just not awake yet." She rubbed her eyes and stifled a yawn. "What time is it?"

"Four thirty."

Lila nearly retched. She'd barely had two hours of sleep.

So much for her promised four hours.

"Where are we going?"

"Sioux Falls, La Verde. Rebecca was taken from foster care this morning, only a few hours before she was scheduled to return home. Her mother asked for you specifically, said you were the only one she trusted to find her daughter. We'll leave as soon as you can get out to NBI. Your father has lent us his plane."

"Okay, give me an hour," Lila said, desperate for a shower even though it was the least of her problems. She still had to get Tristan out of the great house.

"Chief Randolph, we need to—"

"I'll be an hour. If you can't handle that, then leave without me. I was in the middle of something, and I'm more than content to stay where I am."

"Chief, I don't think you…" The implication finally snuck in a little late. "Oh, yes, well, then. One hour," Shaw muttered, and ended the call.

Tristan grinned. "Was that the middle? Because that definitely could have been the middle. Just give me five minutes and—"

"Cute." Lila pulled a sheet over her breasts and typed in the ID of the New Bristol oracle, turning on video this time.

She wanted to look the oracle in the eyes.

"I convinced my father to let the girl go," Lila said when the oracle answered. "You lied to me. What the—"

"It wasn't us, Chief Randolph," the oracle said. She'd evidently been awake for some time, as she'd brushed her hair and held a steaming mug. "We were afraid of this happening, which is why we asked you to free Rebecca. Many of the oracles have had the same vision over the last few days. I even had it again myself a few hours ago. It ends badly, chief, and it's very blurry. Until we met on Monday, I assumed you were the reason for it, but perhaps I should have blamed your father."

"No, we spoke yesterday. I assure you, he was going to release her."

"Perhaps our vision is blurry for another reason, but I don't know why. I don't know what else to do, chief. We know that we can trust you and that you're the one who will help us. Have you made any progress on finding our girls?"

Lila's stomach twisted. She hadn't even popped open the oracle's files. She barely knew the girls' names. "Not yet."

"The oracles will cooperate with you. We'll give you whatever you need, whatever you want. Just find our girls. Please. They're running out of time."

Lila pulled her sheet tighter. "You should tell my father every-thing. I could help you better if I was working with him and Chief Shaw. They have resources that I don't always have on my own. They have hundreds of—"

"No. Rebecca would be at home right now if not for your father. We'll not work with him or the government militia."

"That's not helping the situation."

"As head of the Saxon oracles, I've made my decision, as has the La Verde contingent. You should understand that I won't be able to keep my order from speaking out against him. Many of the ora-cles are furious, and it will only get worse when more of us wake."

"That's a condition of my help, then. You tell the others I won't lift a finger unless you point your collective wrath at someone else."

"You ask for what I cannot promise. We are legion, and my sisters are angry. Give them another target, the correct target, or I fear what they might say."

"You seriously expect me to help the same women who would tear down my father?"

"No, I expect you to help three missing girls who want to sleep in their own beds tonight and who are innocent of the politics swirling around them. It will calm my sisters when the prime minister's own daughter returns their little girls."

"You don't ask much, do you?" Lila broke off the connection and fell back onto the bed, having no energy to get into the shower.

Tristan intertwined his fingers in hers and brought their joined hands to his mouth, kissing hers and giving it a squeeze. "Despite what the oracle says, you don't have to work this on your own."

"I know. I'm just not sure how you can help right now. It's not like I can bring you along." She wiggled her fingers, wishing she didn't have to leave so soon. "I don't even have their files, Tristan. Keep working Oskar's case while I'm gone, will you? Look through the crime scene photos; maybe there's something there I missed. I'll work on the identity of Natalie's friend on the flight to Sioux Falls."

He touched her cheek, waking her body with his warm mouth and languid tongue. "I'll do whatever I can to help. But we already know who took them."

"That's a massive leap, Tristan. Just because a few German mercs took Oskar in New Bristol, doesn't mean they're now behind every kidnapping in the entire country. This girl was taken several hundred kilometers away. The other two were taken before Oskar disappeared."

"What's a few more kids if you're already taking one?"

"It's idiocy," Lila answered, tossing away the sheet wrapped around her body. "If you have the prince, you leave immediately or you risk getting caught. You don't steal the Crown Jewels then loot a few convenience stores on the way home, flashing your ass to every militia patrol in the city for a bit of pocket change."

"Not unless you need to do laundry. Rubies don't fit in those little slots."

Lila rolled her eyes. "I have to sneak you out of here before I leave. Just give me five minutes to grab a shower."

"I'd ask to join you, but my willpower isn't that good. I'll shower at the shop."

Lila slipped into her bathroom and closed the door, stepping onto the cool tiles. The heat and steam of her shower washed Tristan from her skin, and her frown deepened with every flick of soap. It wasn't until she emerged from the water that she winced, remembering she'd left him alone with her electronics.

Opening the door quietly, she peeked out.

Tristan lay in her bed, still naked in the same position she'd left him, sprawled to the world. His chest slowly rose and fell.

Wrapping her hair in a towel, she entered her bedroom, pausing at her dresser. She'd just slipped on a bra when Tristan woke.

"Get dressed," she said, digging out a fresh militia uniform, informal rather than formal.

He peeked into her closet as they dressed.

"Why are you so fascinated with my closet? Is there something we need to talk about?"

"No. It's just that this might be the only chance I get to see your room. I told you before, it's always been so hard to imagine where you go off to when you're not with me."

"So now you can imagine with your cock in your hand?"

"Maybe. My fantasies will be so much more realistic now."

He kissed her lips, then slid a hand under her militia top and all the buttons. "I can daydream about bending you over the desk. Lying with you in your bed." He brushed his fingers underneath her bra and pinched her nipple. "Finishing up in the shower after we're done. Under the water. Against the wall."

He leaned forward to kiss her again, but she shoved him gently away. "Stop it."

"Never. This is only a pause until you come back to New Bristol. I'll keep looking into the oracle's files and try to find something new in the crime scene photos."

He waited while she shoved her Colt into her holster and carefully sheathed her boot knife. Then she opened her window, glancing at the clock to time her patrols, knowing they'd walked by only a moment before. It would be another ten minutes before they had a visual on her window again. "Hide behind those shrubs," she said, pointing at a few bushes near the side of the house. "I'll be out in a few minutes."

"We're not going downstairs?"

"Of course not. This house is rigged with cameras. The only way I could get you down without being seen is to turn on a jammer, and that would bring Captain McKinley's people down on our heads in two seconds."

Tristan stared at the door to her room as though it held a pot of gold behind it. "One day I'm going to see the rest of the house."

"There's no way to swing that and keep you safe. Just trust me, Tristan. I'll be down soon."

Tristan ducked out of the window.

Lila closed it behind him, resettled the drapes, grabbed her satchel, and padded downstairs, emerging into the humid twilight.

Thank gods Sioux Falls would be cooler.

A little flutter of shrubs caught her eye. She pulled Tristan from behind it, leading him through a maze of trees and cameras and blackcoats.

"Wait here," she said, leaving him behind a tree near the garage. "I have to get my car."

"I want to see inside."

"There are too many cameras. I'll be back soon."

Lila opened the garage door, and the lights turned on automatically as they caught her approach. Three blackcoats startled several meters away and spun, hands going to their Colts. A German shepherd sniffed the air.

"Look alive," she called out before they drew.

The group chuckled nervously. "Morning, chief," they murmured sheepishly, putting away their Colts.

"As you were."

She hurried to her roadster as the group pressed on, and pulled out her palm, waving it over the interior and exterior of the car, increasingly annoyed that she bothered with such formalities at all. She'd just driven to the High Council meeting, anyway. It wasn't like anyone would have bugged her roadster between then and—

Her palm vibrated suddenly. Cocking her head, she swiped the screen and studied the weak wiggle of a needle displayed over a field of grid lines. The thin needle on the screen hopped again as she waved it over the back bumper.

Gritting her teeth, she crawled underneath the car, letting her palm guide her. Taking off her gloves, she poked and prodded, finally feeling a little lump behind the bumper, the size and shape of a ladybug. She pulled the device off her bumper carefully, studying it in the light of her palm. The silver lump might have been nothing but a poor weld, but no such shoddy work would have graced a car as fine as her Adessi. Her mother's R&D department had decided to test their new hardware tonight of all nights, a night when she had little time to dawdle.

She grunted and tossed the damn thing on Jewel's Firefly.

She spent another ten minutes carefully combing her car, then connected her palm to her car's GPS and ran her snoop programs.

It didn't take long to discover her mother's second gift, a section of code that wouldn't quite turn off the program when she requested it. If the bug hadn't been on her car, she might not have run her full snoop program on the GPS. She might not have found it at all.

Lila's eyes locked on to her mother's beloved Blanc convertible, smooth lines and curves and an engine that didn't so much purr as growl.

Payback was a bitch.

She'd have it soon.

Since Lila didn't have time to wonder what else her mother's people had done to her car, she downloaded a copy to a star drive, then wiped the entire car, reinstalling its systems from a second star drive she kept close.

At last, she pulled from the garage.

"What took you so long?" Tristan hissed as she stopped beside him, idling.

"Sometimes when I check for bugs, I find them." She popped the trunk and joined Tristan outside the car.

"You can't be serious."

"It's just for a few moments."

"This is ridiculous," he grumbled as he slipped inside, twisting and turning and curling. The car shook on its thick tires.

"I agree. It's extremely ridiculous, but I'll reward you later."

"A naked reward?"

Lila closed the trunk softly.

After a quick drive to the gate, she waved to Sergeant Nolan, barely slowing.

The guard cocked her head, clearly sensing the chief was up to something, but she damn sure wasn't going to ask.

Lila rolled through as soon as the gate lifted. She didn't stop for several blocks, not until she'd left the Randolph dominion. Pulling to the side of the road, she popped her trunk.

A very annoyed Tristan uncurled himself from the trunk, eyeing his location. "Roomy," he said as he climbed out.

Lila opened the driver's-side door with a flourish. She jiggled her keys like a treat bag and jerked her chin toward the wheel. "Your reward."

Tristan cast a bemused look toward the roadster.

"I know you want to drive it. Just don't wreck it, okay?"

"Screw you. I'm an excellent driver."

"I'm sure you are," she said, hurrying to the other side.

Tristan hopped into the driver's seat and pulled back onto the road. He wasted no time zipping down the empty streets, slaloming around the occasional delivery truck. His grin nearly split his face, as though he were a child who'd finally gotten to play with a toy he'd always wanted. Or perhaps it was merely the smile of someone happy, someone not afraid to show childish wonder in front of someone he cared about, someone he'd just bedded.

Lila approved of the look. His eyes had always been a bit too old. The product of too much responsibility thrust upon his shoulders too early. It was something they shared, something that had been pushed onto them by birth or by circumstance, but he still had it in him to be childlike.

Did she?

Lila wasn't sure anymore. It was the first time she felt the age difference between them. Though he was twenty-four, he had not yet attained the breadth of a man, still a touch too rangy and slender.

Perhaps his mind was no different. Perhaps he was still growing into the man he would become, settling into his moods, now thinking twice about charging into the fray half-cocked whenever the chance arose.

Perhaps she should stop being so hard on him, expecting him to have all the answers, trying to make decisions for him when she didn't like the ones he'd made. She'd done that in the past, slighting him when whatever plan he came up with was imperfect or too impulsive.

She'd been trained by the best all her life and sculpted into a leader. She'd been told over and over that it would be her destiny. Tristan had been trained by no one. He'd been forced to wing it, managing to earn the respect she'd only attained from her prosperous birth.

She had to admit, he was doing much better than she would have. Perhaps at twenty-eight she hadn't grown into the woman she would become, either.

Who was that? Who was she?

Was she her mother? Was she her father?

Right now, she didn't want to be either.

Tristan stopped the car two blocks away from the shop. "This is a fabulous car. I really must get one for myself."

"You mean steal one for yourself?"

"Stealing makes it more satisfying. Of course, Shaw would be on my ass in two seconds. Only a handful of heirs in all of Saxony have a car so fine."

"I'll let you drive it again."

He pulled her face to his and kissed her slow and deep. "Come find me after you get back. We'll compare notes."

He grazed her cheek with his thumb and got out of the car, slipping into the night.

Lila watched him disappear, then slid into the driver's seat and turned the car toward the airport. On the way, she typed a familiar number into her palm.

Her mother would feel her wrath.

So would her beloved Blanc roadster.

21

Lila and Shaw flew from New Bristol International on her father's plane, a crowded four-seat affair that left little room for Lila's boots, much less her legs. Dedicated to the principles of austerity, Unity would not splurge for the prime minister, choosing a budget model that would get her father from point A to point B with no added frills.

At least the seats were lush. Lila shifted on the cream-colored leather, careful not to bump her fold-out table for the twelfth time, for her laptop perched precariously upon it. She'd brought it on board in her satchel, knowing that Chief Shaw wouldn't waste her time with a longwinded debriefing of the case. In fact, he'd said nothing about it. He preferred her to remain untainted by his militia and their initial thoughts, claiming it was best all around.

Lila didn't care one way or the other. She had work to do, work she'd rather Shaw not be privy to. Luckily, the chief sat in the seat facing her on the opposite side of the plane. That was the benefit of arriving late. She'd been able to choose a seat away from his curious eyes.

"Militia reports," she'd answered pleasantly when Shaw asked what she was doing.

He'd raised a brow, clearly not believing her story. The brow shot higher when she told Captain McKinley to disengage sections of camera feeds throughout Wolf Tower until nine o'clock. When McKinley pressed for a reason, Lila only gave her one. "It's for a test," she'd said before disconnecting.

"That's not for a militia report," Shaw observed.

"You bet your ass it's not."

Mischief complete, Lila spent the next hour suffering through a spotty net connection while tracking Natalie's friend of a friend. The initial message had come from Teresa Bailey, the lowborn owner of the first chop shop that she and Tristan had visited. Unfortunately, Lila needed an unofficial net ID, a whole host of snoop programs, and far more privacy if she wanted to follow Teresa's trail further.

She'd need the same to follow Xavier.

Instead of taking a much-needed nap, Lila switched gears and used the second hour of the flight to tackle her militia inbox. She managed to handle a third of it before they touched down in Sioux Falls. Her fingers locked in a white-knuckled grip on the armrest as they landed.

Lila gathered her things as soon as the pilot stopped in a far corner of the small regional airport, eager for her boots to touch the ground once more. The plane's steps bobbled under her weight when she descended, and she pulled up her heavy scarf against the cold La Verde air.

To think that only a small flap of metal had separated her from death during the flight.

She nearly tripped when her toe met the tarmac, and she eyed the plane as if it might explode.

Shaw chuckled. "The auction house hero hasn't got her sea legs yet."

"You're going to see my legs kick you in the face in a minute," Lila mumbled, hitching her satchel farther up her shoulder.

"Is that before or after you fall on your butt? You forget. I was there for your hand-to-hand training. It was endlessly entertaining." Shaw pointed into the darkness toward the sound of a wheezing electronic engine. "I think our ride is here."

Lila squinted toward the noise. By the light of the lamps overhead, she made out a blackcoat inside an open four-seater cart.

Chief Vance, the La Verde militia chief, stopped before them, cart shaking as he hopped from the driver's seat. His blackcoat covered a navy uniform lined in silver piping, an orchid stitched on his breast in silver thread. The buttons flashed in the light as he shook hands with Chief Shaw, his blue eyes curious, his blond hair chopped off at the collar. The length was a compromise between his upbringing as a senator and his choice to enter the militia after he could not. He'd been ambitious, talented, charming, and handsome, a perfect candidate. Unfortunately, the doctors had ruled him infertile, barring him from advancing as a senate intern.

No High House and no children, at least not without effort and a lot of money. At eighteen, Vance had been forced to choose a new career. His professors had pushed him toward graduate studies and a potential teaching role with Norrington. He would train great statesmen, they promised.

But Vance hadn't wanted to train great statesmen.

He'd wanted to become one.

Ambitious to a fault, he'd chosen a different sort of power. He'd become the youngest government militia chief in the nation's history, shortly after his thirty-eighth birthday, partly through a convenient set of retirements. Some forced. Some not.

Lila had often wondered about that.

She also wondered how he had attained such a position while spending so much time in the gym. It was evident in every bulge and angle of his blackcoat.

She'd only met him once before, and she'd been greatly tempted to ask him out for a meal. Beautiful? Barren? A man who understood what it meant to be in the militia? A man who knew what it meant to lead multiple compounds stretched over a wide area?

How could she resist?

Chief Vance bowed to Lila, not because she was Chief Randolph but because she was an heir. Old habits and confusion over her status tended to obscure what should have been plain.

Lila inclined her head, acknowledging his bow.

"I heard you were looking into this case for your father," Vance said, his voice deep and rumbling. "I don't like a Saxon heir getting involved with La Verde state business. The point of the state militias is to keep our investigations free from the influence of the families."

Yep, that was why she hadn't asked him out. He didn't trust her. She probably wouldn't have gotten away with half so many things in the last few years if he and Shaw switched places.

"Her father wants her here for a reason. She's—"

Lila cleared her throat, ending Shaw's tirade before it could begin. "Chief Vance, let's not pretend you're pissed about jurisdiction or the sanctity of government investigations or even my father's interference. The oracles won't cooperate unless I'm here, and that pisses you off," Lila said, hopping into the cart. "It would piss me off too, but there's not much any of us can do about it. So let's just save ourselves a bunch of hollering in the cold. You've given your official complaint. I have a two-hour plane ride home, a dozen compounds to run, and a stuffed inbox waiting on me. I suspect you can understand."

Vance frowned as she crossed an ankle over her knee. If there was one thing most militia officers understood, it was work.

"This is highly irregular." He slid into the cart as Shaw folded himself into the back seat. The small wheels lurched forward, and the struggling contraption rattled past the terminals toward a waiting sedan.

A three-legged pregnant turtle could have beaten them there.

Lila ducked into the sedan as soon as they arrived, the car thankfully roomier than the plane. She stretched her legs while Chief Vance dug into a pile of folders on the seat next to him. "I presume you've read our initial reports on the kidnapping?"

Lila shook her head.

Vance's blue eyes narrowed, and he turned to Shaw. "You didn't give her—"

"She knows the basics. Rebecca was taken from her foster home at midnight. No one knows or saw who did it."

"That's not the basics. You've told her nothing."

Shaw raised his chin. "I've told her plenty. It'll only her take five minutes at the scene to deduce what's in your stack of reports."

Lila nearly laughed. Chief Shaw might have been defending her, but it had nothing to do with her and everything to do with the slight against his own judgment.

"This is highly irregular." Vance leaned back in his seat. The leather of his blackcoat strained over his wide chest.

Lila had never been with a man a dozen years her senior, and never one who had spent so much time in the gym. She wondered what it would be like.

Then she wondered what it would be like for Tristan to wear the blackcoat. Perhaps the coat and nothing else. His erect cock peeking out as he entered her bedroom, ordering her to take off her clothes and toss them in a pile, ordering her to turn and face the wall as he slid in between her legs, grabbing her hips as he fucked her, forcing her to grip her desk and moan with each demanding thrust, both of them—

Lila blushed and stared out the window, glad the men couldn't read her mind, glad they couldn't tell how wet she'd just gotten. For oracle's sake, she was visiting a kidnapping scene. A child had just been taken. A child who needed her help.

All she could think about was her lover.

This was why the highborn didn't let themselves get attached.

Lila sank down low in her seat and wiggled her toes. Closing her eyes, she tried to think of anything but Tristan as they drove through the still dark suburbs of Sioux Falls.

She nearly dozed off, but the sedan lurched suddenly, stopping in a well-to-do workborn neighborhood. A two-story house with a metal gate rose above them, its blue paint too bright in the melancholy gloom. Sunflowers lined a small garden in the front yard, their heavy faces turning toward any friend who might appear for a visit. Little red shutters and a red door adorned the house, a collection of pudgy porcelain gnomes standing near the entrance and a freshly painted porch swing. The creatures smoked little pipes, some sitting, others waving at each guest or at one another.

The couple was that sort of workborn, infuriatingly jolly and kind.

At least the kidnapping would knock some of the edge off.

Chief Vance rolled down his foggy window as a Norrington guard peeked inside the sedan, prompting the nervous sergeant to open the metal gate in a rush. It swung forward with a rusty screech, the noise echoing off the sleepy streets.

The driver pulled forward into a line of Sioux Falls cruisers that filled the driveway.

"I'm your tech consult, Chief Shaw," Lila said. "Don't address me by name."

"What am I to call you, then? Hey, you?"

"Works for me."

Lila slipped out of the sedan. She buttoned her blackcoat over her family's coat of arms and left her scarf in the sedan, the entire slash of fabric betraying her inclusion in the House of the Crimson Wolves. The local militia would already be on alert with Chief Vance looking over their shoulder. Having two guests from Saxony would only annoy them further.

Vance eyed the little gnomes down the walk. "The Thomases usually have anywhere from three to six foster children. Not children of oracles, mind you—workborn children, mostly."

"Anything suspicious come up in a background search?"

"They're anything but suspects." Vance bristled. "They're saints."

"Everyone's a suspect. How many kids are inside?"

"Currently, none. Up until last week the couple cared for three siblings, but the children's parents completed all their classwork. After Family Protection Services assigned their live-in counselor, they moved back in with their parents to complete the trial period."

"You think they'll pass?"

"Four months is a long time." Vance shrugged, leading the group toward the house. "FPS chose the Thomases as the perfect foster placement for Rebecca. Not only was their house empty, but the couple is extremely experienced and kind. They have remarkable rapport with children from all backgrounds. They didn't even mind the Norrington patrols."

Lila stopped. "Norrington patrols?"

"Yes." Vance winced. "My men were here during the abduction. They noted some thrashing noises from the north and west sides of the property around change of shift. They investigated and found nothing. We suspect that's when Rebecca was taken. It was quiet for the rest of the night."

"So they fell for the most basic of distractions and didn't think to check on the kid?"

"No, they did not." He nodded at the blackcoat at the front door. The poor sergeant had crossed his hands over his chest, not to look imposing, but because he might send the gnomes tumbling around him at any moment.

Once inside the home, Vance led them toward the parlor, introducing them to the couple, both approaching fifty by the lines on their faces and the gray in their hair. Lila could have used her full name without the couple becoming suspicious. The husband merely scratched his beard and shook hands with anyone who offered it, and his wife barely lifted her gaze from the floor.

They tugged their robes closed at the neck as they sat down.

"Did you find something?" the woman asked, her voice trembling. "Did you find Rebecca? She's alive, isn't she? She's okay?"

"We haven't found her yet, Mrs. Thomas, but we're doing everything we can," Vance assured her kindly. "My two colleagues are here to help."

Shaw sat beside Vance, perhaps keen to dive right in, asking the very same questions that the couple had been asked a thousand times that night.

Lila avoided the couch, choosing instead to sit on the coffee table directly in front of the couple. She took up the wife's hand and gave it a sympathetic little squeeze. As a rule, she didn't like interrogating witnesses, not unless she knew a person was guilty.

She tended to just talk. "I have a little brother. Ten years younger than me, Mr. Thomas. I don't know what I'd do if he was taken in the middle of the night."

Mr. Thomas nodded and bent his head, staring at a frayed cushion on the couch. While he grew lost inside his head, Lila pressed Mrs. Thomas's hand once more. She said nothing more to either of them, just watched their faces, making her own as blank as possible.

Predictably, they began to speak, mostly to fill the awkward silence.

"We were just so tired," Mrs. Thomas explained clearing her throat. "That's no excuse for sleeping through it, though. I'm normally a very light sleeper. We've kept foster children for twenty years, and I've always woken up if one of my kids sneezes or sniffles. Some of them cry, you know. Either they miss home, or they're nervous about what will happen when they go back. There's a lot of calming involved in being a foster parent. Tears and tempers alike, especially before family therapy appointments. But I didn't wake up this time. When it counted the most, I slept while someone took that baby."

She gripped Lila's hand even harder. "Oh gods, she must have been so scared."

"She probably was. You feel horrible for it. I hope I would feel horrible too if someone took my little brother while I was asleep. I suppose that's how you feel when you care."

"I do care." A tear rolled down the woman's cheek, but she didn't brush it aside. "I don't know why I didn't wake up. Why tonight? I always wake up. Why did it have to be tonight?"

"Like you said, I suppose you were just tired."

"We both were," Mr. Thomas said, giving a little cough. He noticed the tear falling down his wife's cheek and pulled a cotton handkerchief from his robe's pocket, putting it in her free hand. She smiled up at him for his kindness and dabbed at her eye.

Oracle's light, they were in love. Real love. Not just soul mates or friends or playmates. They had bonded so completely that they could see no one else but their partner, could never bond with anyone else after meeting one another. Not while they loved, not even after.

They'd married and declared it to the world.

"We were both groggy," Mr. Thomas said. "It kind of hit us at once."

Lila glanced back at Chief Vance.

"We took samples of their blood and sent it back to the lab. We're testing it for practically everything."

"I'd like a copy as soon as you get the results," Shaw prodded.

"Of course."

"I don't think we were drugged." Mrs. Thomas coughed a little as she sipped her warm tea. "I think we're just coming down with something. The tea is helping, though."

Her eyes did seem dark and puffy, but Lila thought it a rather convenient time to fall ill.

A little too convenient.

"Would you like some?" Mrs. Thomas offered. "It's Silver Shark Winter tea."

"No, thank you," Lila answered.

"It's just as well. We haven't been able to make it like the lady from Family Protection Services. Now she's a regular tea aficionado. Perfectly steeped, loose-leaf goodness, straight from the gods."

"Isn't that how it always goes?" Lila smiled. "You stayed up late last night, didn't you? You usually go to bed earlier, but something kept you up."

The couple looked at one another. "Well, you have to understand, we're supposed to foster a new baby in a few days. Abandoned at the hospital, if you can believe it. New mother just got overwhelmed and dropped him off. Rebecca came with us to the FPS office yesterday to pick up our Silver Shark, and we filled out some of Cash's paperwork while we were there."

"Poor baby's only a couple of months old," her husband added. "It's going to take days for Cash's paperwork to go through, what

with the Teddy Stevens Act. I understand the need to lock por-
tions of his DNA profile until he's of age, but he shouldn't have
to stay in the hospital while bureaucrats play pass the papers and
go home at five o'clock to their families. A hospital is no place
for a child that young."

"You don't think you could get Norrington involved, could you,
Chief Vance?" Mrs. Thomas asked, looking slightly hopeful.

"The Norrington militia has little influence over Family Protection Services, but I do know someone at FPS who might put
a word in the right ear. I can't promise anything, but I'll see what
I can do."

Mrs. Thomas beamed. "We owe you for that kindness. We owe
you greatly."

Lila watched their expressions with some interest. Vance was
not wrong in his assessment. The couple really were kindhearted
souls, talking about owing favors over a baby they'd never set eyes
on and who wasn't even theirs. She couldn't help but wonder what
the couple was like when they weren't so unbearably sad.

They probably would have tripped Vance with full-force hugs
and given him a gnome to take home to Norrington.

"Is that what kept you up?" Lila asked, trying to steer the conversation back to the night before. "Worry over the new baby?"

"Oh, no," Mrs. Thomas said, shaking her head. "You see, my
husband climbed into the attic to retrieve our old crib yesterday
afternoon. It's been a while since we had such a young one, so
we were thinking of restaining the wood, since we had a few days
before Cash's arrival."

"That sounds lovely," Lila said, squeezing the woman's hand again.

"I shouldn't have dawdled in the attic, but you know how it is."
Mr. Thomas chuckled. "I got a bit too interested in the other things
we've stored up there. I started digging through a box of toys from
our eldest. Angela just graduated from college in Unity. I ended
up finding a photo album in one of the boxes, and I brought it to
Martha after I got the crib down. One thing led to another and

we were still up an hour past our normal bedtime, looking at all her old toys and giggling and sobbing over her baby pictures. We both just got tired. Nearly fell asleep on the couch. We thought we were just getting old. Even made a few jokes about it."

"We went to bed soon after," Mrs. Thomas concluded.

"Where'd you have dinner?"

"At home, of course," she answered. "All our children help cook and clean up at least one meal every day. Some of them have never learned to cook or clean a table properly, so we make sure we teach them some skills before they leave. I made lasagna, but Rebecca didn't like it. She's a picky eater, but she tried it just the same. That's all I ask of my children. Just try a few bites. She made a peanut butter and jelly sandwich afterward."

There it was again. *Our* children. *My* children. Lila rubbed her chin and glanced back at Vance.

"We're testing the wine that the Thomases had with dinner."

"Did the neighbors hear anything last night?"

Vance shook his head.

"Didn't think so. There's nothing in the wine, mark my words. It will be something they all drank."

"The hot chocolate?" Mrs. Thomas asked, turning toward Vance. "I didn't even think to mention it before."

"What hot chocolate?"

"We always have hot chocolate after dinner. Our children always like it, and it's good to have a routine. That's what my mother always says, and she's ninety. Still sharp as I am, too. If it worked for her, it'll work for me and mine."

"Can you show me the hot chocolate?"

Mr. and Mrs. Thomas led them into the kitchen and pulled down a tin of powdered chocolate. As the group chatted more about the night before, Lila opened the lid and looked inside.

Nothing seemed off about it.

"We also had tea with our dinner, but only my husband and I had some."

"Which tea?"

Mr. Thomas pointed to the mug he'd put on the counter, nothing but dregs in the bottom. While everyone's back was turned to examine the tea, Lila withdrew a vial from her pocket and dipped it into the chocolate powder. After capping it one-handed, she stuck it into her pocket and brushed her gloves against her trouser legs.

No one had noticed.

"The lady at the FPS office just happened to have some handy?" Lila asked.

Mrs. Thomas shook her head. "No, Ms. Royce always peddles a little tea on the side. Silver Shark is one of our favorites."

"Can you grab the packet? I'd like to test it," Vance said.

While Vance and Shaw snatched sample containers from the Sioux Falls militia, Lila turned on the group and peeked from the small kitchen window. Or at least, that was what everyone thought she had done. Instead, she tipped the abandoned mug of tea into a second vial.

She slid it back onto the counter without anyone being the wiser, just as Vance capped their own samples from the tea and chocolate.

"Do you really think we were drugged?" Mrs. Thomas asked.

"I'm certain of it," Lila said. "After all, Rebecca didn't scream."

"Rebecca is six years old," Vance reminded her. "If an adult tells a child to be quiet, she's going to follow that direction, especially if a weapon was involved."

"Perhaps." Lila found it hard to believe that Rebecca wouldn't scream and fight, not when there were armed patrols only a few meters away. After all, she'd been kidnapped once before, though it had been for show.

The couple led them upstairs into Rebecca's room. Since the girl had only been there a few days, there was little of hers inside. A blue bedspread lay atop the bed, with little yellow ducks quacking in wavy lines. A second bed sat nearby, stripped and empty, lonelier in the empty room. Someone had piled a few tattered books on the bedside table between them, the pages crinkled at the edges due to too many small hands turning them. A box of broken colors sat beside it. The Thomases had placed a few wooden toys on a shelf in the back, toys that might have been antiques, if only they hadn't been so roughly bashed against one another. An electronic train track ran under the beds and along the walls.

"We set up the track yesterday. She liked connecting the pieces." Mr. Thomas stood at the door awkwardly, his arm around his wife. "Her bag is in the closet. We didn't make her unpack. She cried when we asked her to. She said she shouldn't have to, that she'd return to her mother's compound soon."

A hovering guard took the couple downstairs so the group could work.

"Have you dusted?" Lila asked after she'd peeked into the girl's bag and found nothing but clothes, a few stuffed animals, books, and pictures.

"We've dusted everything, even the window," Vance said. "We only found Rebecca's prints and the Thomases'. The couple said that they cleaned the room as a family when they first got her home. They did a good job of it, too. It saved us an awful lot of time comparing fingerprints from past children and guests."

Lila opened the window and ducked underneath the sill. A maple shade tree had grown near the window, and Lila could reach out and shake its branches. "They didn't go through the window, not that it wouldn't be an easy move."

"How do you know?"

"The whole family had been knocked unconscious. Why risk breaking your neck or dropping the girl when you don't have to? A six-year-old is still heavy, especially when she's dead weight."

"There are security cameras—"

"Yeah, I saw the security cameras on the way in. You didn't see anything on the footage, I take it?"

"Exactly. That points to an inside—"

"It points to anyone with half a brain. They're hardly hidden, and they've been spaced so far apart that an army could slip inside undetected. The company that designed this security system should be shut down for negligence, and your men should all be retrained."

Vance cut his eyes to Shaw.

"If that's her take, then you should listen," Shaw said. "If you asked her to slip inside this house right now with every man watching the security monitors, even doubling your patrols, she'd find twenty different routes inside. She's slipperier than an eel. Unfortunately, I don't think any of us have the time or the energy for a demonstration." Shaw turned to Lila. "And whatever sarcastic little comment is knocking around in that brain of yours? Don't."

Lila closed her mouth.

"Okay, Chief Randolph," Vance said. "The kidnapper broke into the house and drugged the chocolate so that the family would be asleep when they broke in a second time and actually took the girl? Is that your theory?"

"We don't know if the chocolate is drugged, but it wouldn't be the worst plan in the world. Could be that drugging their food or drink was just a dress rehearsal. This is a workborn dwelling. It's a joke to break into. Why my father decided to stash a future oracle here is beyond me."

"Where else would we put her? Only six highborn families live in Sioux Falls, and all are minor families at best. None of them have seats on the La Verde High Council, and only one has more than three compounds in the region. None of them wanted to take responsibility for the daughter of an oracle. They claimed not to have a large enough militia to protect her. They said there's too much risk involved without a reward."

"Except for bragging rights, excellent PR, and the eternal gratitude of the workborn faithful who have to buy their products from somewhere? No wonder the idiots haven't grown beyond Sioux Falls."

"Well, your father didn't want to place her in Norrington," Shaw said. "He didn't think it would sit well with the oracle."

"Yeah, because stealing her daughter didn't bother her at all."

Lila studied the scene for the next hour, walking throughout the structure with Chief Shaw. They poked a little more in the house and yard, then spoke to the Thomases once more.

The group had a quiet ride back to the airport. Chief Vance sat across from her, messaging his acquaintance at FPS.

The chief bowed respectfully to Lila before she trundled onto the plane. Though Lila spent the flight home clearing her inbox of messages and reports, her fingers stalled more often than they worked. She needed to get the samples to her lab quickly. She knew they'd find drugs in one of the samples, she just wasn't sure which one.

She wasn't sure that it would lead to the kidnappers, though.

After she forwarded her last report to Sergeant Jenkins, she let her mind drift. If tracers showed up in one of the samples, then Tristan's idle, impulsive guess was right. And if German mercs had taken Rebecca, Lila wasn't sure how they'd find her. It was bad enough that she couldn't find Oskar, but adding a few more children into the mix gave her pause.

She drummed her fingers on her armrest, staring at Teresa Bailey's ID.

She would fail the missing children in the end. This time, no matter how hard she tried, she just didn't have the answers, and she didn't have them quickly enough. Usually, she snuck into compounds, most of the time with permission. She downloaded whole databases or stole jewels with the intention of returning them. Other times, she sniffed out illegal sales of drugs and booze and found blackmailers among the highborn.

She'd never had to save someone before, not like this. Not racing against a clock to find victims who might have a gun to their heads, a gun loaded with bullets rather than tranqs. She'd only ever had to dart forward, brandishing her Colt, popping off a tranq to clear a path for her own escape.

She had no adrenaline to aid her this time, only exhaustion and dread. Dread that the girls might be in a dog's cage, just as Oskar had been with Natalie.

Or—

Gods, what if they'd been taken as fodder for Natalie's brothels? Two of the girls had been kidnapped near New Bristol. What if Natalie had taken Rebecca as a last fuck-you to the prime minister and the same government that wished to try her for treason?

Lila stole so many looks at Chief Shaw that his mustache twitched. Should she tell him now? She had a good list of possible locations for Natalie's brothels, but was it good enough?

If Rebecca had been taken by Natalie, was she there yet?

Lila rubbed her eyes and looked away, feeling stupid. She couldn't send Bullstow to the brothels until she knew every location, else boys like Phillip might disappear forever. She couldn't risk losing so many children, not even for the daughter of an oracle.

Besides, what possible use would Natalie have for oracles? By that same token, why would the Germans target the girls? Most Germans who had enough money to hire mercs believed that the oracles had no abilities, except to con people out of their money.

Tristan was grasping at straws.

But if Natalie and the Germans hadn't taken Rebecca, who did? Anyone could meet with an oracle for free. Sure, they might have to wait awhile to be seen—they might even have to wait days if the oracle kept ignoring them—but they'd be seen eventually.

Who couldn't be bothered to wait?

People generally committed crimes for only a few reasons, revenge and punishment among them. Could that be the reason why Rebecca was taken? Revenge because the oracles had not bothered to speak with a pilgrim, taking too long to see an impatient, broken soul? Or perhaps revenge from within the oracles' compounds, perhaps a girl who wished that she had been given a chance to disappear or to shine?

Pulling out her palm, Lila made a call to the oracle for a list of suspects. Her mind was running too wild with too much guessing.

She had too few leads, and she was too damn tired to come up with more.

22

Lila set her laptop down on Tristan's wine barrel coffee table and reclined into the couch, smacking her worn servant's boots beside the computer with two heavy thumps. She crossed her arms over her plain gray t-shirt and let her head sink into the cushions.

A nap sounded like a really good idea.

After Lila sped home and popped into the security office to handle the commanders' meeting, Sutton had gently reminded her that Wednesday was her day off. She'd spent a few hours in her office anyway, dealing with a few pieces of neglected Randolph business. Then she'd dug further into Teresa Bailey. But if the Germans had contacted the woman, it hadn't been through any channel Lila could hack or poke at, which meant that she was stuck. The Germans had either met Teresa in person or the contact had come to her some other way.

To find out, Lila would have to use truth serum. Teresa would squeal about everything then: her chop shop, Natalie, the people behind Oskar's kidnapping. But only the government militia could use the truth serum, and that would only happen if Bullstow put two and two together or if Shaw got the information from Lila.

Unfortunately, Bullstow wouldn't work quickly enough, and Shaw wouldn't ask for her assistance. The chief believed Lila too busy with the oracle kidnappings, especially now that a fresh case had been dumped into her lap. She didn't have time to pull his strings and shove him in the right direction, either. Sending him another anonymous tip so soon would only put herself at risk, for few in Saxony could have hacked Natalie's star drive so quickly, and no one else would use Bullstow to get information they could get themselves through other means.

Chief Shaw wasn't an idiot. He'd figure out that Lila had tipped him off, and he'd have proof that she'd stolen evidence from a crime scene. Shaw would never let that go, regardless of who her father was, regardless of her motivations. Not even if she helped him solve his case and let him take credit for returning the boy.

Besides, the last thing she wanted was to return Oskar.

Breathing out in frustration, she sank deeper into Tristan's couch. She couldn't even track Teresa down herself, because when Shaw finally questioned her, Teresa would likely tell him that they'd spoken.

Lila would still be screwed.

Since she'd had no other leads to dig into and her mother had begun sending her messages about returning to the great house, Lila had fled the compound. She'd known touching her mother's Blanc would bite her in the ass later.

Her eyes flitted to the side of the room.

Dixon had curled himself up in an oversized chair, his eyes half-lidded as though he might fall asleep, his stare fixed on a knot on the floor. When she'd arrived at the apartment fifteen minutes before, he'd barely looked up. He just scribbled a line halfway down the page in his notepad, then shoved it in pocket, returning to his brooding.

Apparently, Tristan had returned to Natalie's for another look.

Before Dixon had closed the notepad, Lila scanned the first entry. He'd written it several days ago. He usually went through an entire notepad in a week.

Lila worried the hem of her t-shirt, unsure how to talk to him, unsure if she should talk to him at all. He'd done nothing but avoid or her brood whenever he had to endure her presence.

Perhaps he'd been doing that with everyone. He seemed so alone, curled up in the oversized chair. He used to sprawl over it like a nonchalant king or a highborn. Even a criminal.

Never a brooding child.

Pax had done the same thing once, looking far younger than his years because something heavy lay on his shoulders, weighing down his mind and his heart. Lila hadn't let Pax fumble with it for long. Two days after Trevor's death, she'd barged into his room without knocking and plopped down on his couch, tuning her palm to a public playlist filled with random music. She'd spent nearly half a bowl of popcorn on him, tossing kernel after kernel onto his back before he got pissed enough to jump up and scream at her.

After he was done hollering, she'd just hugged him. What could you say to a boy who'd lost his best friend and his first love? Nothing anyone had ever said made losing Holly easier.

So Lila didn't even try.

On the second day of music and militia reports and breakfast and lunch and dinner, Pax finally spoke. He didn't talk much, but he talked. Every day he talked a little more until he finally channeled his energy into his schoolwork.

As she watched Dixon's face, she was reminded of Pax lying on the bed, kernels tossed around him. Perhaps Dixon was fumbling too. Perhaps it was harder for him to write something, instead of mumbling it.

Here she was without her popcorn.

"Dixon, come here." She patted the couch next to her.

Dixon's eyes shot up. He looked around the room a little lost, then cocked his head.

"Come here," she said a little more forcefully.

He sighed as if the distance seemed too great. Still he shuffled over, curling himself on the end of the couch as far away as possible.

The knot once again held his attention.

"Not there. Here." Lila patted the spot next to her once more.

His eyes narrowed.

"Don't worry. I'm not going to bust your balls."

Dixon arranged himself beside her, crossing his legs on the seat cushion. It seemed he expected a lecture of some sort.

Lila didn't give him one. She wouldn't have known what to say. Instead, she just put her arms around his neck and pulled him close, running her hand down his neck and back, over and over and again, her gloved fingertips grazing his scars.

He didn't pull away.

After a time, he buried his face into her shoulder. Her neck grew wet, and his breaths grew ragged, sounding like he had been infected with another round of poison. He moaned, noise unlocked by sadness, startling her because she sometimes forgot that the tongueless man could make noise at all.

She held him all the tighter for it.

"I'm here," she said, because she had absolutely nothing intelligent to say.

She'd hoped he would talk to her; she hadn't expected him to cry.

Eventually the tears slowed. He pulled his face away, and she wiped a few drops from his cheek. She pulled his notepad from his back pocket and put it in his lap. "I know you're mad at me and Tristan, but—"

Dixon shook his head.

"It's okay. We know. Tristan's been feeling guilty for what happened. That probably doesn't help, but—"

"Idiot," Dixon mouthed over a little hiss of air. He touched his pen to paper, scribbling out a sentence, the text loose and ragged, so unlike his usual tidy blocks. *I'm not mad. He had to shoot Reaper. I would have done the same thing.*

"Then what's wrong?"

He shrugged and tried to stand, but Lila grabbed his hand and tugged him back down. "Oh no, you don't. I'll always be a shoulder for you if you need it, but I'd be the shittiest friend ever if I just let you walk away now. Whatever is bugging you isn't getting any better. You've brooded for long enough. Talk to me."

His pen hovered over his notepad. *You handle it so well. You walk around like nothing happened. It pisses me off.*

"What am I handling?"

Peter nearly killed you.

"Yes, he did."

You don't seem bothered by it at all. He stared as though some answer had been locked inside her mind, an answer he desperately wanted to get at, an answer he needed.

"That wasn't the first time someone tried to kill me, Dixon. I've lived with that crap my whole life."

I know. And you're fine. You're really fine with it, aren't you?

Lila thought back to how she'd handled the last week of her life. Right after she'd woken up from nearly been killed, she'd almost slept with Tristan in a hospital bed. Less than a week after that, she had slept with him. She was still sleeping with him.

Oh gods, was that why they'd begun?

"I'm coming along."

You had regrets?

"Of course I had regrets, Dixon. I suppose most people do. There were things that I had wanted to do, would never get to do, odd little things I'd never know. I didn't want to die. No one does."

Yours?

It clicked suddenly. When Reaper injected Dixon with that drug, when he fell over onto the ground and had gotten so ill, he'd thought his life was over. He wasn't pissed off about Tristan saving Lila at his expense. His dark moods had been triggered by the thoughts that had come to him while poisoned, while lying on the ground thinking he'd die. He was having trouble coming to terms with it.

In his mind, she wasn't.

Dixon saw it on her face as she figured it out. *I've been hurt, beaten, but I never thought they'd kill me. This time I saw Tristan stab Reaper. I heard Tristan threaten to kill him if I didn't make it. I was scared for us both. I calm him. You do too. If something happens to us, bad things will happen. I don't like that.*

"There are a lot of things I don't like, Dixon, but they are what they are."

Almost dying makes you think, doesn't it?

"About what?"

Regrets. He started to write more, then crossed it out.

"I had them too, Dixon. It's normal. I had regrets about big things and little things all at once. I'd never learned Zoe's name. I'd never found out how you'd gotten all those scars on your back. Tristan and I had never…" She waved her hand, fumbling.

And now?

"Now what?"

Tristan.

"He's trying too hard. He sends me all these messages, wants me to come over constantly, tells me that he misses me all the time. It's too much."

Workborns don't hold back. Workborns find one person they like and latch on. They keep them close. He almost lost you last week. Twice. He's still upset about it.

"I know."

No, you don't. He's holding himself back a great deal, and he's having to try for both of you. That's not fair.

"I'm still here, aren't I?"

That's not good enough. He's my brother, and he deserves to be happy. You do too.

Lila cocked her head. "People don't make other people happy, Dixon. You can only do that for yourself."

What a bunch of highborn twaddle! Dixon smacked her in the head with his notepad.

Lila rubbed her skull. "Very mature."

Love makes fools of us all, Lila. At least the workborn admit it.

"What did you regret?"

He doodled on the side of his page, and Lila thought he might not answer. *I thought Reaper would get away with it. I thought you and Tristan might never get together if I wasn't around to help.* He grinned smugly like a gloating, self-satisfied fairy godmother. *I thought I'd never have a chance to fall in love for real, like the workborns, or have kids. I thought I would die without paying back the ones who hurt me.*

"Who hurt you?"

He looked at her face for a very long time, but it was obvious she hadn't earned the truth yet, or perhaps he just wasn't ready for her to know.

Lila put her head on his shoulder. "Don't sweat it, Dixon. I'll ask again another time."

He nodded, put his arm around her, then leaned back into the couch.

The pair stayed like that for a while, Dixon's quiet way calming her mind, slowing her rambling thoughts.

Lila wasn't sure when it happened, but Dixon's arm grew heavy around her shoulders, and she began to doze. She tried to fight it, but she hadn't had much sleep in over a week, and Dixon's slow breathing cut through her resolve.

A click woke her up.

The click of a gun.

Lila's eyes snapped open. One hand went to her Colt. She'd drawn it and aimed before she even realized it was Tristan.

Holding his palm.

"Jumpy, aren't we?" He scrolled through the device. "Could you point that somewhere else?"

Dixon rubbed at his eyes and gently pushed her tranq gun away from his brother's neck.

"What are you doing?" Lila slid her Colt back in its holster.

"What do you think? I couldn't resist taking a picture. You were both so cute with the drool and the—"

Dixon wiped his mouth. Finding nothing, he cuffed his brother on the chin.

Tristan hopped back, startled.

The brothers smiled at one another.

"Frank and I combed Natalie's place," Tristan said, putting his palm away. "We didn't find anything new."

"It was worth a try."

"Toxic says thanks for sending Natalie's decryption codes for the palms. She also wanted me to tell you about some game she found on them. She put it on a spare and ran it, just to see what it would do." Tristan pulled out the device from his pocket and tapped on the screen, handing it over at last. "She said the code was really weird."

Lila studied the screen, recognizing the alien game at a glance. "Yeah, I saw it. It likely carries a virus. She should be more care—"

"It's a spare palm off our network. She knows what she's doing."

"Fine. Did she play it?"

"She tried, but she said it plays like a broken demo. The aliens fall to the center of the screen, but then they get stuck and the screen flickers. It frustrated her, so she looked into the code."

Lila started the game up again. "Did Toxic tell you anything besides the code is really weird?"

"She said it's trying to communicate with something."

"Of course it's trying to communicate with something. It's sending your passwords and accounts to a server halfway across the globe."

Tristan scratched his chin. "Why would Natalie have that on her palm, then? She's smarter than that."

Lila's lips twitched. She had to admit, it was strange. She woke up her laptop, pulled up the palm data from her files, then ran her snoop programs on the game. When a light flashed red on her screen, she wasn't surprised. "Yep. Virus."

Dixon held up his notepad. *How do you keep viruses off WolfNet?*

Lila and Tristan shared a confused look over Dixon's sudden interest.

"My security programs look for the sending code," Lila said, directing her words to both men now. "If we spot the program trying to send or receive anything but scores or game-related files, we don't allow the download. Reputable game-making families have adopted a standard format for that code. A similar and much more complicated format applies for MMOs and MOBAs."

"Moe-who?"

"Online games where players fight each other or NPCs."

"NP-whats?"

"You never ask me about specifics when we have technical discussions, but as soon as I say games, you suddenly have a burning desire to learn?"

Tristan shrugged.

"Reputable game makers like the Massons follow certain protocols. No one would trust their games otherwise, and it would hurt their bottom line. It's a tentative truce," Lila explained. "No one in the industry can use that code unless they've paid the licensing fee. If the matrons find someone else using the code without permission, the game makers find them, tranq them, and shove them before Bullstow's gate, bleeding from the chest with a note carved into their skin. You don't screw with these people."

Tristan gulped. "The Massons? Really?"

"This game," Lila said, holding up the spare. "It isn't using the standard code. It's either an illegal game or a virus. Given the fact that the game doesn't even work, then it's a virus. Natalie couldn't have downloaded it on any highborn network, that's for sure. Her snoop programs should have caught it as well. That means she must have deactivated them at some point and forgotten to turn them back on. So how's that for clever?"

"The game was on all three palms."

Lila had forgotten about that. She opened the data for all three palms, noting that none of the file sizes seemed to match. She quickly typed in a command to compare the contents of the files. "*Hmmm...*"

"What?"

"The other two copies didn't finish downloading."

"But the one in Natalie's bag did?"

"Yes."

"So what does that tell us?"

"That the devs need to get their shit together before the alpha, or they'll go bankrupt?"

"Alpha what?"

Lila peeked over her laptop. "Seriously, Tristan, play a damn game once in a while."

Dixon grinned, the corner of his mouth twisting upward slightly.

Lila shared his smile. "Did you find anything that might shed some light on Oskar or the girls or their whereabouts?"

"Nothing. Nada. Zilch."

Lila drummed her fingers on her laptop, then broke into Bullstow's files, scanning Natalie's case file for any updates. "They haven't discovered the tracers in Natalie's system. They probably won't if they haven't already. They haven't found much of anything else, either. They haven't even bothered looking deeper into the game."

"Toxic will get a kick out of that."

Lila considered telling him about Teresa Bailey and the brothels, but she wasn't sure what impulsive thing he might suggest. But when she glanced up at his face, she remembered her thoughts from that morning. She needed to give him a break.

Besides, a fresh mind might help.

Two minds, since Dixon seemed to be paying attention to their conversation now.

"I do have a couple of leads. I'm not sure they'll come to anything, though."

Tristan sat across from her on the coffee table as she explained why she couldn't just message Shaw about the brothels or Teresa Bailey. Telling the chief about one brothel might drive the rest underground. A simultaneous raid would be the only way to procure the safety of all the children, and she had to be sure that she'd found them all first. And Teresa couldn't be approached without Shaw being tipped off during questioning.

"I understand about the brothels. I hate it, but you're right. I don't understand your reasoning for Teresa, though. My people and I could talk to her."

"If you go near her, Chief Shaw will know I sent you."

"Because you're the only hacker in all the land who could find Teresa?" Tristan pulled out his palm and tapped on the screen. "I'm sending Fry and Dice to find her."

"Tristan…"

"We already missed Oskar once," he pointed out, his fingers pausing. "Do you want to miss him again because you're too busy trying to be sneaky and covering your ass? Bullstow might not even figure out Teresa is involved."

"They're slow, but they aren't inept, not with someone like Natalie."

"You'd rather keep your nose clean than save Oskar? I thought you were different."

Lila bit the insides of her cheeks, annoyed by how much his censure cut. "Don't forget why we didn't save Oskar at the auction house."

"Maybe it wasn't smart, but I was trying to help a child. What's your excuse?"

Dixon whistled and shook his head at both of them. *Stop being assholes. Lila has a point about Shaw.*

Tristan hopped off his perch on the coffee table, tapping on his palm. "Fine. We'll tail Teresa for now. Maybe we'll get lucky, and she'll meet her German contacts. She might lead us straight to Oskar."

"We should be so lucky."

"Dixon, any other ideas?" When his brother shook his head, Tristan resumed his typing. "Give me the list, Lila. My people can check them out, narrow down the brothels from her other businesses."

Lila clasped her palm more tightly.

Tristan looked up. "Lila, give me the list. I assure you, my people can be trusted."

"I don't even know your people."

"You know me. Isn't that enough for you? We're talking about kids here. They need to be rescued as soon as possible. We can sort out the list and take it to Shaw ourselves. If you're worried about him knowing where it came from, I assure you, I can come up with something that doesn't involve you."

"I don't even know if I have all the addresses yet."

"Bullshit. If that's what you have, then it's complete. I'd bet—"

"You'd bet? I wouldn't. Like you said, these are kids. I'm not perfect, Tristan. What if I don't have them all? What if I don't have one on my list, and they go deeper? What if they've moved all the kids already, and this just tips them off? What—"

"What if you give me the list, and we save most of them? What if my people and I spend the next six months trailing every pervert and pedophile in the city to see where they go for their next fix?" Tristan raked his fingers through his hair. "Damn it, Lila. Natalie was taking workborn. Most of them slaves. It's not your call. What do you think we do all day when you're not here? Fix cars and eat Chinese food? Give me the damn list."

It wasn't even a request this time. It was an order.

Dixon held up his notepad. *Give it to us, Lila. We'll help. This is what we do.*

She looked back and forth between both men, chewing her lip. Reluctantly, she scribbled down the list on Dixon's notepad, not wanting to leave an electronic trail.

While Tristan sent out messages to his people, Lila pulled up a new file sent from Chief Vance to Shaw. As she had suspected, a large dose of sleeping medication had been found in the hot chocolate.

Her palm vibrated in her pocket, and Lila stared at the message, wide-eyed.

Captain Regina Randolph had finished testing the hot chocolate, confirming Vance's findings.

She'd also found tracers in the tea.

23

"Guan will be over in thirty minutes." Tristan shoved his palm into his pocket and sat in the oversized chair, far from Lila.

Lila put the menu back on the coffee table and slipped off her boots, leaving her socks on, overly conscious now about her feet and toes around Tristan. "I didn't know the Plum Luck Dragon delivered."

"Madam Chen started a couple of weeks ago, just for us. She said we were her best customers."

Dixon grinned a little and scribbled on his notepad. *You flirt with a woman once.*

"You didn't?" Lila scoffed.

She's hot.

"She's fifty. She's old enough to be your mother."

If my mother looked that hot, I would flirt with her too.

Tristan and Lila exchanged a glance. On one hand, they were both happy he'd begun joking a little again. On the other…

"You're such a perv sometimes." Lila snorted as her palm vibrated. Director Randolph had received the second tracer sample from the captain. *The extra quantity will help our research. We understand it will be the last you can procure.*

"Who's that?"

"Sutton." Lila shifted in her seat. Giving the tracer to her family's R&D department had been automatic. You found an edge, you found a way to increase your family's profits, and you did it.

She'd begun to have second thoughts, though. Perhaps it wasn't a good idea for the families to have access to such technology. She already tested her room and car for bugs, an act that seemed as mundane as brushing her teeth, taking a shower, or cleaning her Colt. Smart highborns checked for bugs; idiots forgot. It only took once to expose yourself or your family.

Tristan had been shocked and appalled by the need, especially in her own bedroom.

If the director's team succeeded, the highborn would have to test their food the same way they tested for bugs. Everything they ate or drank would be screened by snoop programs. You'd open yourself up for attack if you did not. A whole new branch of etiquette would evolve around dinner. Perhaps they'd invent watches that could scan your food surreptitiously, or perhaps everyone would scan in front of everyone else and damn the hurt feelings.

That hadn't been the only reason why she'd given the samples to her people, though. The Allied Lands needed a reliable test for tracers, a counter to them, what with the German incursions and—

Lila thumbed her palm absently. Who was she kidding? She hadn't been thinking of the empire, and now she'd started something she couldn't take back.

Perhaps it didn't matter, though. The samples had a very short half-life, and the tracers were only half the technology. If the director's team couldn't figure out how the Germans tracked their targets, then all the tracers in the world would be useless.

Lila wasn't sure if that was a good thing or a bad thing.

Tell us about Rebecca, Dixon wrote, interrupting her thoughts. *There were tracers?*

"Yes." Lila told the two men everything she had found in Sioux Falls, even pulling up Shaw's report so they could scan through it. "It makes no sense that these cases should be connected. The Germans shouldn't be interested in nabbing oracles, and whoever is nabbing oracles shouldn't be interested in Oskar."

"Yes, but tracers have been found at both scenes, and only the empire uses tracers. We can only conclude that the culprits want both targets. The cases are connected whether we want them to be or not. Perhaps we can worry about their motives later."

"Motives predict behavior. If we can figure out why they'd snatch oracles, we can figure out if they'll take more. They shouldn't be interested. They think the women are con artists."

"Perhaps King Lucas asked his men to find out if that's true. I can't see any German aristocrats giving a damn about them, and they're the only other ones in the country who could afford mercs."

Dixon sniffed the air suddenly, pointed to his mouth, and left the room.

"Guan must be here. Dixon pretends he can't hear me when I ask him to switch off the heater, but if there's food coming, he can hear the shop door from a kilometer away."

"He's barely moved for food in over a week," Lila said, unable to suppress a hopeful grin. "He wouldn't go down and get it unless he's hungry."

"I see that." Tristan slid beside her on the couch and caressed her cheek, his skin warm and soft against her cheek. "Thank you for that."

"I didn't do anything but talk to him, which is what you should do as well. Stop avoiding him. He needs his brother."

"Thank you all the same." He wrapped his arms around her waist, pulling her in close and tight. She tasted whiskey in his kiss, both of them hungry after a night cut short.

When the door opened, Tristan dropped his arms.

The floor received yet another guilty look.

While they ate, the group speculated at length about possible motives for King Lucas taking the oracles. Motives ranged from the reasonable (to destabilize the oracles) to the downright insane (to create an army of child oracles).

Complete with laser beams and jet packs.

Unfortunately, the longer they thought about it, the less insane it seemed. Not the lasers and jet packs, but the idea of their enemy collecting oracles, especially young oracles who might be coopted. Such a thing had happened once or twice in the past, a traitorous oracle defecting and going over to the enemy. That problem had been solved by sending assassins. Oracles never had visions about themselves. They never saw it coming.

Oracles knew the score, but no one had defected this time.

"How'd they know these girls would be potential oracles?" Lila frowned, plopping back onto the couch with a mug of Sangre after their meal. "Breaking into pediatric medical records takes time."

"Perhaps that's why they stole children from smaller cities. They have less sophisticated security systems." Tristan joined her with his own mug and picked up the girls' files.

"Sioux Falls isn't a necessarily a small city."

"Yes, but they didn't have to dig into Rebecca's records, did they? She was outed as a future oracle during the investigation. It was all over the news. All they had to do was figure out where the girl was being held. That's an easier problem to solve."

"Apparently it is if you have tracers. They must not have been able to break into the FPS database. I suppose that's some relief. It's not easy, but it's not that difficult, either. These mercs aren't technical geniuses."

"What did the oracle mean this morning when she said her vision was blurry?"

Lila shrugged. "She said it happens when someone hasn't made decisions that impact the vision. Like if the mercs hadn't decided how to take Rebecca yet."

"Mercs from the empire are efficient. They have plans within plans and a thousand fallbacks if something goes wrong. They always know their play well before they act."

Dixon whistled, still eating at the counter. *Someone else involved hadn't decided.*

"That's a good point," Lila said. "If the oracle's vision was blurry, perhaps their plan hinged on someone else, maybe someone deciding if the money was worth the betrayal."

"Or someone trying to figure out if they'd rather give up a child, just so mercs would stop breaking their bones." Tristan breathed out sharply. "This is a lot of work for one kid."

"It was also an awful lot of work for Oskar."

They don't care much about getting caught.

"Yes, they do. It's just that no one in the Allied Lands tests for tracers. We don't even know what to look for. It was a fluke that my people noticed at all. The bullets make it look like an obvious setup. Natalie's pissed off half the families in Saxony, not to mention her own. Her partners, too. There are plenty of people in New Bristol who might have done it and had the resources to implicate mercs. The only thing that's hard for me to swallow is that Natalie would accept a drink from any of them. She was smarter than that."

"You sound like you respected her."

"I respected her as somewhat competent. That doesn't mean that I wanted to be best friends." Lila shut down her laptop. "I have to get home. I'll be missed."

"Stay. We'll figure this out together."

"I can't," she whispered in Tristan's ear, her stomach churning, her cheeks burning. "Isabel will know someone was in my room last night, and she'll know we weren't just talking."

Suddenly, Dixon became quite preoccupied with his fortune cookie.

"Isabel?" Tristan whispered back.

"The woman who cleans my room, since Alex hates me now. The woman who does my laundry, particularly the sheets."

Dixon snatched up his food, then shuffled to the door.

Tristan hopped up. "Dixon, wait, I—"

Dixon waved him off and slipped out the door.

"He's okay with us being…whatever we are," Lila said after the door closed.

"Are you sure?"

"Talk to him, not me." Lila shoved her laptop into her satchel. "Besides, I need to get home. I have a great deal of damage control on my plate for this evening."

"From Isabel?"

"Yes. Sweet as she is, she isn't loyal to me. She's loyal to whomever signs her checks. She has to be. My mother knows about you now, and she'll have her spies scrolling through every camera on the property trying to find a glimpse of you."

"She won't find any."

Lila gave him a long stare. "You know this because?"

"Because I'm that good. I do manage quite well on my own."

"Let's hope you kept away from the cameras."

"I kept away from the cameras," Tristan said, rolling his eyes. "Besides, who cares if your mother knows you're screwing someone? Isn't that what highborn do?"

Lila reached for her militia boots, slamming the heels onto the floor. "My mother sees my womb as Randolph real estate, perhaps one of the most important locations. You don't want her attention. Trust me."

"I can handle it."

"Can you handle the auction house? If I seem too enamored of someone right now, she'll start to get suspicious. It won't go well for either of us."

"I don't think you're in any danger of seeming too enamored."

"I don't want to have a fight tonight, Tristan."

"Maybe we should have one anyway."

"Then fight by yourself. I'm tired, and I'm going home."

"I don't need to be protected from your family, you know. Stop using that as an excuse to slink away."

"Slink away?"

"Yes. You're always slinking away, and you're getting your excuses mixed up. What will it be next time, I wonder?" Tristan knocked her boots away with a sweep of his leg.

Lila looked up, annoyed.

She wasn't sure who reached for whom, but Tristan's kiss wasn't nice or sweet this time. It stung with anger and frustration all at once, nearly hurting with its ferocity. He tugged her down to the couch and whipped his clothes off between more nips, shoving her clothes away and tossing them on the floor.

There was no foreplay this time.

Luckily, Lila didn't need any. She'd grown wet the minute he shoved her onto the couch.

He thrust into her, hard.

She didn't even have time to wrap her legs around his waist before he thrust again.

Lila gasped as he kept going, grabbing at the couch cushions to steady herself, his unreadable eyes fixed on hers. Rather than happy or intense or love-stricken, they had completely blanked, but they fixed on her all the same.

She came after a dozen thrusts.

He did the same, gripping the back of the couch rather than her waist, biting back a moan.

They stared at one another awkwardly, as though neither of them quite knew what to do.

"Is this all you understand, Lila? Is this all you'll ever want from me, and only when you're in the mood?"

Lila nearly reached for her boots once more, but his cock flared the moment she looked at it. She no longer wanted to go home. Not yet.

Shoving him on the floor, she straddled him, rode him, but she wasn't fucking him. Not really. She was fucking his incessant need to pull her close, to cling to her, to follow her. She was fucking his continued thrusts into her feelings. The fact that she'd not been able to enjoy their date for fear that a spy might snap a photo. The fact that she had to keep him a secret from her mother to keep him safe, and that he didn't seem to appreciate her efforts. The fact that she had to wear some stupid hood in his shop to protect her identity from his people.

The fact that they were never, ever going to work out.

The fact that she was so damn tired of everything.

She rode him, not fucking him, but fucking all of society like a pissed-off whore turning tricks.

When she came, it wasn't great. It just was.

Tristan gripped her thighs and pumped into her as he finished. After several strokes, his grip slid away and he panted underneath her, his arms slapping on the rug above his head. "That was shit, wasn't it?"

He swallowed.

Lila watched his Adam's apple rise and fall.

She hopped up, not wanting him inside her any longer, then attacked the pile of clothes near the couch. "What are we doing, Tristan?"

"I'm trying to start a relationship. *Trying* being the key word. I didn't realize I'd have to talk you into it every single fucking day."

"And I didn't realize that nothing I do or say will ever be good enough for you." She fastened the clasp on her bra. "You'll always want more."

"All I want is for you to tell me that I'm important to you. That you miss me at least a little when I'm not around. That you want me, at least in some way. Is that too much to ask?"

"It's complicated."

"No, it's really not," he said, tossing her clothes to her as he came to them, then pulling on his trousers before he even found his boxer briefs.

"I have to go home. People are waiting."

"Are they? Last time you didn't want to be here because you worked better at home. Now it's something else. It's always going to be something, isn't it? Always some excuse to leave."

"Do you even care?" She pulled on her boots and grabbed her satchel. "I have to go whether you understand the reason or not."

"Of course, you wouldn't want to be late for Mommy."

Lila's head snapped up. Whatever he'd won over the last week evaporated all at once. "Fuck you, Tristan DeLauncey."

His face crumpled. "Wait," he said, sprinting forward as she grabbed her hood and dashed out of the room.

Tristan was fast, but Lila was closer and faster. She slammed the apartment door in his face and jogged down the hall and stairs.

Dixon sat on the base of them, stopping mid-bite as she blew past.

He stood up, turning back around to his brother, who blew down the steps in a rush of tumbling bare feet. "Will you just wait?"

But Lila didn't stop. She'd had enough. She shot through the back door of the shop and slipped into the alley, nearly knocking Samantha over in her haste to get away.

"Heya, Hood." Lila didn't reply as she sprinted to the mouth of the alley. "Hey, Hood, where are you going so fast?"

The back door opened so hard that it *thwacked* against the brick.

But Lila was already gone. She turned the corner and ran the two blocks to the parking garage that held her Adessi.

She didn't look back.

She was never, ever going to look back again.

After climbing into her sedan, Lila sped through downtown, charging through the streets like a restless panther. She didn't want to go back to the Randolph compound any more than she wanted to go back to Tristan's shop, so she didn't. Instead, she exited onto the loop and circled around New Bristol.

The bluebonnets lulled her into drowsiness as she took another pass. Then another.

It was annoying, not being able to ride her Firefly. Darting around other cars was so much more satisfying with an engine vibrating between your legs, the wind clawing at your skin, the knowledge that you could take a lethal spill if you didn't pay enough attention.

She would have been more awake, that was for damn sure.

She tried to clear her mind, to think about work, to think about Oskar, the oracles, Alex. It didn't take long for her thoughts to circle back to Tristan, her mind on an endless loop, just like her Adessi.

Lights flashed in her rearview.

A haggard Bullstow cruiser turned on its siren, struggling to keep pace.

Lila cursed and pulled over, her sedan bouncing as she slipped off the road.

A fresh-faced Bullstow militiaman knocked on her window with a few sharp strikes. "ID," he said when she rolled down the glass.

He slipped his palm from his front pocket and began tapping on the screen. "Do you have any idea how fast you were going?"

"Not really." She handed him her ID.

The blackcoat nearly choked as he read it, apologizing and stumbling over his words. He bowed and blustered for so long that his palm began to beep, prompting him for the next piece of information for the ticket.

The palm went unanswered.

Lila frowned. The leather blackcoat didn't him fit him yet. It still bagged around his thin frame.

"I didn't recognize you without your family colors," he stammered at last.

"Give me the ticket. It's not like I can't pay it, and I deserve the damn thing. Besides, it'll do my mother good to wonder why I was doing... What was it?"

"Two hundred and ten kilometers per hour."

"Good. It'll shut her up for a while." She rubbed her chin as her brain finally caught up with the number. "Wait, two ten? Really?"

"That's nothing. This car could hit two fifty. The roadsters climb even higher. At least that's what I've read. My cruiser only goes up to one ninety. If you hadn't stopped, I never would have caught you."

"We're militia. We stop for one another."

The young blackcoat nodded and reluctantly tapped away on his palm. "Did you receive your ticket, chief?" he asked as though reading from a script.

Lila lifted her palm and scrolled, finding the message.

Oracle's light. Two ten.

She was almost proud of herself.

"Yes. Remember, never let a highborn off with a warning if you wouldn't let a workborn off as well. It disgraces the militia."

The officer bowed before he darted back to his cruiser and sped away, perhaps worrying she might change her mind.

Lila leaned against the still open window. He'd remember this stop, this lesson she'd tried to impart for a very long time. Not only because he'd dared to give an heir a speeding ticket but because he'd dared to give one to a chief.

And because she'd given him permission to do it, instructed him to do it as though it were part of his training.

She hated that. She hated that people remembered such little things about her, such insignificant annoyances in her life, things that echoed in their memories. The time they gave Elizabeth Victoria Lemaire-Randolph a speeding ticket. The time they saw Chief Randolph eating crème brûlée with the prime minister in Hotel Emeraude. The time they saw the Randolph prime outside a teenage highborn party, taking a break from the ridiculousness inside. The time they saw the heir in El Dorado, eating lunch with a man who couldn't stop grinning.

Shaw would praise her words after he saw the ticket and brought the boy in for a debriefing. He would have done the same at his age, though without her permission. He'd put almost anyone in a holding cell for breaking almost any law, no matter the crime, no matter who they were.

He'd put her in one the moment he found out about the things she'd been doing lately.

He'd only hired her because the prime minister insisted on it, because Bullstow needed her help to solve its most desperate cases, because she worked for free, because he didn't have to put the expense on a spreadsheet and justify it to High House. Because he knew she wouldn't blackmail him.

Because he could trust her.

But he couldn't, and he should never have trusted her at all.

Max was right. She'd been around Tristan and Dixon for too long. Not only was she not covering herself as she should, she was risking herself and others. And for what?

When had everything gotten so damn complicated?

She laid her head against the headrest, letting traffic pass her by, lost in thought.

Half an hour later, Lila awoke with a start, her engine cold.

24

Lila stole through the front door of the great house, her countenance as grouchy as her mood. It was nearly midnight, far too late for anyone to be awake downstairs on a Thursday night. She didn't care if Ms. O'Malley or Isabel saw her, or even if the cameras saw her. She didn't really care if anyone saw her.

Her mother cleared her throat.

Perhaps Lila cared a little.

She turned her head, peering through the entryway into the parlor. Her mother and father lounged on a white couch, sipping Gregorie.

"Sit," Chairwoman Randolph ordered from afar.

Fuck. Lila had seen her mother's Blanc convertible in the garage. The chairwoman had obviously seen what she'd done.

It seemed so funny this morning when she'd been half asleep.

Lila reluctantly shuffled toward the parlor. She propped herself up against the doorway, crossing her boots at the ankles. "You bellowed?"

"I said sit. Not skulk in the doorway like an eavesdropping slave."

Lila shoved her hands in her pockets and plopped down on an uncomfortable wooden chair. The padding was thin, not because it was an antique, but because its maker had been a sadist.

Its owner might be one too.

Slouching, she nearly dropped her heels on the delicate glass table, stopping only when her mother hopped to her feet. "What are you doing?"

Yes, she'd definitely been around Tristan and Dixon for far too long, but that wouldn't be a problem anymore.

Lila sat up, boots on the floor, and cleared her throat. "So, you bellowed?"

Her mother just stared until Lemaire tugged her back to her seat.

"There are oil stains on my rug, Elizabeth. Oil stains. I don't even know how you got my car inside Wolf Tower, much less parked it inside my private apartment on the top floor, but—"

Lila couldn't help herself. She giggled.

Her mother glared. "I could barely get inside, Elizabeth. The door kept bouncing off the bumper. You ruined a rug that's been in the family for two generations."

"Is that sentimentality I hear, Mother?"

"Don't take that tone with me, child. I had to get our mechanics to take the Blanc apart and reassemble it back at the garage. It took the entire day. There were parts left over."

"So buy a new one." Lila shrugged. "Perhaps I'll leave your car alone next time if you stop putting bugs in mine."

The chairwoman cocked her head. "You did all that just because—"

"Because you deserved it."

"So my spies put a few bugs in your car, and you park mine in my living room? Doesn't that doesn't seem a little bit disproportionate to you?"

"It's proportionate to how annoying I find it."

Her mother gulped her wine. "Take over, Henri. I don't have any patience left. I don't know what I will do to my child if you do not."

"I'm not a child."

"Then stop acting like one. If I thought you were in your right mind, we'd be having a very different conversation right now."

Lemaire patted the chairwoman's shoulder. "Settle down, Bea."

"No, I won't. Fix it. Deal with her."

Gods, it was like Lila had been taken back a dozen years.

Her father scooted to the edge of his seat and scratched his jaw. "Elizabeth, Chief Shaw just called. Could you tell us what you were doing driving around the loop at eleven o'clock at night?"

"About two ten."

Her father swallowed hard. "Why were you driving so fast?"

"Apparently, I was teaching a lesson to a very green militiaman. He wasn't even going to write me a ticket, Father. Can you believe that? Bullstow's finest, my ass."

"Language, young lady."

"Ass is a word, Mother. Look it up."

Her father cleared his throat. "And why were you on the loop in the first place?"

"I needed to clear my head."

"You can clear your head while driving the speed limit. If you'd lost control and hit another car—"

"I could have died. Just as I could have died if I'd had a heart attack, if I'd arrested the wrong criminal, or if the plane I was on went down. Or if I drank milk from a poisoned bottle. Need I go on? I'm not going to hide in an armored house. That's not living. I needed to think. I went out and thought. And now, I'm going to bed. I'm exhausted." Lila stood once more, brushing her gloves on her trouser legs.

"Sit," her mother ordered again.

"Why? What exactly do you want to talk about, other than your car and a ticket?"

Lila peered into her mother's face, scanning it like she might inspect a possible forgery. But it wasn't anger she found. That was gone. If she didn't know any better, she'd think the chairwoman hadn't found out about Tristan's visit.

Lila owed Isabel a bribe.

"I humored you once tonight. Don't ask me again."

Lila slipped her satchel over her shoulder, heaved herself to her feet, and stalked away.

"When did she turn into a rebellious teenager?" her father muttered.

"I'm not a teenager," Lila called out over her shoulder. "I'm pushing thirty."

"She never stopped behaving like that with me, Henri. Why did she start behaving like that with you? That's the question."

Lila trundled upstairs, making a great amount of noise, since her mother knew exactly where she was anyway.

When she entered her room, she found Alex sitting on her couch, her pumps on the floor, her legs curled and tucked to the side. The slave worried the hem of her skirt and kept her eyes on the ground.

Lila's grouchiness faltered, but it didn't fade. She wasn't in the right frame of mind for another yelling match.

She dropped her satchel on her desk and fished her palm from her trouser pocket, toeing her kicked-off boots into her closet. Then she turned on her desktop computer and swept the room for bugs.

So far, she'd ignored Alex, waiting to see if she would talk or yell.

She did neither, even when Lila leaned over her to sweep the coat of arms.

Lila finally plopped down in front of her computer, breaking first. "I'm moving you to another Randolph compound after Simon leaves for boarding school, Ms. Wilson. You need a fresh start and a counselor to help you manage. Give me a list of your preferences by the weekend. I'll do my best to meet them."

Alex scooted to the couch's edge and fiddled with her pumps. "That's not why I came."

"It's not a good night to yell at me, Ms. Wilson. I'm done being your punching bag, and you do not deserve to be mine tonight."

Alex looked up. "Something happened between you and that guy you're seeing, didn't it?"

"What guy?" Lila narrowed her eyes.

"I swapped shifts with Isabel this morning. I was going to talk to you then, but you were already gone. I took care of your room."

Lila looked away, embarrassed, finally understanding why other highborn generally didn't speak to the help.

"There was a time when I would have known who you were with. Now, I have no idea."

Lila pushed her palm around her desk. She said nothing because she wanted Alex to leave. She just didn't know how to ask nicely.

She'd wanted to have this conversation for an entire week, but now was not the right time for it.

She just wanted a nice, long shower.

"Your mother was right about some of it," Alex said. "You were too."

"Right about what?"

"Patrick really did those things. It's all true, isn't it?"

Lila nodded glumly.

"Patrick was never bright. At least, I never thought he was that bright. I was so sure that my mother had convinced him to take the blame, that he'd put his neck in that noose, not understanding." Alex faltered. "I made Johnny take me to Bullstow."

Lila's eyes widened.

"He's a Randolph. He's taken me off-compound before. It was actually one of the perks of getting involved with him. Chief Shaw wouldn't let me see Patrick when they arrested me, and my mother was still too sick after the serum to have visitors. Johnny has cousins at Bullstow, though. I was going to threaten to tell your Aunt Georgina about what we'd been doing if he didn't get me inside. I didn't have to threaten him, though. He just took me. He didn't ask why. He just asked for a moment to wash the dirt off his hands."

"He cares about you."

"I know. I almost threatened him. I shouldn't have."

"You didn't."

"I almost did. I was still mad, and I needed to see my brother."

"What did he say?"

Alex turned away and stared at the Randolph coat of arms. "Do you remember the story about Little Red Riding Hood and the wolf?"

"I remember the grandmother was eaten. I once scratched out 'grand' in my book and gave it to my mother after a fight."

"That was mean."

"It was in crayon, and I was five. I didn't know any better."

Alex worried her skirt's hem once more. "I feel like Little Red Riding Hood lately, except that the wolf peeks out from everyone I know. Everyone. Now my eyes are open."

Lila stood up and sat beside her old friend on the couch. "Is Johnny a wolf?"

"What if he is?"

"What if he's not? Am I a wolf?"

"I don't know." Alex's eyes reddened, and she crossed her arms over her chest. "You had me arrested, Lila. How could you have done that?"

"You chose to hit me. More than once, and on more than one occasion. You chose to hit me in front of the council. What was I supposed to do?"

Alex looked away. "I don't know what you are anymore, Lila. I don't know what Patrick is, either. He said horrible things."

"Like what?"

"He said that I should poison the compound's water supply and take my place with him and Mother. That I should make the Wilson name notorious so that everyone in the Allied Lands would remember us from beyond the grave. He's gone crazy. When did he go crazy?"

"I don't know." Lila stood up and dug through a stack of folders on her desk, finding a copy of Patrick's thesis. She'd meant to give it to Alex at some point, but she might not have another chance. "Did you ever read this?"

Alex took the folder and skimmed the title. "*Skepticism and Self-Interest?*"

"It's Patrick's senior thesis. I got it from Bokington."

"No, he didn't do a senior thesis," Alex said, skimming the table of contents. "The Morality of Criminal Activity?"

Alex turned to the relevant section, her eyes passing over the wall of text, her face twisting in confusion. "This isn't right, Lila. He had an internship with the Massons. He bragged about how he received college credit for playing games all—"

"I remember. Doesn't change the fact that he lied. He believed he was hiding his brilliance, I imagine. I had to hack deep into the Bokington network to find that, as well as his advisor's recommendation that he see a psychiatrist. Bokington dropped the ball on that one. They're covering their asses now."

Alex stared at the folder, realization sinking in. "So was he always like this? Did we miss it, or did he hide it? Or did he turn into someone else completely?"

"You were away for a very long time. So was I. I thought I knew him too. When I saw him in the car at the airport, I thought your mother had sent him as a decoy. But the way he spoke to Captain O'Bryan, the passports, Oskar. He admitted to it all."

"We taught him how to ride a bike, Lila. We taught him how to tie his shoes. Did we teach him this too?"

"I don't know."

"I want Dr. Booth to do a CT or an MRI or whatever it is they do on people's minds when they flip like this. He's got a brain tumor or a blood clot or—"

"I asked already. Dr. Booth and Dr. Adams didn't find anything."

"I want an autopsy, then," Alex whispered, unable to hold back her tears. "After he's gone. He's not my Patrick anymore."

Lila bowed her head. "I'll make arrangements with Chief Shaw and Dr. Booth."

Her friend didn't speak for quite a while. When it grew too quiet and too awkward between them, Lila stood up to return to her desk, but Alex grabbed her hand before she could slip away. "I've missed you."

Lila felt her eyes grow hot. "I've missed you too."

Alex dropped her hand. "I'm sorry my family turned out so crap, Lila. I'm sorry they tried to hurt— I'm sorry they tried to kill you. I'm even sorry I hit you. I was so angry that it never registered that I'd almost lost you, and that Patrick would have been the one to do it to you. It wasn't until your mother…"

Lila sat down. "You were right too. I shouldn't have asked you to help me. I just didn't think."

"You didn't make me do anything. I chose to help you. I have to accept my part in it." Alex leaned back into the couch. "I just don't understand how he could have done it. He screwed over our entire family. Some died in the riot. Others were sold at LeBeau's. I have kin as slaves now. Not everyone was prepared for the crash to happen so soon."

"They'll pay off their marks."

"I saw the numbers. It will take ten years for some of them to pay it off. He did that. He ruined my family and nearly killed my—killed you. He's a wolf."

"Your mother—"

"I already knew she was one, and everyone knows my cousins who died in that riot weren't angels. Johnny pulled up the news footage. I saw what they did. It's a humiliation, Lila. My family... Am I a wolf too?"

"Gods, no," Lila said, squeezing her hand.

"Your mother was right about my family, about my breeding." Tears spilled once again over Alex's cheeks. "We're all—"

"Human. You've all made decisions."

"Mine have sucked lately. You have no idea how badly."

"I can assure you that mine have been worse. You know we're going to have to keep tabs on Simon, don't you?"

Alex sat up with a start. "Lila, he'd never—"

"Oracle's light, I didn't mean it like that. I mean we'll have to make sure he doesn't start thinking like you. It'll eat at him."

"I already talked to him. I said that nothing he told you made a difference. You'd already begun poking around." She sniffled into her handkerchief and dabbed at the corners of her eyes. A small smile crept to her face. "So who's the guy?"

"Ms. Wilson."

"Come on, tell me."

Lila stood up and retrieved her palm. "He's no one you know."

"That's not good enough," Alex whined, trying to grin. "Tell me."

"No."

"I'm going to keep asking. You'll get grouchy and annoyed and eventually you'll give in. Why not skip to the end?"

"You can ask as many times as you want. As long as my mother doesn't, I'm happy."

"She won't hear it from me. I'm not going to pretend that we'll be best friends again, but I wouldn't betray you like that."

After an awkward silence, Alex finally slipped from the room.

25

Lila watched the crimson maple leaves flutter and tremble through the glass walls of the morning room. Johnny and his group of workborn knelt among them on the gravel path, pulling out weeds and pruning. They all wore thin coats and thick gloves.

New Bristol had finally embraced autumn once more. The heat wave had finally broken.

It was far colder inside the morning room, though and not as beautiful. Light streamed through the glass walls, casting errant sunbeams on the floor, the scattered light splitting into reds and blues on the wood.

Lila sipped her juice in silence, wincing when a drop stung her wounded hand, free from her bandages and gloves at last. Her skin looked ugly and broken, but at least she could feel her spoon and glass for the first time in almost two weeks.

Her parents barely looked up from their plates.

That worked for her. She didn't feel much like talking. Bleary-eyed from research the night before, she'd barely managed three hours of sleep.

She had little to show for her effort. She'd taken a deeper look into the alien game's code, recognizing that it wasn't a virus and it didn't transmit password or account information. After nodding off a few times, she'd hopped up for coffee, then hacked into Chief Shaw's reports. No new developments had occurred in Rebecca's case. It seemed Chief Vance's men had spent the morning trying to track down Ms. Royce and her tea. Instead, they'd tracked down her body. She'd been killed in a car accident. One car, one pole.

Murdered, by Lila's estimation, though Chief Vance didn't think it likely. After all, the drugs were in the chocolate. There was absolutely no reason to suspect that Ms. Royce was involved. They'd passed her death onto another team for investigation and focused on the hot chocolate and the rest of the staff at FPS, assuming one of them had given out Rebecca's location.

Very sloppy.

Frustrated but not surprised, Lila had pulled up the game's code once more, intent on digging further into the game.

Unfortunately, the coffee she drank hadn't kept her awake. She woke up with her nose pressed into her keyboard, a long string of slashes and semicolons upon the screen.

She'd still had a few keyboard marks on her face after dressing for the day.

Pax's eyes bounced back and forth among Lila and her parents. He scratched his chin and picked up his knife and fork, cutting a bite of his omelet, the knife squealing as it raked across the china.

"About your car," her father began.

Lila sighed. She didn't have the time or the desire to buy a new car today, something she'd do as soon as he tried to bar her from the garage.

"I thought about taking your keys away. I'd be within my rights to do so. You're going to kill yourself one of these days." He placed his fork on the table. "For oracle's sake, Lila, you had a wreck less than two weeks ago. You'd think those stitches all over your hands would remind you to slow down. I have no desire to claim your body when half of it is still smeared on the road. Unfortunately, you're an adult."

"I'm more than an adult. I'm—"

"Don't push me, Elizabeth. You might be the chief of a family, but I'm the prime minister of an entire country. I have an entire army at my disposal. I could have you locked in this compound for the next ten years if I wished."

Lila raised a brow.

"But you'd just find a way to wiggle out of it. Oracle's light, child. Stop being stupid. Whatever's crawled up your ass, find a different way of dealing with it."

The chairwoman turned her head. "Language, Henri."

"Bea? Sometimes you make me want to borrow Lila's Firefly."

Pax chuckled as their mother turned her face away, harrumphing.

At least Lila's mother said nothing for the rest of the meal, likely plotting a way to make her father pay for the remark.

He would pay eventually. So would Lila for her cheek lately, and for the Blanc.

They wouldn't pay today, though. Her mother let the bulk of Lila's attitude pass unchecked, probably because Peter had nearly killed her less than a week before. But the temporary reprieve would soon fade, and her mother would be back to her usual mood and consequences, plotting and scheming.

Lila finished her meal and left the table, pausing at the door while she slipped on her blackcoat, gritting her teeth as the leather pulled on her shoulder. She'd run the obstacle course before breakfast and had taken a particularly nasty fall.

Winding a scarf around her neck, she stepped onto the gravel path.

Her father followed her outside. "Is it the oracles?"

"Is what the oracles?"

"Is that the thing making you so…"

"Would you care if it was?" she asked, thrusting her hands in her pockets.

"Of course I would care. You've always been capable of handling so much. Even when you were a kid."

"So what, now I'm weak because I got a speeding ticket?"

"No, you're just acting like a pain in the ass." He untied and retied his scarf, clearly uncomfortable. "Lila, the staff has informed me that you haven't… That it's been a very long time since…"

"Since what?"

Her father fixed her with a stare. "You're to take a lover this season. That's not an order or a demand, obviously. You're too

WREN WESTON

old for those. It's just a sincere wish on behalf of me and your mother. In the meantime, we've spoken with Commander Sutton and cleared you for two weeks' vacation. You don't have to go to St. Kitts, but take this time to… Well, I'm sure you have an old lover somewhere or a senator you fancy. Rent a hotel room some place beautiful and stay there."

Lila's jaw dropped. "Excuse me?"

"I've worked you too hard lately. What with our work and the council and your job as chief, you haven't had time to get out lately. You're twenty-eight years old, in the prime of your life, and you have no lovers. I blame myself."

"Father—"

"A woman like you should have four or five men blowing up her palm with messages, sending flowers, asking for dinners and weekends away. Instead, all you have is a thousand messages a day about work. Chief Vance and Chief Shaw can find the kidnapped girls. If the oracles really want to find their children, then they'll help, regardless of your involvement. Maybe that makes me an ass, but I'm not going to lose my child to find someone else's."

His face paled. He was clearly horrified at what he'd just said, or only horrified that he'd meant it.

"I'm not going on vacation."

Her father didn't argue with her. Instead, he pulled his palm from his coat pocket, scrolling through several screens before handing her the device.

Lila scowled as the story came up. *Prime Minister Steals Oracle's Daughter.*

"It's over-sensationalized crap, of course, but it's on the first page of the *Unity Post*," he said. "My media consultants are spinning it, making it clear we were looking out for the welfare of the child and the oracles, but the story is gaining traction."

"I warned you to release Rebecca from foster care."

"I listened, just not soon enough." He took back the palm and stuffed it into his pocket. "It's to our benefit that the threat turned out to be real, though I wish it hadn't been. I was just trying to help."

"I know."

"Something is going on—"

"They didn't call for you," she reminded him gently. "They've had your ear for years, and they didn't ask for help."

Her father tugged his coat around himself more tightly. "Why aren't you more curious? You know something, don't you? Something you aren't telling me."

"There's an awful lot I don't tell you. I keep the secrets of lots of people. You, Bullstow, Mother, myself."

"You try to help. Why is it different when I try to do the same thing?"

"Because I don't get involved when I'm not wanted."

"Yes, you do, in your own way. You interfere all the time, just like your mother, just like my media consultants, spinning the story. You've spun me a time or two, and I'm sure you'll do it again."

"Perhaps. Never to harm, though, never to control."

"It's a slippery slope, Lila. One day, you might not remember where the line is."

"Do you?"

Lemaire played with the ends of his scarf. "Did I ever tell you about my boomerang, Lila? It was a toy I had when I was a child, just some oddly shaped stick that came back to you if you threw it right. I used to go out on the grounds in the evenings and spend hours getting the angle right so it would come right back to my hand. My mind would just drop away. It was almost like meditation. I miss that."

"The workborn would laugh at us. Two spoiled highborn, crying with full bellies on the hearth of a palace."

"The poorer classes have their complications. We have ours."

When they parted moments later, her father strolled off to the garage, and she marched down Villanueva Lane to the security office, riding the elevator to her office and a full inbox. She didn't care much about her mother and father's notions of a vacation.

She had work, and she had no leads on the oracles or Oskar.

When she reached the eleventh floor, she nodded to the receptionist and Sergeant Jenkins, then opened her office door. She twirled around, feeling someone's eyes on her back.

Commander Sutton trailed along wordlessly behind her like a shadow.

"Have a seat," Lila said, removing her coat.

"I thought I wouldn't see you here today," Sutton said, plopping down across from her.

"You should know better than that, commander. My parents can't arbitrarily decide when I go on vacation."

"I know, but I can."

Lila steepled her hands upon her desk and studied her mentor's face. "Do you have something to say, commander?"

"Are you going to make me say it, Elizabeth? You've been burned out for months. When you're here, your brain is elsewhere. When you're elsewhere, your brain is here."

"Elizabeth? If I'm slacking, tell me. Don't dance around—"

"You're not slacking. I'd be the first to tell you if you were."

Lila shifted in her seat. "Fine. If I've been dumping too many things on you lately, I—"

"Having the commanders handle a few meetings on our own? Asking me to sign off on the occasional report here and there? That's not slacking. We didn't even have daily meetings under Chief Zoe. We had them twice a week, and she didn't always attend. It took Chief Zoe five days to return reports; you average five hours. The only time you're not replying to messages is when you're asleep, something you haven't been doing much of lately."

Lila lifted her chin to protest, but Sutton cut her off with a wave.

"Don't bother. Sometimes you work elsewhere, but you're always here. Some days my inbox is already full of things you've sent at three o'clock in the morning. Same with Sergeant Jenkins and the other commanders. You even forgot that it was your day off yesterday until I reminded you. Your parents are right. You need to get away for a while, and you need to leave your palm behind when you do."

"I don't need two weeks off."

Commander Sutton frowned. "Two weeks? I suggested a month."

"This came from you?"

"I told you that you needed some time off. When your parents called me in last night and brought it up, I agreed with them."

"Traitor."

"Hey, it's hard when the prime minister asks for your opinion. I may be old and married, but I'm not dead. He's got those eyes that just kind of—"

"Don't finish that thought. That's my father you're talking about."

"Your hot father."

Lila fiddled with her palm. "I just took time off, commander."

"You mean that half-day you took when you got tranqed? Ms. Wilson told me you spend the entire evening puking out your guts in the toilet."

"I took the next day off."

"Wow. A whole day, a day required by militia regulations on several grounds, one being that someone nearly murdered you."

Lila swiveled her chair back and forth. "I don't need—"

"Chief, for oracle's sake, go away. The place will still be standing when you get back next month."

"Next week."

"Three weeks."

"A week."

"Two," Sutton insisted, "and if you come back before then, I swear to the gods, I'll put you in a holding cell until your vacation is over."

Lila wasn't sure if her old mentor was joking or not.

"No one in the militia is going to send you a damn thing for the next two weeks. If something does hit your palm, forward it to me so I can strangle the idiot who sent it you."

"What if—"

"If something comes up that I can't handle? I'll get your dear, sweet mother involved, and you know how I feel about that. Consider it my punishment for this entire conversation."

"Fine," Lila said, tugging the lapels of her blackcoat. "I'll go through my inbox and—"

"No. Forward it to me. All of it. Consider this a practice drill for whenever you finally break your neck on that bike of yours."

"It's called a Firefly."

"It's called a deathtrap when you ride it."

Lila cocked her head.

"Too much?"

"The ice is thin, commander. Very thin."

Lila tapped on her palm for a few moments and sent everything in her militia inbox to Sutton, then set it to forward everything to her commander for the next two weeks.

Sutton escorted her to the elevator. She talked merrily of the weather in Mexico and England. She mentioned cruises to the Caribbean. She even talked of former senators who might be aching to get away. It was only when Lila found herself in front of the entrance to the security office that Sutton finally shook her hand, turned, and hustled back into the building.

Lila stared at the structure, watching the blackcoats move inside, watching them march on the gravel paths during their rounds.

She stared until one of the patrols passed by for the second time.

Lila turned away, shoving her hands in her pockets. They nearly didn't fit, for she'd carried her palm in one and Tristan's spare in the other. She'd found the device in her satchel the night before and carried it with her to work, intending to scroll through the code again while digging through her inbox. The silly game that had bothered Toxic so much had begun to bother Lila as well. The aliens still hovered in the center of the flickering screen. The score had frozen at three thousand.

Three thousand? What was the point of the game? What was she missing?

And why was this stupid, broken game on so many palms at Natalie's hideout?

Frustrated, she shoved the spare back into her pocket and walked down Villanueva Lane, but instead of returning to the great house, she kept going. She had absolutely no interest in seeing her mother's smug face.

Perhaps she was procrastinating, rather than dealing with her blackmailer's message. Max was right. She'd have to pay so that she would have extra time to search.

Militia patrols marched past, as did the highborn in their red coats and business suits, the family's coat of arms stitched upon the breast. Workborn bustled among them, hurrying to and fro in all manner of dress befitting their station and position.

She sat upon a bench in the center of the compound, staring up at Wolf Tower. Like her militia building, the walls had been made of glass, but this glass was impenetrable. She couldn't see in, but the people inside could see out.

It was just somewhere else she didn't belong.

Her palm vibrated, and she reached into her pocket to check it.

Tristan's name popped up on the screen.

Realizing she wouldn't get any peace, she scrolled through his messages, all some mix of *I'm sorry* and *Call me*. Half annoyed, she opened up the latest. *Teresa was found dead this morning. Bullstow is investigating, and my people can't get close.*

Just like that, her leads had all evaporated.

Slumping on the bench, she pinched the bridge of her nose. How was she supposed to go on vacation in the middle of this? Where would she even go? Who would she go with?

She laughed bitterly. Somehow the oracle still believed she would find the girls.

She curled over the bench and dug out the spare palm.

Perhaps she had one lead left.

This time when she brought up the game, the aliens had moved from the center of the screen, trailing in a tail to the left. No matter how she twisted her palm, the aliens always trailed off in the same direction. She'd lost points, too. Her score had dropped to twenty-four hundred.

Intrigued, Lila rubbed at her chin. She'd go home and dig into the code, just like Toxic had done. If she had to, she'd spend all day figuring out how the game was supposed to work and what the virus was supposed to do. It wasn't like she didn't have the time.

At least she'd be doing something to help.

She stood up and took a few steps away from the bench.

From the corner of her eye, she saw the aliens bobble.

Lila looked closer. Not only had aliens moved, but the score had ticked up by one.

"What the—" Lila walked around the block, watching the aliens move and her score tick up and down, though not by much.

Eyes fixed on the screen, she moved in the direction of the tail, letting her score drop lower. She knew it would freeze at three thousand, but what would happen when it hit zero?

The buildings around her didn't make it easy. Occasionally she had to walk a block out of her way before she could follow the tail once more. Other times, she nearly bumped into someone on the street. Lila barely noticed, for they'd always move out of her way.

She was the chief and an heir, after all.

Gradually, the entire compound faded away, becoming only a blur of color and a wash of sounds, barely poking at her consciousness. The only thing that existed was her palm's screen and the eight-bit game.

She didn't see the lamppost until it was too late.

A blonde child in a red dress and black Mary Janes giggled, her laugh echoing in the quiet.

Lila rubbed her aching shoulder, only somewhat thankful she hadn't smacked into the steel with her face, and looked around her. She remained in the northern part of her family's compound, a maze of office buildings, condos, and garages looming above her.

Her palm vibrated, and she removed it from her pocket.

Alex wanted to know if she'd be back for lunch.

Ignoring her palm, the laughing girl, and her aching shoulder, Lila continued on her journey. For another fifteen minutes, the game led her through the estate and toward a pair of glass double doors.

Lila darted inside and roamed a nearly empty lobby.

"Can I help you?" someone called out.

Lila ignored the voice. Her score had frozen on ten, and no matter which way she went, ten was the lowest her score would drop. The aliens refused to show her the way. They had clustered around the center of the screen, darkening, becoming opaque.

Nothing she did elicited much of a response.

A hand gripped her sore shoulder, startling her.

"Are you okay, Chief Randolph?" Director Randolph asked, somewhat flustered, her red lab coat stained with coffee at the neck. "Sara called when you wouldn't answer her. Did we have an appointment?"

The young woman at the front desk picked up her headset and did her best to look and not-look at the confused chief in the middle of the lobby.

"No. No, we didn't." Lila swallowed, her heart beating faster and faster. "What floor is your lab on?"

"The fourth floor. Why?"

"That's about ten meters up, wouldn't you say?"

Lila licked her lips as the woman nodded. The game had led her directly to the Burgess Building. It had led her right back to the tracer samples she'd given to the director the day before.

The game was the tracer program.

26

Lila didn't stop for lunch.

She ran to the great house, scrambled up the staircase, and burst into her room, tugging her boots off before the door had even closed. The slam matched the splat of her blackcoat and her militia uniform falling on the floor, and she dug into her secret compartment for servant's clothes. She put on whatever her hand touched first: a pair of black trousers, a white tank, a gray sweater, and her old, worn boots. After slipping her unmarked motorcycle jacket over her sore shoulder, she replaced the panel and patted her militia garb, searching for the two palms.

"Come on, come on, come on," she chanted, her hands lighting on the devices at last.

Tapping the screen of her palm, she checked her messages. Tristan had not yet replied. It wasn't a good sign, but she didn't have time to wait.

Lila shoved both palms and a few supplies into her satchel, and thrust her Colt into her pocket and her knife into her boot. Then she rushed to the garage and hopped in her Cruz sedan, quickly waving her palm across the car and connecting it to the car's computer.

Thankfully, she found no bugs and no evidence of GPS tapping.

Passing quickly through the gatehouse, Lila sped toward Shippers Lane, jogging toward the shop after parking her car in a garage nearby.

Dixon hopped up from the stool near the dock door. He cocked his head at her frantic pace and rumpled hood. She had told them she'd be over soon, but soon usually meant an hour. This time, she'd only employed a few twists and turns to ensure she wasn't being followed.

There just wasn't time to care about spies.

Dixon opened the shop door and ushered her in. He climbed the stairs two at a time, trying to catch up with her as she burst through the apartment door.

A slightly pale Tristan stood aimlessly in the middle of the room, bootless, staring at the knot on the living room floor. He looked up as the door shot open, startled when she hurried into the room. "That was faster than I—"

"Natalie's a genius," Lila blurted as she crossed the room, throwing her hood and coat on the counter. "Sort of. I mean, she's an idiot, but a genius, too."

"Your message was about Natalie?"

"Of course it was about Natalie. Why else do you think I'd come over here again?" She dug into his trouser pockets for his palm. When she found it missing, she turned around, studying the room. "Where's your palm? I need it. I need as many as you have."

Tristan only stared in confusion.

Lila ignored him and turned to Dixon. "Go get his palm, will you? Yours too. We have to hurry."

Dixon didn't budge either.

"No."

"If this is about last night, Tristan, put it away. We have more important things—"

"It's not about last night. We can't make plans if you don't clue us in, and for the love of the gods, sit down! You're making me nervous."

Dixon grabbed her hand and tugged her toward the couch, putting far too much pressure on her injured shoulder.

"Oracle's light!"

Dixon threw his hands in the air and backed away, his mouth in a little O of surprise.

"What happened to your shoulder?"

"A lamppost hit me." She pouted, rubbing the bone. Dixon retrieved a bag of peas from the freezer and sat beside her on the couch, holding the bag in place. "Give me your palm, Tristan. I'll explain as I work."

Tristan finally slid the device across the coffee table while she dug the spare from her satchel. He reclined in the oversized chair, sitting as far away from her as possible.

"We were idiots to think Natalie didn't have something bigger up her sleeve. Oskar wasn't the point of her last deal at all. He was bait for a much bigger prize." Lila connected both palms with a cable and scrolled through screen after screen as she talked.

"What prize?"

"The tracer system. That's why we found tracers in her blood and the blood of her guards. She used her people and herself as vessels. There's no telling how many palms she brought to that meet, hoping to hack into and download the tracer program. She knew exactly what to steal."

"The game is the tracer program?"

"Yes."

Tristan and Dixon stared at one another. "The broken game?"

"It's not broken."

"Didn't you say that was bad?" He pointed to his palm as she downloaded the game onto his device.

"For fuck's sake, Tristan, don't you trust my judgment by now?"

Tristan raised his hands. "Okay, this is obviously not the afternoon to question your authority."

Lila narrowed her eyes.

"Okay, it's not the afternoon to engage in sarcasm, either."

Dixon poked a finger at his notepad. *How would she fence it?*

"Any family would drool at the chance to study the tracers, even if they only had a day and a half. I suspect she already had a buyer lined up. Two guesses who knew about that deal?"

"Teresa Bailey."

"Natalie would have made a great deal of money if she'd gotten to the buyer. More than enough to escape her charges, flee to Burgundy, and set herself up for life, that's for damn sure."

"How do you know she didn't get to the buyer?"

"If I had just concluded the deal of a lifetime, I certainly wouldn't go back to my hideout and eat breakfast, knowing full well my enemies could locate me. I'd keep moving. That's what made her stupid. She shouldn't have ingested any of it, but I suppose she didn't trust her people. Perhaps she worried they'd hold it hostage for a bigger cut once they got back to the hideout."

"Perhaps she planned on selling Oskar, regardless of whether or not he served as bait. He was worth a great deal of money."

"Perhaps."

"Do you think the mercs knew her plan?"

"No," Lila said. "Natalie wasn't tortured. They just needed her dead so she couldn't say anything about them under the serum. Following her back to her hideout meant they could take Oskar for free, destroy her electronics, and tie up their loose ends. They probably would have looked a little harder if they'd known the empire's crown jewels were hidden in the room."

Lila disconnected Tristan's palm and dug into Dixon's trouser pocket, snatching up his palm and connecting it to the spare. "I also found out last night that Ms. Royce was killed in a car wreck two nights ago. The same FPS employee who liked selling the Thomases their precious loose-leaf tea. That's not a coincidence. It's how they found Rebecca. They spent time on that house, setting up surveillance, all so they could make a clean getaway with the girl. They couldn't let anyone find out German mercs had landed inside the country."

How does the game work?

Lila began the download. "The score indicates distance. The tail indicates direction. If the screen fades to translucence, the tracer is below you. If it becomes opaque, then it's above."

"How'd you—"

"The game led me straight to the tracer samples."

How do the tracers work?

"My lab director took a closer look at the sample," she said carefully. "Turns out, the tracers are just micro receivers encased in some sort of waterproof coating. "

"Waterproof coating?"

Though Lila didn't want to admit just how much her people had learned about the tracers, she couldn't help but grin as she recalled the director cracking one open. "They're small, though. You'd think it was just a bit of sediment in your tea or wine, but they're large enough to feel gritty when you swallow. You might cough a great deal as your body tried to get rid of them on your throat. I don't know how the empire did it, to be honest. Our smallest receivers are a few millimeters in length. You can still recognize them for what they are, even without a microscope."

Dixon and Tristan shot one another an amused look. "You're like a child at Winter Solstice. I've never seen you so excited over anything."

It's cute.

"Do you understand what this could mean for palms if we figure out how they did it? For everything?"

It's not as cute when you yell.

"What are these receivers even receiving?"

"It's just like GPS," she said as she checked the progress of Dixon's download.

But when she looked up once more, she only saw confused expressions. "GPS works by receiving signals from satellites all around the globe, though you only need three to calculate your exact position. Snoop programs intercept this communication between the satellites and the receiver. That's how some of my own snoop programs work when I search for GPS trackers with my palm."

"So if you've ingested these tracers, you become a GPS satellite?"

"No, more like the GPS device. The tracer program behaves like a snoop and can pick up the signal. The system will locate tracers within three thousand meters."

Dixon's eyes suddenly widened. He jumped over the corner of Tristan's chair and ran into his brother's bedroom. Two boots sailed through the air, nearly pegging Tristan in the head.

"What the—"

"Don't you get it, Tristan? Teresa Bailey just died this morning. That means the mercs might still be in New Bristol with Oskar and Rebecca. The same group that searched a city of two million souls street by street until they found Natalie."

"So? We've—"

Tristan's jaw dropped suddenly, and he scrambled from the chair. "Oh shit. We have to go. We have to go now."

Lila yanked the cord from Dixon's palm. "Welcome to five minutes ago."

27

Tristan jogged downstairs with his brother in tow, calling out orders and quickly tapping on his palm with a thunder of boots and a swish of his brown coat. Soon after, Shirley herded Maria and her people into a break room behind the shop, the little bell above the front door ringing over and over again, marking the progress of a swarm. More of Tristan's people entered through the back alley, all approaching from various streets nearby, the back door opening and closing with little noise at all. Even more leapt from the apartments next door, entering the building through the roof. Others came from below.

It was an effort to hide their numbers from prying eyes.

Perhaps Lila had once been prying eyes, for she'd never known that Tristan had begun taking over two apartment buildings at the end of the block. For the first time, she had a true glimpse of the size and scope of Tristan's operation. Perhaps this was the first time a job had been worth it, or perhaps this was the first time he'd trusted her with the knowledge.

Tristan didnt just control a dozen disgruntled ex-slaves and few spies. He commanded his own militia.

Toxic swiveled her stool at Shirley's worktable, her big brown eyes mischievous. Her thick, curly hair waved in the air, like a dandelion in a breeze. Her black skin set off her perfect white teeth like a row of pearls as she grinned, and her electric-blue coat and bright green boots belied her upbringing. "You didn't know there were this many of us, did you?" she asked as she thrust another cable into the mountain of surrendered palms.

"Not until now," Lila admitted, and set up another download.

"This isn't everyone, you know. It's just all he could pull on short notice."

Lila said nothing and yanked a cable from a palm, adding it to the finished pile. Approximately three hundred and fifty souls served in her family's militia on the New Bristol compound, over half of them out on patrol each day spread across three shifts. The rest were administrative staff, investigators, or officers who worked almost exclusively in the security office.

Tristan could pull an entire patrol shift on ten minutes' notice. What he could do with more time?

It was frightening to think about. That, and the fact that no highborn seemed to know they even existed. If the rest of the highborn knew, they might not be so dismissive of workborn needs, for if these people ever got angry enough—

But they were already getting angry, weren't they? How else would Tristan have found so many to join his cause?

Who should she warn?

Her father? Chief Shaw? Her mother? The council?

Everyone?

No one?

Lila swiped the screen of a palm and began a fresh download, eyes washing over the people in the shop. They milled around the crush of cars and trucks, the dock door shut fast with a *Closed for Lunch* sign hung askew on the front door. Most of them wore servant's clothes, their boots cracked and gritty and sun-pale. They'd buttoned up their thin fall coats against the chill and wore fraying, hand-knitted scarves loosely around their necks. Some hid scars from their slave chips. A few others hid the much deeper scar from cutting them out early.

No one hid the telltale bulges of tranq guns and knives.

Tristan maneuvered through the crush, depositing another half-dozen palms in front of Lila and Toxic. The young hacker sighed dramatically as she snatched up a new device, the effect somewhat spoiled when a cable wrapped around the tail of her bright yellow scarf.

"This is the last batch," he assured them.

Toxic untangled her scarf, her face beautiful even when it was crinkled. "I can't believe you guys won't even tell me what the game does. I found it."

"The fewer that know the better. It's better for us all that way."

Lila yanked a cord from a finished palm. "Toxic says this isn't everyone in your group."

"Not even close. Most of my people are at work on the compounds and couldn't get away. Even yours. Scary, isn't it?"

Lila raised a brow, wondering what he knew about the Randolphs. "Servants or slaves?"

"Servants, mostly. Slaves can't leave their compounds or own palms, and their tracking chips make things too complicated." He snatched up a few finished palms. "You're riding with me, by the way."

Lila shook her head. That wasn't why she came. "I can ride with Dixon."

"I need to update you about Natalie and her businesses."

The brothels? Gods, what did he do? "So send me a message."

"Lila, grow up. You're riding with me." He then picked up a few more palms and hurried away.

Toxic paused in her work and watched him go. "So you and Tristan…" She eyed Lila's hood. "I knew it would happen eventually. Everyone did."

"Knew what?"

"Grunting and groaning and orgasms, oh my! Have you guys done it on this table?"

"Stop."

"Yeah, it's not at the right height. The stool would work better. Or did you have a go on his Amazon?" She laughed a little too loudly. "Have you done it on his bike?"

"Shut up, Toxic."

"Not on your life. The way you two always stare at each other…"

Lila peeked at Tristan.

He peered at her from the front of the shop.

Both quickly glanced away.

Toxic snickered. "Tell me something, do you keep the hood on when you two are—"

"I have a gun."

"You won't shoot me. I'm important to this operation."

"There's always after."

Toxic's mirth deflated all at once. She'd been shot by a tranq recently, and the misery still loomed fresh upon her mind. "Fine. You finish. I'll go check on communications."

Lila smirked as the back door *whacked* closed. She cast her eyes to Tristan once more. A dozen of his captains, for lack of a better term, surrounded him in a semicircle, divvying up a map of the city. From time to time, they also looked back at Lila, peering at her hood suspiciously. She couldn't blame them; she'd never met most of them, except for Fry and Frank and Dice.

Not enjoying the scrutiny, Lila finished the palms quickly and retreated, passing into the break room. Tristan had painted it a dark green the week before. A stainless steel refrigerator, microwave, sink, and counter lined one wall. In the middle stood five sturdy wine barrel tables and ten sturdier wine barrel benches. Half a dozen mechanics lay upon them, taking a welcome rest. Two had fallen asleep, snoring softly.

Shirley sat in the corner with Maria, following along as the girl read a passage aloud from a workbook.

Lila frowned. Tristan was playing with the girl's life, having her near so many people with divided loyalties. She should have been hidden away some place much safer. He trusted his people far too much.

Then again, even Lila hadn't known the true size of his organization.

"Hey, Hood," Shirley said as Lila sat down across from them.

"Hey, Shirley."

Maria kept her eyes down, worrying the corners of her reader, seemingly grateful for the interruption.

"Hello, Maria."

"Hello, madam," Maria whispered. Her eyes grew large, and she peered up through her hair. For the first time, it seemed as though she wanted to say something. She just couldn't express it, either from lack of words or fear or petrifying shyness.

Shirley fixed Lila with a hard stare. "All this fuss is for something you brought in, isn't it?"

"It's their case," Lila said vaguely, unsure if anyone had told Maria the reason behind it.

"Don't you get my boys hurt now. Last time Dixon came back a little less conscious than he was before. So did Frank."

"Reaper worked under your nose for years. You can hardly blame me for his actions."

"Not my nose. I just fix the trucks."

"That's not all you do," Lila murmured, glancing at her missing fingers.

It was another fifteen awkward minutes before Tristan pulled open the door. Shirley's people groaned at the sudden end of their break and filtered out, boots shuffling across the cement floor, tossing bottles of soda into the wastebasket near the door with a *pop pop pop*.

Maria didn't rise. She huddled in the corner, still clutching her reader.

"You stay here," Shirley said, patting Maria's arm. "Keep working in that book. It's good for you. Come get me if you want something to eat from across the street, you hear?"

Maria nodded, and Shirley followed her crew out of the room.

Lila hopped up from the bench as well. "I'm continually impressed at what you can pull together in a short amount of time."

There was no reason for her not to be civil.

"You really mean that, don't you?" Tristan asked.

Lila nodded.

"It's nice to be appreciated. My people have already gone, by the way. We should get going too."

Maria put down her reader at last. "I want to go," she whispered, staring at the floor.

Lila and Tristan glanced at one another, both amazed that she'd finally said something beyond yes, no, sorry, and thank you.

Tristan's lips twitched. "Do you even know where we're going?"

"You're going to find my brother. I want to go this time."

"Why?"

"He's my brother. I didn't think you'd let me go the first time." Her voice picked up more and more strength with every word.

"You sound scared. Are you?"

Maria nodded slowly.

"Good. You have more sense than most. You can come for the search, but you'll come back to the shop right after. Understand?"

"Yes, sir."

Tristan stuck his head out the break room door and yelled for Toxic.

"Find something for Maria to wear, will you?" he asked when she appeared. "We bought some trousers and sweaters and boots for Oskar. Try that stuff first. If none of it fits, find some of Zoe's things."

Toxic's bottom lip jutted out. "You must be joking. She gets to go, but I can't?"

"I need you here, monitoring communications."

"Oh, come on. It's such a bullshit job!"

Lila recalled the first and last time Toxic had gone out with them. She'd been so frightened when the Wilson militia found them that she'd almost gotten them all pinched.

Toxic didn't want to go. She just wanted to prove her worth to Tristan. Or perhaps she needed to prove it to herself.

"It's not a bullshit job," Lila said. "We need someone fast and efficient to handle communications. Perhaps it's a bit below your capabilities, but there are too many people doing too many things this afternoon. It's not like Tristan can coordinate everyone and search too."

Her expression eased, but not enough.

"It's not your sibling they took," Tristan said. "When it is, I promise that I'll let you come along."

"I don't have a sibling."

"Thank the oracles for that. I couldn't handle any more of you." Tristan dug out his palm and waved her off. "Maria, go with Toxic. Don't take too long."

Maria ran after the hacker. The break room door slammed against its frame, and their boots thumped upstairs.

"So stealthy," Tristan said as they returned to the shop. Only Fry and Dixon remained, both standing in the center of the room while Shirley's crew popped hoods and jacked up cars around them with *clicks* and *creaks* and a *whoosh*.

"Dixon, Fry. I'm putting the girl with you."

"Who? The mouse?" Fry balked, both men striding over to Tristan's side.

"Watch over her. Keep her safe, will you?"

The big man laughed, the boom of it echoing off the concrete and metal in the shop. "The shy little thing's grown some moxie? I didn't think she'd have it in her."

"I didn't either."

"Is she who I think she is?"

"Probably. Keep her secret. Keep her safe."

"As if she were my own," Fry promised, clapping Tristan on the shoulder.

Lila fussed with Dixon's purple scarf and squeezed his hand, offering him a smile. She wished she could do more, for he'd paled at the knowledge that they'd soon face German mercs, and more specifically, their bullets. She didn't know if he'd gotten a chance to speak with Tristan the night before about all the things he'd been struggling with, and she didn't know if he'd gotten a chance to remedy any of his regrets.

Dixon grinned with a bit of bluster he clearly didn't feel, and encircled her waist in a fearsome hug.

"We'll have wine tonight," she whispered in his ear. "All of us."

Maria opened the shop door in a rush, breathing hard. She frantically searched for them, her head turning this way and that, like she'd been scared that she'd been lied to and wouldn't be allowed to go. She'd pulled her hair into a ponytail and fidgeted in the boots she'd been given to wear. They seemed too large for her feet as she ran toward the group, and the coat swallowed her small frame.

Shirley threw her wrench into her toolbox with a sharp *ping* and marched toward the group. "I don't like this. She's too young for this nonsense."

"I wasn't much older than her once," Tristan replied. "Or don't you remember?"

"That was different."

"No, it wasn't."

"Yeah, it was. You'd already been a punk for years."

"Oh gods, you knew him?" Lila interrupted. "You knew him and Dixon from before—"

Shirley frowned at Lila, silencing her question, then clasped Maria's wrist. The old woman roughly dragged her to a corner of the shop. She unbelted the sheath at her hip and put it around the girl, then motioned for her to practice drawing the knife. Its curve seemed overdramatic for her small hands, the blade too sharp, the handle overlong.

"Keep hold of that while you're out," Shirley said, clasping Maria's chin with what fingers she had left. "You do whatever Fry says, you hear me? Someone might recognize your face, even with the new hair. If he tells you to hide, you hide. If he tells you to run, you run. You leave him behind, you hear me? Even if there's an entire militia patrol on your ass. The big fella can take care of himself." Shirley grabbed one of the spare palms on her workbench and typed in her number then shoved it in Maria's coat pocket.

"You call me if you get separated or lost. I'll come and find you. Wherever you are. I'll find you."

Maria nodded, her eyes a little red. Perhaps no one but her father had ever fretted over her before.

Shirley patted her cheek, then shuffled back to her workbench.

Fry removed his scarf and wound it around Maria's neck to hide her scar. "We should probably go."

He led Maria and Dixon to one of the newly painted Cruz trucks, and they pulled into traffic a few minutes later. Lila and Tristan left in another, heading in the opposite direction.

Lila slipped off her hood and kept her palm in her lap, raptly watching the screen as Tristan drove toward their segment of the city, the same part of New Bristol where Natalie had been murdered.

"My people checked out your list last night," Tristan said. The pair drove past a street of workborn dwellings, well loved and well maintained, a new paint of coat atop cracked walls and crooked shutters. "It was difficult for them to walk away when they found the children."

"How many brothels did they find?"

"Eight. We're not sure how many children are inside each one. It isn't just kids, either." He cleared his throat, squeezing the steering wheel tightly as he turned down another street. "I called Shaw this morning. I threatened to go public against both of you if he didn't have a beer with me at El Dorado."

Tristan watched her from the corner of his eye.

"I told him I'd planned a raid with some likeminded friends, but now that Natalie was dead, I was worried that the brothels might move before I could get them all. I said I didn't have the people to take them all at once and that I'd give him the list if I could come along."

"What did he say?"

"No, but he believed my story. He was left with the distinct impression he owed me one. I even threw something."

"What?"

"His beer bottle. I hadn't finished with mine. Luckily, Dice's sister didn't scream at me to clean it up until after he left."

"You have the manpower to take the brothels, don't you?"

"Yes. A few weeks ago, I might not have thought twice about it, but I can't save those kids and keep my people a secret. Besides, I don't have the resources to help them afterwards. They'll need medical attention and psychologists and fifty other things I wouldn't even know about. Bullstow can help them far better than I can."

"You're using your people now to save fewer children."

"This is different. This is war. I won't stand by while Germans invade our city and kidnap our children. Besides, what will Bullstow do to fix this situation? Sure, they'll send the girls back to the oracles, but what about Oskar? He's a slave. No one else gives a damn about him or his future. He's going to die, one way or another, and Maria will be lost. She's not strong enough to lose her father and her brother. It'll only be a matter of time."

"You're serious, aren't you? You believe this is an act of war."

"Why don't you?"

Lila bit her tongue, unsure.

Tristan turned down another street. "By the way, Shaw might have the impression that I haven't seen nor talked to you since our last job together."

"Why is that?"

"Because I might have said quite a number of disparaging remarks about your character, claiming that you were too busy blocking the little people from your palm to step outside your crimson tower and help a bunch of kids."

"I didn't block you."

"It feels like it. It wasn't that hard to channel my frustration. He bought it. You should have seen his face. He told me to leave you out of my business from now on, that you were an important woman with important things to do. He also said you'd have me in a holding cell if I tried to contact you again."

"So, good meeting?"

"Good meeting. He and his men will take precautions. If there's one thing Bullstow handles carefully, it's children. My people will keep watch over the brothels and who goes inside until Shaw acts. It's killing some of my people not to tear those monsters apart, but they know the score. Besides, those predators might lead us to more locations later."

They reached another stop sign, and he squirmed a little in his seat before driving on. "I'm sorry about what I said yesterday, by the way. It was uncalled for. You have your entanglements, and I have mine."

Lila nodded, some of her anger draining away.

"But using that as an excuse just because you're scared about what's going between us? It isn't fair, and it pisses me off."

"I'm not scared."

"You're scared."

"I've had a lot on my mind."

"Congratulations. We both have. Stop throwing out excuses. It's—"

"I'm being blackmailed," Lila blurted out, wincing as soon as the words were out of her mouth. It was as if someone else had said the words, as if someone else had taken over her body and her tongue, using her as a puppet.

Tristan slammed on the brakes. The truck bounced in place, its frame squeaking.

Lila grasped her shoulder as the seatbelt yanked it back, crying out.

"Sorry." Tristan's eyes darted to the rearview mirror. A red sedan honked behind them in one long, angry curse.

Tristan shifted into park. "Are you okay? Your shoulder, I mean?"

"Yes, I'm fine," she said as she massaged her shoulder. "I shouldn't have said anything. I didn't mean to say anything. I'm dealing with it."

"Lila—"

"I knew Reaper had a partner. All that data wiped the day he died? It didn't add up."

"What do they want?"

"Short term? Money. Long term? Who knows? I haven't had time to do much about it yet. I've been a little busy, what with you, the oracles, Oskar, and my parents forcing me into a vacation I don't want. I have to pay the asshole tonight or else something bad will happen. The message didn't say what."

The car behind them honked again. The driver flipped Tristan off as he drove around their truck and sped past.

"We should go," Lila said. "We don't have time for this right now."

Tristan put the truck back into gear and started off once more down the street. "We'll talk while we look. What do you know?"

"Not much. I hired Max to—"

"Max? Max Earlwell? Gods, I suppose it makes sense that you know him. I don't know whether to be impressed or horrified."

"I'll pretend you said impressed. He's a friend, and he's given me a lead. I'll pay now, but as soon as we've found the kids, I'm finding that asshole. Apparently I have the time now. I have two weeks to fill."

The corner of Tristan's mouth twisted. "What a coincidence. I have two weeks' vacation coming too."

"Focus, Tristan."

They drove for a few blocks in silence, passing row upon row of the same sort of suburban houses with the same sort of dogs barking in the same sort of yards.

Tristan cleared his throat. "You do realize that when I tried to talk about us, you brought up something else? Again?"

Lila pinched the bridge of her nose. "What do you want me to tell you?"

"Something. Anything. But you can't tell me to fuck off one day and come back the next. Just meet me halfway, Lila. Oracle's light, it's not even halfway. It's just one step."

Lila fumbled with her words, not sure what she could or should tell him. She had feelings for him, that much was obvious, but she wasn't sure she wanted the feelings, much less admit to them.

And encouraging him was just cruel.

They always seemed to end up in the same place, didn't they? Pissed off at one another?

The game flickered, drawing her eye to her palm.

"I backed up your messages," she mumbled finally, giving in because it was easier than dealing with the mush in her mind.

"My messages? Doesn't your kind back up every message you receive and seal it in some data vault on your family's compound? You have to access it with a key and DNA scan and..." His joking grin faded as he saw her face tense. "You don't back them all up, do you? Have you ever done that before with any of your other lovers?"

"No."

"But you backed up my messages?"

"Yes."

"I suppose that's something," he said with a little nod.

Lila drummed her fingers on the windowsill and turned her head away, glad he'd been mollified, at least for the afternoon.

Tristan reached out and clasped her hand, their intertwined fingers resting in the middle of the front seat.

"You're driving," she said.

"I know."

28

The trail of aliens had not moved, and the score had not budged. One hour had turned into two, and Lila shifted in her seat, worried and losing hope as time dragged on. Perhaps the tracers were too old to send out a signal.

Tristan's palm vibrated in the silence like a lost swarm of bees humming in the car's heater, startling them both. He pulled to the side of the road and put the call on speaker.

"Our good karma is alive and well," Dice said, his voice pouring into the car. "We've found them."

"Where?"

Dice related the address, promising to contact Toxic and have the rest of the group meet two kilometers from the location. Tristan would give them all further instructions after he got a look at the scene.

"How many mercs do you think there are?" Tristan asked as they sped across the city.

"At least a dozen," Lila said. "You might have sixty, but you'll lose some if you attack directly. The mercs will be prepared, they'll be well armed and well trained, and they'll fight to the death."

"What on earth makes you think I'm going to attack directly? I've learned a thing or two from your sneakiness over the last couple of years. Besides, more than a few of my people spent time in the army. I listen when they speak."

"Good," Lila grunted as her palm picked up the tracer's scent. "My expertise only extends to protecting compounds from stunts like this."

Tristan pulled the truck behind a warehouse, just one in several rows of such buildings, all left in the last two decades when the Perraults tried and failed at expanding their empire from Beaulac into New Bristol. The area had been grand once, a dozen large rectangles climbing several stories and painted in Perrault blue. But the paint had peeled, the tin siding had warped, and the iron beams holding up the structures had rusted. Weeds peeked out from cracks in the sidewalk and vines obscured the broken windows.

The city had never followed through on its promise to develop the land, and Chairwoman Randolph had not yet convinced them to sell it to her at a fair enough price.

Tristan parked, and he and Lila slid behind the buildings. Usually drug addicts took over such places, but Lila saw no evidence of squatters on the abandoned block.

"It's too quiet," Tristan whispered, staring at every window they passed, his fingers on his gun.

Lila did the same.

Finally they reached a warehouse in the middle of the block and slipped through the back door. The inside had been gutted and cleared. Only dust, leaves, small animals, and echoes made it their home.

They heard muffled voices and shifting boots. Lila slipped on her hood, and the pair followed the noise until they spied Dixon and Fry, peering from a window tinted with dust and grime.

A smaller form in a large coat stood between them, ponytail smooth and shoulders stiff.

"You were supposed to take her back to the shop," Tristan said, frowning at his brother and Fry.

The large man dropped his binoculars, letting them swing at his chest. "She threatened to give us a poke if we tried to take her back. I thought I'd let you make the final call. It seems the little mouse has teeth now. Remind me to give Shirley a piece of my mind, will you?"

Maria did not turn around nor surrender her spot at the window. She'd fixed her gaze on the warehouse across the street, her binoculars pressed up against her eyes so hard she likely had a bruise. "I don't see him."

"We had a deal, Maria," Tristan said patiently. "You were—"

"Fuck you, and fuck the deal," Maria said absently, still refusing to turn away, all traces of the demure little girl gone from her voice. "I'm going in there for my brother, with or without you."

Lila blinked.

So did Tristan.

Crickets chirped in the corners of the warehouse.

"Do you see now?" Fry said. "Came out of nowhere. It didn't help that she stole my backup tranq. She said that she didn't need us anymore after you sent us the address. Said she'd shoot us both, steal the truck, and drive herself."

Lila and Tristan blinked again.

Maria turned away from the window. "They're all fools. Workborn and lowborn and highborn alike. But you and Hood are useful fools. You want my brother, and I want my brother. We have the same goal right now, and I figure you're the safest of the lot that wants him, even though you nearly killed my father. From everything I've heard so far, you're the only ones who don't want to send us somewhere he doesn't want us to go. So far," she repeated, before resuming her watch on the window. "I still don't see him."

Lila checked her palm once again. The score flickered between forty-five and fifty. "He's got to be in there. The numbers are a bit fuzzy, but I suspect it's because both he and Rebecca are inside. The program doesn't know which one to focus on. Or perhaps the signals are fading."

"Who's Rebecca?" Maria asked.

"A girl the Germans took. Your people, I suppose."

"They aren't my people. I don't have a people. I have a brother and a father, and that's it."

"What about your mother?"

"My grandmother beat her half to death after she found out that she'd slept with a dirty German slave. The moment their contracts ended, they moved far, far away. My father found us on his doorstep nine months later. At least she did him the courtesy of leaving a note."

"And birthing you and Oskar. I hear it's a little uncomfortable."

Tristan joined the group at the window. "Are you sure your father is really—"

"I know who my father is. He was so damn proud and happy that he hung the certificates on the wall in our room. Bullstow did the DNA test themselves, you know. Twice. They didn't believe anyone would sleep with the dirty German slave. They redid the test when Oskar and I were five years old. Stupid assholes."

Tristan looked helplessly at Lila. "I got nothing."

Lila stole Fry's binoculars, unwinding the strap from his neck. "I like the real you, Maria. Don't ever change."

"That's funny coming from someone who prances around in a hood."

"I don't prance." Lila focused her binoculars across the street, the mesh hood obscuring her view. Nothing moved in the warehouse, except for the occasional head in the dim, dusty windows. "How many mercs have you guys seen?"

"Ten," Fry answered. "We think."

"Could be more. Should be more."

"We'll pretend there are." Tristan withdrew his own pair of binoculars from his coat pocket. "Where do you think they'll be?"

"Roof, perimeter, back entrances." Fry ticked off each suggestion on his fingers.

"Next door," Lila added. "They'll have lookouts."

"We'll account for them. I don't know how much longer they'll stay in the city, so we should move quickly. Fry will come with me. We'll meet up with the others and make a plan. Dixon, Lila, stay here and watch the building. Call me if anything changes."

Lila nodded, completely uninterested in trailing along, just to be caught in a staring contest with people she hardly knew.

After Tristan and Fry left, Dixon pressed his forehead into the glass, withdrawing again, becoming a mate to the shadows he'd hidden behind all week. Lila put down her binoculars and rubbed his back. "We're going to save some children today."

He nodded.

"In a couple of hours, they'll all be safe again. We'll get the girls back with their parents, and Oskar and Maria will be together once more."

Dixon didn't take out his notepad. Whatever thoughts he had, he kept them to himself.

Lila didn't see any patrols, nor did she see anyone in the warehouses but the same few heads in the same few windows.

When the doors in the back opened once more, Lila stiffened.

"Anything new?" Tristan asked as he rejoined them, pulling out his binoculars for a last look. Fry, Frank, and Dice marched in after him, their jaws set.

"No."

"Good. Four teams will surround the building. Another four will hold back, waiting to reinforce where they are needed."

"All those people, and we don't even know what's inside?" Lila grew uncertain as she peered at the quiet structure across from them.

"We don't know *now*. But the six of us will be playing snoops."

"Seven," Maria said. "I'm going too."

Tristan shook his head. "I promised your father I'd keep you safe."

"Yes, I heard. Maybe I'd let you if you hadn't screwed up the first job so badly. This time if you fuck it up, I'll have a chance to get my brother back myself."

"Maria, those are German mercs who have him," Lila said. "Their guns won't be loaded with tranqs. They'll have guns with bullets. They can and will kill you. They've killed more than a dozen people already."

"So? What's my life been so far? Cleaning pots? Always brought back the second I break out of the compound? Pardon me if I don't value another fifty years of that as highly as you do."

Dixon raised his tranq, aimed it at her neck, and looked at his brother for permission.

"We're not going to tranq her."

Another five minutes of arguing didn't help the situation. In the end, Tristan decided it was better to take her along and keep an eye on her, rather than leave her behind in the abandoned warehouse.

"Remember, don't tranq anyone," Tristan reminded them, giving the building one last pass with his binoculars. "We're just getting a closer look. We get a visual on the kids, find the position of the mercs, and relay the information back to Toxic. She'll pass it to the other teams. We're not going to start a fight until the entire building has been surrounded, the neighboring properties searched, and the other teams have gotten into position. Does everyone understand?"

Everyone nodded and reached for their tranq guns and knives, making sure they were in place along with their backup weapons.

"Maria, stay with me and Dice," Fry said. "You hear me?"

The girl nodded, a little of the old Maria coming back as she gulped.

The group moved out. They backtracked two blocks around the warehouse, slipping through a large abandoned field behind the structure. The grass and weeds came up to their thighs. They squinted toward the building, large windows half busted and open to roosting pigeons.

No one patrolled the perimeter, and only a few figures paced in front of the windows, the same people they'd seen before.

Lila peeked through her binoculars. "I don't like this. I can't see anything new, and we can't get any closer. Even without cameras they'll see us the minute we try to cross the field."

A gun cocked behind them, a tiny little snick carried on a frigid wind. "We saw you long before you got to the field."

The entire group spun, lifting their tranqs.

Six well-armed men dressed in black trousers and blackcoats surrounded them, pointing guns at their chests. Guns loaded with bullets. Cold guns made of cold steel held by cold men who had used them to kill.

Had Natalie even seen them before she died?

"You come armed with cute toys," the leader said with a heavy accent. "I will never understand how the empire hasn't beaten you already. Arms up, please."

Lila lifted her arms, cocking her head to side as she tried to place his accent. It sounded like a mix of German and something else, caught up in a warring mix of tones.

The mercs took the group's tranqs from their holsters, and their leader jerked his gun to the warehouse across the field.

Lila stared about her as she marched on. The others would come. Tristan's people would interject themselves into the fray before they entered the warehouse.

But no shots rang out.

No group charged.

No one intervened at all.

Had the others been taken too?

Lila squinted into the dusty warehouse as the group filed inside. The large space had been cleared of all machinery. A few tables had been pushed to a side wall, filled with notepads, computers, temp palms, maps, and food. Another table had been moved to the center, playing cards scattered on top. In the front lay five wire dog cages all in a row. One contained Oskar, and three young girls filled the others. The children's eyes hardly focused on the influx of new people. One merely drooled on a pillow in her lap, her head pushed up against the side of the cage at an awkward angle.

Another empty cage sat beside Oskar's, its door hanging open.

A man at one of the tables stood up to greet them, a silver band tied around his upper arm, a gun strapped to his hip. He thrust his hands behind his back and nodded at his men. "Good work, you've managed to find the last of the set." He crooked his finger at Maria. "Come here, child. You've saved us an awful lot of time."

Maria's bravado had greatly waned upon their capture. Whatever had been left of it melted as she shuffled toward him, her gaze falling demurely to the floor. While one of the mercs piled the tranqs and knives on the table, she raised her faltering, trembling voice. "Are you going to bring me back to my father?"

"Eventually. You've proved quite difficult to find. We almost left you, but now you've been delivered to our doorstep. You won't be any trouble, will you?"

Maria shook her head and strode closer. "They yelled at me and made me clean all the time, just like the others. Are you going to make me do that?"

"Of course we won't. The cages are here to keep you all safe until we can return you to your father." The man smiled an oily smile. "You're a princess, not a slave. We don't practice such barbarity in the empire."

Maria stood beside him and looked down at the ground, the picture of innocence, the epitome of the wronged.

The pacing mercs guarding the warehouse left their posts, joining the rest of the captors. Nearly twenty women and men glared at Lila and Tristan and the rest of the group as if they had been mistreating children, rather than saving them.

Maria was going to get them all killed.

Painfully.

Lila cut a look to Dixon, saw his fingers shaking in the air as he pressed them into bunched fists. Here he was in another life-or-death situation, just a week after his last, and she didn't know how she'd get him out of it. The look that crossed over his face worried her. It was a mixture of sadness, fear, and...

Anger?

"Why?" Lila asked, hoping to buy enough time for Tristan's people to rescue them. "I understand taking Oskar and Maria. After all, you traditionalists harbor some notion of restoring them to the throne, but—" Lila broke off, considering the man's accent and the accent within it. "Oracle's wrath. You're not Germans at all. You're Italians."

The group of mercs eyed one another, shifting in their boots, hands upon their guns.

Their leader laughed and clapped his hands. "Bravissimo," he said, his vowels and consonants changing completely. "It's hard to speak your language with a German accent. Harder still to speak it perfectly, though a few of my men can fool your people well enough. It's a pity you figured it out. I would have let you and your friends scamper back to the little police force at the capitol so you could tell them all about the bad German people who stole the prince."

Lila's shoulder ached, and she struggled to keep her hands up. "Why take Oskar?"

"Why not? Everyone wants him. Your highborn want to sell him to the highest bidder, your government wants to send him to Head Councilman Abbot so America can get a shiny gold star on its collar, and the German traditionalists want to put him or his father on the throne. Even the German loyalists want him."

"The loyalists? I thought they wanted him dead?"

"Only the idiots, but they pay like crap." The man snatched up one of the tranq guns on the table, peering at the trigger and darts loaded inside.

"King Lucas doesn't pay like crap, does he?"

"King Lucas is the slyest one of all, maybe more than King Felipe. You know the easiest way to sway the public? Turn your enemy into a villain or a clown. King Lucas has never wanted Peter dead. He'd rather not make Peter and his children into martyrs, into sad legends the populace can rally around whenever they don't like something he does or says. He hasn't even had to do much. Give Peter a few drinks, put him around in front of the cameras, and let him make an ass of himself. It's been delightful watching King Lucas work. I may not like the man's politics, but you can't doubt his sense of humor."

"What about King Felipe? He wants to own the next king of Germany?"

"The next best thing to being an emperor is to control one. If the children are good and do as they are told, he might even send us to Germany to collect their father. Everyone will think King Lucas has finally gotten rid of the foolish man. That will take some explaining on his part, don't you think?"

He dropped the tranq gun on the table and padded toward Maria. Squeezing her shoulder, he tossed a careless glance back at Oskar's cage. "Does that sound good, boy? You can have your father back if you cooperate. You'll be a prince and then a king and maybe even an emperor. You and your sister will wear nice clothes and eat delicious food, so long as you do what you're told."

Oskar didn't say a word, his glazed eyes staring at the floor.

"Why take the oracles?"

"King Felipe wants proof that the witches are false before he agrees to war."

"The militia will figure it out. You shouldn't have used tracers to find Rebecca."

"Ah, that's how you found us," he said with a shrug. "It was an acceptable risk. A few bugs in the FPS office, and we learned all about Rebecca's new parents and their tea habit. It wasn't much to go on, but it was enough, and it was much easier than hacking into the FPS files."

"But—"

"Oh god, take off the woman's ridiculous hood. I want to see her eyes while I shoot her in the mouth."

Lila's hands immediately went to her hood, but one of the black-clad guards held her arms in place. The mesh brushed against her skin and hair as it was pulled off.

Fry and Dice couldn't help themselves. They turned their heads, their eyes bulging at the sight of Elizabeth Victoria Lemaire-Randolph, chief of the Randolph militia. To their credit, they cut their eyes away before their captors noticed they'd caught such a big fish.

But the black-clad Italians knew her face, too.

"Well, well, well." Their leader grinned. "It appears we have—"

A shot rang out.

Blood sprayed from the Italian's forehead.

29

The recoil nearly knocked the gun from Maria's grasp, but she held on, firing at the next merc before she'd even aimed properly. Her shots were as wild as her eyes, but she managed to put two bullets into a fleeing merc's chest before spinning to find a new target.

The mercs nearest Maria cursed in Italian and scattered. They did not draw their guns. The girl was worth too much money to harm.

They weren't the only ones moving.

Lila had crouched as soon as the Italian's head exploded, and not because she was frightened. She grasped at an empty sheath before she remembered they'd taken her boot knife. The drop had been lucky, though, for she'd dodged a merc's arms.

They closed around air.

She escaped purely by accident.

Lila pretended a weapon and swung, slashing toward his throat. It was a feint, just enough of a threat to make him wary, just enough for her to get close and snatch his gun.

A gun he had not drawn so that he would not destroy another prize.

Predictably, the merc dodged.

His burly arms closed around her.

Lila elbowed him in the neck, wiggled in his grasp, and grabbed his revolver. She fired at the man's kneecap through his holster.

He shifted at the last instant, right before the crack of the pistol erupted at his waist.

The recoil shot up her arm, shaking her bones.

The man's screams tore through the air as he fell, clutching at the space between his legs.

Now armed, Lila turned to the next merc, who rushed at her with outstretched arms. She knew she couldn't aim in time. She knew she didn't have the skills for hand-to-hand.

She knew she had to move.

Before she could do so, his body jerked, and half his skull erupted. He fell to the side, collapsing into a bloody mess on the gritty cement.

Maria didn't bother watching him fall. She merely aimed at another scrambling merc, too greedy to go for a gun.

But these men were professionals. They quickly abandoned the idea of rushing Maria and Lila. All swarmed the table, having the same thought. Too much money breathed in the room, and they couldn't risk destroying any of it.

They needed tranqs.

The others had also moved. Tristan, Dixon, Frank, Fry, and Dice had all lunged at the nearest mercs, fists punching, boots kicking, all scrambling to get to a weapon.

Lila left them to it, unwilling to risk a shot so close to her friends. Instead, she aimed her gun at the neck of the closest merc, just as she'd done in practice so many times before.

The blast kicked her arm, and she nearly lost hold of the gun.

Her target collapsed, gasping for air, clasping his hands around his neck to stem the tide. He paled and twisted, from both pain and the realization of his approaching death.

Did his regrets march before his eyes?

Lila watched the pool of crimson underneath him grow, wondering what a merc regretted about his life.

She knew what she regretted.

She'd killed him. She'd actually killed someone this time.

A hand gripped her leg. Her first target yanked at her ankle, attempting to topple her.

No second thoughts passed through her head. Turning her aim, she shot his neck, just as she'd been trained to do.

He fell, back-pedaling futilely in a second pool of crimson.

Then he stopped moving altogether. His regrets floated away.

Swallowing hard, she stole his gun, then aimed again toward the crowd of mercs. The press of bodies made them easy to hit, but this time her target fell before she'd even managed to fire. A little dart had struck his head, rendering him far luckier than he might have been.

Tristan had rushed the table and snatched the last tranq.

A wetness creep down her cheek.

Perhaps she'd been hit.

Squeezing her eyes, she breathed out sharply. Most of the mercs had pointed tranqs at her and her friends, scattering now that they had weapons. The ones who hadn't scored a tranq fumbled for their guns. Bullets would come from both sides, and the sides were still uneven. There was nothing to hide behind, nothing that a bullet couldn't burn through.

She was moving too slowly.

Time was moving slowly.

Dixon fell nearby.

Raising her gun, she called upon every lesson she'd ever taken from Commander Sutton, every hour spent at the range with Sergeant Jenkins. She gritted her teeth and began to fire as she'd been taught.

Rapid. Efficient. Accurate.

Head shot.

Sutton's chuckles when Lila's time was a tenth of a second too slow to best hers.

Head shot.

Jenkins spinning his wheelchair and popping a wheelie, chanting that neither of them would ever best him.

Head shot. A row of little paper targets.

Head shot. The wetness creeping into her eyes, making it harder to focus.

Head shot. Moans and groans and screaming and writhing on the floor.

Head shot.

Head shot.

Multiple times in the same body if the merc didn't go down. *Click. Click. Click.*

A switch of guns.

Pulling the trigger until ear-splitting bursts turned into *clicks* once again.

Lila looked at her guns, empty of bullets. She looked around the room, empty now of anything more to shoot. She felt as though she'd knocked back a few shots of whiskey, and she embraced the warmth that loosened her muscles.

It was like walking on a cloud.

It was like breathing a cloud.

She was a cloud. Transparent. Weightless. Floating through space and time. Raining.

Her legs did not touch the floor.

Tristan leaned over his brother, tying a gray bandana over his leg. Blood trickled down the length of it, wetting his black trousers. Dixon didn't seem to mind. He panted a bit, grinning like a man happy to be alive after a storm churned through the city, leaving nothing but his home, perfect and untouched in its wake.

"It's okay. The bullet didn't hit an artery," Tristan said to her unanswered question.

Unanswered because Lila hadn't thought to ask.

Fry ran toward the cages, opening their squeaking doors to check on the children inside. "Oracle's light, the gods were watching," he called out, cradling the head of one of the girls. "There were a few close calls, but none of them got hit."

"Thank the gods. Get them out," Tristan ordered as he pulled hard on Dixon's knot.

Fry did as he was bid, laying the children out carefully, their heads resting on pillows, their shoulders covered by the blankets that had once lined their cages.

"I never knew you could shoot like that," Tristan said to Lila, finally turning away from his brother. "No wonder you've never taken me up on hand-to-hand training."

His half-smile dissolved the second he spied her face. Jumping up, he tugged her toward the front of the room and sat her in a chair. "Hey, talk to me." He caressed her cheeks with raw, swollen hands.

"Did I get shot?"

"No. You're just…crying."

Maria stared at the pair, wide-eyed, clutching the gun she'd stolen. She seemed not to know what to do with it or herself.

Tristan gently took the weapon from her grasp and placed it on the table.

"I knew he was full of shit before he even opened his mouth," Maria said, glancing at Oskar, who still hadn't looked up from his drooling stupor. "I don't want to go to Germany. My father has that look in his eyes, the one he used to get when Oskar and I were little and the chairwoman called for him."

The teen kicked the merc leader in the head. "He put my brother in a dog's cage."

Tristan pulled her away from the corpse, and she panned her head at the carnage.

So did Lila. Not because she wanted to but because she couldn't help herself. Blood and bodies and brains spilled over the cement floor. Shaking death throes. Scraping boots and twitching hands. All of it mixed amid the snoring of those who'd been taken out by tranqs and the moans of those who'd been beaten into unconsciousness and hadn't yet been tranqed.

Tristan picked up a tranq gun, clenched in a dead Italian's hand, and fixed those who might wake. They finally slumbered with closed eyes while the dead stared back.

Regrets played in her mind. Regrets that were not her own. The regrets of nearly a dozen people, for her hand had dealt death to most in the room. She'd never erase the sight and smell of so much blood. Not the sounds of the fallen. Not the moans of the injured.

The oracle had been right after all. Tristan had dragged her into the mire to drown. She was a killer now. These were her victims.

And she didn't feel a damn thing.

Lila focused on Maria. She heard her own voice speak from far away, sounding strange even to her own ears. "Where'd you learn to shoot?"

Maria fiddled with the scarf wound around her neck. "One of the blackcoats used to let me play on the range at night when no one else was around."

"That's against protocol."

"He wasn't thinking with his protocol. I've been perfect so many times. I didn't do well here, not even close. It's not the same, is it?"

Lila shook her head, and the cloud of numbness carried her thoughts away.

"The assholes deserved it. They were Italian mercs. This was war. We wouldn't be standing here right now if either of you hadn't done what you did."

Tristan pulled his palm from his pocket. "Toxic, tell me you got that."

"Is everyone okay?" Toxic asked, her voice echoing in the large room.

"Yes, did you get it?"

"I hit record as soon as you dialed."

"Do you see now why we left you behind? Where are the others?"

"I told them to hang back until the idiot stopped talking. Then all I heard were gunshots."

Tristan clenched his teeth. "Toxic, next time we have sixty people ready to rush in and save us, you let them do that, okay?"

"Okay. I'll tell the other teams to meet up at your location."

"Good. Have them meet us in the field behind the warehouse. Tell Gwen to start up the fireworks. We don't need anyone to get suspicious and take a closer look."

"Already done."

"Good. Then I need you to make a new AAS flyer. Print up as many as you can."

"Wait, what?" Toxic asked. "I don't even know what was on the first one."

"That's why it has to be you. Don't dig up the file for the old one. It can't look or sound the same. It needs to read like someone copying Peter. Print it on the new paper we bought, and wear gloves. No prints. Tell Shirley to fetch the nitro from the hotel. She has another job."

"No," Lila said quietly.

"What?" Tristan dropped his palm to his thigh. He knelt beside her chair, wiping her cheek with his thumb. "We can get it easily. Bullstow's been too busy to look for it."

"No, you're not going to blow something else up." In her mind, Lila saw bodies exploding. Not just those of the dead, but the bodies of the tranqed.

"This is war. What else can we do? We'll print off every blueprint we can find of the oracle's compound, then blow this warehouse to ashes. We could even fake Maria and Oskar's deaths, make everyone believe that they were killed in the blast. Shaw will get the idea of what they were planning, all the kids will be safe, and none of them—"

Lila shook her head. "I'll not let you be that person. We're already drowning. If you do this, we'll never touch the bottom."

"Drowning?" Tristan squeezed one of her hands and fumbled with his palm. "Toxic, delay my previous order. Just have everyone meet in the field, you got that?"

"Yes, sir."

He disconnected and slid his palm into his pocket, then flipped on the jammer in her pocket. "They saw you, Lila. They did this to themselves. I'll not let them reveal your identity under the serum. I need to protect you. I need to protect—"

"There are more important things. You kill these men now, and no one knows anything. We need to know what the empire is planning, Tristan, not just what they told us while I was stalling. We need real information. We need the truth serum."

"You want me to drop them off at Bullstow's front gate? That's not happening."

"No. I want to call the oracle."

His eyes widened.

"The woman could put a bullet in all of us, confess to Chief Shaw, and still go home for dinner. We partner with her on this one. This is the oracles' fight, anyway. More theirs than ours, that's for sure. They should get a say, and it's more than my father will give them."

He fixed his gaze upon the sleeping children. "Okay. Fine. We'll see what she wants to do, but I'm not agreeing to anything. Not yet."

Lila took out her palm, still numb, her brain barely chugging along. She didn't need much of it, though, for her call was short. Lila had barely said hello before the oracle interrupted her.

"Are they okay?"

"Yes."

The oracle breathed a sigh of relief. "I just need the address."

Lila gave it.

In the front of the room, Maria knelt beside her drugged brother. She'd snatched up Oskar's hand and brushed her lips upon the back of it.

Oskar dozed on, lost and oblivious to the world.

Tristan might have been as well. He stood beside Frank's and Dice's bodies, cursing the tranq darts lodged in their cheeks and noses. They'd been closer to the mercs than the rest, and had suffered for it.

Fry knelt beside them, checking their pulses, then pulled out the darts and flicked them onto the floor. "Frank's going to be pissed when he wakes up. This is the third time he's been tranqed in two weeks. I just hope the sensors didn't malfunction. He got dosed pretty hard."

"You think he'll quit?"

"I think he'll be glad he wasn't shot. If he's not, I'll remind him of what could have happened. It would have been a lot worse if they hadn't gone for the tranqs."

"And if they hadn't wasted so many darts on our coats rather than our skin." Tristan crouched before Frank and checked his pulse. Satisfied with what he found, he put his friend's arm gently back on the floor.

"So much for overcomplicated plans, eh," Fry said as both men stood up. "How about next time, we just bring along a princess who knows how to capitalize on a distraction."

"Did I mess things up?" Maria asked.

"Quite the contrary. You did much better than me and Dice. We were too busy gawking at the chief."

Lila's stomach should have twisted in knots at Fry's words, but it didn't.

Hood had been revealed.

How quickly would word spread among Tristan's people?

How quickly would word spread to Chief Shaw and her father?

"I didn't see you steal the gun," Tristan said.

"Of course you didn't," Maria said. "I learned how to be ignored a long time ago. Sometimes I borrow things when no one's looking. He was so busy yapping that he didn't even feel me take it."

"It seems you developed quite the skillset as a Wilson slave."

Dixon scooted back to the wall, using it as a crutch to pull himself up. His gaze fixed on one of the mercs and the bloody puddle underneath him.

One of the many that Lila had killed.

She looked away.

"Let's go," Tristan said. "We need to get the others away from here. There are far too many eyes for the number of secrets in this room."

Fry retrieved Lila's hood from the floor and tugged it over her head. "We'll keep your secret," he promised, squeezing her her shoulder, the same one that had hurt so much all day.

This time, Lila didn't feel a thing.

30

It turned out that the closest teams who might have helped them in the warehouse had encountered problems of their own. Italian patrols had slipped behind several groups, guns drawn, ready to kill. Luckily, the reinforcements had spotted the Italians before the mercs could creep behind their friends. Palms buzzing with advanced warning, they'd all done some creeping of their own, and the mercs had all been darted before they even had a chance to fire.

Superior numbers had saved them.

In the end, three dozen foreign soldiers had entered New Bristol.

Tristan had been more than a little disturbed by the number. Lila should have been disturbed as well.

But Lila was a cloud.

Whoever she had thought herself to be was not who she had become. She had become the oracle's worst fear. A vision cutting through the her peace. A horrible, grating migraine. A path she'd tried to divert. A darkness. A storm cloud.

The mire.

This was what drowning felt like.

She sat on the tailgate of Tristan's truck, parked near the warehouse, her feet swinging back and forth. She'd slid her tranq back into her holster, but the guns she'd killed with lay in easy reach. The crickets chirped in the early evening, and the sun had not yet set. Her hood hid her face while she followed the moon's progress. It floated above the horizon on an assigned course, a path that had been planned by the gods.

Had hers been planned so neatly?

Had this been the plan? Had she done it right, or had it gone horribly wrong?

Had she held the gun, or had it been the gods?

She hadn't cared much about the gods before, not even when she dreamed of the oracle the week before, but now it all seemed important. If the oracles were the gods' emissaries, and they'd used her and Tristan's people to save the children—

Lila retreated into her coat. Her thoughts were too heavy, and she liked floating better.

She liked it very much.

Fry and Tristan carried Dixon out of the warehouse and into a waiting car. They'd buckled Shirley's knife and holster around his waist. Blood still oozed down his trousers, staining the gray fabric. He'd given Lila more than a few concerned glances as he passed, but there wasn't time for a chat. His grin had dissolved, as had the adrenaline, and his jaw had clenched tightly against the pain.

Tristan was too worried to let him dawdle.

The driver had peeled away, set on getting Dixon to Doc's room at the shop.

Tristan's people had brought the snoring bodies from the fields, friends and enemies alike, for a few friendly fire incidents had occurred during the mercs' attack. Their scarves trailed in the field, flashes of color popping amid the thigh-high weeds. They loaded up their friends in two loud trucks, chosen because their rumbling engines would cover the snores. Fry and Tristan added Frank and Dice, then slapped the sides of the trucks.

The vehicles pulled away.

Tristan sent all but ten of his people back to their homes and jobs in New Bristol. Those who remained looked as though they'd spent time on a battlefield. They brought out the sleeping young and set them to doze in the back seats of a few cars, with warm blankets tucked over their shoulders. They brought out Oskar next and put him in the back of a truck so that Maria had plenty of space to sit beside him. Her suspicious eyes followed everyone's movements.

The group then began a search of the surrounding area, finding nothing of interest but the Italians' vehicles. The four delivery trucks looked new, and none of them had been stolen.

The oracle arrived soon after, her small gray electric car bouncing up and down on the broken road behind the building, flanked by two large trucks. Her door closed in the quiet, and she emerged. She had exchanged her purple robe and slippers for a long gray coat, draping sweater, jeans, and boots.

Workborn clothes.

Six figures disembarked from the other vehicles, all orbiting the oracle as though she were the sun, all wearing workborn clothes as well. They scanned the warehouse as though it were a battlefield.

Lila had never seen a purplecoat before.

Perhaps she saw them now, as anonymous as their mistress.

Tristan led them to the cars that held the children. The oracle peeked in on them, touching their faces. Once she was satisfied, Tristan led her into the warehouse.

Lila didn't follow. She didn't want to see the people she'd killed.

It felt like hours before the oracle returned, followed only by Tristan. Their faces were far more determined than their footsteps, which shuffled upon the concrete.

The truck dipped as they both sat upon the cold tailgate beside Lila.

"You found the girls," the oracle said, as two purplecoats emerged from the warehouse, keys jingling at their fingertips. "Tristan told me what happened, though I'd already seen most of it in my visions."

Lila licked her lips. "So I didn't stop anything, then."

"You stopped enough. I saw much worse. Believe it or not, this is one of the better outcomes."

Tristan raised a brow. "I feel as though I'm missing something."

"You are, but it's none of your concern. Nor is this mess. It belongs to the oracles. You were right to get me involved, chief. You are not your father's daughter."

Lila didn't know what to say to that. Judging from the blood on the warehouse floor, she was far from being his copy.

Car doors slammed in the distance. Two engines sputtered to life.

"I'm going to finish it. I'm going to take the mercs back to my compound, the dead and the sleeping alike. Their computers as well. I don't trust your father or his lackeys to investigate this on our behalf."

Lila wondered if the oracle referred to her or Chief Shaw. "You should tell him about this. You need to be protected. He only did what he did to keep you safe."

"We don't need him to keep us safe. Everyone forgets that not so very long ago the oracles were battle queens. We made the decisions for our tribes, not the matrons, not the senate, and certainly not the prime minister or the Allied Council. We answered to the gods, and only to the gods. We saw the paths that triggered our visions, and we saw the same paths. Some we wanted to trigger, others we did not, but we could adjust and adjust quickly when the time called for it. The senate is blind, and so is your father. Perhaps it really is time for the oracles to take charge once again."

"Do you really mean that?" Tristan asked.

"Maybe, maybe not, but others of my kind think it. I've tried to be the voice of reason. Life is so very different these days. We've not been a collection of tribes for quite some time, but the prime minister pokes his head into our affairs too often for me to be comfortable, and my sisters are angry and worried. The sleeping empire is waking once more. It grows impatient."

"You believe war is coming."

"I know it is," the oracle said. "We'll investigate this on our own. We'll tell the prime minister what we want, when we're ready to tell it, and say it came from our visions. We have access to truth serum, and the immunity to use it. These men's lives are forfeit."

"So you're asking me to keep my mouth shut?" Lila asked.

"I should think you'd want to. Both of us benefit from this arrangement. Isn't that what the Randolphs are all about? Mutual benefit?"

Lila said nothing as two delivery trucks backed up to the warehouse. The drivers hopped out and reentered the structure. People streamed from the building, carrying bodies to the trucks. They put the dead in one, and the sleeping in another.

"Tristan, I need a moment alone with your friend. Could you make sure my people have begun cleaning the blood from the warehouse floor?"

Tristan nodded, and the truck rocked again as he stood up. "I'll load the computers into your car while I'm at it, madam. Lila is good with that sort of thing. You might consider asking for her assistance when you begin your investigation."

Lila watched him drift away, surprised he'd followed her orders.

Perhaps he'd begun to believe. Perhaps she'd begun to believe a little as well. The oracle had gotten to the warehouse far too quickly. She'd been in the neighborhood. Waiting.

"What would have happened if I hadn't stopped Tristan? He had a plan."

"He didn't have a plan," the oracle replied. "He had intentions. I told you before, he's making decisions. He knows what he'll fight for. He'll fight against those who would threaten his home, and he'll fight for those he considers his family. You have other concerns, other priorities. Luckily, yours prevailed today."

"Only because you warned me."

"You didn't need me to warn you about this."

Lila stared at a clump of dirt, unsure if she believed the oracle.

"You don't fight, chief. You never do. You don't attack. You defend. It's why you refuse your birthright, and why you wouldn't have agreed with Tristan's plan even if I hadn't said a word." The oracle pursed her lips. "In some of my earliest visions, not all the children made it out. In others, none of them did because you weren't here. Things would have been far worse if you hadn't come along and stopped your friend."

"Worse enough to spark the war?"

"As I said before, it will spark regardless."

For the first time in an hour, Lila felt something stir in her belly, a feeling that she could not name.

Fear? Worry?

"I've had the same vision over and over for some time. We all have, and I fear that all paths will lead to it eventually. It's only a question of degree. There are some among us who are more hopeful. I am hopeful." The oracle sighed heavily. "But you don't care about any of that right now, do you?"

Lila looked down at her hands, both folded in her lap. She followed the stitches that crisscrossed her palms. One stitch leading to another like a little chain.

The oracle picked up the German guns and slid them into her coat pockets.

Lila let her.

She didn't want to see the instruments of death ever again.

"What would make you feel better, chief? If I said the gods aimed your weapons or that you did it of your own free will?"

"I don't know."

"Good, because I don't know the answer. But let me assure you, the people in those trucks weren't good people. They were monsters, long before they ever took our daughters, and they would have done worse things than kidnap them if they knew our visions were real. I've seen it, over and over. I have no sympathy for any of them."

Lila poked at her stitches.

"Come see me tomorrow."

She shook her head.

"Then stay with him tonight," the oracle said gently.

Lila hopped off the tailgate and strode to the warehouse toward Maria, not sure how to answer, not wanting to answer.

The oracle followed, her boots muddy in the wet grass.

They rested their elbows on the truck bed, watching the dozing Oskar. Maria turned her head briefly, then resumed her watch over her brother.

"If you want to thank us for letting you handle this, then take them with you," Lila said. "They have nowhere else to go."

Maria's head snapped up.

"You won't give the oracle any trouble, will you? No more stealing weapons and threatening people?"

The oracle stared at Maria's face, at her hair, and at her slumped shoulders. "You're Peter Kruger's daughter, aren't you?"

Maria bit her lip, refusing to retreat.

She nodded.

A warm touch landed on Lila's back. "You beat me to it." Tristan rested his chin upon her uninjured shoulder and wrapped an arm around her waist. Lila didn't know whether to sink into him for comfort or pull away. "I had planned to ask the oracle the very same thing."

"Yes, your people told me as much last week. Stop trying to slip a spy in amongst the oracle children. It won't work. I have too many people amongst yours, and they like me better."

Tristan stared at the tires.

"So what do you say, Maria?" the oracle asked, tugging Oskar's blanket higher upon his shoulder. "From what Tristan has told me, you were instrumental in rescuing Rebecca. The old ways are still nurtured among the oracles. Rebecca's mother and her family are indebted to you for the rest of your life. Have you ever seen pictures of Sioux Falls?"

"No, but one place is as good as another."

"Ah, that's not true. Sioux Falls might be cold in the winter, but it's extremely beautiful and it doesn't get nearly so hot in the summers. Few places are as nice."

Maria shrugged.

"Well, in any case, it will be a safe place for you to stay while your brother recovers. You wouldn't be a prisoner or a slave there, though it would be best for you to stay within the compound walls. You're old enough and shrewd enough to understand that. If you decide that you don't like it, I'm sure we could find somewhere else to suit your tastes. An oracle lives in every city in the commonwealth. You'd have your pick of compounds."

Maria played with her brother's collar.

"They can keep you far safer than I can," Tristan said. "Perhaps one day your father can join you there. I'll get him a message. I'll let him know that you are safe."

Maria nodded. "All right, but just for now. Just until my father comes back."

"For as long as you want," the oracle said.

31

Lila hopped out of the shower. Wet and shivering, she stared at her reflection in a steamed mirror. Purple and green bruises still marred her skin from the fight at LeBeau's, from Alex's outburst, from too many tumbles in the gym, and from the fight in the warehouse. They coated her as though she were a rotten piece of fruit, dropped and bumped and stepped upon.

Her insides were just as bruised. She'd become a killer, and no one knew.

No one but Tristan and a few of his people. She thought of going to see him at the shop, but she'd worked so hard to get away after they returned from the warehouse.

Besides, she didn't have the energy to figure things out. She needed time to think.

Or perhaps time to sleep.

Turning away from the mirror, she dressed in a militia t-shirt and workout pants. She then transferred one hundred thousand credits into her blackmailer's account and slipped under the sheets.

Her head had barely touched the pillow before Isabel knocked upon her door. "Your father and Chief Shaw are downstairs," she said, peeking inside. "I'm sorry, madam, but they insisted."

Lila didn't even bother changing clothes; she merely slipped on her boots and her blackcoat and trudged downstairs. She'd worn worse when training, and she was too tired and too irate to care how she looked.

Lemaire and Chief Shaw stood as she shuffled into the parlor. She flopped into a sofa chair next to the white couch they sat upon, her damp hair wet against her arm as she tiredly propped up her head. "I'm on vacation," she said, imbuing the last word with a growl, adding more force than necessary. "A vacation you're interrupting. I'd almost managed to fall asleep."

Shaw shifted in his chair. "Rebecca has been returned."

"Good work."

Her father drummed his fingers upon his knee. "You already knew about Rebecca, just as I thought. I suppose you also know about the other two girls taken in New Bristol?"

Lila raised an eyebrow.

A lying eyebrow, and her father knew it.

"Damn it, Lila, this is an official investigation. When were you going to inform Chief Shaw and Chief Vance that you'd found a break in the case?"

Lila looked at her father and Shaw for quite a long while, then sat up with a great deal of effort. "You were right about one thing this morning, Father. I'm tired. I'm tired of this. I'm tired of bending over backwards trying to help you, only to have you go behind my back and negotiate with members of my own militia as though I'm a child."

She glanced at Shaw. "I'm tired of both of you, expecting me to be at your beck and call, then meeting me with suspicion anytime I answer. For gods' sake, do you think I enjoy your inquiries every time something's been hacked? Do you think I enjoy having to defend the people I've chosen to help us? Do you think I enjoy anything about these little chats?"

The two men eyed one another and said nothing.

"I'm done. I'm done with both of you for a while. You were missing children. The children have been returned. Case solved. Good night."

Shaw turned his gaze back and forth between them. After a quick study of their faces, he stood and straightened his coat. "I think I'll take a walk among the maples. The trees are lovely here in the autumn."

Lila watched him go, all too happy to see the back of him.

Her father leaned back into the couch. "You're angry because I talked to Commander Sutton and took you off the oracle case."

"Oh please, like you could take me off anything."

"Lila, where were the girls?"

"They aren't your concern any longer. Neither am I for the next two weeks."

The pendulum swung back to mistrust. Her father peered at her as if trying to read her, trying to figure out if she'd become such a skilled liar that he couldn't tell anymore or if he'd become so paranoid that he couldn't even trust his own daughter.

Lila didn't know which one she wanted him to pick.

One thing was certain. He no longer trusted his own judgment about her.

"Elizabeth, where were the girls?" he asked again, threading his fingers in his lap.

"I told you they're safe. Don't ask for more."

"You're playing in an official investigation. If you've—"

"An official investigation!" she whispered. "You don't hire me for anything official. The oracles aren't your playthings, Father. Don't prod where you don't belong."

He recoiled at the remark, his own daughter biting back. Lila realized she'd stepped over a line. She might have disagreed with his choices occasionally, but she'd never told him no. She'd always supported him, always agreed to help him, always caved to his every whim.

She felt lonely sitting before him now. Like she'd lost something.

He seemed to as well. As though he'd shot himself with his own gun.

"They're hiding their own children," he reasoned. "It's the only reason why you'd tell me to back off. Why? Why are you helping them?"

"I cleaned up your mistake with Rebecca. She's been found and returned to her parents, and the other two girls are safe. There were never any kidnappers, just clever girls who didn't want their futures. Surely you have some sympathy."

"It's not the same as with you."

"Why not?"

"It just isn't."

"I never realized you were such a believer."

He looked away.

"Leave it alone, Father. You've swiped at the oracles for long enough. Find some other way to make a legacy or learn to be content with the one you have."

With that, Lila stood and trudged back upstairs. She opened the door just in time to catch her palm as its vibrations sent it skittering over the edge of her bedside table.

Snatching it up, she tapped the screen. *Thanks,* her blackmailer had written, including an attachment. After scanning it with her snoop programs, she opened the file. A news story with a very familiar heading appeared on her palm.

The same heading she'd read a week before on Reaper's server.

Her eyes wandered to the top of the message. She drew in such a sharp breath that she nearly dropped the device.

The asshole had sent it to her mother.

She felt like a whore who'd been forced into an act she hadn't agreed to and then been kicked downstairs in lieu of payment.

Her head snapped up, and she looked toward her mother's room. They might have been transported to Max's home, for she could almost see through the walls and watch her mother opening her palm, reading the article, wondering if it was true.

Knowing it was.

It would only be a matter of minutes before she'd summon Lila to explain herself, before she'd kick her out of the militia, out of the family, off the estate. Perhaps the chairwoman might even turn her in to Chief Shaw if she was angry enough, if he still wandered around the maples.

Perhaps she'd even call for the family's blood squad.

The thought of her mother being angry at such a little thing she'd done weeks ago seemed funny in comparison to what had happened that afternoon.

She'd killed people.

She was a killer, a murderer.

A little parade of regrets marched through her consciousness. Regrets that she'd been too busy planning Oskar's escape from LeBeau's to search for her blackmailer. That she'd wasted too many hours in Tristan's arms when she had other matters in need of her attention. That she hadn't gone to Max's house, just for an hour or two, to track her blackmailer down.

Regrets that she'd slept instead of working.

Regrets that she'd paid.

All her regrets slipped through her mind, one by one by one, her chest tightening until she could barely breathe. It was like a little death, and she had no more time to spare, not when she'd reached the point where they crashed into consequence.

Footsteps echoed down the hallway.

Her doorknob turned.

Other Titles by
the Author

Fates of the Bound
Disreputable Allies
Stolen Lies
Barren Vows
Forged Absolution
Exile Bound
Manufactured Deceit
Elected Rebellion

About the Author

Wren Weston grew up writing fantasy and science fiction stories, but one chance book club encounter with a romance novel changed her favorite genre forever.

She became addicted.

Not only can she not stop reading them, she can't stop injecting shades of the genre into everything she writes.

You have been warned, darlings.

To contact Wren, visit www.wrenweston.com or drop her a line on Twitter or Facebook.

www.ingramcontent.com/pod-product-compliance
Lightning Source LLC
Chambersburg PA
CBHW030802260626
47169CB00001B/157